Frank M. Robinson
The Dark Beyond The Stars

A TOM DOHERTY ASSOCIATES BOOK
NEW YORK

This is a work of fiction. All the characters and events portrayed in this book are fictitious, and any resemblance to real people or events is purely coincidental.

THE DARK BEYOND THE STARS

Copyright © 1991 by Frank M. Robinson

All rights reserved, including the right to reproduce this book, or portions thereof, in any form.

A Tor Book
Published by Tom Doherty Associates, Inc.
175 Fifth Avenue
New York, N.Y. 10010

TOR® is a registered trademark of Tom Doherty Associates, Inc.

Cover art by John Harris

ISBN: 0-812-51383-5

First edition: July 1991
First mass market printing: March 1992

Printed in the United States of America

0 9 8 7 6 5 4 3 2 1

PRAISE FOR
THE DARK BEYOND THE STARS

"An exciting story in the grand tradition."

— *The New York Review of Science Fiction*

"Full of intriguing ideas, thought-provoking speculations, and personality."

— Gordon R. Dickson

"[A] generation-ship masterpiece . . . Robinson has composed *The Dark Beyond the Stars* with a lot of heart."

— *Los Angeles Times*

"This classic science fiction adventure is complex, ingenious, and thoroughly riveting. I couldn't put it down."

— Elizabeth A. Lynn

"A first-rate thriller." — *Booklist*

"I think Frank Robinson is incapable of writing a poor story. *The Dark Beyond the Stars* is one of his best."

— Mike Resnick

For the memory of Thomas N. Scortia

and

For Vincent Di Fate, Richard Berry, and Alex Eisenstein

for encouragement above and beyond . . .

NOTES AND
ACKNOWLEDGMENTS

The author is indebted to the following for their advice and suggestions:

Mark Hall of Berkeley for his modern views of ancient man; Dr. John O'Brien for information on broken arms and emergency room traumas; Professor Sidney Coleman of Harvard for the vagaries of time relative to interstellar speeds; Maude Kirk for reading portions of the initial draft and offering valuable insights; Robert Austin of Synetic Systems of Seattle for input on "artificial realities" and future computers; Jeff Windle, who cheerfully shared his enthusiasm for rock climbing; Charles N. Brown, who had helpful views on subtext in novels; and Chuck Frutchey, Bob Stephens, Sherry Gottlieb, David Moloney and Richard A. Lupoff, all of whom gave valuable suggestions.

My special thanks to Debbie Notkin, my official editor, and John Locke, my unofficial. I hasten to blame them for misplaced commas, less than felicitous phrasing, and anything else with which the reader finds fault.

And, of course, a deep bow to the "long voyage" stories of Don Wilcox, Robert A. Heinlein and a myriad of others. They sparked a youthful imagination and led to my own eventual offerings in the subgenre.

Readers interested in the possibility of extraterrestrial civilizations are referred to the arguments in *Are We Alone?* by

Robert T. Rood and James S. Trefil (Charles Scribner's Sons, 1981). I admit to appropriating some of them and recommend the book to those interested in an in-depth view.

Finally, a hail and not-too-fond farewell to the lobster men of *Galileo III*. Sadly, our love for fantasy has encouraged our reluctance to face hard reality—if we are alone in the universe, with what respect should we treat each other and the rest of the life forms that inhabit the fragile Earth?

                                    Frank M. Robinson,
                                    San Francisco—March 1990

Part One

She looked over his shoulder

For vines and olive trees,

Marble, well-governed cities

And ships upon wine-dark seas;

But there on the shining metal

His hands had put instead

An artificial wilderness

And a sky like lead.

—from "The Shield of Achilles."

W.H. Auden

The only thing I remembered was that I had seen extraordinary sights on the morning of the day I died.

I had gone in with the crew of the Lander at 0600, just as the system's sun began to cast a delicate lavender haze over the valley floor. I was the last one down the ladder, snagging a boot on the bottom rung so I had to make a desperate lunge to keep from sprawling on the planet's surface below. Nobody seemed to notice, but the stress indicators inside my helmet whirred and a dizzying series of readouts whizzed by in my heads-up display, stopped, then scrolled past again.

Pulse rate up, respiration up, body secretions up . . .

There was a flicker in the smooth sequence of numbers where a tiny circuit had burned out, and I swore to myself. I had inspected the electrical harness and the helmet display on board ship and I knew somebody else on the team must have checked it again after me.

It shouldn't have happened.

I took a firmer grip on my small hand ax, readjusted the position of the sample bag on my equipment belt, then turned to watch as the rest of the exploration team climbed into the Rover. I was looking directly into the sun and had to shield my eyes against the glare. The visor polarizer wasn't working, either. I wondered if it ever had, then realized it must have

been the first thing I had checked, if for no other reason than
that it was the easiest. I couldn't have missed it.

I glanced around again and promptly forgot about it, caught
up in the overwhelming beauty of the planet.

Dunes stretched for half a dozen kilometers down to a shallow canyon and its dry creekbed while pink hills huddled under a peach-colored sky. Porous reddish rocks were half
hidden in the drifted sand—*sand!*—and I kicked at one of the
rocks with my flex-boot, grinning proudly at the little puff of
dust I raised. On impulse, I laboriously scratched an *H* next
to the rock.

Instant immortality. At least until the next windstorm.

On the far side of the canyon a shield volcano jutted up a
good ten kilometers, the scarp at its base within easy reach of
the ancient riverbed. We would take samples from the
creekbed and scarp, record the terrain, and then . . .

I grinned. We would do all of that but we would also gawk,
scuff our boots in the dust, and take only half as many readings as we should. There were no seasoned explorers on
board—there were too few opportunities for exploration.

I glanced again at the figures in the Rover and waved, unable to wipe the smile from my face. The first planet I had
ever walked upon, the first rock I had ever kicked, the first
sunrise I had ever watched, the first clouds I had ever
seen . . .

The stress readouts flickered again. My pulse rate was edging higher, as well as my secretions . . . the inside of my helmet was rosy with warning lights. Well, what had I expected?
I was lucky that sweating was all I was doing. Besides, the suit
weighed; the planet had a gravity of 0.8, while on board ship
there was none at all outside the gymnasium.

There was a crackle in my headset. I waddled to the Rover
and climbed in, still staring openmouthed at the volcano and
the shadows along its base. I shifted on the metal seat so I
could see the Lander and the dark silhouette stretching away
from its broad footpads toward the cratered horizon. The
planet was ideal, the fourth solid-surface planet out from the

primary, the last one before the two gas giants. An atmosphere with a pressure of 47 millibars, primarily carbon dioxide laced with argon and traces of water vapor and oxygen. An average surface temperature of 210 Kelvin . . .

The Rover jolted to a stop at the bottom of the creekbed. I turned around, startled. Either the Rover had made better time than I thought or I had been too absorbed in gaping at the landscape.

Once more my headset crackled. I cocked my head and tried again to make sense of the words but couldn't. One member of the team hoisted himself out, took a few steps, stretched, then trudged back for his sample bag. The sunlight glinted off his visor, turning it into a golden mirror speckled with worn spots through which I could glimpse the vague outlines of a face. I couldn't make out who it was.

Another burst of crackling. I frowned and hit the side of my helmet with my gloved right hand, then leaned forward and tapped the crewman in front of me. He swiveled around but the sun gilded his visor as well and I never saw his face. He watched in silence as I pointed at my headset, then shrugged and climbed out to join his companion.

They weren't going to return to the Lander just because I couldn't communicate with them—not with an entire planet out there to explore. The driver started the Rover and once again we bounced along the creekbed heading for the nearby scarp, leaving behind two team members to survey the flatlands.

I stared at the scenery, fascinated. It was the standard landscape for an iron-core planet of this size and surface temperature and at this distance from its primary—a mixture of rocks, sand, stony outcroppings, dry riverbeds, endless dunes, innumerable craters, and gigantic volcanoes. Almost everything reflected various shades of iron oxide, though an occasional streak of yellow was undoubtedly sulfur. The landscape had color and form and texture—everything I had expected and more.

I wondered what the others would think if they saw me

smiling, and I inspected the landscape with a more scientific eye. There were distinct signs of weathering, the results of a thin atmosphere and millions of years. We had been warned that the planet was still geologically active, that there was plate motion and—

And what?

There was no life, there had been no signature of it from space, I remembered that from the briefing.

I felt the first quivers of uneasiness. I couldn't recall the rest of the briefing, who had given it or who else had been present or what else had been said. I worried for a moment, then put it out of my mind. The grade was becoming steeper. I concentrated on gripping the safety bar across my lap as the Rover climbed out of the creekbed and jostled over the rocks toward the scarp three hundred meters away.

A few minutes later we stopped at the edge of a debris fan running along the bottom of a small landslide. I climbed out, clutching my ax and sample bag. I tried again to talk to somebody but there was only the irritating crackle in my headset. I had a sudden urge to throw a rock at the driver and his companion, now fifty meters in front of me, just so they would turn around and I could see who they were.

Another twinge of worry. I didn't know their names, I couldn't recall their faces. . . .

Fifty meters of climbing over rocks and the exertion started to bother me—my life-support systems weren't handling it very well at all. My helmet was fogging up and I could hear the faint *sluffing* of the internal vacuum pump. By now we should have learned to keep the suits in better repair. . . .

The rise was sharper than it looked and the boulders were getting larger—we had to thread our way between them instead of stepping over. At the foot of the scarp my headset crackled once again. I looked over at the figures inspecting the cliff face. This time, their helmets were in shadow. The smaller of the two pointed up at a light-colored sedimentary layer and waved at me.

I caught my breath. It wouldn't be easy, not with my sample bag and the weight of my suit. And I was afraid. You never fell on board ship, nor did anything ever fall on top of you. But it would be an all-too-real possibility climbing up the side of the cliff.

The face of the scarp was badly fractured; there were dozens of minor outcroppings and chimneys in the reddish rock. My boots were flexible enough for toeholds and I had a length of rope, a safety harness, and a rack with plenty of protection—chocks and hex nuts and small, serrated expansion cams that I could wedge in cracks to hold the rope.

And maybe in that pale sedimentary layer I would find what we were all looking for—the faint, fragile outlines of something that had been there before us, something that had once called this planet home and to which the endless wastes of sand and rock were more commonplace than beautiful.

I turned again to glance at the landscape behind me, the rolling dunes we had crossed, the craters in the distance, the spidery network of dry riverbeds and gullies—all of it bathed in the brilliant light from the system sun.

It was a perfect day for heroes.

Half an hour later, I was more than sixty meters up, clinging to the flaws in the cliff's rocky face. I could see the Lander from that height, and the range of mountains behind it, no longer hidden by the low dunes. I looked down at the other figures hugging the face of the scarp. Twenty meters below me was my belay man, and another ten below him, the third member of my team. I knew both of them were watching me intently, though once again the reflection of the sun hid their faces from view. At times the primary painted them in shining gold. The next moment it revealed them as tiny, fragile figures draped in dirty expanses of what used to be dazzling white permacloth, streaks of green verdigris dappling the metal fittings of their antique suits.

I thought I remembered the name of the smaller of the two but it had slipped from my memory as easily as somebody erasing a writing slate. I felt another surge of panic, then forced my attention back to the rock face in front of me.

I had seen image pix of the different strata formed by layers of ocean bed and sediment that had buckled upward into sharp-ridged mountains, the result of colliding continental plates. The crumpled sheets of rock before me didn't look much like the pix, but this was the first time I had seen geologic reality.

I finished recording a three-meter strip of the surface, hooked the image camera on my harness, and pushed back with my legs to swing at the crumbling rock with my ax. I remember thinking that I just might be the one—

I wasn't expecting it at all.

There was a slight shimmer to the landscape and the scarp trembled. The rope sagged as two of the chocks slipped out of the suddenly shattered rock. I swung in toward the cliff, scrabbling for a handhold, terrified that I might be hit by something falling from above.

Before I could find a grip, the last of the chocks jerked out of the rocky face and I plummeted through the thin air, screaming into my helmet. A moment later, I was swinging from the harness around my chest and the rope tied to my belay man. I twisted slowly, just beyond reach of the stony surface. I was facing upward and I could see the other figures on the scarp looking down at me, each holding on to the rock with one hand and the rope with the other.

Suddenly, just above my suit, the rope unraveled like a piece of worn string as it rubbed against a sharp finger of stone. I fell once more, bouncing off ridges that exploded in small rock slides, desperately grabbing at the surface of the cliff that flashed past me.

I struck a boulder at the bottom, then slid to the ground, stunned, my left arm pinned beneath me. I was afraid to move, afraid to take a breath. I lay on my side looking at the field of orange boulders spread across the plain below. They looked as if somebody had painted fuzzy gray streaks on them; then I realized it was because the curved plastic of my helmet was covered with fracture lines. I was suddenly aware of my shallow breathing, the faint noise of the suit's pump and a high-pitched hissing sound.

I was losing air fast through the cracks in my helmet.

I couldn't believe that I had fallen, that the day was going to end like this. I moved slightly, uncomfortable because the rough weave of my ventilating garment was rubbing against my skin. The sweat that coated my body was starting to dry and I felt chilled.

My head was clearer now, the shock fading. My arm had started to throb and when I took a deep breath, I gasped—it felt as if my rib cage had been crushed. My feet were warm and wet and I was afraid the tubing had broken in my inner-weave. Or worse, that my urine bag had ruptured and I was lying in my own piss.

Then I felt the slickness around my chest and waist. I was bleeding and the blood was collecting in my boots.

I pleaded into my headset for help. Once again it crackled and once again I couldn't understand what was being said. I began to shiver. It would soon be 210 Kelvin on the inside as well as on the outside and I would be frozen stiff in minutes. Even if I weren't, I wouldn't last very long trying to breathe 47 millibars of CO_2 and rare gases.

I didn't realize I was crying until I felt the tears freezing on my eyelids. I ignored the pain in my arm and chest and shifted so I could see the landscape beyond the field of boulders.

It was a beautiful morning on a not particularly important planet circling an obscure G-class star and I was bleeding to death.

Unfair.

2

I lay there gasping for air, watching the numbers on the stress indicators flicker past before the displays frosted over from my breath. But I didn't need to watch their slow decline to know my life was gradually seeping into the cold. Minutes later I sensed footsteps behind me on the debris fan, two sets of them. I had never doubted that somebody would come for me; no exploration party could afford to leave anybody behind.

". . . a good thirty meters, probably dead . . ."

The words cut through the static this time, but I was too cold and in too much pain to feel overjoyed. I peered out at the darkening world through slitted eyelids. The jagged breaks in my helmet were thick with frost and my face was numb. I could feel the cold wash down inside my suit, chilling my stomach and my groin.

I rolled slightly, crying out as my fractured ribs grated against each other. I smelled urine and felt vaguely embarrassed, knowing for sure that I had pissed in my suit.

". . . all the way, careful . . ."

Hands grasped my shoulders and turned me on my back so I was staring up at the peach-colored sky. It was a deeper hue now, the pinkish red of sunset. I couldn't believe I had lain there that long, that it was now almost dusk. I wondered why my teammates had been so slow in working their way off the cliff face and why I hadn't frozen to death by the time they got there.

". . . sealer . . ."

". . . spray it on, hurry up . . ."

A face loomed over me, the first I could remember having seen all day. A woman, not old but not too young, her face distorted by the curvature of her helmet. She looked worried.

". . . hear me . . ."

Her voice bellowed in my ears. I tried to nod. Ripples of something cloudy washed over my helmet and froze in thick, opaque smears. The hissing inside my suit faded. I could hear my own breathing again, ragged and deep. I also began to feel warmer as my life-support systems started to catch up.

". . . on his side . . . have to try his arm or his buttocks . . . careful . . ."

Another shift and my cloudy helmet turned dark. I felt the suit bump against the rocks and promptly voided what was left in my bladder. They had turned me the wrong way so I was lying on my broken arm. I screamed with pain, though it came out more like a squeak. Somebody held the left leg of my suit and there was a brief prick as a hypodermic needle was shoved through the suit's disconnect, just below my bum.

". . . don't know if I got it . . . have to try the arm, too . . ."

". . . we're losing him . . ."

There was another prick through a shoulder disconnect. A moment later I couldn't feel anything from my neck on down.

". . . internal injuries, heavy bleeding . . . he won't make it back to the Lander . . ."

". . . he can hear you . . ."

". . . then he's in better shape than . . ."

". . . shut up . . ."

The inside of my suit was now warm and comfortable. I drifted off into a world that had suddenly turned vague. I didn't feel it at all when they lifted me up and carried me to the Rover.

I was unconscious during most of the bumpy trip along the dry creekbed to pick up the others, jerking back to awareness only when they hoisted me into the Lander. Once they put me down

to get a better grip on my suit and something tore inside my arm.
There was a sudden spurt of warmth and I cried out again.

I was bleeding to death, didn't they realize that?

I had a hazy impression of a control room jammed with
banks of finger switches and amber readout screens. My res-
cuers stretched me out on an acceleration couch and the four
of them huddled over me.

". . . helmet . . ."

One of them worked the thumb locks on my neck disconnect, then lifted off the plastic bubble. There was a rush of air
as the pressure equalized. The air inside the Lander was warm
and smelled of sweat but at least it wasn't laced with the acrid
stink of piss.

A woman stared down at me, her helmet off. She was the
same one who had inspected me at the bottom of the scarp. A
meaty face, gray eyes, brows heavy enough to have been
daubed on with greasepaint, short black hair, and the same
worried look she'd had before. Tears glistened on her cheeks
and I wondered vaguely what I meant to her or she to me.

Her voice was harsh, commanding. "Get his suit off—hurry
it up but don't kill him."

My body had been numbed by drugs but it still hurt when
they shelled me out of my cocoon of permacloth and metal.
The woman knelt on the deck beside me and ran her hands
over the bloody inner-weave, testing for broken bones with
the expertise of a surgeon.

"Compound fracture of the left humerus, torn brachial artery—strip off the weave and get some tourniquets."

I gazed at the overhead, only half conscious, indifferent to the
cold metal of the automatic shears against my skin as they cut
through the cloth and tubing. One of the crewmen started to
adjust a pressure bandage on my arm and I turned my head to
watch him. He had slipped out of his suit and inner-weave,
kneeling naked on the deck as he worked with the sticky-cloth.

He looked about nineteen, perhaps twenty. High cheekbones, a large mouth, pale skin, pale hair chopped at the
shoulder, pale eyes that masked whatever he was thinking,

and a thin, hairless body that looked more agile than strong. There was a delicacy about him that had eluded his teammates and he was cursed with the type of prettiness that some young men have before all the cartilage and baby fat turn to bone and gristle. He wrinkled his nose.

"He stinks."

The woman bent down for another quick inspection. "Clean him up. Strap on an IV pump, cover him with blankets, and lock him in."

The pale eyes made a judgment. "He won't make it to In-between Station." I wondered how he knew but there were no clues on that pale face.

They rolled me on my side. Another crewman—thicker muscled than the first, with rough features that looked not quite finished—fumbled with some toweling, doing his best to sponge up the blood and urine that had soaked the weave around my groin. He was stubby-fingered, clumsy and close to tears.

"I think he's going to die."

The crewman with the pale hair slipped the needle end of a thin tube into a vein in the back of my hand and adjusted the flow from the pump. He nodded at the woman behind him, murmuring, "She doesn't want to hear that."

But she had, and cut in curtly, "Everybody to stations."

They slid into their control chairs and seconds later I felt the mattress beneath me harden as the Lander leaped into the sky. I started to drift again, the sensations of my body fading. If I were going to Reduction, this was a better way than most.

After a minute or two of acceleration, the couch relaxed and I knew we were floating in the dark of space. The pain had long since vanished; the only thing that still bothered me was that I couldn't put names to the faces around me. I watched them as they worked their control panels and wondered who they were. Once the woman studied me for several minutes before going back to her board. Her expression was one of deep sadness and loss. I moved slightly on the acceleration couch just to reassure her that I was still alive.

The crewman who had sponged away the blood and urine, and another whom I hadn't noticed before—smaller and faintly apprehensive—were busy with their instrument panels. The first glanced back several times to check on me. The other only looked at me once, embarrassed for someone who was dying.

It was obvious they all knew me. I didn't know them at all.

The crewman with the pale hair was busy punching in calculations at his computer console. It was half an hour before he swiveled around to stare at me. I remember thinking he was more than just pretty, he was beautiful. But I didn't like him and I knew he didn't like me. For just a moment the pale eyes flared with feeling and he silently mouthed a few words.

What he said was: *"I hope you die."*

I didn't know whether it was a hope or a threat or a statement of fact—my mind was too fogged to make much sense of it or even to feel much reaction. What worried me was not so much that I might die but that I might die not knowing who the other crew members were.

Or who I was.

Then the control room and those in it faded away. I wasn't aware of it when we transferred to Inbetween Station; I had drifted into unconsciousness and the first of many nightmares.

In my dreams, I relived every second spent in exploration that morning, starting from the moment I stepped on the first rung of the ladder and climbed down to the surface of the planet. There was something before then—not much. I was in a metal coffin with my arms folded across my chest, staring through the clear plastic lid at a jungle of thick, silvery worms that were reaching out for me. Behind them were faces, hundreds of faces. The most vivid was that of the woman who had been in charge of the exploration team below. Another was of a man with a faint smile and sardonic eyes who could see into my very soul—a cold man in a trim black uniform who frightened me more than the worms.

More than once I woke from the nightmares screaming and sweating and had to be sponged off by the nurse. "Drink this," was all I remembered her saying, though I know she talked to me frequently and even held me when I woke up shaking. She was a soft woman; everything about her was soft—her face, her hands, her olive-colored skin, her voice . . .

If she had been a hard woman, I would have died.

She was young, her chubby sixteen-year-old's body covered by a white waistcloth and a thin halter. I worried that her youth meant I was so close to death an experienced nurse would have been wasted on me. But I didn't worry all that much. Most of the time I slept, lost in my nightmares.

Then one time period I woke up and stayed awake. I was in a sick bay with the railings on my bed raised and thin plastic straps holding me down so I couldn't float off. There were other patients in the compartment, maybe a dozen all told. Several had IV pumps dripping fluid into their veins like I did and I assumed they were crewmen from other exploration teams.

A transparent glassteel partition blocked off an operating theater that was a forest of polished machinery. The bulkheads, the deck, and the overhead gleamed with soft white light from glow tubes inset where the bulkheads and the overhead met. Brightly colored anatomy charts enameled on one of the bulkheads were illuminated by light panels set to either side. Just beyond the hatchway's shadow screen I could see a corridor, alive with crewmen, that seemed to stretch for kilometers, the end of it fading into the distance.

The ship was *huge*.

Mounted directly over my bed was a small screen with pictures constantly flickering across it—entertainment, I supposed, though I seldom had enough interest or energy to try and make sense of the images.

But the real show was on the other side of the three large ports in the exterior bulkhead. From my bed, I watched the stars wheel slowly past and caught an occasional glimpse of a planet's surface far beneath us. I gradually realized the ship was in orbit over a world a thousand kilometers below.

"Drink this," my child-nurse said once again.

She handed me a drink bulb filled with a grayish liquid. I sucked on its plastic tubing and tried to keep from gagging.

"What's your name?" I mumbled.

"Pipit." Behind her smile, her expression was watchful and curious. It would have made another girl look sly, but on Pipit it only made me less sure of her age.

"What's mine?"

She didn't answer, but leaned closer to stroke my forehead with her soft hands. "Shush," she whispered. "It'll come back to you."

Then one sleep period, when the sick bay was dark, somebody woke me up, murmured, "Down the hatch," and held a drinking tube to my mouth. But the voice didn't sound like Pipit's and the hands didn't feel like Pipit's. I twisted away, crying. The hands became more insistent, trying to push the tube into my mouth. I fought back, calling faintly for help and flailing at my enemy, too weak to do much damage but strong enough to keep the tube away from my lips. I suspected that if I swallowed the liquid in the bulb, I would never wake up.

Then whoever it was, was gone and Pipit was cradling me in her arms, calming my pounding heart. She asked me who had been there but I hadn't seen their face. Exhaustion finally closed my eyes and I slept once again. There were more dreams and nightmares, mixed with brief periods of wakefulness. The woman on the Lander came to see me often and I had distinct memories of the pale-skinned crewman leaning over the bed rails. He watched me for hours, his pale eyes as speculative as they had been on board the Lander.

He said nothing at all.

Once Pipit showed up hand in hand with the crewman who had been so clumsy and so concerned for me aboard the Lander. He wasn't wearing cling-tite sandals and had to grip the side rails so a sudden movement wouldn't push him halfway across the compartment.

"How do you feel?"

I remembered the harsh planes and angles of his face but I had forgotten the long brown hair that swirled about his head like a halo, lending him a grace his features lacked. But I didn't pay much attention to him—I was watching Pipit work the meal dispenser at the far end of the compartment and thinking how hungry I was. Then I blinked back to my visitor.

I didn't know his name but guessed he had come to see me because we had once been friends.

"Where am I?"

He looked worried. "On board the *Astron*."

"The *Astron*," I mumbled. It sounded familiar. "Who are you?"

He didn't bother masking his disappointment; he had wanted badly for me to remember.

"Crow."

Once he said it, I recognized the name, but that was all.

"Thank you," I said.

He looked blank.

"For your help on the Lander."

Pipit now drifted over and fastened a meal tray to the side rails. I pried off the plastic covering with my good arm and sniffed the steam from the meat and the thick, gooey gravy that held it to the plate. I filled a scoop spoon and swallowed a mouthful, enjoying the lingering taste of the gravy. Then I promptly vomited.

I lay back, turning my face away as Crow frantically tried to catch the floating brown globules with the loose end of his waistcloth. Whatever other purposes Crow had in life, apparently one of them was to clean up after me.

He looked down at me, stricken. "I'm sorry, I—"

"Go away," I said, and pulled the sheet over my face, too ashamed to talk any more and too filled with an envy that neither he nor Pipit would ever understand.

The memories of their sixteen or eighteen years filled their heads like sugar in a bowl. But I had no memories. For all practical purposes, I had been born a few weeks before. I had no recollections of a mother or a father or a brother or a sister or friends or enemies or lovers. The only memories I possessed were those of the planet below, the Lander, and my nightmares in sick bay.

They weren't nearly enough.

Pipit was always there now, usually with several small children who fingered the bedding and studied me with a grave curiosity. When she wasn't attending me—she never seemed to nurse the other patients at all—Pipit played with the youngsters as they floated about the compartment. She seemed to enjoy the role of older sister or surrogate mother and she was very good at it. She anticipated what the children were going to do before they did it, even plucking them out of the air to hold them over the vacuum of a waste chute when they needed it.

I discovered later it wasn't nearly as simple as motherly anticipation.

Finally, one time period when I awoke, the tube was gone. Pipit was waiting for me with a bowl and a scoop spoon, her chubby face starched with a grim determination.

"You'll have to keep this down." Her voice was surprisingly hard.

She fed me a mouthful of porridge. When it started to come back up, she clamped my mouth shut with her hands until the spasm passed and I had swallowed both the porridge and the bile that had risen with it. After ten minutes of turmoil, my stomach no longer had the strength to rebel. Several meals later, I was eating solids.

It wasn't many time periods after that when Pipit floated into the compartment, trailed by two more visitors. Both were old men wearing white halters, both had a caduceus stenciled on each shoulder, and both carried writing slates tucked in their sashes.

One was fat and bald and red-faced and looked as if he had better things to do. The other was thinner, more awkward in his movements, his eyes bright behind a pair of ancient spectacles whose wire frames had been wrapped and rewrapped with tape.

At my bedside, the fat one dropped three magnetic lines to anchor himself, folding his plump legs beneath him. He studied the instruments set in the bed's headboard, clamped chubby fingers around my wrist, and took my pulse by hand, obviously lacking faith in the automatic readouts. His grip had the clammy feel that too much flesh always seems to have.

I looked up at the thin one and mumbled, "Where am I?"

"On board the *Astron*—didn't Crow tell you?"

"He didn't tell me what it was," I said, sullen.

He gave me a reassuring smile. "The *Astron*'s an exploration ship, interstellar. So far as we know, the only one. From Earth." Somehow I knew that, though I knew nothing about the planet itself.

Both of them waited expectantly for me to ask something more. The thin one was patient, his smile bright. The fat one was nervous, frowning and plucking absently at his sash to let me know his time was valuable. I guessed that both of them were acting, that the thin one was really impatient and that there was no other place the fat one would rather have been.

"I'm Noah," the thin one offered. "My friend here is Abel. They're names from the Bible."

It surprised me that I knew what the Bible was.

"They're just names," I said, still sulky. "Who are you?"

Abel glanced at Noah, then back at me, annoyed with both of us. Noah smiled again, patiently playing the game. "We're the ship's doctors. Abel is a body doctor. I'm more concerned with the mind. But that isn't what you wanted to ask, is it?"

I was reluctant to answer. I had no memories, no name, and no knowledge of the *Astron* or my relationship to it, and that made me the most vulnerable person in the compartment.

"Who am I?" I finally asked.

Noah looked secretive and nodded to Pipit. She closed the shadow screen so we were alone with the other patients, none of whom were paying any attention to us. Noah and Abel hunched closer to the bedside while Pipit lingered a discreet distance away.

"Who—"

Abel interrupted, peevish. "It would be better if you told us."

"I don't know," I said, turning my face away so they couldn't see my anger. "If I did, I wouldn't have asked."

"You don't remember," Abel corrected. He leaned closer, his breath heavy with reminders of his dinner. "Look at me," he said curtly. "It makes it easier if I can see the eyes of the person I'm talking to."

Whoever I was, I was young. You used that tone on boys, you didn't use it on men.

"I don't remember," I repeated, even more surly.

Abel snorted in disgust and glanced at Noah. "I told Huldah it would be no use," he muttered. "We're wasting our time with dangerous business."

Noah ignored him, his eyes huge behind lenses that were so full of scratches they were almost opaque. They went well with the antique spacesuits but not with the highly polished technology of the operating room beyond.

"Tell me what you do remember. Go as far back as you can."

I told him about exploring the planet below, about falling from the face of the scarp, and about my teammates who had carried me back to the Lander.

"Nobody ever called you by name?"

I shook my head.

"You don't remember anything before climbing down the ladder?"

For just a moment I stood before a door behind which were crowded all the memories I could no longer recall.

"I started down the ladder," I said. "I caught my foot, then I was on the surface and . . ." There was something more but it vanished quickly. "I've told you everything since then."

"We're wasting our time," Abel complained once more to Noah. But he made no move to leave.

"It's a form of amnesia," Noah said, watching me closely. "Retrograde amnesia. You remember the accident and what you did after stepping off the ladder. Before then it's . . . gone. The obvious cause was the fall from the scarp. It came very close to killing you."

"My memories will come back?" I asked.

He and Abel shared a brief glance, then Noah tried to reassure me.

"Memory loss is usually selective. You haven't forgotten how to talk, you'll relearn how to get around the ship, you'll start to remember a lot of little things. The first memories to return are those closest to the trauma. You'll remember more experiences and one will lead to another." He hesitated. "If the condition persists, we can always try hypnosis or drugs."

There was no hint of guile on his face but his voice was full of it. My memories were gone—probably for good—and, for reasons of his own, he was as bitterly disappointed as I was.

"Who am I?" I cried once more.

There was no more pretense at reassurance; that game was over. "Somewhere inside, you know," Noah said in a voice as full of desperation as my own.

I was tired and started drifting off to sleep. "I don't remember," I muttered.

"Somebody's coming," Pipit interrupted, her ear against the hatchway.

Noah pushed away from the bedside and Abel yanked at his magnetic anchors. I watched them as they scrambled for the shadow screen. For the first time I realized that both of them had been badly frightened all the time they were talking to me—afraid not only of the questions they were asking but of what my responses might be.

At the hatchway, Noah turned and blurted: "You're a tech assistant on board the *Astron*. You're seventeen years old. Your name is Sparrow."

Sparrow.

Unlike "Crow," the name didn't mean a thing to me.

3

As my nightmares tapered off, I spent more of my waking hours exercising in bed and trying to talk to the other patients. Pipit never served them, though occasionally I saw one sitting on the edge of his bunk eating from a tray. There was a steady buzz of conversation as they talked to each other, and a few of them groaned with pain as they slept.

But they never looked at me or answered when I spoke. I wondered if my accident had scarred me, though my hands could find no evidence of it. I tried to catch a glimpse of my features in the polished metal of the bulkheads, but for some reason it would not yield a clear reflection of my face.

One time period I tried to strike up a conversation with the crewman in the next bunk, a man about my age who wore a cast on his right arm. He was obviously in pain and my first try was sympathetic.

"The planet took me by surprise," I said. "I guess it did you, too."

He ignored me and started talking with a friend in another bunk. Ordinarily I would have shrugged and turned away, but I had been ignored for almost a month. It finally proved too much.

I raised my voice. "You can at least say you don't want to talk to me."

He looked right through me, not acknowledging my presence at all, and began to rearrange his sheets.

"You can go to hell!" I shouted. I scrabbled about on my mattress, searching for something to throw at him.

Pipit appeared then, frowning.

"What's wrong, Sparrow?"

I turned away from her, still grumbling. I made a note to resume the conversation once we were out of sick bay—but then, I would do my talking with my fists.

Eventually I gave up trying to communicate with my fellow patients and concentrated on Pipit as she played with the youngsters. Once it sounded like she was holding class. I stayed awake to listen as the children chanted their "begats."

"Cuzco was begat by Ibis who was begat by Ophelia who was begat by Wrasse who was begat . . ."

Cuzco was perhaps three years old, a little girl who laughed a lot and was one of Pipit's favorites, though in reality they were all her favorites. I had no idea who Ibis was until I met a thin, nervous woman, a little older than Pipit, who was her coconspirator in farming a secret spice plot in Hydroponics. Ophelia was the woman who had been in charge of the exploration team on Seti IV, the planet where I'd had my accident, a planet now light-weeks behind us in the void.

The mothers usually picked up their children after shift. They were greeted with squeals of delight, but few of the children failed to wave good-bye to Pipit and some were reluctant to leave at all. It was Pipit who kissed it and made it well when they bumped themselves floating around the compartment, it was Pipit who hugged them when they needed it most, and it was Pipit who entertained them with simple fairy tales before nap time. . . .

Crow and Ophelia still came to see me, but for Ophelia it had become more professional than personal; whatever deep concern she had felt for me on board the Lander had withered as I grew stronger. On the other hand, Crow seemed less formal and more open, joking and talking with me as he might

have with any crew member. Occasionally I caught a wistful
look and was reminded that when I had lost my memories,
both he and Ophelia had lost someone close to them, someone I doubted that I could ever replace. Or ever know.

Then the time arrived when Pipit lowered the rails, untied
the straps, and pulled me over to the shower stall.

"You smell," she said primly. "You need a bath."

She helped me strip off the bandages, then pushed me into
the cubicle and scrubbed my back—hard—as the water jetted
out to be sucked up by the intake vacuum.

Nudity didn't bother her, though I was painfully aware of
her naked body and olive skin. I bit my lip in a vain attempt
to prevent the eventual erection. She ignored it and finally I
did, too. It obligingly went away. At the same time I resented
the fact that after numerous sponge baths she knew my body
as well as her own. The baths and her touch had become a
source of erotic pleasure for me: I resented that, too.

She finished vacuuming the water off my back, then handed
me a clean waistcloth. There was a mirror just outside the
shower stall—it had been steamed over when I entered—and
I wiped it with a corner of the cloth. For the first time in my
"life" I saw myself.

I thought I was very handsome.

I was thinner than Crow and looked older—I didn't think
by much. I was neither as tall nor as muscular, though there
was no hint of adolescent babyfat. I had thick auburn hair, a
reddish beard, and a straggling moustache. My eyes were a
light green. Sometime in the past my nose had been broken,
though I was convinced it made me look romantic. My skin
was white even for someone with reddish hair—I hadn't spent
much time under the sick-bay health lamps—and my shoulders were slightly hunched. I had a flat stomach, big hands
and feet, and a curly mat of rust-colored fuzz on my chest. My
fingers were spatulate, though the rest of me looked normal
enough.

*My name is Sparrow; I'm seventeen years old and a tech
assistant on board the* Astron.

I was vastly pleased with myself.

"Everything's there," Pipit said matter-of-factly. "I checked."

She had read my every thought. In the mirror, my face turned pink.

"I hope you enjoyed yourself," I grunted. I slipped the cloth up and around my waist and knotted it, realizing a moment later that whatever else I had forgotten, I hadn't forgotten how to do *that*.

Pipit took off her cling-tites and slipped them beneath her waistcloth. Then she switched off the shadow screen over the hatchway.

"Would you like to see the ship?"

I looked at the brilliantly lit corridor just beyond and watched the crewmen jostling each other as they floated down it, eventually to be lost in the distance.

I wanted to see the ship very badly.

We drifted through the hatch into the passageway outside, lined with color-coded piping that served as directions to the various living and working quarters. Names and assignments ran in a continuous illuminated strip along the bottom of the overhead. Pipit grabbed a ring jutting out from the bulkhead and pushed herself along, braking the same way.

"Do exactly as I do," she said. "It's more difficult than it looks."

But it wasn't—it was something I had done before and it didn't take me long to relearn it.

On that first tour, the *Astron* was a world spread over a dozen different levels, with compartments filled with gleaming machinery and passageways that went on forever. Pipit showed me the machine shops where they worked on maintaining the equipment, the enormous hangar deck for Inbetween Station and the Lander plus the balloon and submarine probes, then took me through the various tech shops where I saw exploration suits and support gear hanging in neat rows along the partitions.

I even caught a glimpse of a crowded mess compartment with crewmen eating at stainless-steel tables and working in the galley. None of them glanced up when I paused in the hatchway to watch, reminding me of the patients in sick bay. Pipit finally nudged me away, saying that most of the divisions, my own included, had their personal mess.

The next stop was Communications, a large, gleaming compartment jammed with radio equipment and a dozen personnel too busy to pay much attention to us. On the bulkhead outside was a clipboard with a sheaf of the latest weekly messages from a remote Earth printed on crisp plastic sheets. I glanced at one or two, brief summaries of politics and economics, and then Pipit was tugging me away.

Hydroponics was in the after portion of the ship. I stared openmouthed at the troughs of green plants racked from deck to overhead in rows that stretched for hundreds of meters. Pipit motioned me to follow her and floated toward a distant section of the compartment, where some plant troughs were hidden beneath the nutrient piping. She pinched off a leaf, crushed it in her fingers, and held them out for me to smell. The fragrance made my nose itch.

"Mint," she said, reaching over to break off a leaf from another plant. "Anise." She put her fingers to my lips. "Don't tell."

She shot off and I trailed after, still bemused by the different smells on her fingertips.

In the stern, I was awestruck by the huge water-filled pool, blue with Cherenkov radiation, that housed the ship's Locke-Austin fusion engines. The compartment was three levels high, and I spent several minutes gawking at the nearly naked technicians, protected by their shields, hovering around the huge machinery. Then Pipit tugged at me once again, saying it was time to go.

The crew's quarters were small cubicles off the main corridors, subdivided by shadow screens into living spaces for families or singles. All of them were filled with comfortable foam furniture and magnetic tapestries that clung to the bulkheads. I wanted to stop and talk to the crew members I saw inside but Pipit shook her head, frowning.

"There's too much to see," she protested.

A number of the crewmen in the passageways wore clear plastic masks that covered their eyes and ears. I supposed they worked in the drive chamber, where the glare of the lights was almost blinding. Unlike the crewmen in the mess hall, several of them nodded and called me by name. I wondered how well I had known them and if we had ever worked together.

One crowded passageway was filled with flickering lights, flashing signs, and colored cloth awnings at which I stared, fascinated.

"It's the ship's bazaar," Pipit said, uneasy.

I took a closer look and decided this was where crew members traded or sold articles they no longer desired or objects they had made. I wanted to see what was for sale but Pipit clung to my arm, shaking her head.

"You're doing too much," she warned. "It's time to go back."

I was tired, but not *that* tired, and Pipit's concern had begun to irritate me. I dodged past her down the corridor, losing myself among the awnings and the piles of goods and crowds of crewmen.

But even though the shelves were piled high with bolts of cloth, musical instruments, toys, and bedding, the counters themselves were nearly bare. There wasn't much actually for sale—two or three books of thin plastic sheets, some tiny hangings knotted from colored string, a slate similar to the ones Noah and Abel carried tucked inside their waist-cloths . . .

What finally caught my eye was a bookseller's stall. I fingered an ancient volume of poetry lying alone on the counter. The book was beautiful, the print on the plastic pages still crisp and black. I leafed quickly through it, entranced by the words that danced before my eyes.

"How much is this?" I asked the old woman who was selling it. The shelf behind her was thick with volumes but she was only willing to part with the one thin book of poems.

"A thousand hours," she murmured. "I can't read it anymore." For the first time, I noticed the cataracts that clouded her eyes. They shouldn't have been a problem, not considering the equipment in the infirmary.

Pipit caught up with me and clutched my shoulder. "We should go back," she warned again. "It's time to go back."

I laughed and darted down the corridor. When I spotted a hatchway, I dove through it—and suddenly had to catch my breath. I was at the hub of what looked like a gigantic wheel slowly turning around me. Crew members stood on the distant rim, working with exercise apparatus. Handholds on the rotating bulkhead led to the rim and I grabbed at the nearest one, eager to see what the crew members were doing.

I had no idea I would be among them so soon. I clung for a moment to my handhold; then it was torn from my grasp and I fell to the rim. I clutched at the handholds as they flashed by, breaking my fall, then flattened out on the deck at the bottom, staring up at the oblong hatchway twisting round and round far above my head.

I now had weight and found it difficult to move. My breathing was labored and I could sense that my heart was under a strain.

"You managed to find the gymnasium," I heard Pipit say behind me. Then, with less sarcasm and more concern: "You ready to go back now?"

I nodded weakly and she helped me to my feet.

"Easy does it," a voice said. I turned to find Crow steadying me. His skin was shiny with sweat, his eyes as worried as Pipit's. Others had stopped their workouts with the springbars and the exercise cycles to stare at me. I felt foolish, even more so when I noticed the pale-faced crewman among them. Crow and Pipit helped me back up to the hatch. My body ached where I had struck the handholds on the way down and I winced with every movement.

Reentering sick bay, I forgot to brake. I grabbed frantically at something to stop myself, then crossed my arms in front of my face as I sailed toward one of the beds close to my own. I braced myself for a jarring collision with the patient in it, my mouth already forming apologies.

The bed and its occupant turned out to be as insubstantial as the air itself. I didn't stop until I struck the opposite bulkhead, slipping through two more beds and their patients. They winked out of existence as I passed through, then flickered back into view as I receded.

I froze, concentrating on the other patients as they talked among themselves or sat on the edges of their cots while they ate their meals. None of them seemed aware of my sudden entrance or, as usual, that I even existed. I reached out to touch the nearest one and my hand passed through him with no resistance whatsoever.

I had watched them for weeks but never noticed their obvious lack of reality. They slept in beds with no restraints to hold them in, they ate from standard food trays and they sat as flat upon their mattresses as if the sick bay were planet-bound.

I glared at Pipit, then made the connection with the crewmen in the corridor who had been wearing masks.

"Give me a mask," I said in a voice blurred by anger.

A dozen strips of transparent plastic were tied to a nearby bulkhead peg and Pipit handed me one without a word. I clipped it around my head, staring openmouthed as the familiar surroundings disappeared.

The sick bay was actually a small, almost empty compartment that held half a dozen beds. I was the only patient. The bulkheads were dull and oily looking; I could never have seen my reflection in any of them. The deck was a beaten sheet of metal worn by the passage of generations of magnetic sandals. A few of the glow tubes flickered where the bulkheads and the overhead met; two of them had burned out. The anatomy charts were discolored and chipped; one light panel was broken, the other was dark.

There was no glassteel partition through which I could see banks of shining machinery in a spotless operating theater. In fact, there was no operating theater. Nor were there any ports through which I could stare at the stars or watch a planet revolving majestically a thousand kilometers below.

I had been looking at the ship as it once had been, not as it was now. Beneath the images formed by the intersecting planes of light, the *Astron* was *old,* old past anything I could imagine.

Pipit stood there, biting her lip as she searched for words to calm me. I ignored her and dove for the outer passageway.

On my tour with Pipit, the ship had been spacious and clean, sparkling with chrome and stainless steel. Now it was ancient and cramped, the passageways shorter, the compartments tiny, the bulkheads stained with blotches of rust. The sight and feel and taste of aging metal was everywhere; the stink of oil was like a fog. I wondered why I hadn't noticed it before, then realized my eyes had blinded my other senses—I hadn't smelled the stench or noticed that the bulkheads were damp with generations of human sweat.

Communications was a small, cluttered compartment with three crewmen who stared at me curiously, then went back to idly checking their instruments. A writing slate with the latest communication from Earth—a brief message of encouragement—scrawled on it, hung on the bulkhead outside. It was dated from the year before.

The racks of hydroponic tubs were real, though not nearly as extensive as I remembered. The plants were just as green, but some of the grow lights were dim and others had burned out. The compartment that housed the fusion drive, while still huge, seemed smaller than before. There was no mess hall, no files of crewmen waiting in line to be served, no galley filled with gleaming bake ovens and ranges. Where it had been was a small, empty compartment that contained no odors of cooking, no crumbs of food.

The old woman was still in the now-bare corridor selling her one precious volume. There was no shelf behind her jammed with other books. She looked at me with pity peeking out from behind the clouded lenses of her eyes. I felt the same for her—the *Astron* held neither the equipment nor the knowledge to heal her sight.

On the way back, I glanced into several of the living cubicles, now devoid of their rich tapestries and elegant furniture. They were tiny cells, equipped with string hammocks, an occasional worn plastic table, a shelf attached to a bulkhead. . . . There was very little else.

I braked more expertly when I entered sick bay this time and yanked off my eye mask. The ports and stars promptly reappeared, as did the compartment beyond with its make-believe machinery. My fellow patients went on about their business, as oblivious of me now as they had been before. I held the mask before my eyes and once again was alone with Pipit.

I was seventeen years old, I thought bitterly, a youthful mariner on an ancient ship bound for God only knew where.

Pipit winced at the expression on my face. "You've forgotten the compartment falsies," she said. Then she burst into tears.

I was young and cried too easily, but this time tears were beyond me.

4

I spent two more time periods in sick bay, most of it undergoing tests by Abel, who apparently wanted to make sure that my broken bones were healed and I was fit for duty. He poked and prodded, full of unconvincing "hmmms" and variations of "Does it hurt?" I was wearing the mask over my eyes and ears but neither he nor Noah mentioned it.

"You're healthy," Abel finally grunted. "You're well enough to work so you can earn what you eat."

I resented his attitude, resented the ship, and was full of sarcasm. "I'm your only patient but you seem to eat well enough."

Noah smothered a grin but Abel's plump features hardened with outrage.

"Nobody gets sick on board the *Astron*, they just grow old. Do you want to blame me for that?"

"We work at many tasks," Noah sighed. "Be patient with us, Sparrow. And with yourself." He meant well but I was too newly cynical to appreciate it.

The next time period Pipit told me that I had been reassigned to Exploration. I was to report there immediately.

There was nothing to pack; my waistcloth was my sole possession. I hesitated outside the hatchway, Pipit beside me, not knowing how to say good-bye. I hadn't spoken to her since I had discovered the real *Astron* and accused her of deliberately deceiving me. I recalled too late how she had probably saved my life. I flushed and turned away; I wanted to thank her but a seventeen-year-old's shyness had made me mute.

Pipit was smarter and more compassionate than I was. She said, "I hope your memories come back, Sparrow," kissed me lightly on the cheek, and ducked back inside the shadow screen. I was left with my apologies dying on my lips.

It was the end of a shift and the passageways were filled with crewmen hurrying to their living cubicles or to the various shops. They were naked except for their waistcloths, color-coded for the division in which they worked, and their instrument belts. Like the caduceuses worn by Noah and Abel, their specialty insignia were stenciled on their shoulders. A few of them called out to me, but the children playing in the side corridors stared in silence as I drifted by.

I was a man without a past, a freak, and everybody knew it. I anticipated being pitied or patronized and was prepared for it.

I wasn't prepared for the reality.

Exploration was three levels down and I slipped in unnoticed. The first time I had seen the compartment, it had looked neat and scrupulously clean, the equipment racked in tidy rows against the bulkheads or strapped down in military files along the deck.

Everything was still tightly secured but now the compartment reeked of age, the dust hard-packed in the corners, the ancient exploration suits still holding the shape of the crew members who had worn them last. It was already crowded with tech assistants like myself and the stink in the air was a thick stench of sweat and herbal perfume.

Ophelia had placed a star chart on the bulkhead and stood over it, pointing to various areas as she talked. Her bored audience hung from cluttered work tables or bulkhead rings like so many bats in a cave. I pushed my way past racks of ancient life-support gear and small heaps of motor parts cov-

ered with a dense frosting of dust and grease. There was an
abandoned Rover in the corner, gaping wounds showing
where it had been cannibalized for parts. I drifted over and
sprawled out on its one good seat.

I stole a quick glance at Crow and his friend who had been
with him on board the Lander, both perched nearby. Neither
had noticed me. A few meters away, in another Rover lacking
both wheels and a rear seat, a tech assistant my age dutifully
stared at Ophelia with the unblinking gaze of one who is
sound asleep. Next to me, hidden by a row of ancient exploration suits, a young machinist's mate explored other interests
with a girl, both of them oblivious of my stare.

The crewman who had once wished me dead, and who had
spent hours in sick bay studying me, slouched against the far
bulkhead. I would have recognized him by his pale skin alone,
skin so fine and free of hair that you could see the twitching of
the individual muscles beneath. He chewed on a fingernail,
ignoring Ophelia and watching me. I looked away but I could
feel the hair on the back of my neck ripple.

I forced myself to forget the others and concentrated hard
on what Ophelia was saying. There would be landing drills on
the hangar deck, equipment familiarization, required atten-
dance in the rotating gymnasium so we could adapt to a gravity-plus environment, and an endless list of lectures on
possible planetary flora and fauna.

All of this was would take up a major fraction of our lives,
Ophelia assured us. We were coming up on Aquinas, which
had at least one planet in the CHZ—the continuously habitable zone surrounding the primary. As we approached it and
the spectrometers picked up more information, the drills
would become increasingly intense and specific. The estimated time of arrival was expected to be eight months.

Eight months!

Too soon, I thought, startled. Even traveling at near light
speed since leaving Seti IV, it was still too soon. Planetary
systems didn't occur that close together. . . .

"That's all," Ophelia suddenly announced. "Same time,

same place two shifts from now. Sleepers will draw extra duty—your names will be posted."

There was a collective groan. My fellow techs broke for the corridor, heading for their living quarters, the gymnasium, or the division mess.

"Duncan," a voice suddenly said. An older, thin-faced engineer had drifted up to pump my hand. "Gannet," a young woman offered, with just the right amount of reserve and interest. Next was Roc, a chubby electronics expert with a nervous smile, then Crow's cocky little friend with the crooked grin and the cracked voice, who slapped my back, laughing when I jumped. "Loon—glad you're back, Sparrow." He had been a lot more restrained on board the Lander but that was when he had thought I was dying.

Most of the others filed up after him, with the pale-skinned crewman last in line. He was taller than I by a centimeter or two and looked in his early twenties. His skin had an odor that was vaguely pleasant, like the spices Pipit had crushed with her fingers. His pale eyes were steady and open, though I still couldn't read what was behind them. He shook my hand before I could pull it back.

"I'm glad you survived," he said. "My name is Thrush." His voice was husky and smooth as heavy silk.

I stared, uncertain how to react, while he searched my face, reading the state of my health with more accuracy than Abel ever had. I was still physically weak and psychologically vulnerable, and he knew it. He touched me lightly on the shoulder, then turned and dove down the passageway. A few meters away, he twisted into a graceful somersault, glancing back to flash a broad smile.

"Welcome back, Sparrow!" The words trailed after him like a ribbon of velvet.

I was still staring when behind me Ophelia said sharply, "Sparrow."

I grabbed a ring and spun around. Ophelia's eyes were narrow and faintly hostile, her voice brusque. "You've got a lot of catching up to do. You'll have to do most of it on your own but Tybalt will help you and so will I. If you need assistance, ask—you'll be disciplined if you don't."

It was more of a command than an offer. She didn't wait for an answer. I watched her as she left, her muscular legs kicking hard against the bulkhead when she rounded a corner. She was almost a matron but still an impressive woman, one that I admired in the same way you might admire a beautiful painting or a piece of sculpture.

Only Loon and Crow were left. I guessed that Crow had been assigned to keep an eye on me and suddenly felt irritated. I didn't need a keeper or a bodyguard.

"Ophelia asked you to watch out for me, didn't she?"

He looked hurt.

"I volunteered, Sparrow. And it's not to watch out for you, it's to show you around."

I recalled his clumsy concern for me on board the Lander and felt ashamed.

"I don't know where I live," I admitted.

His smile was quick. "Friends?"

I nodded and felt the chip slide off my shoulder. He laughed, hit me on the arm, then turned and shot down the corridor, followed by Loon. I sailed after them, leapfrogging over their shoulders when I caught up and almost panicking when Crow nearly collided with the metal deck. He caught a ring to slow himself and we continued to chase each other down three levels and over two decks, ignoring the annoyed shouts from crewmen in the more dimly lit passageways where some of the glow tubes had burned out. As adept as Crow and Loon were in flying through the corridors, I surprised myself by being even better.

They finally braked to a halt in front of a small, shadow-screened compartment halfway down a short corridor. "This is ours," Crow panted. "You're next door. Come on in."

I followed them through the shadow screen into a cubicle much like the ones I had seen before. There was a worn plastic pad sealed to the deck, a narrow ledge that jutted out from the bulkhead to hold an ancient palm terminal, a wider ledge that served as a table, and two string hammocks that were stowed on hooks next to a small locker. On the other side of the locker was an exercise rig of springs and cables. Judging by Crow's arms and shoulders, he used it often.

The opposite bulkhead was covered with a large foam model of an Earth-like canyon and above it a slate painting of a stream and a forest clearing. Both were exquisitely done.

Loon rummaged around in the locker for a battered harmonica and settled in a corner, hooking his feet through a floor ring. He watched me, curious, while he quietly played scales. He was a little more reserved than Crow—wary of me and protective of his friend.

Crow used the end of his waistcloth to wipe the sweat from his chest. "Take off your eye mask, Sparrow, I want to show you something."

I hesitated. I had been lied to once, I didn't want to be lied to again.

Crow shrugged.

"You want to wear your mask forever, go right ahead—but you'll go crazy looking at the same things all your life." He searched for the right words, trying to make me understand what Pipit hadn't been able to. "You're not on a sailing ship, Sparrow. If you want to see something different, you can't stare at the sky and watch the clouds change shape." He grinned and patted the terminal. "Besides, you've never seen it and I want to show it off."

Loon put down his harmonica, expectant. I unsnapped my mask. The falsie for the cubicle was a shock, though the first thing that struck me was the low murmur of music.

"It took us a long time," Crow said proudly.

The compartment was now a spacious room with huge windows overlooking a square two stories below. The windows were open, "sunlight" streaming in from a recessed glow tube and lace curtains moving in a breeze that really wasn't there. It was a nice touch. The painting of the clearing and the model of the canyon still hugged the far wall but now there were colorful tiles on the deck, an eating nook where the table ledge was, and a recessed pit holding a bed whose level was the same as that of the deck mat. There were overstuffed chairs, a swinging sofa suspended from the overhead in the same position as the hammock, and a large screen in the corner, alive with swirling colors.

They could sleep on the mat or in their hammocks, eat off the table or use the screen as a terminal for the ship's computer. There was little they might do that would spoil the illusion. I followed Crow over to the "windows."

"They called it St. Mark's Square," he said, filled with enthusiasm for his own creation. "Don't ask me who St. Mark was."

The plaza below was thick with flocks of birds and with pedestrians threading their way past them. Just beyond were an ancient bell tower and a canal with small boats bobbing on the choppy waves. Each boat carried several passengers and had a boatman manning an oar in the stern. In the far distance, several rocket trails marked the location of the local spaceport.

Crow had even included background sounds of birds pecking their jerky way over the stones of the square, the distant rumble of the rockets, and the muted murmur of people talking.

"Loon did the sound," Crow added.

"It fits," I said.

Loon winked at me. "I didn't think he'd mention it."

I turned to Crow, accusing. "The two of you had help."

Crow nodded, pleased by my doubts. "We copied it from an image in the computer's memory matrix."

He leaned out of one of the open windows and I felt a touch of vertigo before I realized he had programmed his fantasy wall a dozen centimeters in front of the real bulkhead. His movements were practiced, the illusion perfect.

"I keep wondering who owned the boats and who traveled in them," he mused. "Or if they regularly collected the bird droppings and sent them to Reduction. I think they must have, don't you?"

I had no idea. Crow sat on the window ledge and for a moment I thought the compartment had gravity.

"I wish I had lived then—and there," he said slowly. He waved at the scene outside the window. "It's beautiful, isn't it?"

He was homesick for a planet he had never seen, a city that no longer existed. He stared out the window for a moment longer, then "slid" off the ledge and swung into the hammock/sofa in one practiced movement. It wasn't just that the falsie was a work of art, it was how he moved inside it.

He curled up in the hammock, laced his fingers behind his head and looked at me with a face that was a study in innocence.

"If there's anything I can tell you, Sparrow, ask me. I won't lie to you."

The moment he said he wouldn't, I knew that he would. With the best of intentions and for my own good. And because, for some reason, he was oddly anxious to please.

I hugged my chest and floated with the air currents. "You and I were good friends, weren't we?"

He nodded in confirmation.

"What was my job—what did I do?" I asked.

"You worked in Exploration with Ophelia, myself, and the others. Planetary profiles, equipment checks, team monitor for drills—that sort of thing. You were pretty good at all of them."

Which wasn't really what I wanted to know from him. I'd find out soon enough what my job description was.

"What made me different?" I said slowly. "What made me . . . me?"

He was suddenly hesitant, trying to translate feelings into words—or trying to figure out what was safe to say and what wasn't.

"You liked to play chess—you used to play with Noah. You liked all kinds of games. You read a lot, you were hardworking, sometimes you were funny. And you were easy to be around."

He listed more of my virtues, but there was nothing personal, nothing of substance. Did I belch after I ate, did I talk in my sleep, did I wait too long between showers, had we ever raided Hydroponics together? Who hated me and what had I done to deserve it? And if that wasn't the right question, then who loved me? And why?

Maybe Crow and I hadn't known each other very well after all. But I *knew* that we had.

When he finished, I said, "We didn't find anything on Seti IV, did we?"

By now both Crow and Loon were sweaty-faced and I wondered if they would contradict each other if I asked them the same questions separately.

"On Seti IV? No, we didn't find anything, Sparrow."

How long had we stayed? I wondered. Had there been any hint that life had touched the planet, if only for a moment? I could ask Crow but I couldn't trust what he might tell me.

"My mother—she never came to sick bay."

"She died years ago," Crow said quickly.

Besides the unexpected sense of loss, there was the suspicion that he had answered too fast, that perhaps he had rehearsed his answers with Noah.

"And my father?"

"Biological?" He looked genuinely surprised. "None of us know our fathers, Sparrow—you've forgotten that." His voice suddenly caught and he turned his face toward the windows so I couldn't see his eyes. "Your father is . . . whoever takes an interest."

It was very quiet in the compartment now, the only noise that of the crowds and the squawking birds in the square below.

"Somebody must have taken an interest," I said desperately.

"A lot of people did." Then, even more hesitantly: "There was another casualty on Seti IV. Laertes. Volcanic eruption, the hot gases cooked him in his suit." Crow must have been there when it happened, but he said it with all the emotion of a man who had memorized it.

"He was my father?"

"He took an interest."

I clipped the mask around my face, the plastic covering my eyes and curling into my ears. The windows and the fluttering curtains disappeared, the city below vanished, the murmurs of the birds and the people stopped. The three of us were alone in a tiny cubicle with sweating bulkheads.

"I want to see where I live," I said quietly.

Crow pushed off the ledge and disappeared through the shadow screen behind him. I followed, finding myself in another small compartment not that much different from his own. A table and a mat, a hammock and a locker and half a dozen waistcloths tied to a bulkhead peg.

Plus a bookcase with twenty or more volumes.

I gently broke the slight pull of the magnetic headband that held one of them to the shelf and opened it, the plastic "paper" feeling greasy and fragile in my hands. There were volumes of fiction, more of essays and history, a few of poetry, and some technical manuals that were close to crumbling.

Books were enormously costly and I wondered how I had ever acquired them. I glanced around the compartment again but the only thing remarkable about it was the books. Still, there was the indefinable air of somebody having lived there before me. It was difficult to accept the irony. The compartment was haunted by myself.

Crow wasn't sure how to judge my silence. "The division has its own mess, Sparrow. We usually eat together. If you want me to show you—"

"I'm not hungry," I said in a distant voice.

"Friends?" he repeated. There was an agony of uncertainty in his voice.

I turned cold.

"Privacy, Crow."

He looked wounded and vanished through the screen.

"You're a fool!" Loon cried. "He would die for you and so would I!" Then he, too, slipped through the shadow screen.

I was seventeen years old, I held grudges, and I knew Crow had lied to me about my father and my mother and even about myself.

All of them had lied to me, I thought sullenly, starting with Pipit.

I read for ten minutes, then slipped quietly out of my hammock and went exploring—I wanted to see the ship for myself.

The corridors were almost deserted; those few crewmen floating through them acknowledged me with a nod or ignored me altogether. There was a glow tube still on in Exploration but the compartment was empty. I pushed past it into one of the long residence passageways, listening to the faint sounds of slumber or the quiet hum of conversation from the other side of the shadow screens. By the time I reached the end of it, I was having second thoughts about my tour. I was tired and I wanted nothing more than to curl up in my hammock and drift off to sleep.

I had just made up my mind to return when a quarantine sign by one of the shadow screens caught my eye. I hesitated, curious. If somebody was sick, why weren't they in sick bay? I thought about it a moment longer, but my imagination had been too busy conjuring up mysteries about the ship and curiosity got the best of me. I pushed silently through the screen, all primed to apologize for intruding.

The compartment was empty. The only signs of occupancy were some loose waistcloths floating in the stray air currents and a few books on the terminal ledge. I glanced at the titles, noting that a page had been turned down in one of them, sacrilege for anything that fragile. I picked it up and read the marked paragraph about life and death. The mere reading of it made me shiver.

I started to back out, then noticed there were dark stains on the floor mat and on the bulkhead around the waste chute. I ran my fingers lightly over the mat. The stains weren't quite dry; the mat was still damp to the touch. My fingers came away faintly streaked with red. I shivered and kicked back to the shadow screen.

I paused again at the hatchway and took off my eye mask. The compartment falsie was far different from that of Crow and Loon's. I was on a hillside just below the ruins of a castle whose main tower was circled with stone steps. The plain below was bare of grass, the few trees on it stripped of their leaves, their trunks blackened by fire.

My eyes lingered on the steps around the tower and automatically followed them to the top—or tried to. Something was wrong with the perspective: The steps never quite got there. You went up and up but at the same time you were going down. . . .

It was a clever optical illusion. I guessed the falsie was meant as a joke, though a dark one. Then I coupled it with the passage in the book and wondered if it had been programmed as a commentary on life itself. For the first time, it occurred to me that there might be crewmen on board with problems more serious than my own.

I pushed through the shadow screen and returned to my own living quarters, more tired than before and more thoughtful. I read for a few minutes, then turned off the glow tube, my mind preoccupied with the strange compartment, who had lived there, and what had happened to them.

Just before I fell asleep it struck me as odd that the falsie had been left on and the deck mat was still damp with stains. The only reason I could think of was that an investigation was in progress and the dark-stained mat and the falsie were evidence that somebody had died in that compartment.

And that they might have had help.

5

"Sparrow! Wake up, mister!"

I sat up, startled, reaching in a reflex action for a book, which was now clinging to the metal bulkhead. I had dozed off before I had a chance to put it back on the shelf.

"Let's go, Sparrow."

I twisted out of the hammock, blinking in the sudden flare of light, and looked over at the man who had called my name. His features were almost lost in the gloom of the shadow screen, though I could make out the chevron of Security stenciled on a bulky shoulder and the bulge of a pellet gun in his waistcloth. I was annoyed at being woken up, I objected to the stink of him, and I resented the obvious pleasure he took in his own authority.

"The Captain wants to see you."

The Captain . . .

He shoved me into the corridor while I was still rubbing the sleep out of my eyes. We shot through almost empty passageways, at one point passing through the corridor where I had seen the quarantine sign. It was gone now and I wondered if I had seen it at all, if the strange compartment hadn't been one of my nightmares.

I had no time to brood about it. We spiraled upwards through the different decks of the ship, my guide staying close behind and showing me the way by blows to alternate shoulders. On the last level there were two guards outside the hatchway to what I guessed was the bridge. Before I could enter, Abel suddenly filled the opening, and I flattened against a bulkhead. He glanced at me sourly, then sailed down the corridor like a balloon. I didn't have time to wonder what he was doing there; the next moment I was pushed into the compartment.

The bridge was enormous. Suspended in the middle was a small halo of light surrounding the figure of a man seated behind a floating control panel. The panel itself encircled a plotting globe of Outside, all of it clinging to an almost invisible arch of crystal that grew from the deck. The globe with its three-dimensional projection of the galaxy was the center of a compartment whose bulkheads were the *Astron*'s hull and whose windows were huge ports that extended the equivalent of two levels from deck to overhead.

Outside the ports was a slightly-above-the-ecliptic view of the galaxy, a brilliant fuzzy ball of light, orangish-yellow at its core, surrounded by spiral arms of cloudy blue flecked with bright dots of red and white and smudges of green.

The dark of space, lit by a thick sprinkling of diamonds and emeralds and rubies. It was a color-enhanced simulation beautiful beyond belief.

My eyes were getting used to the dark now and I could make out the technicians hovering about other control panels around the periphery of the compartment. Scattered among them were crewmen wearing the Security chevron. There were a lot of them and I felt tiny prickles of fear, wondering why there were so many. I put on my eye mask but there were no changes in the compartment nor in the view through the ports.

"What you see is what you get, Sparrow. Please come here."

The voice was soft but it cut easily through the murmur in the compartment. I pushed over, trailing my hands against the crystal arch so I slowed to a stop perhaps half a meter from the control panel. The light from the plotting globe outlined the man sitting in a sling beside it, his face partly hidden by a haze of smoke coming from a small bowl he held in his hand.

The Captain.

I looked down, both embarrassed and frightened, and noted the small metal plaque inlaid in the desktop. CAPTAIN MICHAEL KUSAKA. His name was unique to him, I thought with surprise; he wasn't named after a mountain or a bird or a character from the Bible or Shakespeare.

The fragrant smoke from the bowl tickled my throat and I coughed. He held it up so I could see the stem curving away from its bottom.

"It's called tobacco, Sparrow. Pipit raises the plant in Hydroponics and I have it dried and shredded so I can smoke it in this pipe." He smiled. "Private stock—rank has its privileges, so they say. I'll put it out if you prefer."

He didn't wait for me to answer but shook the glowing embers into a small vacuum catch-all in front of him. He stood up and held out his hand and I grasped it. The palm was thick and muscular, the fingers long, the back hairless. His grip was strong enough to make me wince.

The smoke drifted away and I could see his face clearly, though I was careful not to stare, preferring to sneak an occasional glance. The hair on his head was black and straight, just starting to gray above the temples. He had a thin black moustache, neatly trimmed, that accentuated his high cheekbones. His eyes were dark, partly hidden by heavy black brows. Later, I was to remember those dark eyes better than anything else. He had very little body hair. His skin was a golden brown from sun lamps, fine-pored and faintly damp to the touch. His face was narrow, the nose sharp, the mouth thin, his expression intelligent and searching. He also looked like he frowned more often than he smiled. I guessed he was about forty years old.

When he stood up, I didn't get the impression of a big man so much as a powerfully built one—larger than me but smaller than Crow. His skin was parchment thin and his muscles were tight and well defined; you could see their interplay whenever he moved. He looked immensely strong, but the impression of strength went beyond muscle. He was used to having his way, to being obeyed, and I was smart enough to recognize that as a superior kind of strength. He wore black shorts and halter but there were no captain's insignia stenciled on his shoulders. He didn't need any.

I never got over that first impression. I started to shiver then, my skin developing tiny bumps.

"Anything wrong, Sparrow?"

The murmuring in the control room died away and I knew that everybody was watching us, listening to every word we said. I felt very small.

"No, sir," I lied, "nothing at all." My voice squeaked and gave me away but there was no helping that.

He smiled again, whether in recognition of my shyness or in an attempt to calm my sudden fears, I wasn't sure.

"I'm glad you're up and around, Sparrow. Your division was worried about you. So was I."

He convinced me without really trying, the concern and the friendship obvious in his face, and I was deeply flattered. He had deliberately lent me stature in front of the others.

I mumbled an almost inaudible "Thank you, sir."

It was difficult to continue meeting his eyes, and my own wandered once again to the control panel. I was fascinated by the projection of the galaxy in the plotting globe, noted the various writing styli clinging to the panel top, then fastened on a small cube of transparent plastic. It contained tiny white and blue flowers whose roots were embedded in a thin layer of sand and pebbles, all of it preserved for eternity within the solid cube. It was beautiful and strange but oddly out of place on the panel.

The Captain leaned back comfortably in the sling. "Tell me about Seti IV and your accident. I have Ophelia's report but I'd like to hear yours."

His tone invited confidence: He was a fellow crew member asking about my adventures on that now distant planet. I told him how beautiful Seti IV had looked that day, about my accident and how I had been convinced that I was going to die. He seemed immersed in my story, his eyes never leaving my face. I realized with amazement that nobody else on the bridge mattered to him right then quite so much as I did.

"You don't remember anything before the landing on Seti IV?"

"No, sir."

"Nothing about your life on board? Nothing about your friends, maybe a love partner?"

I looked at the deck and mumbled, "I've tried my best to remember, sir."

He shrugged. "It'll come back. You're not the only crewman who's suffered from amnesia."

I thought later that his casual reassurance was the only false note in the entire conversation.

He pushed out of the sling and glided over to the ports, motioning me to follow. I thought I was good at maneuvering in free fall but he was much better. He twisted gracefully in space, his feet barely brushing the arch, to slow to a halt a few centimeters away from Outside, his outstretched fingers resting lightly on the thick glass. I drifted up beside him and he put a hand on my shoulder. My skin promptly broke out in bumps again.

"Do you know why we're here, Sparrow?"

He didn't raise his voice but somehow it filled the bridge. I could sense those in the compartment coming to attention— the Captain was talking as much to them as he was to me.

"Out there are the Deeps, Sparrow. We're the first ship sent out from Earth to explore them, we're the advance party for civilization. We've been entrusted with the most important mission given to any group of human beings—to find life forms other than our own. There's no event in human history as important to the race as the task of this ship."

I shivered on cue. He waited a moment before waving a hand that took in all of Outside.

"It's vast beyond imagining, Sparrow—a galaxy teeming with billions of stars and millions of planets and hundreds of thousands of civilizations and untold numbers of creatures that crawl or swim or fly or live out their lives in the muck."

There was a note of exaltation in his voice, and I stared at him with awe. His head was silhouetted against the vast field of stars, his face backlit by the faint glow from the plotting globe behind us, his mouth open, his eyes glittering in the semidarkness.

"Do you ever wonder what we'll discover, Sparrow?" He didn't look at me, but his hand squeezed my shoulder so hard it hurt. "Most of those civilizations will be friendly. Some of them won't. Whatever the case, we'll be the first to take back word that we're not alone, that the same God that guides our destinies guides theirs as well."

He paused for a long moment, lost in the immensity of Outside. Then he ruffled the hair on the back of my head and his voice dropped to a more personal level.

"Your name will go down in history, Sparrow. So will mine and that of everybody else on board."

He had listed me first and I was almost sick with pride and excitement. If he had asked, I would have given my life for him right then and there. Then he turned away from the port and drifted back to the plotting globe and the soft bubble of light that surrounded it. There was a low murmur in the compartment as the crewmen picked up their duties again.

"We haven't found life yet, Sparrow, but we very well may on Aquinas II—we've detected radio frequencies in the waterhole range." He fumbled with his pipe and tamped in some tobacco from a small pouch. "I think this time we'll find it. We'll need the help of everybody on board then, especially the younger members of Exploration like yourself. I may even go in with you on the first Lander."

"I'd be honored, sir."

I had noticed a slight quiver around his mouth when I had spoken before and now I noticed it again.

"If not on Aquinas II, it will be soon enough," he murmured as an afterthought. Then he promoted me to friend and confidant with a quick, self-deprecating smile. "A race whose drive systems have attained one-tenth the speed of light could colonize the galaxy in something like ten million years, Sparrow. We could do it ourselves. In the lifetime of the universe, ten million years is hardly a blink."

He concentrated on his pipe for several moments and when he started talking again, I wasn't sure whether it was to himself or to me.

"We're overdue to start running into the colonies of something else."

There was an unmistakable note of worry in his voice and I glanced toward the ports, half expecting to see a telltale streamer of light that would indicate another ship close by, one that was alien and dangerous and a threat to the entire human race. I was acutely aware that we were a picket ship probing the unknown, that we represented mankind's furthest reach and were the only ship out there that could warn Earth of an alien invasion.

I thrust out my hand to shake the Captain's, to show him that he could count on me. In my haste, I brushed aside the small plastic cube with its tiny flowers trapped inside. I grabbed it before it could float too far away from the control panel and gripped it tightly, panicked at having disturbed it.

It didn't feel right. There should have been hard edges where the sides of the cube met but there weren't any. It was subtly, oddly deformed.

"It's a paperweight, Sparrow—a memento of Earth." The Captain was smiling faintly, watching my face.

I opened my fingers and stared at the cube. The edges were rounded where the plastic had . . . slumped? Heat, I thought, then realized the *Astron* had probably been at a constant temperature since the day it was launched. The edges must have been worn from . . . handling? And if so, how long would it have taken? I set the cube down, its magnetic base gripping the panel top.

"The *begats*," I said, my mind numb. "How far back do they go?"

"A hundred and two generations." He concentrated on his pipe again. "On board ship, a generation is approximately twenty years."

The *Astron* had spent two thousand years, give or take a few decades, in the depths of space. More than a hundred generations of crewmen had been born, lived, and died during its voyage.

The security guard was drifting toward me; my session with the Captain was over. I shook his hand for the last time, smothering my surprise at what he had said.

"The previous captains would be proud of you, sir." I sounded as pompous as only a seventeen-year-old can sound, but I wanted to assure him that I was ready to march in his army.

He shook his head, still faintly smiling, still watchful, still curious which way my thoughts might jump.

"There's been only one captain of the *Astron,* Sparrow. It's an honor I've held since Launch."

For a long moment I couldn't say anything. "I'm s-sorry, sir," I finally stammered. "I didn't know." I sounded like I was offering condolences rather than trying to hide my shock.

His smile turned sardonic. "I bear up, Sparrow."

The guard was by my side then and I followed him into the passageway, still unwilling to believe what I had heard. The Captain as old as the ship itself? I could think of no reason why he would lie, so I accepted it—and suddenly felt angry.

How many times had he given a still-wet-behind-the-ears crew member the same enthusiastic speech he had given me? Two thousand times? Ten thousand times? And how often had he heard the same response? The slight quiver around his mouth as I had talked to him . . . He knew all the variations by heart, he had been mouthing what I was saying at the very moment I was saying it.

I'm sorry, sir, I didn't know.

It struck me then just how short my own life was when compared to the Captain's, and I was both envious and afraid. He had enlisted me as friend and follower with ridiculous ease. Well, why not? He knew everything there was to know about human beings; he'd had more than two thousand years in which to study them, to learn how to manipulate them.

I wanted to hate him for it but I couldn't. The truth was, I wanted desperately to believe in a Captain who told me that he needed me, who had let me know that I was both friend and companion, whose outstretched arms had briefly encompassed the entire galaxy with its billions of stars and myriad life forms, who had given me the one thing in life I needed above all else—purpose. I would be willing to do a great deal for the man who gave me that.

As I drifted down the corridor back to my compartment, I reminded myself that he had borne a crushing responsibility for those two thousand years. He had not only watched over all of us, he had led the crew in fulfilling the destiny for which the *Astron* had been launched so many years before.

If I had to die for anybody, it would be for him.

And then I started to shiver uncontrollably, no longer able to deny what I had known from the start. If he wanted me to die, I would die all right. He was The Captain, and as such he held the power of life and death over everybody on board.

He was also the man from my nightmares, the man in black who could see into the depths of my soul.

6

I didn't sleep well the rest of that time period, and gratefully floated free of the hammock when the wake-up light came on. The division mess wasn't hard to find: I followed my nose to a cluttered storage compartment down the same passageway where Crow and I had our living cubicles. Clustered around a few metal crates in the middle were Ophelia, Crow, Loon, Thrush, and a dozen others, including a pleasant-faced older woman. All of them were sipping collapsicups of hot coffee.

Members of other exploration teams were clinging to the compartment's racks and stanchions—Hawk and Eagle, two wide-eyed fifteen-year-olds who were as new to the division as I was; Swift, beautiful but nervous and almost as shy as Pipit; Heron, sly and pimply-faced, who apparently had found a hero in Thrush; and a thin, flat-muscled girl named Snipe, with close-cropped brown hair and that air of superiority with which so many young girls antagonize immature boys.

Ophelia was present, as were some of the other team leaders. The one nobody could ignore was Portia, fat and sharp-tongued, whose saving grace was that she was as hard on herself as she was on others. Her lover and second in command was an untidy little man named Quince who seldom had anything to say except in support of whatever she said.

I almost didn't notice Tybalt, but then nobody noticed

Tybalt at first. He was a weathered, gray-bearded man, minus a left foot. I was later told he had lost it in a landslide on Galileo III twenty years before. He was chief of the planning division and my immediate superior when I wasn't on call for Ophelia. He had a reputation as an easy man to work for—if you knew your job.

The last one, Banquo, was heavy-eyed and yawning. Muscular but larded with fat, he was a member of Security as well as an assistant team leader. He took both much too seriously and made a point of sitting by himself. It was Banquo who had woken me up and taken me to the Captain a few hours before.

I said "Good morning" to nobody in particular. Most of them murmured something in reply and all of them studied me, trying to figure out what I was like now. In turn, I studied them and wondered what I had been like before.

Thrush roosted in a corner, apparently his favorite spot for watching the others and taking mental notes. His hair was still matted from sleep, his face occasionally distorted by a yawn. He noticed me when I slipped in but his eyes were fixed on Pipit, who was busily pushing various pouches of leaves and powders into the food dispenser.

Crow glanced at me once, his expression hostile. I wanted badly to tell him about my visit with the Captain, but I couldn't talk to him if he weren't talking to me. Loon was right; I had been a fool.

Ophelia caught my eye and nodded to the woman next to her. "Huldah, partnership Noah." She sounded curt and looked as hostile as Crow, though I couldn't think of any way I had antagonized her.

Huldah was a plump little woman, eager to smile at anybody and anything. A working matron, I supposed, some minor duties in Hydroponics and a life that revolved around her partner. I nodded out of a vague sense of politeness.

"You should talk to Huldah sometime," Ophelia said pointedly, dropping her voice. "She knows all about the families on board."

I dipped my head, embarrassed. Huldah smiled the same empty smile that she had before.

Thrush smothered another yawn, then said loudly so everybody would hear, "Did the Captain tell you all about the *Astron,* Sparrow?"

I didn't know how he knew but I didn't try to hide my enthusiasm. "He said he wanted to go in with us at Aquinas II."

"I'm impressed," Thrush mocked. "He hasn't been off ship in a thousand years."

Tybalt came alive then. He glanced at Thrush with contempt, then back to me. "Pay no attention, Sparrow—if the Captain says he's going to go in, he'll go in." He sipped his coffee, studying me as intently as Thrush had. What did they hope to see? I wondered.

Thrush shrugged. "He's an old man, he won't remember what he said."

I suddenly felt ashamed. The Captain had befriended me but I had yet to defend him. I slitted my eyes and glared.

"Say it to his face, Thrush."

The compartment fell silent. Thrush had disliked me before, but from now on he would be an active enemy. I didn't think it would be any great loss.

Heron looked at me and smirked. "Two thousand years old—he must creak when he walks."

Tybalt turned on him.

"You have to be as old as the Captain to have vision, Heron. You wouldn't understand that."

Whatever Thrush's faults, he didn't strike me as a coward. I wasn't that sure about Heron.

Thrush grinned and scratched his chest.

"*A* vision, at any rate."

Ophelia said sharply, "Shut up, Thrush." He shrugged and went back to watching Pipit. Through it all, Banquo held his tongue, leaving the reprimands to Tybalt and Ophelia. That surprised me—I would have thought Banquo was the Captain's man if anybody was.

The buzz of talk started up again while Pipit distributed the breakfast trays. I was as interested in the people in the compartment as I was in the food. It was easy to figure out the chain of command, which followed generational lines. There was the Captain and then probably a few right-hand men. After that came the heads of departments, like Noah and Abel, and finally the Seniors, team leaders like Ophelia and Tybalt.

Most of the talk over breakfast was of Aquinas II, with the younger team members bragging about what they would do once we landed. Ophelia, Crow, and a few others said nothing at all, making a point of not even looking at one another though it was plain they all agreed on something.

Breakfast was textured protein flavored with Pipit's secret store of spices and served in edible casings to keep it together; I had no idea what it was supposed to be but it tasted very good. Halfway through the meal, there were squeals in the passageway and three youngsters burst through the shadow screen. The smallest had misjudged his speed and I grabbed his legs to keep him from colliding with the bulkhead. We spun through the air, the contents of my tray spattering over the others in the compartment.

While I tried to stop, the boy clung tightly to my arm and stared gravely into my face. He was a chubby three-year-old with brown hair and overly solemn eyes. I recognized him: K2, one of the children Pipit had been tutoring.

Hawk and Eagle scrambled around the compartment with spare equipment rags to clean up the mess. The others in the compartment were annoyed, while Thrush watched with a sour smile on his face, amused by the flurry of activity.

We settled back around the crates. Huldah absently brushed K2's hair and asked him if he knew all his *begats*.

He looked away, suddenly shy. I interrupted, saying, "I don't know mine."

There was an abrupt hush. Huldah cleared her throat and began in a sing-song: "Sparrow was begat by Nerissa who was begat by Abigail who was begat by Hake who was begat by Fox . . ."

I held up my hand after the first dozen. "You know them all?"

Another vacant smile. "They're in the computer—you can look them up."

Nobody was listening to us now, the *begats* having bored all of them.

"You know my family history?" I asked anxiously.

Huldah's smile vanished and she bent closer, her eyes filled with speculation. In that brief moment she became a different person, though nobody else seemed to notice the change.

"People telling you about your past is not the same as you remembering it, Sparrow. You should look for your past in your present. Your memories may be gone but *you* haven't changed."

As quickly as it had vanished, the empty smile reappeared. I had misjudged her. But then, it hadn't been the first time I had misjudged somebody, and it wouldn't be the last.

K2 shoved away from Huldah and settled in the crook of my arm, helping himself to the bits of food that still clung to my tray. Pipit floated over to the food dispenser to get another one and as she passed Thrush, he stroked her leg possessively. She brushed his hand away without visible resentment, but when she returned she made a point of sitting next to Crow. Thrush now stared at Crow and Pipit in much the same way he had stared at me on board the Lander.

The last person to enter the compartment was Abel, brusque and officious; he ignored the sudden silence and went directly to Pipit for his tray. He glared at Noah, which surprised me since they had been friendly in sick bay, then anchored himself in a corner.

"Keep right on talking—nobody has to be quiet on my account."

But everybody watched what they said after that and even Thrush guarded his tongue.

Once again I had misjudged someone. Banquo may have been the Captain's man but he wasn't nearly as close to the Captain as Abel. The more serious implication was that the

Captain had informers among the crew and Abel was one of them. For what reason? I wondered. I felt uneasy, suspecting that I had become a player in a game whose rules I didn't know and whose penalties might be more serious than I could imagine.

I shivered and went back to feeding K2 and myself. A moment later the glow tubes flickered red and the crew members finished their breakfast and drifted out the hatch to start their shift. Ophelia touched my arm just before she left and said, "You've been assigned to Snipe for indoctrination. Check in with Tybalt when you're through."

K2 twisted in my arms, trying to find the best position for a nap. I glanced at the young woman named Snipe. "Where's the nursery?"

She wiped her hands on her waistcloth and said, as if I should have known, "Where you were—sick bay." She held K2 by one arm; I took the other and we pushed out of the compartment.

"Who's his father?" I asked.

"For now? You." I looked surprised and she sniffed, "It's ship's custom, you took an interest. Anybody can take an interest—sometimes it's women who never had a chance to be birth mothers but when men do it, they become fathers, at least for a while. I think everybody should take an interest in one of the children, don't you?"

I didn't think I was all that involved with K2, though I was sure that of the three-year-olds on board he was probably the smartest and the strongest and the best looking. Then the whole subject struck me as maudlin and I refused to think about it any more.

What I did think about was Noah, who hadn't said a word during the meal but had roosted quietly by himself, watching all of us while we ate. And I thought about those who had remained silent while the rest of us talked, and realized there wasn't one crew aboard the *Astron*, there were two—though what the differences between them were, I wasn't sure.

But mostly I wondered why all of them had spent so much

time studying me. And why nobody had mentioned the crewman who had died that sleep period.

"I expect I'll have to show you everything," Snipe said, "right from the very beginning."

We were standing at one end of the darkened hangar deck where they kept the Landers and Rovers and where they docked the huge Inbetween Station, the planetary orbiter they used when they couldn't bring the *Astron* in too close. The rest of the bay was empty. A gigantic shadow screen covered the glassteel docking doors that formed the immense overhead, hiding the view of Outside.

"Pipit already showed me the ship," I said, annoyed. "You don't have to."

"Pipit showed you *her* ship," Snipe corrected. "She didn't show you *my* ship."

Which irritated me even more, but this time I bit my tongue. I waved at the huge hangar deck surrounding us.

"Why are we up here?"

"Because this is where the stage is."

I looked surprised. "Stage for what?"

"Plays," she said, impatient once again. "Plays about the *Astron* and its mission. It's one way we keep our continuity with previous crews and with the Earth itself. It's not the only way but it's probably the best way."

"Plays," I said, mystified.

"Plays," she repeated. She drifted over to the palm terminal. There was a flickering on the hangar deck and I was suddenly looking at a vast expanse of purple sand dotted with small hillocks sweeping upward toward a range of pink mountains. It was an alien planet at dusk, with two moons overhead and an impossibly large spaceship settling to the ground a kilometer away. Two odd-shaped military tanks came clanking around one of the small hills between us and the ship but I could see nothing else moving. I stared, fascinated, hastily shielding my eyes when flares exploded above the ship.

The scene faded and Snipe said, "That was the invasion of Pilar, this is—"

"Did that really happen?"

"It could have." The difference didn't seem to matter to her. "We use it for training."

"I didn't see any people."

She made a face. "Of course not, that's just the set."

"And the actors?"

"Almost everybody acts in them from time to time." She looked me up and down, obviously unimpressed. "If you can act, maybe we can find a part for you. But Ophelia said she didn't think you would be very good."

The projections were changing now, from the alien battle-field to a jungle of huge trees with trailing vines and many-colored birds flying through the branches overhead, to an outer-space battle between a ship I took to be the *Astron* and vessels crewed by intelligent insects.

There were at least fifty "sets" that flickered in and out of existence so fast they became a confusing blur—a universe of alien creatures and civilizations, the purpose of the *Astron* made fresh every time actors appeared to bring that purpose to life.

The last of them faded and I said, "Do you ever act in them?"

Snipe became surprisingly shy and said, "Sometimes."

"Which ones?" I persisted.

She gave me a sidelong glance, debating whether to trust me.

"The historicals—those where I can dress up. You know . . ." She opened her eyes wide and suddenly looked small and demure and three years younger.

"'Thou know'st the mask of night is on my face, else would a maiden blush bepaint my cheek for that which thou has heard me speak tonight.'"

She relaxed into herself again. "That's from *Romeo and Juliet* by Shakespeare. He's . . . very good."

I was astonished. For a moment she had become a charac-ter who had lived and died in imagination thousands of years before. I took a closer look at her as she floated in the flickering glow from the terminal. She was skinny, her nose was too big, her hips stuck out, and she was much too quick to tell you the truth about yourself even if it hurt—or maybe especially if it hurt.

But despite all of that, she was very pretty. And fragile. And she had trusted me enough to let me see her fragility.

"Which plays are the most popular?"

"The historicals, of course. We like to live other people's lives because our own are so dull."

I was surprised. "Do you really believe that?"

In a small voice: "Most of the time." Then, irritated by her own weakness, she burst out: "You have eyes. Can't you see?" She immediately followed it with a contrite "I forgot, I'm sorry."

I didn't ask what she forgot, but changed the subject to something more important to me. "Did I ever act in the historicals?"

"Everybody on board does at one time or another." As Crow had when I asked too many questions, she suddenly became evasive. "I really don't remember, I didn't know you very well."

In seventeen years, it would have been difficult for Snipe *not* to know me very well. But whatever I had been like before, Snipe wasn't about to tell me. She was no different from Crow in that respect.

Thinking about Crow made me remember something from breakfast. "Crow and Pipit," I said casually. "They're lovers?"

She pursed her lips. "Pipit's a friend of mine. I won't talk about her."

I smiled to myself; she *would* talk about Pipit, and probably as soon as possible. "How did Thrush know I had been to see the Captain?"

She sniffed. "Thrush knows everything. Or thinks he does." Without a pause she added: "He's jealous with no reason to be. He and Pipit have already been with each other, why should he begrudge Crow?"

At first, I didn't realize what she meant. I wanted to ask her more, then decided against it. "Tell me about Tybalt."

"He's my father." She said it with an affectionate enthusiasm and I knew she meant he "took an interest." She was relaxed and talkative now and I asked her about other members of the crew. She had an endless supply of gossip and a ready imagination. I don't think she ever consciously lied but I wasn't always sure when she was telling the truth. To Snipe, what might have been was just as exciting as what was.

She told me almost everything I had wanted to know about the crew on the *Astron* and quite a bit that I hadn't. But of all her store of gossip, she hadn't mentioned the one thing I thought she would.

"Somebody died the other time period," I said.

She paused, her face suddenly pale.

"People die," she said in a faint voice. "All the time." For once, she didn't want to talk about it, and that surprised me more than anything else.

The glow tubes suddenly flickered red around the palm terminal. It was time to report to Tybalt in Exploration.

"I can't stay with you this sleep period," Snipe said casually. "I'm on shift."

I wondered how she knew. It had been a stray thought at best; I hadn't been about to ask and I knew my body hadn't given me away.

"We're still friends?" I remembered when Crow had asked that and had a glimpse of how much it had meant to him when I realized how much it now meant to me.

"Oh, yes, we're friends." And then a speculative look crept into her eyes. "But we're not friends, too."

It wasn't until after we parted that I realized all the time I had been asking Snipe questions and judging her character, she had been judging mine. On a personal basis, I knew instinctively that I had passed.

But she had been passing judgment on another level as well; what its qualifications were, and whether or not I met them, I had no idea. But I suspected that the dead crewman in the strange compartment had played a part.

7

Tybalt clung to the railing of the observation deck over-looking the main control room, watching me while I watched the crewmen swarming over the huge plotting globe in the control room below.

"You don't remember any of this, do you?"

I shook my head. "No, sir, I wish I did—I've tried."

He slipped over the railing, motioning me to follow. Waving the operators aside, he pressed his hand to the palm terminal on the control board. The galaxy in the plotting globe exploded outward in light streaks that made the surface of the globe look like the working end of a brush.

The streaks thinned and vanished, replaced by a single yellow star surrounded by seven planets, the two outer ones gas giants and the five inner ones iron core. The first was too close to the primary to have any prospects for life. The second was far more likely; the rest were too far away.

"That's Aquinas II," Tybalt said, pointing. "We'll be there in eight months. No sign of alien scouts, though there's a chance we might run into some."

"Have you run into any before?" I asked, surprised.

He nodded. "No doubt about it, though only a few ever caused us any trouble. Probably as frightened of us as we would have been by them."

Scouts. I felt the sudden thrill of danger and promptly

strained my eyes by looking into the globe for exhaust glows impossible to see. Aquinas II was still too soon after Seti IV—but that was a fading thought.

Tybalt palmed the terminal again and a column of statistics scrolled over the surface of the globe.

"It's your job to match physical descriptions with needed supplies when we go in. Watch for anything unusual that might require Shops to make special equipment." He turned thoughtful as he read the flowing rows of numbers.

"Composition reminds me a lot of Midas IV—did I ever tell you about Midas IV, Sparrow?" He caught himself, muttering, "No, of course not."

He lifted his hand and the scrolling in the globe vanished. "Try it." He pressed my hand against the palm terminal. "Each pad is programmed for a specific number of functions. Move your palm and your fingertips—remember what happens and see if you can re-call the graph we just looked at. Don't forget, pressure is as important as touch."

The soft face of the terminal molded itself to my hand. It felt like living flesh, sensitive to pressures and shifts of direction and the faint stroking of my fingers. It was quieter and less confusing than speech, faster and more precise than keyboarding.

My mind remembered nothing but my palm and fingers remembered everything. It took only instants for the original graph to swim back into view.

Tybalt grunted approval. "You learn fast, Sparrow, but then it was second nature to you before, no reason it shouldn't be second nature now."

He scanned the columns again. "You know, we almost died on Midas IV," he said. "Our shields were up going into orbit, nothing should have gotten through—but something did. Sucked out a dozen compartments before Damage Control closed the hatches. Never did know what they hit us with."

My admiration for Tybalt grew with every word.

"What happened when the exploration teams landed?"

He shrugged, still studying the image in the globe.

"Not much of anything. The bastards were well hidden, we never found a trace. But camouflage is the oldest form of self-protection—we probably looked right at them a dozen times and never saw them."

After a few minutes Tybalt turned the palm terminal back to the chief computerman, a fat crewman named Corin. He had been working at another station and occasionally glanced over to check my progress. I was reluctant to leave; the terminal felt familiar and comfortable and I was very proud of my ability to operate it.

In the small compartment where Exploration was headquartered, Tybalt pointed out the two types of suits: those that needed repair and those so far gone they were only good for cannibalizing parts. I inspected the cloth and the fittings, did a quick inventory, and felt the sweat start in my armpits. As a generational ship, the *Astron* must have had a huge surplus of suits at Launch, but that had been long ago. Those currently available had been patched and mended hundreds of times; few of their fittings were original issue.

Tybalt hooked a leg around a shelf upright and folded his arms across his chest. We were alone and it was lecture time.

"You're very good with the palm terminals, Sparrow, you're one of the best fingermen on board. Always were. You have a rapport with the computer that I wish I had, that everybody wishes they had. I used to fight with Ophelia—"

He caught himself in the middle to sneeze and when he started talking again, he didn't bother to finish the sentence. I wondered just what it was he used to fight with Ophelia about.

He fumbled in his waistcloth and pulled out a small pipe similar to the Captain's. Pipit was generous with her crop, I thought.

Tybalt inhaled deeply from the pipe and held his breath. His eyes read my expression. "We don't compete in our vices, the Captain and me," he said in a strangled voice. "He doesn't mind; I'm slated for Reduction someday and he's not." He let the smoke drain out his nostrils and relaxed but I sensed he was studying me again, wondering how much I had changed. "Don't be ashamed of what you were before, Sparrow. You were hard working, loyal and a good friend." He gave me a long look. "Still are, I hope."

"I've been told I was easy to work with," I said with a trace of sarcasm, thinking he was repeating Crow.

He shook his head. "Actually, you were a pain in the ass—you knew it all and let everybody know you knew it all. You and Thrush, you both knew too damned much."

If Crow had catalogued my faults instead of my virtues I might have believed him.

"Thrush dislikes me," I said casually.

"Thrush dislikes everybody. But I'd watch myself around the bastard if I were you, he's the one person . . ." He let the sentence fade into the air.

I changed the subject. "What was Laertes like? You worked with him."

He shrugged. "Competent, brave, no malice in him. We were on the same team on Galileo III. Did I tell you that's where I lost my foot?"

Both he and Crow had dismissed Laertes in a sentence or two, and I wondered why. Had they disliked the man that much? "Laertes—" I began.

Tybalt slipped the knee-high cling-tite off his left leg and twisted his stump from side to side.

"You don't remember, but I have a prosthesis that fits inside the sneak. I hardly miss the real thing when I'm down below."

Laertes was forgotten. I couldn't take my eyes off Tybalt's foreshortened limb, the skin pale and laced with scars. "How did it happen?"

"They said it was a landslide. But that's only partly true." He stared at the smoke drifting toward an exhaust vent, not seeing me at all.

"I'd been acting as scout. Galileo III was a dry planet, thin atmosphere, but we all knew there was a possibility of life. Water flowed under the surface—you wouldn't have had to dig very deep to find it—and the polar caps were largely water ice. I was in a Rover, maybe two kilometers ahead of the rest, when I saw them."

He inhaled deeply again and I burst out, "Saw who?" while he was holding in the smoke.

"There were three of them," he said after he finally exhaled, "standing by some sort of flyer. They were my size, maybe a little larger. Red chitin for skin, arms and legs articulated like a lobster's. A head where you would expect one to be, segmented eyes on stalks. Horrible to look at. I imagine I looked pretty horrible to them, too."

He tamped out the ash in his palm and held it close to the exhaust vent, where the ashes vanished in a puff of glory.

"We saw each other about the same time. They had a weapon, I didn't. I ducked when they shot and they hit the rocks above me. I was trapped by the landslide—buried me up to the waist. But before the rest of the crew caught up to me, my three red-skinned friends jumped in their machine and took off, flying low over the hills. Don't know how they did it in that thin atmosphere but they did."

"Nobody saw them?" I asked, openmouthed.

He shook his head. "That was the irony, Sparrow. We were looking for life but nobody believed me when I saw it. They said it was part of my delirium while I was waiting to be rescued."

I nodded. "And that's when you lost your foot."

"Amputation on the spot," he said proudly. "No anesthesia. I felt it for a long while afterward. Abel called it a phantom limb sensation."

The glow tubes started blinking red. The shift was over.

"I turned in a report—the Captain commended me. Some of the crew disagreed, but I was there and they weren't."

"How many planets have you explored?" I asked. I was already wondering if I could be transferred from Ophelia's team to his.

He spread out the fingers of his hand. "Five. Aquinas II

will make it six. But this time if I meet something planetside, I'll bring it back."

He unhooked his leg from the upright and pushed toward the hatchway. "You been to Communications yet? Cato was talking about you." He grinned. "Speaking of someone who never liked you . . ."

An hour later, when we parted, he left me with a glow of confidence and the certainty that we had once been good friends and true equals.

I had no memory of what I had done to deserve either friendship or equality, but for the first time I had a sense of the person I had been before. I was a good fingerman, I was one of the best at maneuvering inside the ship, I liked books. As Huldah had suggested, I was finding my past in my present, I was putting myself back together.

My only disappointment was that Tybalt hadn't told me anything about Laertes. I made a mental note to ask more about him the next shift.

But when I left, I really wasn't thinking about Laertes. I was thinking about alien ships firing on the *Astron*, about creatures two meters tall, with red chitin for skin and eyes on stalks, who could be found hiding behind the next hillock waiting to ambush heroic explorers like myself.

I knew that I would dream about them the next time I slept.

Life quickly settled down to a routine once I had my job assignments. At mealtimes, I got long looks from Crow and Ophelia, but Hawk and Eagle were friendly and joked with me, as did the others. At first everybody had taken an extraordinary interest in what I had to say and fell silent when I talked. That gradually changed, though nobody lost interest in me completely.

Surprisingly, Thrush sometimes smiled when we met, but he never let me see what was going on behind those pale eyes. I distrusted him even more because Heron remained unfriendly. He still dogged Thrush's footsteps and I thought: Like dog, like master. If there had been any sincerity in Thrush's occasional smile, Heron would have known and blessed my heels with a lick or two.

When we ate, I sat next to Noah or Huldah. Tybalt and Ophelia were team leaders and I found myself tongue-tied when with them. Crow and Loon had drawn a circle around themselves and if I wanted to enter it, I knew I would have to dip my head and say I was sorry. I still didn't have the knack for apology.

Noah seemed oblivious of it all, talking quietly about the ship and the mission. Had he ever seen signs of alien life, as Tybalt had? He smiled and said, No, but then he hadn't had Tybalt's opportunities since he usually didn't go in with a landing party. But he knew very well what went on below and asked questions about planets and CHZs that I frequently had to check out with the computer before I could answer them.

To my surprised delight, Noah and Huldah started to "take an interest" and often invited me to share meals in their compartment while they filled me in on the history of the ship and the crew. Sometimes they invited younger crew members and once they made a point of introducing me to Swallow and Petrel, who worked in Engineering. Petrel was polite and standoffish, Swallow gawky and embarrassingly flirtatious, though there came a time when we were not so embarrassed with each other. I guessed that's what Noah had in mind.

I thought less and less about Laertes, finally accepting that I would never know him. But it no longer seemed to matter.

At one meal break in Exploration, Noah brought along a worn metal chessboard and a set of ancient chessmen and asked me if I cared to play.

I fingered one of the men and studied the board, then hooked a foot in a floor ring and sat beside Noah while he set up the pieces.

It all struck me as familiar and remembering what Crow had once told me, I said, "I used to play, didn't I?"

He nodded. "You were very good. Of course"—he smiled—"you weren't as good as me."

It took two meals before I was at ease with the game. Then I found myself gulping down my food so I could spend the last fifteen minutes of the period in deep thought opposite Noah, studying the pieces on the board and trying to decide on my next move. Nobody paid attention to me at all now and I could watch them with ten percent of my mind while the other ninety percent concentrated on bishops, knights, and pawns.

Crow and I made up shortly after that, when I was alone in my compartment and felt the bulkheads pressing close around me. The touch of claustrophobia made me envy Crow his falsie of the ancient city and its lagoon. What *I* saw was what I got. Then I wondered if there might be something more.

I untangled myself from the sling, drifted over to the palm terminal, and retrieved the inventory of furnishings for the compartment—the standard inventory for every living space on board. It didn't take much searching to find the program and switch it on.

When I turned around, my stomach tightened. The compartment had become an ancient library, with books racked on varnished wooden shelves that extended from floor to painted ceiling. Windows looked out on a green lawn and distant rolling hills. A thick carpet covered the floor and there were leather chairs with nearby lamps that cast a pleasant glow for reading. Outside, I could hear faint shouts and the crack of what I guessed to be a cricket bat. Inside, there was classical music.

One shelf of books was real, the others illusion. I reached for one volume and the book vanished at the same moment that my fingers touched the metal bulkhead. There was a sudden glow from the terminal's viewing screen. When I glanced at it, I saw an image of the book with the pages slowly turning.

It was a compartment for an older man and I wondered why it had been assigned to me. Probably because if I were to design it, it would be the same—I wouldn't change a single detail.

"I wondered when you would look at it," a voice said behind me.

Crow and Loon had ducked in through the shadow screen. Crow smiled half apologetically. "Do you mind, Sparrow?"

I shrugged, glad they had come but reluctant to admit it.

They drifted in and sat in the two chairs opposite me. It took a moment before I realized they had brought in metal crates and were sitting on them. They were familiar with the falsie from . . . before.

"It was kind of you to ask us in," Loon said, trying to hide a grin. Crow took a small pipe from his waistcloth, lit it and handed it to me.

"Want some smoke?"

I took it, inhaling cautiously. The smoke made me cough, but after a moment it also made me feel very much at ease.

Loon accompanied the classical music with a few bars on his harmonica, then suddenly asked, "Did you hear about Quince and Portia in the equipment room?"

He said it with a wink. I looked blank so he filled me in on all the details, including some I'm sure he made up on the spot. I started to giggle and found I couldn't stop. Crow's smile grew broader. They offered me more smoke and gossiped about other members of the crew and I spent half that sleep period alternating between shock and fits of laughter.

It was the first time I had ever felt completely at home on board the *Astron*.

One time period, after my shift was over, Crow took me down to Reduction, a compartment on the lowest level. My skin was crawling before we even got there, and once there, I didn't want to stay very long. It was a small, tidy room with a low overhead and a metal ledge jutting out from the bulkhead to which you could secure yourself if you wanted to sit. There were tightly covered, well-scrubbed vats with a lot of piping along another bulkhead. Against the far one was a squat, sealed chamber with distillerylike apparatus on top. The compartment reeked of efficiency; it was the only one I had seen whose metal piping still shone and whose bulkheads still gleamed.

It also smelled far different from the rest of the *Astron*. Buried beneath faint whiffs of disinfectant were odors of age and human waste and something else. Despite the glisten and the shine, I knew we were in a charnel house. The thought made me sick.

At first I didn't notice that one of the glass-fronted storage chambers against the near bulkheads was covered by a black sheet. Memories struggled within me and I was tempted to go over and lift the cloth; then I deliberately turned away. I had fought my nightmares once, I didn't want them to return.

Microscopes and other equipment were secured to a laboratory table in the center of the compartment. I floated over and put my finger beneath the objective lens of one of the 'scopes, working the stage controls until the ridges of my fingerprints had become mountains. I let Crow look, then drifted down the table, running my hands over the other equipment. Set into the overhead were shelves holding bottles of different-colored reagents and lockers filled with laboratory glassware.

"There's more medical equipment here than in sick bay," I murmured.

"People don't get sick on board," Crow whispered, "but they do die."

We didn't hear anybody come up behind us, though I could usually tell if someone was approaching by the disturbance in the air currents.

"Crow's right, nobody gets sick. But nobody lives forever, either. On the *Astron*, nothing ever goes to waste—we're a closed system, we can't afford the loss of mass."

Abel had drifted through the hatchway without my being

aware, a warning that big as he was, his size was no handicap in getting around. Following close behind was Thrush.

There were no RESTRICTED signs but I felt guilty anyway. "Crow was just showing me the ship," I said.

Abel glanced at Crow, who nodded vigorous assent.

"I planned on showing it to you soon enough. Everybody on board has to acknowledge their own mortality, and a tour of Reduction is the first step."

It was logical that Abel, as the ship's doctor, would be in charge of Reduction, but I had no idea why Thrush was there. He answered my question before I even had a chance to ask it.

"I'm assisting, Sparrow—one of my duties." He drifted over to the bank of storage chambers and lifted one end of the black sheet. To my surprise, an expression of clinical detachment suddenly replaced his usual arrogant smirk. It was the first time I had ever seen the look of a scientist.

Abel joined him for a moment, then turned back as Crow and I edged closer to the hatchway. His look of perpetual irritation had vanished.

"You understand, Sparrow—when people come here we have to ease them out of life and make sure their water and minerals and proteins are preserved for the ship."

"When people come here," I repeated, feeling stupid. I couldn't visualize anybody deliberately going to Reduction to die. At least, I had never seen one. Then I realized they probably went during shift, when the passageways were mostly empty and few would be watching.

A flash of Abel's usual impatience returned. "I told you that people only die from accidents on board. There is no sickness, they just get older and older. There comes a time when the quality of one's life is such it's no longer worth living. Eventually they come here."

Crow was standing behind me, tugging at the back of my waistcloth. He wanted desperately to leave and so did I.

I looked over at the chamber, where Thrush was still inspecting something beneath the black sheet.

"Who was he?"

"Judah." A shadow passed over Abel's face and I vaguely remembered a slender, middle-aged man with a perpetually worried face at breakfast. Judah had been one of Abel's few friends.

I bowed and said formally, "I regret your loss and thank you for the gift of knowledge."

Abel bowed slightly in return. Thrush looked up from the vacuum sink where he was washing his hands and said quietly, "Don't get lost, Sparrow."

"I won't," I said, antagonistic as always when it came to Thrush. "You're not the one who's showing me around."

"Your loss," he murmured, smiling.

Then I had one of those flashes of insight that sometimes come to a person. Abel had lied to me. Judah hadn't been old and he hadn't been ill and he hadn't come to Reduction. He had died in his own compartment—the compartment with the quarantine sign that I had explored a dozen sleep periods before.

I really didn't know much about the ship or its crew but I was learning that there were informers and plots and deep differences among the crew members. I suspected in that atmosphere it might have been easy for a man to die.

8

Within a few time periods Crow and Loon and I became inseparable. We explored the distant recesses of the ship, drifting down deserted corridors and poking into empty compartments that held faint reminders of their former occupancy: a face mask that had been thrown in a corner, a piece of writing slate, a wadded-up waistcloth . . . Everything was thick with dust and at times the emptiness and the silence were so overwhelming we spoke in whispers.

Once, Crow and I were alone in a large compartment—Loon had come along but hadn't caught up with us yet—when the cabin suddenly filled with the noise of clinking dinner utensils and ghostly voices.

Crow glanced wildly around and whispered, "Be quiet!" I froze, drifting slightly with the eddying air currents. But it wasn't Crow's command that had frozen me, it was the voices themselves, crisp and clear in the silence.

". . . a day for a picnic . . ."

". . . called him . . . Lincoln's getting better . . ."

". . . hurt in the fall on Bishop VI . . ."

". . . visual drama where the hills meet the sky . . ."

". . . this was called punch . . ."

Loon floated in through the hatch, laughing. Crow cuffed him, half in anger, and Loon fled to the far end of the compartment, still cackling.

"I couldn't find the projection, only the audio. It sounds like some sort of party."

Crow was watching me intently, ignoring Loon, who caught the expression on my face and promptly shut up.

"What's the matter?" Crow asked.

"The voices."

I concentrated, trying to sort them out so I could follow conversations. Names, I needed names—but the names wouldn't come.

Crow sighed. "They're from a long time ago, Sparrow."

I shook myself. "A long time ago," I agreed. I didn't tell them that the voices had jogged buried memories, that several of them sounded like people I had known. Familiar faces had bobbed in the back of my head and then vanished before I could associate a name or experience with any of them.

Hydroponics was another favorite stop; once I got sick from eating what I found out later were green tomatoes. Another time we consumed half a row of strawberries before guilt finally caught up with us. Crow grew very quiet and I knew he was thinking that Pipit would accuse him of stealing the fruit and then she wouldn't talk to him for a half a dozen time periods.

I envied Crow her attentions and I even envied him her anger. There were times when he shared Pipit's compartment and I particularly envied him those moments. In my mind, I frequently cast myself in his role, only with Snipe playing the part of Pipit.

I often went to the plays on the hangar deck because Snipe was in them. I fell in love with her as Juliet and had lewd thoughts when she played Cleopatra opposite Noah's Caesar. She had a flair for playacting that few of the others had, though Ophelia seemed perfectly cast as Lady Macbeth.

To my amazement, one of the best of the actors was Loon, who starred as a character named Bottom in a play about ancient Greece. He played his harmonica and danced to a tune he had made up to go with the words "the raging rocks and shivering shocks" from the play. The applause was tremendous and Loon was the star of the show, though even he grew sick of the words and tune: Everybody sang them when he showed up for breakfast or when they passed him in the corridors.

As we got closer to the Aquinas system, Crow became more preoccupied and troubled. When I was with him, there were long stretches of silence when he seemed about to tell me something, then changed his mind and drew back. One time period after we had seen a training play, he waited until the corridor was deserted, then tugged me into an empty compartment. He closed the shadow screen and pressed his hand over the palm terminal to activate the falsie.

A moment later, we were standing in a cave with a warm fire at our backs and a night sky blazing with stars beyond the cavern's mouth. Somewhere in the darkness an owl hooted and small animals rustled in the brush. I shivered when a wolf howled in the forest below.

"I come here when I want to be alone," Crow said quietly. "I like to look at the stars and think."

He sat on the rocky floor of the cave and I sat beside him, shifting my cling-tites slightly and pressing my knees to my chin so my bum was actually in contact with the metal deck. I should have kept silent and given him a chance to talk but for some reason I had started to think about Reduction. I couldn't shake the image of the black sheet draped over the storage chamber that held Judah.

"Where do we go when we die, Crow?"

It was a child's question and I felt embarrassed the moment I asked it.

"Where do we go?" Crow repeated, surprised. "To Reduction, of course."

"After that."

He shrugged. "Back to the Great Egg, I suppose—it's where all life eventually goes."

Sitting in the darkness next to Crow was the closest I had been to another human being since Pipit had held me after one of my nightmares. For just a moment, I let myself be carried away by my emotions.

"Do you ever get lonely, Crow?"

I wasn't thinking of Crow, of course—I was thinking of myself and Snipe.

"No, I don't get lonely," he said finally. "I suppose some people do. Some people will always be lonely, they were born that way."

He didn't add "poor bastards" but I supposed he was thinking it and I wondered if it included me. He shifted uneasily in the darkness.

"Sparrow?"

"What?"

He hesitated a moment, then changed his mind and said, "Forget it."

I should have encouraged Crow to tell me what was bothering him, but perception usually comes with age and I was too young.

"Do you think we'll ever meet them?" My mind had drifted once again and I was searching for exhaust trails among the stars.

"Meet who?"

"Tybalt's aliens."

Curtly: "No, I don't think so."

"You don't really believe they're out there, do you?"

Crow didn't answer but stood up and pushed over to the glowing palm terminal. The night sky and the cave faded. "We've got a shift coming up, Sparrow." He didn't look at me but grabbed a bulkhead ring and kicked out through the shadow screen.

I finally sensed his disappointment and suddenly wondered what he had wanted to talk about.

I didn't have to wait long to find out.

For a week, the rumor was that after Aquinas II there would be a major change in the *Astron*'s course. I hadn't paid much attention, on the ground that it would affect my life not at all. But one time peiod, after her early lecture, Ophelia asked me to drop by for a meal, suggesting that I needed help to catch up. I worried about it enough so that when I did drop by, I had no appetite at all. She wasn't alone and I couldn't decide at first whether to be relieved or disappointed. My imagination supplied motives for both her original concern for me and the hostility to which it had gradually changed.

Crow nodded when I drifted in; he didn't look very friendly. Loon had been quietly playing his harmonica and now stopped and secured it in his waistcloth. Corin, the chief computerman, was present but seemed so nervous and upset I wondered why he was there. Snipe nodded at me, her expression reserved and distant.

Crow said, to nobody in particular, "I'll secure the hatchway," and started to dog down the actual metal hatch. I was astonished. Shadow screens had always been enough for privacy; nobody ever violated them. The dogged-down hatch was an added precaution but I had no idea why or against whom.

Ophelia was working with Noah at the small food dispenser. She looked up and said, "We'll be ready in a moment, Sparrow." Her voice was neutral and told me nothing. Everybody had fallen silent when I drifted in and I realized dinner had been a pretext—this was a meeting of interested parties and the subject of interest was me.

The meal was a bland protein mush with no spices or forming. I had choked down about half of it when Noah said, "You should ignore Thrush, Sparrow. He's no respecter of authority."

I felt bewildered; I hadn't been thinking about Thrush at all. But I said, "He should be—the Captain's a great man."

Ophelia looked up from her tray. "Tybalt thinks so." She obviously thought I was parroting him.

There was another long pause with only the click of utensils against the trays to break the quiet.

"Michael Kusaka was a good choice for captain," Noah

said, and for some reason that struck me as far different from saying he was a good captain. No one added anything and I took their silence as a challenge.

"When I saw the Captain, he told me the purpose of the *Astron,* why we're here and what we're supposed to do." I felt some of the enthusiasm returning and smiled in remembrance. "He said I was as important to the ship as he was. It's not true but I thank him for saying it."

Noah nodded in apparent agreement. "All of us are important to the ship," he said, which also wasn't quite what I meant.

Ophelia fought to hold her tongue, lost the battle and burst out: "At Launch, Kusaka might have been a good choice for captain. He isn't now."

I stared at her in shock. I didn't know what to say. Everybody else concentrated on their trays; that all of them agreed with Ophelia was obvious.

"If the Captain died," Noah said, not looking up, "who would you be . . . honored . . . to serve under, as a replacement?"

It was a strange question but the answer was easy.

"Tybalt."

"I thought you might say that," Noah murmured.

"He has the same feel for the ship as the Captain," I blurted. "Probably more than anybody else, he knows why we're out here. He even gave his foot for the mission on Galileo III!"

"Amputated on the spot, wasn't it?" Ophelia's sarcasm was thick.

I looked at her, startled. "What?"

"Tybalt had his foot amputated on the spot on Galileo III. Isn't that what he told you?"

I glanced over at Corin, who hastily looked away. He had told her about my conversations with Tybalt, I thought angrily. The Captain wasn't the only one who had informers.

"Yes," I said, indignant at the betrayal. "He was very brave to—"

"Galileo III," Ophelia interrupted coldly, "is a planet with virtually no atmosphere. It would have been instant death if we had opened his suit. They took off his foot in the Lander while he was still out of his mind and babbling from exhaustion." She sneered. "It's easy to see aliens if you're out of your mind."

I looked at the others for support, but none of them met my eyes. I had once considered them friends; now it seemed they had all become my enemies.

"I was there," Corin affirmed nervously. "When Ophelia and I found Tybalt, he was delirious. There was no possibility of doing anything for him until we got him back to the Lander."

They hadn't believed Tybalt's tale about the aliens. And I didn't want to believe them. If I did, I suspected I would have to believe the next thing they told me and the next thing after that. Eventually, I would find myself believing everything they told me and I desperately didn't want to. I also realized they really weren't attacking Tybalt, they were attacking the Captain, and for that I despised them.

"What difference does it make how he lost it?" I protested, sullen.

Ophelia stared at me. "You and Tybalt recently inspected some suits, didn't you?"

She apparently knew everything I had done during shift. I nodded and she said, "How many expeditions do you think they've been used for?"

I shrugged. "Hundreds."

"And how many more do you think they'll be good for?"

I didn't want to answer.

"Well, Sparrow, how many?" she repeated.

I cleared my throat. "A dozen," I said slowly. "Not many more."

"And how many more generations do you think the *Astron* will support?"

"I don't know. I have no idea." I had never consciously thought about it until then.

"Guess," Ophelia said in a tight voice. "A hundred? Two hundred?"

I was no engineer, I was a seventeen-year-old tech assistant who had lost his memories and had little knowledge of the ship. But I remembered the glow tubes that had burned out, the worn decks of the compartments and the passageways, the layers of dust on the hangar deck and on the equipment in Shops, the cannibalized Rovers, the rotting fabric of the exploration suits, and the all-pervasive stink of thousands of years of oil and sweat.

"Not two hundred. Not one hundred. I . . . don't know how many."

I glanced at Crow for moral support but his only expression was one of pity. Corin was studying his hands, probably worried about what I might say the next time I saw Tybalt. Loon nervously fingered his harmonica; neither he nor Snipe looked at me. Oddly, Noah met my stare but with a look of such desperation that I felt as much pity for him as Crow obviously did for me.

Ophelia kicked over to the palm terminal and pressed her hand to it. The bulkhead fell away, to be replaced by Outside. The deck of the compartment now stopped abruptly at outer space, the illusion so convincing that I grabbed for a floor ring to keep from floating out.

It occurred to me that the Captain had not been entirely truthful when he said that what I saw on the bridge was what I got. Perhaps that was true of the bridge itself, but Outside had been a simulation and I had looked at it with eyes that gilded it with color and a sense of wonder. What I looked at now was stark and forbidding, a universe of harsh light, glowing dust, and filaments of flaming gases. No part of it reminded me of diamonds or emeralds or rubies.

Ophelia was outlined against Outside, floating against a background of broken crystal. She pointed out the limbs of the galaxy and the blackness between.

"Kusaka wants to take the *Astron* to a region where the stars are closer together and older and where, presumably, there would be more planets to explore. Theoretically, that would increase our chances of finding life." She placed her palm on an edge of one of the limbs of the galaxy, two-thirds of the distance from the center. "We started here." She moved her hand to a nearby spur of stars, closer toward the center. "We're going there. But to get there, we have to cross the Dark."

She pointed at the blackness between and was silent for a moment. I stared at the empty space covered by her hand and tried to translate it into distance and time. I shivered.

"It would take a thousand generations. The planetary systems are very few and far apart. We would run out of mass for the converters as well as most of the elements we need for subsistence and repairs. And we would run out of them in a generation—*this* generation, Sparrow." She hesitated, then said flatly: "Even if that part of space weren't empty, we would never see the other side. The *Astron* is falling apart, it can't make it."

"The Captain knows the ship as well as you," I objected, jittering on the inside with panic and anger. "Why would he risk it and his crew?"

"Because he can't help himself," Ophelia said bitterly.

I felt confused—she wasn't making sense. Noah edged into the argument, ticking off the points with his fingers.

"The requirements for captain at Launch were very specific. They didn't want a man who lacked courage or determination and they didn't want a man who would return to Earth too soon. So they picked a man whom they were sure . . . believed."

Ophelia broke in, impatient.

"Read his bio in the computer's memory matrix, Sparrow—that's one thing that *is* in it. Kusaka was an atmosphere pilot on earth, then ran freight to the Moon and the O'Neill colonies. When he volunteered for the interstellar mission, they grabbed him because he was one of the few who could take the medical treatments. He was the most important member of the crew and they made sure he was immune to any of the degenerative diseases—nobody knew that long life would be one of the side effects. The treatments also made him sterile but I doubt he cared about that.

"Equally important, Kusaka sincerely believed there was alien life in the universe. They strengthened that belief with intense psychological indoctrination and sent him out knowing that he wouldn't return—*couldn't* return—until he found it. They were hugely successful in programming him. More than a hundred generations later, he's still searching."

"He'll find it," I said confidently.

"That's a religious assumption!" Ophelia snapped.

"He convinced me," I said, my voice squeaky with anger. "He'll convince you, too, if you've nerve enough to ask him."

Ophelia looked at me with contempt.

"Ask him? I don't *have* to ask him! It's a hundred lifetimes later, Sparrow—we've explored a thousand systems and fifteen hundred planets, from gas giants to lumps of airless rock, and we haven't found so much as a flea or a germ or a single living cell! The only life in the universe is what's inside this ship and in that thin green layer of scum covering the Earth!"

She paused for breath. In the sudden silence I could hear my own breath rattle through my nostrils. I was suddenly afraid of her and her convictions. Tybalt was a believer and so was she but they didn't believe in the same things. I was terrified I would have to choose between them.

"There's you and me and three hundred others on the *Astron*. We're all the life there is for light years around. There are no lobster men on Galileo III and there isn't any advanced civilization of intelligent slugs on Quietus II. There isn't, there wasn't, there never will be!"

She spread her arms to take in the whole view of Outside, much as the Captain had done on the bridge.

"There's nothing out there, Sparrow! Nothing at all!"

9

O phelia touched the palm terminal and the image of Outside faded to the sweating surface of the bulkhead. I
glanced at Crow and Loon for help but both of them had
turned to stone.

"I don't believe you," I said desperately.

Noah sighed. It was his turn to try and convince me.

"Men have always hoped they weren't alone in the universe, Sparrow. Long before the *Astron* was launched, they
believed there might be life on Venus and Mars. There
wasn't. Then they thought there might be life on some of the
satellites of the gas giants. They were disappointed once
again. Before they built the *Astron,* they spent decades with
radio telescopes listening for signals from other systems. They
never heard any. We haven't, either. Oh, our equipment will
pick up what we think are signals, but inevitably they turn out
to be due to phenomena that have nothing to do with life. We
haven't run across anything yet that could be traced to sen-
tience, not even any Dyson spheres."

"We will!" I cried. I was close to tears.

"That was a joke, Sparrow." He took off his glasses and
polished the thick lenses with his sash. He was going to lecture me and I didn't want to listen. I didn't have the knowledge to refute him and if he convinced me he was right, he
would destroy everything that I had come to value.

"Sparrow, only so many stars are formed each year in the galaxy, and only so many of those can possibly support life. The development of life takes time. Some stars are too massive and have too short a lifetime. Others are binaries and can have no planets, while still others are unstable for a variety of reasons. The result is that only a small fraction of stars can support a planetary system at all."

His voice seeped through the chinks of my beliefs like smoke. "You know that, don't you?"

I thought of all the questions he had asked at mealtime and the dozens of occasions he had sent me to the computer to check for an answer. He had been educating me for this meeting.

"We seem to have found a number of systems," I said, sullen.

He nodded. "We were lucky, if you want to call it that. But the only planets that matter are those in the CHZ, the continuously habitable zone. If they're too close to the primary, the gases and liquids with low boiling points will boil off. If they're too far, all the volatiles remain and you have the gas giants. The only chance for life lies with those in the middle, the iron-core planets with water and an atmosphere."

"So life is rare. We know that."

"Perhaps you don't know how rare, Sparrow." He paused, the fussy teacher carefully choosing his words.

"You have to have water and you have to have an atmosphere. If the planet is too close to its sun, the water vapor can't condense into oceans, it stays in the atmosphere. The carbon dioxide from volcanoes stays in the atmosphere as well and the temperature of the planet's surface will become too hot to support life. If the planet is too far out, its water freezes and you have a lifeless, frozen waste."

"I know that," I said sarcastically. I had a pretty good idea where he was going.

"The CHZ is small," he continued, ignoring me. "Alarmingly small. Some scientists thought that if the Earth had been five percent closer to the sun, it would have been another Venus. One percent farther out, another Mars—those are the planets flanking Earth."

I promised myself I would check on it later, even though I was certain he wasn't making it up. The others were studying my face for my reactions, but I kept it as blank of emotion as I could.

Noah cleared his throat. "Even on a planet in the CHZ, there has to be a reducing atmosphere with an energy source that will produce the amino acids that make up the proteins that in turn make up life."

He paused, waiting for me to nod in agreement, and smiled slightly when I did so.

"The next step is crucial. The simple organic molecules have to be shielded from the ultraviolet radiation of the primary. That requires a large body of water—an ocean—to protect them. No protection and the molecules break up as soon as they're formed. And oceans of water are . . . extremely rare."

I desperately wanted to clap my hands over my ears.

"But something else is rarer still. The next step in the creation of life is when the amino acids form into long chains. Left in the ocean, they drift apart as easily as they join together. There has to be a means of concentrating them. Once a certain level of concentration is reached, they'll form long chains, more complex molecules, automatically. Heating isolated bodies of water would help, say tidal pools warmed by hot lava and occasionally replenished by the sea."

He looked at me quizzically. "I had you check that out in the computer, didn't I?"

I didn't answer and he leaned closer, as if proximity would convince me.

"Do you understand, Sparrow? Tidal pools implies tides and that means a moon large enough to raise them—though not too frequently, because you might dilute the pool too much. A combination of the primary and the moon would raise larger tides less often, and that would be a happy medium. What's required, then, is a planet that has land surfaces, oceans, and a large enough satellite to raise suitable tides. The action would concentrate the simple amino acids and they could combine into the longer chains."

From somewhere, a latent knowledge of physics came to my rescue.

"You could concentrate them by freezing," I said smugly.

He nodded his approval. "A good thought. But reducing the temperature would slow the process, it would take too long."

I cursed myself for having listened to him. "How long?"

"Probably longer than the lifetime of the universe."

I didn't have the facts and figures to argue with him, though I was sure the Captain did. Then a stray thought popped up and I grabbed at it as I might have grabbed at a bulkhead ring.

"You're talking about life—"

"—as we know it," he interrupted, anticipating my objection. "A carbon-based life. Carbon is plentiful and it forms chains long enough to make DNA, which contains millions of atoms. Silicon is also plentiful and makes chains, but its chains are only thirty to forty atoms long. On a planet with liquid nitrogen, the chains would be longer—but at that temperature, the process might take forever."

I could feel the blood drain from my face. Ophelia had been right. Whether there was other life in the universe wasn't a question of science so much as it was a question of faith. And Noah was attacking my faith.

"Some of the requirements for life are met relatively easily. Others are remote possibilities. Put them all together and you come up with a statistical improbability, so improbable that we know of only one anomaly in this galaxy. Perhaps only one in the universe."

He leaned back in the sling and sighed, knowing he hadn't convinced me. "I agree with Ophelia, Sparrow—there's nothing out there. The *Astron* has spent more than a hundred generations looking for something that doesn't exist."

"And how much of the galaxy have we actually explored?" I sneered. "A millionth of one percent? Maybe two?"

"A lot more than that," Ophelia snapped back. "The radio telescopes on board have searched space for two thousand years—hundreds of thousands of stars and millions of frequencies." It was her turn to be contemptuous. "There's nothing out there," she repeated, "nothing at all."

"That's n-not true," I stuttered in outrage. "The Captain said we had discovered signals in the waterhole range coming from Aquinas II."

Noah shrugged. "We've discovered signals in the waterhole range before, hundreds of times. I told you—all of them were explained by causes which had nothing to do with any form of life."

"You want to go back," I suddenly blurted. "You want to seize the ship and go back." I was a slow study but not so slow I couldn't recognize mutineers when I saw them.

Ophelia looked relieved that at last I understood what they were driving at. "That's exactly what we want to do. Take over the *Astron* and go back—go back to the one planet where we know there's life."

"So why don't you?" I cried. "Choose a new captain and go back. That should be easy enough for you to do, you only outnumber the Captain three hundred to one!"

Ophelia stared at me in frustration.

"The ship's drive is tied to the computer and the computer only takes orders from the Captain. Only he can run the ship—they made sure of that at Launch. They didn't want the crew seizing the *Astron* and returning to Earth too soon. Since they couldn't program everybody, they settled for programming Kusaka. If you want to be poetic, it's a dead hand that controls the *Astron*, Sparrow."

I stared at them, more bewildered now than angry.

"Why tell me? I don't believe you and even if I did, there's nothing I can do—" I broke off, finally aware of what the meeting had been all about. "You w-want me to join you! You want to start a mutiny you can't p-possibly win and you want me to join you!"

I was trapped halfway between tears and laughter. They wanted me to join them in a mutiny against the man on board whom I admired the most, and in so doing destroy what little meaning I had found in life. And Crow and Loon, supposedly my best friends, were part of it. Even Snipe . . .

"Why are you telling *me*?" I repeated. "I'm nobody."

Another long silence, broken when Ophelia said tightly: "Don't flatter yourself that you're the only one we'll talk to."

"You can't be that foolish," I said angrily. "I would never join a mutiny against the Captain."

Then I realized what was at stake and all the bravado seeped out of me. They had told me too much, they couldn't afford to let me leave the compartment alive.

"What good would I be to you?" I said slowly. "I know nothing about the ship, there's no way I could help. . . ."

As I spoke, my eyes flicked around the compartment, desperately searching for something to use as a weapon. I finally found it, a piece of a broken writing slate clinging beneath the ledge that held the terminal pad. I dove for it, then waved it at them like a knife. I tried to look fierce, curling my lips away from my teeth as I fumbled at the hatch with my other hand.

What astonished me then was the look of shocked surprise on their faces.

"What are you doing, Sparrow?" Snipe asked. There was a tremor in her voice; she was badly frightened.

Ophelia held out her hand toward me and closed her fingers so they formed a fist, then uncurled them one by one.

"There's nothing else in the entire universe that can do that, Sparrow—but it's taken us more than a hundred generations to realize it." She twisted her wrist and bent her hand back and forth and I followed it with my eyes. "Life is too rare and too valuable. None of us would harm anything living. None of us could."

I kept a firm grip on the piece of slate.

"Somebody killed Judah," I accused. "I saw the bloodstains on the deck mat."

For the first time since I met her, Snipe looked close to tears.

"I wanted to tell you before, Sparrow. Nobody killed Judah; he killed himself."

"He committed suicide?" I was stunned. On a ship where life was so highly valued, it was difficult for me to comprehend—perhaps even more so for them.

Snipe nodded. "None of us can take a life, Sparrow. Except our own."

Noah looked grim. "If the *Astron* goes into the Dark, we couldn't replenish mass and minerals at some planet every five years or so. We'd run out of vital elements very quickly and die within eight to ten generations."

"A lot can happen in eight to ten generations," I said coldly.

Noah's expression faded to one of sadness.

"We won't have that long, Sparrow. Judah lost faith and others will, too. The danger is right now, this generation."

When crew members went to Reduction, it was with the hope and understanding that they were bequeathing themselves to future generations. But for Judah, there had been no future.

I lowered my hand that held the piece of slate and stared at them, trying to make up my mind what to do.

"I'll tell the Captain," I said at last. "He'll have an answer."

Ophelia laughed cynically. "And implicate us all."

"If he did," Crow said hotly, speaking for the first time since the argument began, "he'd implicate himself as well."

"You're lying!" I shouted.

He shook his head, ignoring a whispered objection from Noah.

"You were with us before, Sparrow—it was you who persuaded Loon and me to join in the first place."

I didn't really know if Crow was lying, but for the first time since I had lost my memories on Seti IV, I didn't want them back. I didn't want to know who I had been or what I had believed or how I had been involved. I was safe enough from the mutineers: If I could believe Ophelia, in a hundred generations the crew members had learned to so love life they could not take one even if their own depended on it.

But the Captain had been raised on a world where life was commonplace and I knew instinctively that their reluctance didn't apply to him.

10

I had nothing more to say to them or they to me. Noah let his tray float to the deck and glanced in consternation at Ophelia. Neither of them spoke. Crow put his hand lightly on my shoulder as if he were about to reason with me some more but I was tired of words and arguments I couldn't win and brushed him aside. I undogged the hatch and slipped out through the shadow screen.

My duty was plain, and that was to report them to the Captain. I kicked up through the different levels but found myself growing increasingly reluctant the closer I got to the bridge. What I had to tell the Captain would mean punishment for the plotters. Two of them had been good friends. I was afraid I was falling in love with another, while still another had "taken an interest" at a time when I desperately needed somebody to show me both attention and affection.

But the Captain *would* punish them, and what his punishment might be gave me great pause.

I was still thinking about it as I kicked past the level with the passageway bazaar. I ducked in to glance at the few books offered for sale while I made up my mind what I would do about the mutiny. Two pages into an ancient astronomy text I decided to do nothing. I would wait for a period or so and see what happened. Ophelia and Noah must have talked to other crewmen besides me and certainly not all of them would remain silent.

The next meal period, Ophelia ignored me as usual. On the surface, Crow and Loon were as friendly as always, but there was an undercurrent of tension strong enough to make Thrush glance at Crow and me, his eyes full of curiosity. Fifteen minutes before the end of the period, Noah set up the chessboard and studied the pieces as if he were going to play against himself. After a minute or two I drifted over. Maintaining a routine was all-important, otherwise Banquo might notice and Abel certainly would.

I straddled a crate so I wouldn't drift and tried to decide on my opening gambit, my mind still full of revolts and mutinies.

"The first move is always the most difficult," I said, making excuses for the time I was taking.

Noah didn't look up from the board. "Not if you have a game plan."

I pushed a pawn forward, then pulled it back. "We didn't decide who plays white."

He shrugged. "You go first, Sparrow. It's your move."

I looked at him sharply. We were fencing about the mutiny and that was a game I was bound to lose. I decided to concentrate on simply playing chess.

So I didn't go to the Captain. Gradually I found myself nodding to Crow when we passed in the corridors, and then we were going out of our way to be civil to one another. Finally, one sleep period, I slipped into his compartment to admire the view from the balcony and share some smoke and the latest gossip with him and Loon.

I didn't mention the meeting then but later, when Crow and I were alone in an empty corridor, I said, "You're not afraid?"

"Of what?"

"That I might go to the Captain about your meeting."

"If you were going to go, you would have done it immediately."

"I still might," I said, annoyed.

"You lost your chance, Sparrow—it's too dangerous now."

I was puzzled. "What do you mean?"

"The first thing the Captain would ask is why you didn't tell him sooner."

"I didn't tell him sooner because I didn't want to inform on my friends," I said, offended.

"You're not thinking." Crow lowered his voice. I could feel the faint movement of air at my back—somebody was coming. "The Captain's not going to give you a medal for putting your loyalty to your friends above your loyalty to him. He'll think you delayed because you were considering joining us."

I was indignant. "But I wasn't."

Crow sighed. "Use your head, Sparrow." He slapped my shoulder and kicked off down the corridor, leaving me to wonder if he was right. They had risked too much by trying to recruit me. Crow might have been telling the truth at the meeting; maybe I had been involved before, though how or in what capacity I didn't know. But if I had been that important to them before, I was probably still important to them now. They would approach me again.

The risk was that somebody else would find out about them and tell the Captain. And because I had kept silent, I would be found as guilty as they.

The key was who I had once been and what I had once done. The one person who could help me was Huldah, but she hadn't stepped out of character since the time in the mess when she had suggested that if I wanted to discover my past, I should study my present.

I had never had a chance to talk to her alone to ask her what she had meant. Even when I shared supper with her and Noah, she always played the part of the dutiful wife who dialed the meal on the food machine, then sat quietly in a corner reading at the terminal screen or working on a string tapestry while Noah and I played chess.

I waited for my opportunity; one time period when Noah had been called to a meeting in Exploration, I slipped through her shadow screen after first announcing myself and receiving permission.

She offered me a collapsicup of tea, then relaxed in the compartment sling, a plump little olive-skinned woman with eyes much too bright and intelligent for the matron whom she played. She did me great honor by not making me waste time trying to coax her out of that role.

I didn't know how to begin but she made it easier by saying, "I've been hearing about you, Sparrow, from Noah and Ophelia. Crow and Loon mention you from time to time. So does Corin, when he stops by. And Snipe."

I said, "You know."

"About the meeting? Of course. But you make a mistake if you think those six are the only members." She read my face and smiled. "The mutiny is an open secret, Sparrow. You can spare yourself a trip to the Captain, though I believe you already have."

"You have your loyalties. I wouldn't impose on them."

"I don't talk," she said dryly, "I watch. Everybody respects that."

"And the Captain?"

"He has his own eyes. He doesn't need mine."

"Who do you watch?" I asked casually.

She smiled and squeezed a small bulb of liquid into her cup. I caught the odor and wondered what it was. Later, Loon told me about the secret distillery on board.

"Children." She sipped at her cup and relaxed still more. "And their parents. I watch genes work their way from generation to generation, not only in the shape of bones and the color of eyes and hair but also in actions. I watch children when they get angry or when they laugh and I know I'm watching their parents and their grandparents as well. You watch long enough and you can tell who mated with whom— it's not that difficult."

My respect for her was turning to amazement and I said so.

She smiled. "Anybody can do it, Sparrow. I'm just the one who takes the time."

"Nobody knows who their father is," I said. "Why?"

"You can't hide maternity, Sparrow, that's why the *begats* follow the mother's line. But there's no easy way of determining the father."

She drained her cup and let it drift to the bulkhead, where it clung. "Life is very rare and valuable in the universe. It's also rare and valuable on board ship. Mass is limited, so nobody can have a child until food is assured. That usually means somebody has to die before a child can be born."

She leaned forward, her eyes glowing in the soft light of the compartment.

"Think of it, Sparrow—the creation of life! For both men and women, the birth of a child is a miracle. It's also an act of pride and possession, especially for the man. So impregnation is not restricted to one man. Because nobody knows who the father is, one child is everybody's child."

Her words were a revelation. I had been too young to realize what it might mean to a woman to have a child—or to a man to father one.

"How's the woman chosen?"

"Usually by lot. Sometimes by the Captain's fiat."

"And the . . . father? How many men have a chance to impregnate her?"

"Not fewer than three. Perhaps as many as a dozen."

It struck me as barbaric, then I realized I had no basis for comparison. Huldah read my expression with disapproval. "It's a matter of ceremony, Sparrow—probably the most moving one in which you'll ever take part."

The honor of fatherhood would be diluted. So would the man's feeling of possession of either the woman or the child. Long-term relationships would not be based on blood, at least not from the man's viewpoint.

"The *begats*," I said uncomfortably. "Aren't they all in the computer?"

"On some things," she said with emphasis, "the computer is . . . unreliable."

"Nobody ever knows the father?" I asked again.

She shrugged. "Not the biological one, though occasionally that's obvious. But everybody has to feel they had the chance to create life, everybody has to feel they played God at least once."

I remembered what she had said about genes. "But *you* know," I said. "You always know."

"I watch people, Sparrow, that's all."

"My father—"

"Biological?" She shrugged. "I don't know, Sparrow. Even if I did, it wouldn't help you remember your past. Nevertheless, it's important for you to struggle to find out. The very process of trying will help you."

"And Laertes? Crow and Tybalt said he . . . took an interest."

"A lot of crewmen took an interest, Sparrow."

For some reason, that didn't comfort me.

"Crow said my mother died early. Laertes must have been very important to me." I had fixed on Laertes; if Nerissa had died when I was very young, then Laertes must have been the most important person in my life. What I didn't tell Huldah, though I think she knew, was that I desperately wanted a father, wanted somebody whom I could claim and who would claim me.

"You have the means, Sparrow," she sighed. "Why don't you use them? Find your own answers and perhaps they'll have some relevance for you. If I answered all your questions, you would only have more questions."

It was a rebuff, one I deserved. "The ship," I said. "Life on board has always been the same?"

She looked at me sharply. "You mean, does it change from generation to generation? No, Sparrow, it remains the same. Life remained the same in Egypt for hundreds of years and so did life in the shtetls of Russia. Change comes from the outside, seldom from within. And I think, right at Launch, they made sure that nothing would really change on board."

I didn't understand that, and wanted to ask more questions, but her eyes had dulled and her shoulders had slumped back into the posture of the plump little matron. It was time to go.

"I thank you for your time," I said formally. I turned and almost ran into Pipit coming through the screen with several packets of herbs in her hand. She looked surprised and started to back out.

"Don't go," I said, "I'm leaving." And then I stared hard at her and glanced back at Huldah. "Your daughter?" I said. I couldn't believe I had missed the resemblance before.

"You used your eyes," Huldah said approvingly.

Pipit floated over to her mother and the family portrait was complete. I couldn't be sure who her father was but I thought I saw traces of Noah in her. Then I remembered sick bay and the many sleep periods when she had sat up with me, and her insistence that I get well.

"I should have thanked you long ago," I said.

She looked embarrassed. "I did very little, Sparrow."

I kicked over and kissed her lightly on the cheek.

"Then I thank you for very little," I said and slipped away into the corridor. It was my first apology, but I knew it wouldn't be my last and I was very proud of myself for having made it. Pipit was kind, she was generous of spirit, and she was beautiful. I could understand Crow's adoration.

The sleep periods slid by and I became increasingly aware—at times painfully so—that I was sleeping alone. Like most young men, I found an outlet in my dreams. Sometimes I dreamed of Pipit, feeling guilty enough when I awoke that I would avoid her for several time periods. One period I awoke sweating and wet and realized with a shock that I had been dreaming of Ophelia. It didn't make any sense, though I blushed when I saw her in Exploration and stammered when she asked me a question. She looked at me curiously and after lecture asked what was bothering me. I assured her nothing was wrong, then proved I was lying by fleeing from her through the corridor.

But most of the time I dreamed about Snipe, in situations and positions I was sure nobody had thought of before. I watched her in plays and found excuses to visit her on the hangar level. At the time, I was certain she didn't know why; I was to discover later that at seventeen, I was far younger emotionally than most crew members my age and Snipe was far older. I finally talked about it with Tybalt while on shift.

"Snipe?" he said, disbelieving. "She's a skinny little thing. I was afraid nobody would ever see anything in her."

"I do," I said, blushing still again.

He grinned. "I guess it takes all kinds. Why don't you just ask her to sleep with you?"

I stuttered that of course she had no interest in me, that her only possible reaction would be rejection. Tybalt's half smile faded.

"I keep forgetting," he said slowly. "Sparrow, nobody on board the *Astron* ever turns anybody down the first time. Nobody. And nobody asks the second time unless they've been assured it's mutual." He paused, searching for words. It was obvious that it was a ship's custom he wasn't quite sure how to explain.

There was a moment of awkward silence, broken when I blurted: "Babies, what about—"

"Contraception?" He raised an eyebrow. "It's in the food—I thought you knew that." Then he mumbled, "Of course you didn't," and finally grumped, "It isn't healthy for people to be a mystery to each other, Sparrow. We live too close together." He shrugged. "It's a small enough thing to do. I don't know anybody for whom it's a problem."

But it turned out to be a problem for *me*. I finally stammered out my request to Snipe, who seemed neither overjoyed nor depressed by the prospect. She came to my compartment that sleep period and I made what I thought was love and then spent the rest of the period apologizing. Physically, Snipe was no

longer a mystery but love itself remained one. I'd had no idea I
could be so close to Snipe and yet not be close at all.

. I went to the hangar deck as often as before to watch her in
plays and discovered to my shocked surprise that there was
still something I wanted from her. I wept when she died as
Juliet, was won once again by her Katherine played against a
very wooden Crow as king, and found her irresistible as a
lithe and vivacious Rosalind pretending to be a boy.

There was more to Snipe than a rag and a bone and a hank of
hair, as Tybalt frequently put it. I wanted desperately to know
just what that "more" was. She fascinated me at the same time
she irritated me; she could be coolly pragmatic one moment
and wildly illogical the next, superior and aloof at the start of a
conversation and warm and understanding by the end.

It didn't help to realize that Snipe's personality would stabilize
with time and eventually she would irritate me less and fascinate
me even more. At seventeen, I was in no mood to wait.

On station, Tybalt and I worked well together, and he was
quick to admit it. I also found myself achieving a rapport with
the palm terminal. As Tybalt had told me, its fleshy surface
responded faster to a delicate touch than a hard push. I pared
my fingernails and rubbed lotion into the palms of my hands
so the skin was soft and supple. Sometimes I even scraped my
fingertips so the nerve endings were closer to the surface. In
the viewing globe, I could make the charts and equations flow
so fast you couldn't tell one from another, but I could still
stop the display on the desired graph.

I could make the numbers dance. Nobody else in the division could.

One shift Abel came by with Thrush in tow and they
watched while I put the terminal pad through its paces. When
I was through, Thrush said in a noncommittal voice: "You're
very good. Show me."

It wasn't a request, it was a command, and I glanced at
Tybalt for his approval. Abel didn't wait for Tybalt's permis-

sion but nervously growled, "Do it," so I showed Thrush a simple series of movements. He watched my hand with the same intent look I had noticed in Reduction, then duplicated my movements without a mistake. I ran through another, more complicated series.

He made one mistake this time, then leaned back in the operator's sling with a small smile of triumph. "All it takes is practice, right?"

"It takes more than that," I said through clenched teeth.

He twisted smoothly out of the sling and hit me lightly on the arm.

"I don't think so, Sparrow."

He smiled again when he left and this time I read his expression with no difficulty. We were competitors, he and I, though I had no idea what for, nor did I know what the winner's prize might be.

A dozen work periods passed before Tybalt mentioned his adventures again. By now, I accepted them for what they were—memories of things not quite seen—and did my best to sift fact from fancy. I had been wide-eyed with awe before but now, thanks to Ophelia, I had growing doubts—and hated myself for having them.

We were alone and Tybalt settled into the headquarters sling, taking special pains so his foreshortened leg was free of the webbing. He reached for his pipe and turned the exhaust vent on high.

"I told you about the first landings I ever made, didn't I?"

"Tell me again," I encouraged. The names of the planets kept changing and I was no longer sure just which *were* his first landings.

"They were Alpha and Omega, twin planets in the Tau system," he began. "They were dead planets—no moons and no tectonic activity, frozen to their cores. We had no hopes of finding life there, we knew those planets had never served as a cradle for it. Alpha was a cursory exploration, all ashes and pumice and ice. Omega was the more interesting—by far."

Once again I was rapt with attention.

"Omega was as dead as Alpha, of course. But we found the remains of *something* that had been stranded there. We ran across slabs of rock that formed a huge lean-to—you could even see the blast marks where they had been cut from a nearby cliff. And there were tracks in the pumice surface where something huge had dragged itself over to the lean-to for shelter. The tracks were almost obliterated by small craters; the creature had been shot and wounded."

As Tybalt talked, I could see the creature in my mind as clearly as if it were a projection on the hangar deck. Something with four stumpy legs and gray, rocklike skin with a shielded braincase out of which tiny eyes glared defiance at a hostile world.

The picture hung in my mind for a moment, then wavered around the edges and started to fade as doubt set in. The biggest handicap in believing Tybalt was that I wanted to so badly.

"You found the body?" I asked, knowing that he hadn't.

"Its friends had come back for it," he said with a note of regret. "You could see where the rescue ship had landed." He used a stubby finger to draw a picture in the sweat on the bulkhead. "First there were the tracks of something pulling itself through the pumice, then those were partly erased by small craters during the fight, then a dozen of the craters were crushed in turn by the rescue ship settling on them."

I was tempted to argue that the craters and the tracks had been made by meteorites, then thought better of it. He wasn't trying to convince me, he was just telling me what he thought he had seen. Another time, I would have believed him implicitly, but the meeting in Ophelia's compartment had introduced doubts.

"And nobody else saw them," I said, prepared for disappointment.

"You're right, Sparrow," he sighed, "nobody else did." He concentrated on filling his pipe. "It would be worth my life if I made that up."

I thought I had done a better job of hiding my skepticism, then realized I was doing him a disservice by not being honest.

"Ophelia doesn't believe you," I said bluntly. "She claims there's a rational explanation for everything you've ever reported."

He banged his fist against the bulkhead. "Ophelia doesn't believe in a damned thing!" He fought his anger for a moment, then shrugged. "Skepticism can blind you as much as faith. If you had never seen an elephant, there would be no end to the reasonable explanations for the path it left in a forest—none of which would include a lumbering beast with a small tail at one end and a large tail at the other, with an enormous head and two huge fans for ears."

He smiled at his own imagery. "Look up 'elephant' in the computer's memory, you'll see what I mean." He leaned forward in the sling to poke me in the chest with his forefinger. "The galaxy is huge, Sparrow. To think we know all the requirements for the creation of life is hubris—and the gods don't take kindly to that."

I agreed. But I couldn't shake the memory of Ophelia crying that there had been a hundred generations and a thousand systems and fifteen hundred planets and the crew of the *Astron* had yet to find a single living cell.

Ophelia and Noah had been very convincing in their arguments and they had scientific logic on their side.

But so, in a sense, did Tybalt.

It didn't take long for my shift at the palm terminal to become boring. I was skillful and fast and never made mistakes, though occasionally I came close. Those were the times when Thrush came to the compartment to practice. I never saw the results of what he did but I could tell by his frequent look of self-congratulation that he was gaining in dexterity and speed. Nobody ever told me why he was learning to work the palm terminals and I never asked.

Eventually, of course, I couldn't resist checking out Tybalt's landings. Unauthorized use of the computer was strictly forbidden but I was willing to risk it. Who would know what I did during those times when I was the only one on duty at the terminal?

Tybalt's stories had become a part of his personality and were easy to forgive, if for no other reason than that they were entertaining. But whatever else they were, it turned out that Tybalt hadn't made them up to pass the time with me. The reports of his landings on Alpha and Omega, Galileo III, and Midas IV were all logged in the computer. The official accounts were stripped of the romance of his stories but the details were the same, buried in the jargon required of a report to the Captain.

I listened to him with more respect after that. I'm sure he knew I had checked his reports, but if he was offended, he never let me know.

It was much easier to check out Tybalt's reports than it was to research the genealogy of the crew. Tybalt's reports were finite but the genealogy went on forever. Researching the families on board was tedious, but it took courage to check out my own background. I was afraid of what I might find out.

I waited until I was alone in the compartment with no danger of being interrupted, then took a deep breath and punched in my name. The earliest information that appeared in the viewing globe was the medical records from sick bay, detailing my time there after the accident on Seti IV. I asked for additional background but the words scrolling through the globe read:

ALL DATA CONCERNING SUBJECT
SEALED BECAUSE OF
ACUTE STRESS DUE TO AMNESIAC
ILLNESS. GIVING
SUBJECT LIFE HISTORY INFORMATION
PRIOR TO HIS
OWN RECALL WILL HINDER COMPLETE
RECOVERY.

Forbidden to tell the truth, my friends had invented clumsy lies whenever I badgered them about my past. As usual, I owed them all an apology.

But nothing had really changed. All the statement said was that nobody could tell me about my past. It didn't say I couldn't find out for myself.

I rubbed my hands together, cracked my knuckles, then placed my palms back on the terminal pad and watched the words go tumbling through the globe. Nerissa was real, though, as Crow had told me, she had gone to Reduction a few years before and her mother—my grandmother—two decades before that. There was also a Laertes who seemed to fit both Tybalt's and Crow's descriptions. Unfortunately, the information on him seemed strangely sketchy.

I frowned and traced him back through his mother and grandmother. He and his ancestors were mentioned less and less frequently until, about the fifth generation back, no further information about them appeared in the records. The intricate weaving back and forth of his genetic lines feathered and after five generations Laertes' line vanished from the ship's company.

There was only one possible reason. In addition to Tybalt and Crow lying to me about Laertes and Huldah evading my questions, somebody had made false entries in the computer. They had been prepared for my questions about my mother. They hadn't thought I would take an even greater interest in my "father."

I sat there in shock, my hands lying loosely on the terminal's skin. Why? I wondered. Why the lies and the elaborate pretense? Why the attempt to tamper with the computer, however crudely?

But there was no arguing with the conclusion.

"Laertes" had never existed.

11

Instead of accusing my friends of breaking faith and lying about the nonexistent Laertes, I withdrew into myself, resolving not to trust those who had been closest to me. Inexplicably, I chose to trust the one whom I had good reason to trust the least.

I returned to see Huldah but was greeted by a pleasant, vacant-faced matron who responded to my angry questions with a look of hurt bewilderment and an offer of some of Pipit's herbal tea. I reminded her that we had talked before but she claimed she couldn't remember.

Later, I wondered why I hadn't asked Huldah about Nerissa, or even pursued her through the computer's memory. But she and my grandmother had died years before; their line stopped with me. There was no end to the information I found out about her, most of which indicated that she was much like any mother and did all the things that mothers usually do. Everybody I talked to remembered her in excruciating detail—leading me to suspect they didn't really remember her at all.

Knowing Laertes would have lent me dimension and identity; knowing him would have meant knowing myself because I would have known the person I had patterned myself after. If he had ever really lived, even in death he would still have left some traces of himself behind.

But once again I found myself existing in a vacuum, dating my life from my memories of Seti IV and from when I had awoken in sick bay. What little I had gleaned about myself from Tybalt and Crow was now suspect. If they had lied about Laertes, why wouldn't they have lied about me?

So I kept to myself, avoiding those I had been close to before, even Snipe. I still smarted from the knowledge that she had slept with me because it was ship's custom not to refuse, not because she had wanted to. She had given no indication that she found me attractive or even liked me and I wasn't willing to confirm her indifference now that she was free to refuse.

I begged off dropping by Crow's compartment for smoke and gossip and while on shift I discovered reasons to continue working with the palm terminal when ordinarily I would have taken a break with Tybalt. I practiced long hours with the terminal, discovering nuances in its operation that I hadn't suspected before. When I wasn't working, I read the books in the "library" that served as my compartment. Some of them seemed familiar to me and I hoped they would provide a clue to the type of person I had once been.

After I made it plain that I wanted very little to do with anybody, my friends were offended and reluctantly left me alone. That hurt me even more and the hurt fed upon itself. What I wanted, of course, was to be reassured of their friendship and talked out of my dark mood.

The one crewman who didn't leave me alone was Thrush. He sensed something was wrong and watched me closely at mealtimes, when I played chess indifferently if at all with Noah, and in Exploration, where my relationship with Tybalt had grown more distant and professional.

Thrush made his first overture of friendship one time period when I was flying down a corridor lost in my own thoughts and missed the bulkhead ring I would normally have caught to change direction. I had just flipped in midair so I would hit the bulkhead bum first when a hand grabbed my arm and jerked me to a halt.

"Slow down, Sparrow, you're not that good yet." I twisted and stared full into the pale eyes of Thrush.

I shook free. "Everybody overshoots once in a while," I said in a chilly voice. I started down the corridor again, afraid I would be late for my shift in Exploration.

Behind me he said, "You don't like me very much, do you?"

I turned to face him. Thrush was a logical target for my hostility.

"Not many crew members do."

He shrugged. "At times, I regret it." That surprised me and without thinking, I found myself drifting down the corridor with him. Right then, I was as much of an outcast as he was, and mutual misery accomplished the impossible by turning Thrush into acceptable company.

"You're very good at the terminal," he said with a sideways glance. "It will take me a while to catch up."

I felt a surge of warmth for him at the same time I heard a dozen warning bells. Thrush was being friendly and Thrush never did anything without reason.

When the conversation limped to its natural death, he suddenly said, "You've seen the ship?"

"Too many times."

"Do you know how it works?" I looked puzzled and he explained patiently, "The ship is a machine, Sparrow. You don't know how it works if you only know how pieces of it work."

He had the same expression on his face that I had seen in Reduction and when he was at the palm terminal. It had nothing to do with lust or anger or joy or contentment. It was the expression of a man who wanted to know more than he did, who would always want to know more than he did, and it indicated an attitude that I would eventually admire above all else.

But at the time I misunderstood him and said, "I don't want to know how Reduction works."

"I wasn't going to show you—not yet." He said it with a sly smile that was both an offer and a dare.

I knew my own job and knew it well, but I didn't know much beyond it; I had never thought of the ship as a single mechanism.

It was Thrush who showed me, describing how the huge fusion motors in Engineering were tied into the memory matrix of the *Astron*'s biocomputer. Then he explained the inherent fragility of the latter. It was living, he said, and subject to its own illnesses and diseases. The piping was sealed and if it were ever breached, the memory fluid would become contaminated, the neural net would die, and in short order the ship would become a drifting hulk.

He also explained that the *Astron* was actually a "cluster ship," not a single cylinder but a group of three, two of which had long been abandoned. I had no idea that so much of the *Astron* was deserted and vacant, that as the crew had shrunk, it had gradually receded into the central cylinder. Even though the ship was a closed system and everything was recycled, there were still unavoidable losses. Over the generations, living in the *Astron* had been like living in a balloon with a slow leak.

There was nothing that Thrush didn't seem to know about the *Astron,* from the plants in Hydroponics to the vacuum vents and the recycling system that kept the air breathable, if not completely free from the stink of the crew. His thirst for knowledge was a part of Thrush's personality that I had never seen before. Or maybe it was a different personality entirely.

With that new assessment went both respect and admiration. From time to time, I had a glimpse of what was really happening, but it was lost in my own eagerness to learn. Thrush was showing me his personal treasures and I felt more and more in his debt.

I wondered how I could have misjudged him so badly.

Once, Ophelia cornered me and said, "Thrush has no use for you, Sparrow. Be careful." When I grew sullen and didn't answer, she shrugged and said, "My God, you're such a fool," and drifted away. Crow and Loon were the next to try and reason with me.

"He means you no good, Sparrow," Crow warned.

"How would you know?" I cried. "All of you combined against him a long time ago, you never gave him a chance."

"He never gave us one," Loon said in a dry voice.

"He doesn't lie," I said hotly.

"Not with words, Sparrow."

I didn't know what he meant and turned away. Behind me, Crow murmured: "Be careful, Sparrow. He's one of the Uncounted—he violates ship's customs."

I never asked what he meant and I never noticed what was so obvious to Crow and Ophelia and everybody else. I envied Thrush his intelligence and his knowledge and I envied him in other ways as well. I went out of my way to watch him as he exercised in the gymnasium and to admire the play of the muscles beneath his parchment-thin skin. When he sped through the corridors, his movements were fluid and precise, the mark of a man who knew exactly where he was in space at any given moment. More than anybody else on board, he was graceful.

In short, I was blinded by his brilliance, his physical beauty, and what I had come to consider his generosity of mind. What I never would have believed, and what nobody could have told me, was that I was being seduced and the whole ship was witness to it. I should have guessed, of course; Heron's jealousy should have been enough to warn me.

What I clung to later was that I never confided in Thrush as I did in Crow, nor did I joke with him or gossip. And while I was relaxed during most of the time I spent with Crow or even with Snipe, I was never relaxed with Thrush. At times I tried to talk to him about my lost memories and what they meant to me, but he never encouraged it and I knew that I was boring him.

In turn, he seldom talked about himself. But it came as no surprise when he finally told me the Captain had "taken an interest" in him. Once Thrush told me that, I should have anticipated the invitation to share a meal with him and the Captain. Thrush hid his feelings of self-importance but I was properly impressed and, of course, properly grateful.

I told nobody else but showed up early on the bridge, telling the guard that I was waiting for Thrush. Abel left just before Thrush arrived, his mouth turning down at the corners when he saw me, his greeting sour and perfunctory. Then Thrush arrived and we kicked through the bridge area into the next compartment, the Captain's private quarters.

The Captain was standing at a huge port, staring at the stars beyond, one hand lightly touching the glass and the other behind his back. I wondered if it was a pose for my benefit, but when we eventually left, he had resumed it. I knew I would never see Outside the same way he did and envied him his view.

His nod to Thrush was casual, the one to me slightly less so. He offered his hand and I shook it once, formally, then glanced around the compartment while he greeted Thrush. There were paintings on the bulkheads, along with intricate string tapestries and comfortably padded slings; a desk and a dinner table stood in the middle. When I took a closer look, I discovered the paintings were of deserts and forests and canyons on a planet that only the Captain remembered first-hand.

There was a murmur of conversation coming from somewhere behind me and I glanced around, startled—I had thought we were the only ones there. Where the bulkheads met the overhead, there was a bank of view screens, dozens of them, showing compartment interiors with crewmen eating or sleeping, and corridors with tiny figures floating to their shifts in Hydroponics and Engineering.

It bothered me that the Captain could look into any area of the *Astron* any time he wanted, that while shadow screens gave us privacy when it came to each other, there was none at all when it came to him. I had seen the view screens scattered throughout the ship but nobody had told me they were the eyes and ears of the Captain.

"Don't look so concerned, Sparrow—the peep screens are precautionary. I seldom watch them."

He gestured at the table and Thrush and I floated over. A stony-faced crewman, Escalus, served us in silence, then quietly sat guard just outside the hatchway to the sleeping compartment. He kept an eye on us while we ate, and I decided Escalus was watchdog as well as waiter.

The food was well-formed and tasty but no better than what I had enjoyed with Noah and Huldah or that Pipit served at division mess. If anything, it was a touch below the latter, the only indication the Captain wasn't aware of *everything* that happened on board.

"Tybalt says you've become very proficient with the palm terminal."

This time, I wasn't quite as naive. It was going to be a game of conversational chess and I suspected he was better at it than Noah.

"Thrush is learning fast, too," I offered.

The Captain looked mildly surprised. Thrush shot me a wooden glance and I realized too late that he hadn't wanted the Captain to know. Another bite of food and then: "What else is happening in your life, Sparrow?"

I guessed that he wanted me to fill him in on the details of the mutiny but I sidestepped the opportunity.

"Tybalt's told me about his landings." I realized immediately that I had made a mistake.

"Oh? And what did he tell you?"

"He told me about his encounters with aliens—his near encounters."

There was a sudden silence except for the slight sounds of eating. Thrush was intent upon his plate but the Captain pushed his away and leaned back in his sling, his dark eyes curious.

"Why do you say 'near'?"

"Because nobody else saw them," I said defensively.

His smile tightened. "Perhaps nobody else was looking for them." He twisted out of the sling and kicked over to the port, motioning me to follow. At the port, he put his hand lightly on my shoulder and once again I felt as if I were back on the bridge.

"Not everybody still believes in the mission, Sparrow, I know that." I tensed, then cursed to myself, knowing he was reading my reactions with his hand as easily as I could read a palm terminal.

"Relax, Sparrow, I already know their names."

He said it with just the right note of hurt in his voice that not everybody shared his faith. I didn't say anything and realized too late my silence told him what he wanted to know. I, too, no longer quite believed.

"We haven't found life yet, though Tybalt's reports have been encouraging. I know some members of the crew have told you differently, Sparrow. I'm curious about what they said."

I searched his face but saw only honest curiosity. I didn't want to say anything at all but it was his opening gambit and I couldn't stand there mute.

"That it's been a hundred generations and fifteen hundred planets and we haven't found anything," I said in a shaky voice.

"Fifteen hundred planets . . ." He smiled. "That many." He stared through the port a long moment, then said, "And how many planets do you think are out there, Sparrow? Care to guess?"

"Millions," I said faintly.

"More like tens of millions, I should think. And the chances of life, Sparrow? What did your friends say about that?"

I tried desperately to keep my voice from fading away entirely.

"That it wasn't very likely."

He smiled again but with no trace of humor. "I didn't know we had so many scientists on board."

He waved his hand at Outside and I remembered how on the bridge he had made me feel important and filled me with a sense of purpose. I suspected he knew I didn't feel quite the same way now. But he couldn't know how much I regretted it.

"I've lived too long, Sparrow. I've seen stars explode and fill the void with light so bright it blinded all our view screens and I've watched them shrink to blackened cinders—stars whose moment of dying was just as brief as that of anybody on board. I've explored planets where red suns filled a third of the sky at dawning, I've seen worlds where the tides were made of molten rock, I've stood in rain that had been falling for a hundred million years, and I've heard the crash of thunder under a sky so covered with clouds no living creature would ever see the heavens."

I knew he could feel my trembling but it didn't matter. I would change my mind later—I knew that, too—but once again I would have died for him. He turned me around and held my shoulders with both hands while he stared into my eyes, reading what was passing through my mind as easily as he read a book.

"The galaxy is huge beyond conception, Sparrow. We come from an infinitesimal portion of it and we don't even know all of the laws that govern that. Knowing so little about our own small corner of it, does it make sense to propose theories about what's possible in the rest of it? Does it make sense to you, Sparrow?"

"No, sir," I squeaked.

He let me go and looked at Thrush.

"What about you, Thrush? Does it make sense to you?"

Thrush shook his head. "No, it doesn't, Captain." He managed to say it without sounding obsequious and I wondered if he truly believed or was just a better actor than I.

"What else did they tell you, Sparrow?" His mood had turned dark and I felt a pinch of fear.

"That you want to take the *Astron* into the Dark."

"And?"

"That we couldn't possibly make it."

"What do you think, Sparrow?"

For just a moment, I had the feeling he wasn't asking the question of me, that he was asking it of somebody else. And that he had asked it many times before.

"I'm not the one to judge, sir."

He frowned. "I'm not asking you for anybody else's opinion, Sparrow. I'm asking you for yours."

I took a breath. "The *Astron* is falling apart. I don't think the ship could make it."

I waited for the overhead to fall and the bulkheads to collapse, but instead the Captain turned back to the port and once again put his arm around my shoulders.

"Are you familiar with Magellan, Sparrow? He sailed from a country called Spain back on Earth, centuries ago, hoping to circumnavigate the world. He had five leaky ships and a few hundred men. Some of his ships were wrecked and most of his men died, but three years later one of his vessels returned to Spain. He had accomplished his mission, he had proved the earth was round."

I fidgeted during the silence that followed while he stared, bemused, at Outside. Finally: "Do you know what was really important in all of that, Sparrow?"

I shook my head.

"All anybody cared about was that he had done it. Nobody asked if his ships leaked. Nobody asked if his crews endured hardships. In the end, the only thing that mattered was whether or not he possessed the will."

He turned away from me and looked back at Outside. I hadn't finished eating but I no longer had an appetite. Thrush mentioned that it was time for shift, and the Captain nodded absently. Just before we floated out the hatch, he said, "What mattered was the will of one man, Sparrow. Only one."

The Captain had come close to persuading me once again. He had almost recreated the brief moment of hero-worship that existed for me the first time I met him. Almost, but not quite. The change was not in him so much as it was in me. I

was perceptibly older and more aware of the ease with which
he changed roles. He could inspire, he could lead, he could
debate, he could instruct, he could be persuasive.

And he could, I suspected, be cruel.

Later, I looked up Magellan in the computer files. What the
Captain had failed to tell me was that Magellan had died on
the trip and never made it back to his ancient country of
Spain.

Once in the passageway, Thrush asked casually, "Interested
in the creation of life, Sparrow?"

I was still thinking about the Captain and said offhand,
"Sure."

He drifted down the corridor. "Follow me. I'll show you
how it all begins."

It didn't strike me until later how confident he seemed, how
very sure of himself he was.

We ended up once again in Reduction, but this time the
chambers were empty; there were no black sheets over any of
them. Still, my heart was beating faster than usual and I
wanted to leave. Thrush was in no hurry. He explained all the
equipment in the compartment and how it worked while I dutifully drifted after him and tried to learn as much as I could.

When the short tour was at an end, he reached inside his
waistcloth and pulled out a pipe similar to Tybalt's and
Crow's. "Want some smoke, Sparrow?"

I glanced around to make sure the exhaust vents were on
and he said, "I turned them on when we came in," and I said,
"Why not?"

We sat there for a while trading the pipe back and forth
while I thought of what the Captain had said and realized he
hadn't told me much of anything at all. My fault, I supposed,
because I had never asked him the same questions that Noah
had asked me. But I would the next time. By the time I remembered why we had come to Reduction, my head was
swimming and I had a case of the giggles.

"Life," I said to Thrush, reminding him.

"Life," he agreed. He put the pipe away and set up the microscope, then picked up a thin glass slide. "Human life," he said. "This is how it all begins, Sparrow."

He unknotted his waistcloth. I watched, disbelieving. A few sweaty minutes later he pushed the slide under some holders on the viewing stage and adjusted the focus controls as he looked through the eyepiece. When he had the proper focus, he stepped away. "Take a look, Sparrow. The little fish with tails on them. They fertilize the woman's egg and we grow from that."

I leaned over the eyepiece and watched the wriggling sperm with fascination. This was the Beginning, from which would grow creatures with fingers and toes, hearts and brains. Creatures that could walk and run, eat and think and feel—the only creatures who could do that in the entire universe. The wriggling things were what made Thrush and me and everybody else on board . . . gods.

I didn't learn until much later that what Thrush had done was something every male medical student on Earth tried at one time or another—and for the same reason.

When I finally looked up, Thrush handed me a slide, grinning. "Those were mine, Sparrow. Let's see yours."

I was lightheaded from the smoke and felt oddly disoriented and free. I hesitated only for a moment. I was vastly curious and besides, it was for science. I was shyer than Thrush and it took longer but soon I was looking at my own sperm through the lens, thinking that on the slide below were hundreds of embryonic replicas of myself.

I was still studying them through the lens when I felt Thrush's hand touch my shoulder. I was suddenly acutely aware of his closeness, of his nakedness, of the smoothness of his skin, of the smell of his body, of the times I had admired his grace in the gymnasium, of his kindness in explaining the operations of the ship, of how long it had been since I'd had sex with Snipe, and of how many times I had slept alone since. I was dizzy and disoriented from the smoke, but very much aware of the warmth and privacy of Reduction. I was totally relaxed and passive, limp in Thrush's arms holding me from behind. My feelings were those of a gratitude and admiration that verged on love.

Afterward, when I was readjusting my waistcloth in the corridor outside, Thrush laughed and said, "You're easy, Sparrow." I watched him as he kicked down the corridor, feeling a slow flush build until it seemed like my skin was burning.

My mind was blank until I got back to my own compartment, then I was knotted with rage. I hit the side of the bulkhead with my fist, once, twice, then huddled in the sling and held my head in my hands. Thrush would not, of course, keep it to himself.

"Something wrong, Sparrow?"

Crow had stuck his head through the shadow screen.

"Go away," I grunted.

He looked at me in astonishment. "What happened to you?"

"You'll laugh," I said. "You and everybody else."

Something in my voice kept him from retreating.

"You know I won't," he assured me.

I wouldn't look at him for fear he would see my tears of anger. He saw them anyway.

"Thrush," he said.

I nodded. It would have been easy for anybody to guess the outcome of my brief friendship with Thrush.

"What happened, Sparrow?"

My mind was a confused mix of injured pride, impotent anger, and most of all a desperate need for reassurance of personal worth. I tried to explain it all to Crow but what I said didn't make much sense even to me. The heart, I learned then, is a poor thing to think with.

When I was finally through, Crow looked puzzled.

"Thrush has been with almost everybody on board. Nobody's going to think the less of you for it."

I stared at him. "Were you ever with him?"

He shrugged. "Nobody refuses anybody the first time, Sparrow. Ship's custom. It's not that important."

I tried to tell him that it wasn't just what other crew members might think of me but what I thought of myself. For the rest of my life I would hear Thrush's laughter and know that he had played a game and I had let him win.

"So you lost your pride. That's not much of a commodity on board."

"I want it back," I gritted.

"It's foolish to let somebody have power over you because of that," Crow said gently. "That's why Thrush did it, you know."

What he was saying would make sense to me the next time period or the one after that. But right then I was too fragile to be able to think about it logically.

I rocked in the sling and Crow said, "Do you want me to leave, Sparrow?" I tried to answer but couldn't. Crow frowned, then said, "Do you want me to stay?" I sat there, mute, and he stroked my chest and said again, "It's not that important, Sparrow," and spent the rest of the sleep period with me.

When I woke later, alone in the compartment, I realized wryly that I had gone through essentially the same experience twice in the same time period. But despite the similarities, Thrush had become more of an enemy and Crow had become more of a friend.

The difference was that one had taken away my pride and the other had given it back. Nobody but Crow ever understood that.

12

I didn't know what to expect at breakfast; I was prepared for any comments. My fellow crewmen watched as covertly and as intently as they had when I first got out of sick bay, but nobody said anything. A few speculative looks made me flush but there were no jokes, no laughter. Apparently nobody considered what had happened important, though my reaction to it was of great interest to them. I was relieved; I couldn't tell whether Thrush was disappointed or not. I glared at him and felt my anger surge when he stared blandly back. We were two apes, he and I, and I had presented—Thrush had proved to himself that he was the alpha primate.

I choked down my meal and when Noah got out the chess pieces, I tried to forget Thrush and concentrate on the board opposite me. I played very badly.

There would be other games with Thrush, I thought, and next time the outcome would be different. But for now, Crow was right—there were more important things to worry about.

During the next dozen shifts, when I was alone at the terminal pad, I checked through the ship's inventory of EVA suits, helmets, sets of inner-weave, life-support packs and exploration supplies. According to the figures, we had suffered only normal attrition from the thousands we had started with, considering the centuries that had passed. There shouldn't be any problem for the exploration parties.

I didn't believe it.

I told Crow my worries and one time period, between shifts, we went to Exploration to inspect the suits racked along the bulkhead.

"Look at this." Crow held one out to me by the sleeve and I floated over. "Would you be willing to wear this?"

He tugged gently where the cloth met the metal disconnect at the wrist. It stretched slightly, then parted evenly at the metal. Anyone wearing the suit and putting pressure on the disconnect would have lost his air supply in an instant.

The suit was *old,* as old as the Captain himself.

"They'll check them before they're actually used," I said, not completely convinced. But I didn't leave it to anybody else; I still had vivid memories of the rotten length of rope on Seti IV. I checked the suits, and I checked the helmets as well to make sure they were fully transparent, that the plastic hadn't fogged over with age so you couldn't see the faces of those wearing them. Finally, I inspected the life-support packs and the transceivers; there would be no communications failure this time.

As we got closer to the Aquinas system, the rest of the teams checked everything once again and both Crow and I felt foolish. I was assured the teams always took great care in inspecting the equipment. But nobody yet had come up with a credible explanation for what had happened to me on Seti IV.

Even though we were still months away from Aquinas II, the lectures by Ophelia and other Seniors in Exploration grew more frequent and intense, the audience more alert. There were few sleepers now. For those members who had never been through a landing, their first planet would be a rite of passage entitling them to full membership in the crew.

The watches in the plotting room and at the terminal pads became longer and more nerve-racking. Information on the Aquinas system was flowing in and had to be broken down and analyzed so Shops could make the necessary adjustments in landing gear. Would we be using balloon probes or would we actually go in with the Lander? Was there an atmosphere, was the surface temperature compatible with human exploration?

There had been no signature that would indicate any form of life, but excitement was running high, especially among those for whom this was a First Landing—they had yet to be disappointed at finding nothing but rock and sand or methane ice and a swirl of deadly gases. I discovered I wasn't nearly as dubious about the possibilities of life in the universe as I had thought.

Finally, one particular time period, Crow and I were scheduled to go Outside on a simulated repair and rescue mission of Inbetween Station. No problems were anticipated—the gear had been checked and so had Crow and I, even down to our pulse rates and response times. It was a first-step exercise, meaning they wouldn't actually launch the station itself. We would leave the *Astron* through a lock and meet at a predetermined spot a kilometer away in open space. The object was to familiarize us with the use of tether lines and teach us maneuverability in space.

"Suit up! Let's go, Sparrow!"

A group of us were standing in the first-level airlock: Crow, myself, Thrush, Snipe, Loon, and Heron, all of us looking eager—with the possible exception of Thrush, who took great care never to look eager about anything. I took off my waistcloth and pulled on the inner-weave, making sure the connections were tight and the small tubing was leakproof, then the main suit.

Tybalt helped me on with my helmet and tightened the grippers around the neck disconnect. I ran a quick check of the support system, switching on the transceiver for a final check.

"Can you hear me, Crow?"

I could see Snipe and Ophelia wince. Tybalt motioned with his hand for me to cut the volume.

"Too loud and too clear, Sparrow."

Crow was smiling in his own helmet and I had a sudden premonition, remembering all too well how the system sun of

Seti IV had glinted off the helmets and turned them to gold, completely hiding the faces of their wearers.

There was a yellow glow off to one side in my helmet and Tybalt's voice filtered through the helmet speakers. "You all right, Sparrow? Your perspiration rate's way up."

"Just remembering Seti IV," I said.

"Seti IV?" Then, sharply, "Forget Seti IV—concentrate on what you're doing."

"Time!" Ophelia called. I waved a gloved hand at her, winked at Snipe, and crowded into the airlock behind Crow. There was a short wait and I could feel the suit stiffen as the air was evacuated from the lock. A moment later, when the hatch rolled open, Crow and I stepped out into nothing.

Position, I thought, concentrating on the direction indicators in the heads-up display set in the plastic of the helmet. The course had already been predetermined by computers; all I had to do was keep a small red circle in the crosshairs of the indicators.

I gave the maneuvering jets a brief squirt and watched the ship dwindle beneath me. For the first time I saw the *Astron* from the outside. I could see the three individual cylinders that made up the vessel, located where the hatch was, and then tried to guess the location of the various compartments. The main cylinder was easy: There were the glassteel doors of the hangar deck and the bulge that held Hydroponics and the engine compartment. The bridge was easy, too, and the Captain's cabin just behind it—plus a whole section directly behind *that*, which I hadn't even known existed. He lived like a king, I thought. Rank did indeed have its privileges, as he had once told me.

"Quit gawking, Sparrow—pay attention!"

Ophelia's voice in the headset was so tinny I could tell it was her only by the harshness. I squinted up at the direction indicators, noting the red circle was far off the crosshairs. It was easy to adjust if you were only a little off. If you were way off, it was easy to overshoot.

Which is what I did.

Crow's voice was a little fainter than Ophelia's.

"Aim to your right and down, Sparrow . . ."

I missed the first time but made it the second. Right on course, I thought with relief. The lights inside my helmet had turned a deep orange. When I got back, they would have to drain the sweat from my boots.

The ship had become a small blob of light almost a full kilometer away. A few hundred meters distant were the faint flares of Crow's maneuvering jets, cutting in and out as he maintained position. A little more and we would have circled opposite sides of an imaginary Inbetween Station and met at the "top." A brief handshake and back to the *Astron* so the next pair of would-be space explorers could step off.

"Watch your course, Sparrow."

Ophelia again. I swore to myself. She was one of the few Seniors who could make me sweat, and my helmet was fogged enough as it was. I turned slowly, taking my eyes off Crow for only a second to stare at the universe around me. There was the thick glow indicating the center of the galaxy, still hidden by the dust clouds in Sagittarius; the clumps of stars outlining the arms; and then the rifts of almost total blackness that marked the space between the arms and between the various spurs that jutted out from them.

The Dark.

The sense of solitude was overwhelming and I quickly turned toward the ship again. This was no time to lose my nerve.

"Heads up, Sparrow."

Crow was drifting maybe five meters away, his locator lights bright against the blackness. I reached toward him but he stubbornly remained a few meters distant. The arcs that both of us had traveled had straightened into parallel lines but my tether cord was short. I gave a short blast with the maneuvering jets and without thinking tugged on the tether line for more slack. I shot past Crow, my tether line trailing behind.

It had parted somewhere behind me . . . worn out by how

many centuries of use? I felt the same sharp disbelief that I had felt on Seti IV when the climbing rope parted. I panicked. I gave the maneuvering jets full throttle to get back on station and ended up cartwheeling in space, the stars spinning lazily around my head.

"Slack off your jets, Sparrow." Ophelia's voice was sharp. "Crow, get back to the ship—that's an order." Then, to me: "Use your maneuvering jets to stabilize, Sparrow. Do it. Now."

I tried several short blasts and the field of stars settled down.

"Turn toward the ship, try a short burst to see if you're headed right, and then a series of short bursts. Watch your fuel."

There was a note of worry in her voice.

I pressed the hand switches for a brief burst on both jets. Nothing happened. She was too late with her warning about the fuel; I had already expended the last of it.

In my headphones, Ophelia muttered, "Christ."

There was chatter from a number of sources now.

"—distance—"

"—half a kilometer, opening fast—"

"—I can get him—"

"—orders, Crow, back to the ship—you haven't fuel—"

"—have to rescue—"

"—who's practiced the maneuver?"

"—triage . . . triage . . . *triage* . . ."

The *Astron* had shrunk to a small bulb of light that was rapidly growing dimmer. I didn't know my own velocity, but I knew that in a few minutes I would be beyond rescue. It would take hours to get a Lander ready for operation. By that time my life-support systems would have failed and I would be nothing more than a frozen, drifting derelict.

Twice within a few months I had come close to death and this time I was convinced it was the end. There was no one to hold my hand, no fond farewells; there would only be an increasing sense of loneliness until I finally suffocated in my body wastes. It had been a short "life" and not an entirely happy one, but this time I couldn't blame fate or ill luck. I had been foolish.

I stared out at the stars and tried to think of nothing at all. I was past panic or even regret. When next I met Crow and Snipe and the others on board, it would be as part of the Great Egg.

I floated there in silence, a tiny speck in the immensity of space, staring out at the multitudes of distant stars, shattered bits of crystal set against depths of absolute blackness. Here and there the stars were obscured by faint stretches of luminosity that marked vague clouds of gases heated by the suns buried within.

The darkness itself was smothering, reminding me of times on board the *Astron* when I had been alone in closed compartments and the glow tubes had failed. I was buried alive in a thick, silent blackness where *nothing* had both texture and substance.

The loneliness hit me first. Inside the *Astron*, I had been sandwiched between layers of life, from the hundreds of crewmen who crowded the corridors and the working spaces to the racks of dense foliage in Hydroponics. I had been immersed in the stink and the sweat and the feel of life and now I was alone, surrounded by nothing at all. If the *Astron* had shrunk to the size of a grain of sand, the nearest star system— aside from Aquinas—would have been an impossible ten thousand kilometers distant. I had been a creature on that grain of sand wondering about the possibility of other creatures on other grains of sand on a beach a continent away. . . .

In all that vast arena of nothing, the only life was on board the *Astron*. I suddenly ached for the presence of my fellow crew members. I would have given all my meager possessions just to hear Tybalt belch or smell Abel's rancid breath.

I shivered and thought of the Captain staring at the stars

through the huge ports on the bridge. To me, space was bleak and cold and dead. But when the Captain looked at the stars, he saw only the possibility of life. And if life was not to be found *here*, then perhaps it would be found *there* . . . or there . . . or maybe there.

The trouble with possibilities is that there is no end to them.

I shivered inside my suit and had my final revelation. All that was blessed in the universe was on the *Astron* or represented by "that thin green layer of scum," as Ophelia put it, that covered distant Earth. Like Tybalt, the Captain *believed* and because he believed, he was going to risk us all. Unlike him and Tybalt, Noah and Ophelia and Crow had lost any interest in searching for life without because they had become obsessed with saving the life within and . . . and . . . and . . .

A moment more and I might have solved at least one of the mysteries that had slowly grown in the back of my mind, but the bubble of thought burst with the renewed chatter in my headphones.

"Sparrow! Turn toward the ship!" The voice was a tinny rattle in my helmet, distorted and hollow. I couldn't tell who it was but from the bark and sense of command, I thought it must be Ophelia.

I jerked around and made out the pinpoint of a maneuvering jet and then the faint blur of helmet lights coming closer. It wasn't Ophelia: The movements were too smooth, too graceful. But even closer up, I couldn't tell who it was. Their helmet was as foggy as mine and all I could see was a diffused yellow-orange glow with vague features hidden within. Crow, I thought. They had sent Crow back to get me.

When we were ten meters apart, the figure stopped and once again I was drifting away from it. They had tied two or three tether lines together but it was still too short. The figure didn't hesitate a moment but cut free of the cord and came after me, catching up with short bursts of its maneuvering rockets. It clamped an arm around my own and turned us both back to the small globe of light that marked the ship.

"Are you all right?"

It was hard to make out the words in the distorted rattle that filled my headphones.

"I'm fine," I said. I couldn't believe that I was as calm as I sounded.

"Have to find the tether line . . . short on fuel."

We would have to search for it in the dark; the tether line didn't glow by itself and there was no light from a primary that might reflect off it. We both moved our hands around in space feeling for it. Neither of us could see anything in the darkness and the chances were very good that we were drifting away from it.

"The stars," I blurted. "The line will blot out the stars behind it."

And then I spotted it, a thin black snake moving across the field of broken crystal. There was a sudden blur in front of my helmet, lit by the glow from my warning lights, and I grabbed for it.

We pulled ourselves along the line in silence, both afraid to speak for fear we might congratulate each other too soon. The lights of the *Astron* grew rapidly closer—those on board were reeling us in as well. At last the hatch came into view and gloved hands reached out to tug us on board.

Moments later I heard the hiss of air, then felt somebody working the grippers at my neck disconnect to lift off my helmet. I gulped fresh oxygen and managed to smile at Tybalt, who tried to look stern but didn't quite make it. At his side, Crow was grinning in relief.

I gaped. It hadn't been Crow who had gone out to get me. He hadn't even suited up.

I whirled around to stare at Snipe, behind me, shucking off her suit.

"You," I said, bewildered.

As usual, she kept her poker face. She said, "I didn't think anybody could be that clumsy."

Ophelia interrupted. "Triage, Sparrow. The logical choice was to send somebody who had practiced a rescue maneuver before but whose absence wouldn't cripple the ship if they failed."

They had sent Snipe because they could afford to lose her. For a crewman who felt as unimportant as I did, that bit of knowledge was to cement a relationship that lasted for as long as Snipe lived.

Ophelia gave Snipe the smallest of approving pats. "You'll go out again two shifts from now, Sparrow—and next time do it right."

I went back to Crow's compartment, only half listening to his words of sympathy. Loon sat in a corner and played his harmonica while Crow tried to cheer me up. I stared moodily out at St. Mark's Square, watching while the projection recycled twice.

"You're not listening," Crow said, suddenly worried.

"Who was in the lock?" I asked.

He looked surprised. "You know who. Snipe, myself and Loon, you, Thrush, Heron, Tybalt, and Ophelia."

It was so obvious, I thought.

"I want to go back there."

I slipped out through the shadow screen, Crow and Loon following in silence. There was nobody around the lock area and the tether lines had been returned to Exploration. I ducked back into the corridor, not caring whether Crow and Loon followed or not.

It was between shifts and Exploration was deserted. All the drums of tether line were stowed against the far bulkhead—all except one which had been left out for repair.

"We'll have to unwind it," I said.

Crow looked uncertain and Loon said slowly, "Why do you want to see it, Sparrow?"

"It was a faulty tether," I said. "I want to see just how faulty."

Crow shrugged and they set the drum on the cable spindle with an empty at the other end. I watched it intently as the

cable slowly unwound. It would be at the very beginning, I
thought, where it had snaked back into the ship and attached
to a ringbolt just beyond the lock.

Crow was still uneasy. "The shift will come by soon, Sparrow."

"I don't care."

He shot a glance at Loon. Both of them looked unhappy.
I slowed the tether when it was nearly unwound and let it
run through my hands, then held onto it when the end finally
slipped off the drum.

Crow examined it and said carefully, "There's nothing
wrong with it, Sparrow."

The end, where it had been secured to the ringbolt, was
wrapped, as were all tether lines, with no indication of fraying
or cutting. Crow was right; there was nothing wrong with it. I
rocked back on my heels, frustrated, then grabbed the end for
a closer look. The tether line would have been threaded
through a ringbolt, and the end then whipped back on itself
and clamped to the main portion of the line that ran out
through the open hatch.

The line would have been squeezed by the clamp and I
should have been able to feel and see where the clamp had
been—it would have taken more than a few hours for that
part of the line to "recover." But the line was supple and
there was no difference in thickness where a clamp might
have bit into it. I knew without even asking that Thrush or
Heron had been in charge of securing the line, that they had
threaded the end of it through the clamp but had never tightened down on it. Any slight pull and the line would have run
freely through the clamp and out the hatch.

"Somebody tried to kill me," I said.

Both Crow and Loon struggled with the idea but it was too
novel a concept for them, even when I carefully explained
what must have happened. If the line had been cut or frayed,
maybe it would have been easier for them to believe.

I read the doubt on their faces, but all I could think of was
Seti IV and the time in sick bay when somebody had mur-

mured, "Down the hatch," and held a drinking tube to my lips.

Crow shook his head, the sweat flying off his nose in little droplets.

"You're wrong, Sparrow," he said earnestly. "Nobody tried to kill you, nobody could." Loon nodded in hasty agreement, though neither of them offered an alternative explanation of why the line had pulled free.

They couldn't accept the conclusion I had so eagerly jumped to. But I was convinced I was right. Somebody was trying to kill me. And on board the *Astron*, where life was revered above all else, that should have been impossible.

13

Nobody on the exploration team agreed with me, but I remained convinced that somebody on board had tried to murder me. Even Ophelia struggled with the idea and couldn't accept it. To her, as to the others, it was impossible. She was the first to suggest that I had become obsessed with Thrush. In the back of my mind there was the growing belief that perhaps she was right.

She pointed out that the fault might lie with the clamp itself, that perhaps the threads had been stripped and it wouldn't tighten down. I couldn't prove it either way; the clamp had been tossed on a small heap of other clamps, some of which had stripped threads. Thrush could have deliberately chosen a faulty one, I said, at which point Ophelia lost her temper.

Even when it was proven that other crew members could have had access to the clamp and the tether, I persisted.

"It was Thrush," I said bitterly to Crow when we were alone in his compartment. "He was on the inspection team."

Crow wasn't sure whether to humor me or be realistic. "So were others." Then, cautiously: "Why Thrush? What motivation?"

"He hates me. You know that."

Crow looked blank and for once, even Loon struck me as slow-witted. "Enough to kill you?"

I nodded.

"Because of the time the two of you were alone in Reduction?" Crow struggled with his disbelief. "You hated him for that; I don't think hatred was what he felt for you."

I opened my mouth to reply, then changed my mind. Thrush had disliked me when I had first seen him on board the Lander and had gone out of his way to humiliate me, at least to myself if not to the crew. But murder . . .

In the end I had nothing more than my own convictions, but my hatred of him was strong enough that I didn't want to question them.

After that, Thrush and I exchanged hard looks whenever we met. I was close to being out of control and he sensed my inner violence and avoided me. He didn't come around to practice with the computer and was usually early or late for meals so we spent a minimum amount of time glaring at each other over our food trays.

It was different in the gymnasium. Thrush would have lost face if he had left upon my arrival. We competed in the gym, he and I, no matter what apparatus was in play. And then Tybalt introduced physical contact drills on a just-in-case basis, to the great distaste of most of the members of the exploration teams.

Oddly, it wasn't Crow who was the best at tumbling or putting-your-partner-on-the-mat. He was afraid of his own strength, with the result that he tended to be too slow and cautious. Hawk and Eagle, the youngest members of our team, were easily the most skilled. They were evenly matched, and probably because they were young, relatively small, and unafraid of each other, their matches were quick and almost a pleasure to watch. Heron was good, which surprised me, and so was Snipe.

Thrush and I were in the middle range—not as good as the best but better than the worst. Tybalt watched both of us closely, especially when we were pitted against each other. The first time he raised an eyebrow, the second time he prefaced the bout with a warning. There was no third time. It was apparent to even the dullest that Thrush and I were perfectly willing to hurt each other, something other participants avoided at all costs.

I might have anticipated the reaction of the crew. That somebody would deliberately hurt somebody else was appalling. Nobody had particularly liked Thrush; now they went out of their way to avoid him. And they avoided me as well. We were antagonists and our fellow crewmen gave us plenty of room in which to circle each other and maneuver. They made no attempt to hide the fact that they found the situation distasteful, that because Thrush and I were capable of a violence they abhorred, there was a gulf between them and us.

Between most of them and us.

But not all.

Matters came to a head with the rape of Pipit. Crow and I had gone to Hydroponics after shift one time period, intent on sampling the new crops. We were halfway back in the huge compartment when we heard muffled sobbing three rows over. We glanced at each other in surprise, then hastily circled around the intervening nutrient troughs.

Pipit was clinging to some vines, naked, her waistcloth stuffed in a nearby trough. The tears rolling down her cheeks emphasized the bruises on her face and breasts.

I knew what had happened without even asking. I remembered what Snipe had told me. I remembered the first meal I had taken in Exploration, when Thrush had stared with hatred at Pipit and Crow. And I remembered Crow telling me that Thrush violated ship's customs. Whatever beliefs the rest of the crew held, Thrush obviously didn't share them.

Crow held her in his arms, and I gently stroked her head and asked, "What happened?"

"Thrush," she confirmed, doing her best to hold back the sobs. Crow gripped her tightly, murmuring reassurances in her ear. "I refused . . . he had no right. . . ."

This time, Crow couldn't deny that evil had been done—

the evidence was at hand. The struggle was apparent on his suddenly pale face; he desperately wanted to hurt another human being but could barely bring himself to think about it. Doing anything about it was beyond him. His great strength was no help and I suspected Thrush had known that.

For a moment it looked as if Crow would be sick.

"Why did he do it?" Crow asked.

He was staring at me when he asked it but he wasn't seeing *me* at all. Nor was he talking to me—he was talking to somebody else, somebody he had known before. I felt helpless. I could give him no answers.

"Take her to sick bay," I said. "Give Abel something to do for a change."

"Thrush," he whispered.

"I'll report it to the Captain," I said. But I had a score to settle with Thrush first.

Crow nodded and helped Pipit past the rows of nutrient tubing to the far hatch, holding her against his chest with one free arm while he used the other to propel himself along the bulkhead rings.

I watched them go. Once they had left, I sped through the corridors to Exploration, glancing through the hatch just long enough to determine that Thrush wasn't there. The next stop was the gymnasium. Thrush wasn't among the sweating crew members. I shot through the hatch to the other side.

Once outside the gym, I slowed down. Thrush couldn't be that calm; I doubted even that the rape had been premeditated. He had probably run across Pipit in Hydroponics and hadn't been able to resist taking what he wanted when he wanted it. As I had found out for myself, lust is the enemy of logical thought. Afterward, he would have gone someplace in the ship where he could plan what to do next, what story he might offer, whom he could go to for protection.

He might go to the Captain, I thought. But I didn't think even the Captain would help him and I suspected he knew that.

I finally found him on the dimly lit hangar deck. Heron was

with him, talking fast and low while Thrush listened with obvious contempt. I guessed that Heron was urging him to go immediately to the Captain with his own explanation of what had happened. I gave Thrush credit for realizing there was no explanation to offer.

At first they didn't know I was there. Then Thrush noticed me standing inside the hatchway and said, "I thought it would be Crow."

"He's taking Pipit to sick bay," I said.

"She isn't hurt. Nothing happened to her that hasn't happened before."

He was watching me, gauging my reactions. I was different from the rest of the crew and so was he. Nobody else would have anticipated violence but I knew he was prepared for it.

"You left marks," I said.

He grinned. "She wasn't as easy to persuade as you were."

I almost lost what little control I had left.

"Why Pipit?" I asked. It was hard to keep my voice from shaking.

For the first time since I had known him, his facade broke.

"I love her," he said fiercely. "Everybody knows that." His face was pink with anger and the anger made him ugly. He was laying claim to property he considered his own and he couldn't understand why anybody would dispute it.

"You shouldn't have touched her," I said in a dead voice. I braced myself against a bulkhead, bent my knees, and sprang at him. He dodged easily, taking refuge in a corner where the tether lines were racked.

"What do you think you're doing, Sparrow?" There was no alarm in his voice; he knew what I intended.

"Beat you," I grunted.

I couldn't admit even to myself that I was thinking of something more than just a beating.

I grabbed for Thrush again and he scrambled deeper into the tangle of tether lines and life-support cables. He showed no fear, though he had every reason to be afraid of me.

Contemptuously: "You'll have to come after me, Sparrow."

I burrowed into the nest of lines and he dodged farther back, hoping I would entangle myself in the ropes. I managed to grab his ankle but he shook me off and then was free, floating in the middle of the hangar deck, waiting for me as I struggled out of the snarl of rope. Heron danced beside him, shouting curses as I pushed through the last of the tether lines.

A solitary glow tube illuminated the middle of the broad metal prairie, leaving in shadow the corners and the sides where the curving overhead met the deck. I sensed vague movements in the darkened recesses, evidence we had attracted an audience. Crow had probably left Pipit in Abel's safekeeping and tracked us down, picking up Loon and others along the way.

I pushed off from a deck ring but Thrush anticipated me, darting forward to butt his head into my stomach. I grabbed him and whirled him around, locking an arm around his neck.

"You tried to kill me," I said in a low voice, holding my wrist tight with my other hand so he couldn't get away. "You used a faulty clamp on purpose."

"Don't be a fool," he gasped. "I'm the first one they'd suspect."

His logic distracted me and I didn't expect it when he jammed an elbow in my ribs, knocking the wind out of me. I loosened my hold and we spiraled away from each other, then grabbed floor rings and came back to slowly circle each other again.

"Thrush, catch!"

The shrill voice belonged to Heron. Something flashed in the dim light and Thrush caught it. I felt a moment of panic then, wondering what Heron had thrown him. Thrush disappeared into the shadows and I slowly turned, not knowing where or when he would come at me. But he wouldn't leave the hangar deck, he couldn't afford to turn down a challenge—not from me. . . .

He suddenly sped out of the darkness, missing me by what seemed mere centimeters.

It took a moment to realize that he hadn't missed at all, that he had slashed me across the arm and chest with something sharp and blood was welling from the slits. I shook myself and small red droplets went flying through space. A collective gasp came from our frightened audience in the shadows.

I twisted slowly in the air, too late to stop Thrush from gashing my right thigh. It wasn't a knife, I thought, or I would be dead by now. It was probably a piece of metal or broken plastic, scavenged from a cannibalized Rover.

Thrush had tasted victory and when next he flashed by, his eyes glittering in the dusk, he was careless. I caught him by the wrist and twisted hard, catching a sharp piece of metal when it flew from his hand.

"My turn," I murmured. I slashed his cheek and caught his upper arm with the metal, then wrapped my legs around his waist, slippery with sweat, and held the metal strip to his neck. I could feel his muscles relax; he knew if he made any movement at all I would cut his throat.

"Tell me why," I said in a low voice.

"I told you."

"Not Pipit," I said. "Me. All along, why me?"

"You know why," he whispered. "I'm the better man."

I didn't have time to wonder what he meant. There were hurried movements in the shadows now, a scurrying, and then the remaining glow tubes started to flicker on.

"Go ahead, cut it," Thrush muttered. "It's the last chance you'll get."

I wanted him to whimper, to be afraid, to plead. But he wasn't going to do any of those—and by not doing them, he was going to win once more. I fought with myself, then abruptly made up my mind. I couldn't afford to lose again. I tensed my arm to pull the blade across his windpipe and only then did I catch any tremor of fear from him.

For his sake and mine, it was enough.

I held him a moment longer, then cursed and let him go, throwing away the bloody strip of metal. Suddenly Tybalt grabbed my arm and yanked me to one side while Banquo did the same to Thrush. The overhead glow tubes were all on now and I stared at the audience with surprise. It looked as if half the crew had assembled to watch the fight.

"You're a fool," Tybalt grunted as he hustled me toward the hatch. "You never were before but for some reason I don't understand, you've become one now."

Abel attended to both of us in sick bay, Banquo and little Quince standing by as guards. Quince was shy, unwilling to look directly at either me or Thrush. Both he and Banquo carried short rods of thick metal which I supposed were meant to be clubs. I wondered if they would actually use them and guessed that Quince definitely wouldn't but that Banquo might. Thrush and I glared at each other but both of us knew better than to start the fight all over again.

Abel worked quickly, carefully squeezing together the edges of the cut on my thigh and spraying it with an antiseptic adhesive. It stung and I winced, not afraid to show it. Thrush had made a face when Abel closed the wound on his arm, and that gave me permission to do the same, or so I felt.

"You should have thought it might hurt before making idiots of yourselves," Abel said. "But neither of you were thinking, were you?"

"My face," I said. "Will it scar?"

He shrugged. "Both of you will probably scar. But nobody on board is going to feel sorry for you if you do."

I looked at Thrush only once and that to verify what my nose had told me. Some time during the fight, he had pissed in his waistcloth. I took grim satisfaction in that, then remembered he had challenged me to cut his throat even though he had been scared to death. A brave man and a dangerous one—I had humiliated him and he would never get over it.

But the overwhelming hatred I felt for him had burned itself out. So had any attraction.

Abel had just finished stitching up Thrush when there was a small commotion in the corridor and the Captain pushed in through the shadow screen. He nodded at Abel. "You can finish up later."

After the fat doctor had gone, the Captain sat on the magnetic counter top, gripping the edge so he wouldn't float off.

"I don't suppose either of you has an explanation," he said quietly.

Thrush looked away and said nothing. Finally I said, "Did you talk to Pipit?" I was surprised by the antagonism in my voice.

He nodded. "I saw her and talked to her. Right now I'm more interested in why the two of you tried to kill each other."

I glanced at Thrush. "He would have killed *me*," I said.

The Captain looked irritated. "And in all likelihood you would have killed him if you hadn't been stopped."

"I stopped myself," I said, sullen.

His eyes were very bright and very thoughtful.

"Answer my question, Sparrow. Why?"

"I'm a friend of Pipit's," I said.

"So was Thrush—at one time." My jaw dropped. He shot a contemptuous look at Thrush and said, "Not a very wise one or a very compassionate one. You were in love with her, weren't you, Thrush? And when she didn't return it, you began to hate her."

Thrush looked away, sullen, and didn't answer. The Captain slipped off the counter and floated in silence for a moment while he devised a punishment. "Both of you are in Coventry until we arrive at Aquinas II. When not on station, you're confined to quarters except by special permission. There'll be no talking to each other or to anybody else except in the line of duty. All crew members are likewise forbidden to talk to you or have anything to do with you. If they do, the same punishment applies to them."

He turned to at Thrush. "You're dismissed. Sparrow, I want to see you in my quarters—now."

I floated after him, trailed by a nervous Quince and Banquo. Once in the Captain's office, they were excused and we were alone, the Captain lounging in his sling and I floating unhappily in front of him, the huge port with its view of Outside on my left and the array of peep screens with their subdued chatter on my right.

"You fought for Pipit's honor," he mocked. "How noble."

"Crow couldn't," I said in a brittle voice.

"You're right, he couldn't. I imagine he went through a very personal little hell when the two of you discovered Pipit. But that doesn't mean that nobody else would have fought for her—or that the crew wouldn't have thought of some suitable punishment for Thrush. You were a little too eager, Sparrow. Why?"

Objections flooded my throat but I choked them off. Anything I said would only succeed in condemning me.

"Pipit will recover, Sparrow. But if you hadn't been interrupted, Thrush never would have."

"Thrush . . . violated ship's custom," I finally said, quoting Loon.

"Ship's custom." The Captain thought about it for a moment. "Sparrow, we have our drills and our duties on board but we can't work all the time. Sex is the great leveler, what people do to fill up the empty hours, the empty feelings. Nobody's exempt from sharing themselves with their fellow crew members. At least once."

"Thrush had already been with her," I said in a low voice. "It was her right to refuse him after that."

"You're so sure she did?"

"Yes," I said. "She wouldn't lie."

He looked in my eyes and I would have sworn he read my mind.

"Tell me, Sparrow, were you thinking of Pipit when you were getting up the nerve to slit Thrush's throat?"

The hot words died on my tongue. He waved at the peep screens behind him. "There are no secrets, Sparrow. I thought you knew that."

I paled. The Captain had watched Thrush and me in Reduction.

"So you know I had reason to hate him," I said in a husky voice.

"Before, during or after?" The Captain leaned forward in the sling. "Not before, you'd found a friend you empathized with. And not during, certainly. Only after. Why, Sparrow? A sense of betrayal when he said you'd been an easy conquest?"

I stood there, white-faced and mute.

"Well, why?" he roared. "Because you felt ashamed? Because you'd lost your pride? Thrush is the only real scientist we've got on board and you would've slit his throat like a pig at slaughter over something schoolboys have done since time began!"

"We were smoking—" I started.

"—so you could lose the inhibitions you didn't want anyway." He looked at me in disgust and relaxed back in the sling, clasping his hands behind his head.

"Were you hurt in the heart, Sparrow?"

I could feel the color rise in my face, and shook my head.

He smiled faintly. "I didn't think so, you're not the type. So it must have been your ego." Sarcastically: "He hurt your feelings."

"He . . . humiliated me," I said desperately.

"I didn't say he was wise, Sparrow, only valuable."

The silence gathered and I waited to be dismissed but he was in no hurry.

"I don't know why he did it, Sparrow." He shrugged. "Maybe he wanted to know you better—that's one way, especially if you're lacking in empathy. For a young man, sex is the fool's gold of the emotions."

He turned to look at the peep screens and I knew a quick scan told him everything he wanted to know about what was happening on board.

"Two thousand years," he said quietly. "I did everything there was to do in the first two hundred and then I got bored.

I had sex with everybody in the crew, I found all the buttons you can push, all the possible movements and positions, all the phrases you can utter, all the promises you can make. I indulged in all of my fantasies and all of theirs. Then my interest turned clinical and I merely watched. Now I look away because it sickens me. Monkeys, masturbating in a zóo."

He looked back at where I stood sweaty and embarrassed.

"That's not cynicism, Sparrow, that's reality—my reality at any rate. Unlike the rest of the crew, I can't make permanent liaisons, I can't take lovers or become attached. What's a moment for me is a lifetime for others, and I have to watch them grow old and dry and feeble. It's like a time-lapse film of a rose whose petals curl and brown and eventually drop off." He paused and looked at me quizzically. "You don't know what time-lapse photography is, do you? Or even a rose. Sorry, Sparrow, I forgot."

The meeting was over and I turned to leave.

"I regret what happened to Pipit but she'll get over it. So will you. Thrush won't. He wants something very badly but he can't have it."

He waved a hand and I left, wondering why he had defended Thrush when it was obvious that Pipit and I were the aggrieved. At least Pipit was. I wasn't so sure of myself anymore and the more I thought about it, the more I despaired. Nobody else on board would have reacted as I did; that convinced me once again that I had little in common with the rest of the crew.

I had begun as a freak and a freak I would remain.

14

I got used to the silence easier than I thought. It spared me defending behavior the rest of the crew found irrational and for which I really had no defense. We neither thought alike nor felt alike and any explanations I cared to offer would have made no sense to them. I wasn't sure they would have made sense to me.

Not everybody disapproved, if that's the word. I noticed at mealtime that Pipit always found something extra to put on my plate. And when we jostled through the hatchway entering or leaving Exploration, Crow would be at my side and find a moment to squeeze my shoulder. If the Captain had been watching, he would have seen nothing. Or so I thought. At least, Banquo and Abel never did.

As for myself, I had changed. Until the fight, I had been seventeen. Now I had almost killed a man and seventeen was long ago. Most of the crew ignored me, but Tybalt and Noah did little things to show they remained friends. After meals, Noah played games of chess with himself and I would float over to watch. I quickly discovered that I was always his unseen opponent. He would open with one of the moves I usually used and then play the game as if I were sitting opposite him. He was a master player and seldom made a move on "my behalf" of which I disapproved. Occasionally he caught my eye and I thought I could see a smile, though it was nothing any peep screen could have detected.

Tybalt was stern and, for him, officious, but there was always time for an impromptu "lecture" and smoke in the privacy of the small Exploration office.

I quickly discovered there was certain benefits to living in Coventry. Forbidden to talk, I found myself listening and observing more acutely. I silently cheered on the lovemakers in Exploration who hid behind a Rover and explored each other while Ophelia rattled on about what we might find when we explored Aquinas II. And Quince's occasional nuzzling of Portia now struck me as both affectionate and funny.

The first real break in Coventry came when Abel inspected our wounds in sick bay.

"You're healing fast," he noted. The only signs that I had ever been cut were now faint traces of pink snaking over the flesh.

"You're disappointed," I said.

"Satisfied," he corrected me, then lowered his voice and added, "Don't snap at the hand that helps you, Sparrow."

"You're talking to me," I pointed out. "The Captain wouldn't approve."

He ignored the sarcasm. "It's permitted in the line of duty." And then, in a quiet mumble: "You've made enough enemies, why make another of me?"

He had a point, and I shut up. I watched intently when he examined Thrush. The pink tracery on his skin was as faint as my own; though Abel made no comment, I knew that he was surprised, which in turn surprised me.

Before I left, I asked again if we would scar. He shook his head.

"Apparently not. Both of you will be as handsome as you were before, which wasn't . . . very."

It was more conversation than I'd had in two weeks and I enjoyed every syllable.

Thrush had become even more of an enigma to me. Like

myself, he was noticeably older. He now took little interest in the crew members around him, not even looking at Pipit when she served him at mealtimes. He worked hard—and he worked all the time. At his computer station, he was becoming almost as good as I, though my ability to manipulate the palm terminal came to me naturally while Thrush's was learned reflex.

Between us, there were no bitter looks, no words, no feelings. But I never turned my back. I knew instinctively that he still had plans for me, though I now suspected his plans involved more than just me. Not that he ever said anything, though Heron couldn't resist dropping hints until Banquo warned him that he, too, could be subject to Coventry.

Heron was also a mystery to me. Everybody knew he had thrown the blade to Thrush, but somehow he had evaded punishment. I watched him carefully after that. He was a lumpish man with few graces who skulked through the corridors rather than floated and was constantly at Thrush's heels. Since he was good at fetching and carrying, Thrush treated him more as a convenience than a companion. I guessed that Heron would have wanted more, but he had to settle for what he got.

"It's not over yet, Sparrow," he once whispered as we passed in the corridor.

I ignored him, but when Crow broke Coventry, I mentioned it to him.

Crow risked punishment one time period after a lecture in Exploration when I brushed past him in the hatchway and he quietly murmured in my ear. An hour later I met him in the compartment with the falsie of the cave, the roaring fire at its back, and a night sky dusted with stars. Loon was with him and grinned at my apprehensive face when I floated through the shadow screen.

"The peep screen failed months ago, Sparrow—we helped it along."

I was overwhelmed with gratitude and love for both of them.

"You're taking a chance," I warned.

"Not much of one."

I edged closer to the fire, squatting on my heels and holding out my hands to warm myself. I knew it was all psychological, but right then I wanted to believe in it and I swore I could feel the heat.

"How's Pipit?"

"Recovering. She's staying with Loon and me. When we're not there, Ibis is."

Nobody interfered with partners, but Crow realized as well as I did that Thrush didn't play by the rules.

I stared into the firelight and drifted into a mood.

"Heron said it wasn't over yet . . . between me and Thrush."

Crow shook his head. "It's over, Sparrow. The two of you will never be left alone now. Thrush knows it. They say the Captain talked to him privately and when Thrush left, he carried marks."

I was shocked.

"The Captain *struck* him?"

He shrugged. "That's what they say. I haven't seen him."

"He should've hit Heron," I grumbled. "He's the one who threw Thrush the strip of metal."

"Nobody talks to Heron," Loon offered. "They extended Coventry to include him without the Captain's orders."

I didn't want to ask, but I had to.

"What do they think of me?"

Crow shrugged. "They don't understand you. Most of them."

"You mean some do?"

"Some want to."

"And you?"

He looked uncomfortable.

"I appreciate your wanting to punish Thrush. I . . . couldn't."

"And if I'd killed him?"

"What do you expect me to say?" He sounded agonized. "Thrush is *alive*."

"And everybody thinks as you do."

"Not everybody."

"I almost killed him," I repeated, the black mood deepening.

He edged away from the fire, which made it feel even warmer.

"Sparrow," he said slowly, "if you had, would it have been just because of Pipit?"

I sighed. "No, it would not have been just because of Pipit."

He looked immensely relieved. "That would have been an enormous burden for us."

In a sense, I had done his dirty work in trying to punish Thrush. But the moment I thought this, I knew I was lying. Pipit had been an excuse. The truth was that I had harbored murder in my soul and I had gone after Thrush for reasons of my own.

"We're different, you and I," Crow said at last. He sounded as if it broke his heart to say it, and I knew another line was being drawn.

"Tell me how," I said somberly.

He was silent for a moment, then: "Pipit is beautiful," he burst out. "But so is Loon, so is Thrush, even Heron and Quince and Abel and Banquo! They're beautiful because they're *alive*. They move and walk and talk and think and feel! Can you understand that, Sparrow? Even when they do something . . . bad, they're still beautiful! I can't imagine *killing* any one of them, I can't imagine killing *anything*!"

Crow wasn't just being a good person who was incapable of hurting somebody else. His attitude came from two thousand years of hurtling through space in a metal tomb, of being alone in an immensity of nothing with no other life of any kind around you. Under those conditions, you would come to revere life. In saying what he had, Crow was also saying that he couldn't help being himself any more than I could help being myself.

"But not everybody thinks that way," I said.

"No," he said reluctantly, "not everybody thinks that way."

"They think more like me?" I asked, puzzled.

He looked away. "No, they don't think like you, either, Sparrow. There's no possible way they could."

I was very different from anybody else in the crew; I already knew that. Hearing it from Crow didn't make it any worse. Or better. But it confirmed that loneliness was all the future held for me.

"Make me laugh, Loon."

It was a difficult five minutes but Loon had the gift and I was a more than willing audience. Once again I found myself entangled in Loon's version of the latest scandal concerning Quince and Portia, of the rumors about the upcoming change of course after we finished exploring Aquinas II, and of the momentary break in training plays, which let Snipe reappear in some of her favorite roles.

The last interested me the most and I found myself talking about Snipe and asking for gossip about her. Who she had been with, whether or not she had partnered—though I was sure I would have known *that*—and whether she ever mentioned me. In Coventry, I had become adept at reading and interpreting expressions; sometimes whole conversations were summarized in a look. But I had never known what, if anything, Snipe meant by her occasional enigmatic glance.

"So she doesn't talk about me."

Loon shook his head. "She doesn't talk about you at all."

I tried to shrug it off.

"Snipe talks about everybody, all the time," Loon continued slyly. "But she never talks about you."

I stared at him. "That's strange."

Loon grinned. "I thought so, too."

*   *   *

I had no idea whether Snipe would break Coventry or not; I didn't plan to tempt her. But sometimes the most significant things that happen to a person happen with no plan at all.

I had obtained permission from an indulgent Tybalt to see Snipe's plays, and after the latest one I followed her back to her compartment, convinced I was actually on my way someplace else. It deceived others, and I even deceived myself, but it didn't deceive her. When she got to her compartment she slipped in through the shadow screen but not before motioning me to follow.

Once inside, I said, "The Captain—"

She smiled. "You can relax, Sparrow—not every compartment has a peep screen."

She wiped the last bit of spray-on costume from her arm and flushed it down the waste chute, then relaxed in the string hammock and looked at me expectantly.

"Of course," I said. I took off my eye mask. It was the polite thing to do. I was also curious—I had never been in her compartment, she had come to mine.

The falsie was surprising in its simplicity—a pleasant meadow with a small stream and a multicolored tent by its shore. Nearby, a horse chewed the grass that grew along the water's edge. In the distance, almost hidden in haze, was a range of mountains. That was all, though I realized it would look considerably different under an evening sky blazing with constellations.

The simplicity itself made sense. Snipe worked with projections every shift, most of them military fantasies. She was probably tired of the complex and the alien.

Then I took another look at the horse and changed my mind. It was all white, with an absurd twisted horn growing out of its forehead.

Before I could comment, she said, "I think it's quite good," and I murmured, "It's beautiful."

She looked at me sharply. "You're not just saying that?"

"No," I said, then ruined it by adding, "Though the horse—"

"Unicorn," she corrected with a trace of irritation. "I wasn't sure how the horn grew—the horns on all the deer of the same period grew backward but it didn't seem right for the unicorn."

I suspected she was talking as fast as she was because I made her nervous, then decided there was no chance in the universe that I could make Snipe ill at ease. So much for my powers of perception.

"It would look better if it pointed straight up," I said, trying to be tactful.

"The computer mentions them but I couldn't find a pic of one," she said.

She had probably overlooked a file hierarchy. There are real animals and mythological animals and no data taxonomist would have combined them in a single file, though Snipe probably hadn't known that. What a strange, fertile world Earth must have been, so teeming with life they could even make up animals!

She walked over to the unicorn and stroked its mane. Like Crow, she had a knack for making the falsie something to live in as well as something to look at. It struck me then that if I ever went blind, my own little world on the *Astron* would be unspeakably barren.

She watched me watching her and suddenly looked away. "You never told me you wanted *me*," she said in a low voice.

I flushed. "Wasn't it obvious?"

When she looked at me, for the first time I saw the woman hiding behind the girl. "Obvious?"

"I asked for you," I said, embarrassed. "I'd been told it was ship's custom."

"Some things are." She concentrated on the tangled mane.

"I . . . wasn't very good," I said.

"Those who are the most sincere are frequently the most awkward," she murmured. Then: "Would you have been unhappy without me?"

I tried to edge away from the subject. "I've seen all your plays. I look for you at mealtimes. I've . . . followed you in the passageways."

"You should have told me how you felt."

Right then I felt miserable.

"I . . . didn't know how," I said.

She smiled, the woman in Snipe completely in control. "I think you do."

I reached for her and she dodged away. A moment later I was clutching my nose where I had banged into a bulkhead, doing my best to blink away the tears. She floated back to help wipe them away.

"You could have told me I did a good job with the falsie."

"I said it was beautiful," I squeaked through my fingers.

"You're clumsy," she said, but without her usual arrogance.

"Not always," I defended, aware of her closeness but not knowing for sure how to act.

Her sponging had changed to a quiet stroking. "I shouldn't have had to go Outside to get you."

Which was true. If I had been more aware during the walk-about, she wouldn't have had to risk her life trying to save mine.

"You're right," I admitted with more than a touch of humility, "you shouldn't have had to go Outside to get me."

I had finally made up my mind to put my arm around her when she moved away, pushing over to the nearby tent and pressing the palm terminal in the middle of the coat-of-arms on the tent flap. The stream, the unicorn, and the tent faded away. The real compartment was more homelike than most, decorated with large string tapestries into which she had woven the same scene that was in the falsie. I hadn't noticed it when I had first floated in; my eyes had been too full of her.

"I activate the falsie for guests. I seldom wink it on for myself—I see enough fantasy in the plays."

She had turned Ophelia-like, efficient and mature, old beyond her years. Huldah told me later that I had come into Snipe's life when she was at an awkward age. Despite her best precautions, she was growing up, and those moments when she put aside her playthings were becoming more frequent.

"I'm sorry about the drill." I felt like I was apologizing to a Senior.

"You're not to blame," she said. "They told me about the tether." She looked at me, curious. "Is that why you tried to kill Thrush?"

"One of the reasons," I said cautiously.

"Don't try it again. He'll kill you instead. Or Heron will."

"I can take care of myself," I said, flushing.

She relaxed back into Snipe.

"No, you can't," she said. "Not yet."

I was glad that nobody was around to tell Loon what happened next or an exaggerated and undoubtedly very funny version would have been all over the ship the following time period. I reached for her again and she moved away, but not too fast. Then we tangled with the hammock, and at what should have been a very tender moment we both burst out laughing. After that it was all play and laughter and jabs to the ribs. It gradually became more serious and gentle as we grew more familiar with each other. It was, I thought later, nothing at all like what I had seen in some of the more erotic image pix or what had been described by some of my fellow crew members. It was especially unlike what I had experienced the first time with Snipe.

Taking off each other's waistcloths was enormously exciting, as was merely touching each other and hugging; afterward, she complained that her ribs hurt. We took turns going limp and letting the other feel wherever they chose; then I would lightly stroke the hairs on her arms and watch them quiver as the skin tightened. I wondered what idiot had divided the body into erogenous zones when all of her was erogenous, at least to me.

We spoke volumes without speaking at all and I knew without thinking about it that, whether either of us proved faithful to the other or not, right then we were partnering at some subconscious level that would last the rest of our lives.

But making love to Snipe was not without an element of guilt. A part of me kept insisting on comparing Snipe to Crow and even to Thrush.

I swore quietly to myself, realizing honesty had crept up on me as innocently as sleep, though it wasn't nearly as welcome. The Captain was right; one of the reasons I hated Thrush was because he had encouraged me to feel something for him and then betrayed it. . . . And I would not deny my feelings for Crow, though I insisted to myself that they were . . . different. For one, I wanted very badly to protect Snipe, even though I knew she could protect herself far better than I ever could. . . .

I struggled with my emotions, then gave up and snuggled closer to Snipe. You loved who you loved when you loved them, it was as simple and as complicated as that.

Just before we finally drifted off, Snipe said, "You're very gentle with women, Sparrow—you're very different from what they told me."

She was half asleep when she said it, or she wouldn't have said it at all. But it was like hearing a tumbler fall in a lock when you start to work the combination.

Who had told her, and how had they known, when Snipe was the first woman I had ever made love to?

15

We were three weeks out from Aquinas II and now had accurate measurements of its gravity, the composition of its atmosphere, the mean distance from its primary, and its range of surface temperatures. It was a cold planet, colder than Seti IV, without any signature of life at all. That was no surprise, though some of us still had hopes.

The Seniors made up a training projection in which Crow, Hawk, and Eagle rolled across a desert planet in a Rover heading for a distant mountain range. I watched, fascinated, as they climbed one of the steeper slopes. We were neglecting something, I thought, and caught up with the brilliance of my idea I approached Ophelia once the play was over.

"We took image pix on Seti IV," I said. "Why not review those? It would be better than actors in a projection background—we would be dealing with reality rather than with astronomical models."

"Seti IV?" She looked at me with suspicion, then shook her head. "It's a good idea, Sparrow, but the image cameras malfunctioned and we have no records of Seti IV." She turned bitter. "It shouldn't surprise you, you know the state of our equipment. In any event, there was nothing there."

She had missed the point—it wasn't what we had or hadn't found, but how we had gone about it that would have been helpful to us. I thought she was too quick to dismiss the idea

and wondered if it wasn't because it was my suggestion. I
brought it up with Tybalt but to my surprise he was snappish
and unfriendly.

"You know better than to complain to me about another
Senior, Sparrow."

"I'm not complaining," I protested. "I just think it's a good
idea. In a few weeks, we'll be on the surface. A review of
what happened on Seti IV would be invaluable."

He shook his head. "Ophelia was right about the cameras.
No great loss, there was nothing much to record."

But he didn't meet my eyes and I couldn't believe he had so
little to say when ordinarily he would go on for hours about
any planet on which he had set foot.

When I was alone at the palm terminal, I retrieved the data
we had on Seti IV and was disappointed once again. There
was little information, much less than for a standard exploration survey of any planet, and most of it struck me as random.
The planet was notable, it seemed, primarily because it was
where I had fallen from a cliff.

I tried to forget about it, but it came back to me again when
I was watching another training projection in which a survey
team tried to rescue Heron, lost somewhere on a distant
planet. This time I was so fascinated I almost forgot it was
Heron and that I hoped the team would exercise its better
judgment and leave him there.

I went back to the computer and tried again, scanning every
file that might have data on Seti IV. There was next to nothing. Then one sleep period I had an inspiration and stole onto
the hangar deck. The corridors were empty, there were no
guards, and since it was off shift, nobody was on duty. I
placed my hands on the terminal where Snipe activated the
projections for her plays. Most of the planetary surfaces that
floated across the empty hangar deck were meant for instruction. By now I had seen and been bored by most of them.

On impulse, I retrieved an inventory. It was possible that
any image pix of Seti IV might have been misfiled. I scanned

the list of hundreds, noting that at the bottom a dozen more were under computer lock.

I started to sweat, afraid somebody would walk in and report my unauthorized use of the terminal. I rubbed my hand against my thigh to increase the circulation and sensitivity, then nervously started to "pick" the lock.

The last few projections were far more complicated than the ordinary training plays or even the compartment falsies, mere three-dimensional images meant only to be perceived. These were artificial realities with which the observer could interact. You were not only *in* your surroundings, you could reach out and touch objects and even move them about as you desired. To crewmen wearing the necessary data suits, the "realities" were very real indeed.

The hangar deck filled with ghostly images framed by the intersecting planes of light: A water planet with crew members from the *Astron* climbing over a reef in a lifeless sea; a frozen planet with glaciers of methane ice and rock formations that looked like ancient castles; a world of iron and granite that constantly shook beneath the explorers' feet and where thousands of volcanoes belched lava at an angry sky.

I slowed the action until the realities solidified, catching my breath when an explorer in the first one ripped open his exploration suit on a rock and drowned in seconds. On the world of ice, one of the explorers fell down a crevasse and was buried forever. Still another crewman was lost in a sudden unexpected lava flow on the volcano world.

These were cautionary tales of what might happen if we weren't careful. They were probably scheduled for showing immediately before we ventured down to Aquinas II. If shown too soon, they would lose their impact. Give Loon enough time to invent a parody and their warning would be lost in laughter.

The last of the realities was of a desert planet with a team in a Rover bouncing along a dried-up riverbed on its way to a distant mountain range. There were jumps in the action, as there had been in the others. You established the crew in the Rover, then you cut to getting out at the base of a cliff, and finally you focused on one explorer dangling against the rocky face.

I watched, stunned, as the rope that held him frayed against the cliff and he plummeted to the stones below. A few moments of a closeup on the ground, then another scene shift to dusk and the rest of the team gathered around him, spraying quick-freeze on his cracked helmet to prevent the loss of air. The action was badly timed—with his fractured helmet, the crewman would have lost his air long before the rest of his team got to him.

But that hardly concerned me. The planet was Seti IV and the face of the crewman in the fractured helmet was my own.

I turned it off and sat there in the dark, feeling the sweat grease my skin and trying to control the sudden skipping of my heart. It was an artificial reality—which meant that Seti IV and my fall from the face of the scarp had never really happened at all.

But everybody on board the *Astron* had conspired to make me think it had.

Once again, they had all lied to me and once again I had no idea why. The lies had been clever and had involved everybody. What little information there was in the computer about "Seti IV" had been planted there in the event that I became curious. Even the warning in the computer not to give me my life history had been a lie—nobody on board had been about to. Quite the contrary, they had kept it from me.

I went back to the beginning and reviewed the entire projection, from climbing down the ladder to the rocky surface below, to the ride in the Rover with crew members whose faces I never saw, to the fall from the scarp and Ophelia bending over me, to the ride back to the Lander.

It even included scenes inside a mock Lander and an Inbetween Station. But, of course, I really had been in sick bay.

None of it made much sense, but what made the least was the sincerity of Loon's embarrassment and of Thrush's hostility and of the loss that I read on the faces of Ophelia and Crow.

If they had been acting, then it had been great acting. But I had seen them in some of Snipe's plays and they had been anything but great. Ophelia was always too formal and Crow usually looked confused trying to fake emotions he didn't feel. For Pipit, I had been a bona fide patient; even though I never had any real injuries, my suffering was real enough.

I played the projection one more time, convinced that the answers were buried within. I watched myself appear in the hatchway of the Lander, then cautiously descend the ladder, pausing for just a moment as I stepped onto the rocky ground. I left the palm terminal and pushed into the scene, standing beside "myself" as I kicked at a small pebble and laboriously scrawled an *H* in some drifted sand.

Back at the terminal I stopped the scene and stared at it. Just the one letter, nothing more. Why would I have done it? Why would anybody? Of course. An initial. Except that my name began with an *S*.

Only my fingers were working now. My emotions were frozen and I didn't dare let them thaw. I accessed the crew's roster and ran through the *H*'s but I knew everybody who was listed. Then, on impulse, I dropped back one generation. Most of that crew were still alive; the others were strangers to me and I guessed they had made the journey to Reduction. But the crewman I was looking for had to be listed—after all, he had consumed food and air and water and had taken up living space.

I planned on reading the biography of each vanished crew member whose name began with *H*, but I didn't have to go beyond the first.

Hamlet.

I moved my hand slightly on the terminal pad to retrieve more information, and the words dissolved and flowed into a brief notice:

ALL DATA CONCERNING SUBJECT
SEALED BECAUSE OF
ACUTE STRESS DUE TO AMNESIAC
ILLNESS. GIVING
SUBJECT LIFE HISTORY INFORMATION
PRIOR TO HIS
OWN RECALL WILL HINDER COMPLETE
RECOVERY.

The data were protected by a guardian shell and there was no way I could break it.

I sat there in shock, staring at the screen. I could not imagine amnesia victims in successive generations. The odds would not allow for it. I put my hand back on the pad and went still another generation back. Most of the names were unfamiliar now and I had nothing to guide me—there was no *H* scrawled in the sand to serve as a clue. Unfortunately, time was running out; in another hour or so they would be using the hangar deck for more instruction plays.

But the biography I was looking for was very short, and the names tumbled through the screen faster than I expected. This time, the name was the very first.

Aaron.

A dozen more and I shut the computer down and drifted off the darkened hangar deck. There was no possible way there could have been an amnesia victim in every generation. But there was exactly one approximately every twenty years. The information on them was far more fragmentary than that on Laertes had been. In fact, there was no information at all; in each case an identical guardian shell served as a computer block. What did the shells contain? Or were they empty?

I struggled against the obvious. But before I could accept it, I had to find some way of proving it.

The obvious was that there was no new amnesia victim in every generation.

We were all the same victim.

* * *

When you eliminate the improbable, you're left with the impossible. But I couldn't confide in anybody on board, I couldn't ask for help in searching for clues. There was only the artificial reality itself, the names that had bobbed up in the rosters of the different crews, and the guardian shells in the computer. And, of course, there was myself.

I was sweaty and unhappy, finding it difficult even to speculate about what I should do next. I floated through the corridor back to my compartment, my mind mostly blank, absently trying to scratch my thigh where a small drop of sweat had nested in the hairs. The itch was persistent; I glanced down and once again my mind froze with shock.

It had been two weeks since Thrush gashed my leg. It had been a deep cut and I had lost a lot of blood, but the cut had vanished without a trace. I fingered where it had been, pressing hard against the flesh. There was no pain at all, only the pressure of my fingers.

I was terrified by what this hinted. I was healthy; I healed faster than anybody else on board. Abel should have been surprised but hadn't been, and that was a clue I had been a fool to ignore.

I drifted through the corridors, oblivious of the few crewmen who passed silently by, then floated through the lower levels to Reduction. Nobody was there, the peep screen was off, and there were no guards—there was no need of them. My skin began to crawl but I drifted in and quickly examined all the equipment, desperately trying to remember everything Thrush had told me. For the first time, I was glad of his tour and the education he had given me, even though the price he charged had been far too high.

I kept returning to a large, transparent cylinder in one of the corners. A body-scanner, Thrush had called it. He had run through its operation, more interested in displaying his knowledge than making sure I knew how it worked. We had been smoking and the details were fuzzy but I thought I could manage it without help.

I floated over to it and ran my hands down the glassite walls. How do you tell your age? I mused. The skin loses its elasticity as you grow older, and muscles atrophy from lack of use. The teeth are probably the best indicators of all—they rot with time, they wear down over the years. But mine had never hurt and I guessed they would tell me nothing. If what I thought was true, I probably grew them the way a salamander grows tails.

That left the skeleton. I might knit quickly but it was doubtful that I could grow a new tibia at will.

I set the dials and ducked in. Once inside, I felt nothing; the only signs that the body-scanner was even operating were two metal rings that floated up and down the transparent walls. On the bulkhead opposite, a screen lit up; I watched with interest as the rings slowly painted the picture of a skeleton as they passed over my body.

A few moments later I was inspecting a portrait of my own insides. I wasn't sure what I was looking for, though I could make out the vague blur of cartilage. Wasn't it compressed in older people? I assumed it was, though I was less sure it would be under weightless conditions. I couldn't tell whether mine was or not and finally assumed it wasn't—I suffered from no aches or pains, I had no difficulty moving or working my joints.

Then I caught my breath and looked closer at the screen, my heart pounding. The bones in my arms, legs, and rib cage were covered with dozens of faint, thin lines.

Bone fractures. Healed breaks.

How many times in his life did even the most active explorer break a bone? Once? Twice? Maybe three times? How many lifetimes would it have taken to accumulate all the breaks in my bones? How many lifetimes of roaming the surfaces of strange planets, of falling from cliffs or skidding down slopes of methane ice or scrambling out of the way of sudden lava flows?

For all I knew, I might be as old as the Captain. Perhaps, like him, I had been attached to the first crew. Attached in the same sense that he had been attached—after all, we had outlived the others by a hundred generations.

I panicked at the implication and fled through the different levels back to the hangar deck. I wanted to look at Seti IV again and watch myself descend the ladder to its rocky surface and scratch an *H* in the sand. Somewhere in those simple actions were the reasons why nobody had told me about myself, why nobody could tell me.

Months ago, in sick bay, Noah had said that I was seventeen, a tech assistant on board the *Astron*. He had been more wrong than right—and he had known it all the time.

I was far older than seventeen. And whatever I was, I was much more than a simple tech assistant.

I ran the projection once more from the beginning, taking note of every detail. This time I could see that my spacesuit was a skintight data suit, rigged to function like a palm terminal and give tactile feedback. The result had been overwhelmingly real, at least for me.

I watched it to the end, once again impressed by Ophelia and Crow, so convincing here and so unconvincing in the historicals that Snipe staged.

I had frozen the last scene in the Lander and was studying it when I sensed somebody slip in through the darkened hatchway behind me.

"You're breaking Coventry coming here, Sparrow—that's a reportable offense."

I moved slightly so Ophelia had a better view of the projection.

"Sparrow's in Coventry. Hamlet isn't."

I could hear the surprise in her sharp intake of breath.

"I'll live forever, won't I, Ophelia?"

"Not forever," she said in a flat voice. "But long enough."

I couldn't read her expression in the dark of the hangar. I

waved at the ghostly image of the artificial reality in front of me.

"All of it was a charade, wasn't it, Ophelia?" I didn't wait for her answer. "Your acting was very good. And Crow—Crow was excellent; I didn't know he had it in him. Anybody watching the two of you would have thought you were mourning a lifelong friend."

Her voice was inexpressibly sad. "We were."

"How could you be?" I sneered. "I wasn't dying—and you knew it."

"No, you weren't dying," she agreed. "Hamlet was."

As she had gradually become convinced that Hamlet was gone forever, that "Sparrow" was somebody she had never known, her attitude toward me had changed. Hamlet had been a friend, "Sparrow" a stranger, and she had reacted accordingly.

"And Pipit," I said, not wanting to let my anger slip away. "She should get an award."

"She should," Ophelia agreed once again. "For patience. If the body thinks it's been hurt, then it's been hurt. You'll live a long time but you're not immortal, Sparrow, you can die. And you can be killed. You have a lot to thank Pipit for."

If she meant to sober me, she succeeded.

"Why did they do it?"

"They knew the voyage would last a long time. They didn't want the crew to forget."

"Forget what?"

"What it's like to be human." She corrected herself. "What it was like to be human at the time of Launch. You haven't changed since then."

Another tumbler fell into place.

"The crew studies me, don't they? You study how I react, how I think, how I talk, the importance I give to the things I do. Or you do. You watch me watching you. I'm a living mirror in which you can check your own image—that's it, isn't it?"

Huldah had told me that nothing ever really changed on board. She hadn't told me that I was the reason why.

"I wouldn't make that comparison. You're more like a Rosetta Stone, a link between what we are now and what we were when we left the Earth. That's very important to us, Sparrow."

"You could have studied the Captain," I said.

"Kusaka's many things, but one of the things he isn't is the same man who left the Earth two thousand years ago. He's not at all like you, Sparrow. He remembers everything, he forgets nothing. He can't."

Then all the tumblers fell into place—or I thought they did.

"I'm only good for one generation, right, Ophelia? After fifteen or twenty years I've adapted to the ship, I react to situations just like any other crew member. My reactions are no longer . . . fresh . . . so I have to start all over again. I'm the phoenix that rises from its own ashes, the firebird. How do you do it, Ophelia? Drugs? So I can't tell the real from the unreal? And then when I'm out of my mind and my memory is hazy, I find myself on Seti IV climbing a cliff that exists only for me."

She was still staring at the scene in the Lander; I wasn't even sure she had heard me.

"What happens then, Ophelia?"

I could sense her shiver in the darkness.

"Your memory's flatlined; you remember nothing before the accident."

I recalled my nightmares and the host of faces that had surrounded me, the faces of all the crew members I must have known through the generations. And then Ophelia's own face and that of the man in black. The Captain. I suddenly felt as helpless as I had in sick bay.

"Why?"

"Because it was your assignment!" she burst out. "Centuries ago, you must have volunteered for it! You knew what it was all about back then—you're the feedback loop that keeps all of us human! My God, how else would we even know what 'human' is?"

"I'm a living relic," I said bitterly. "You compare yourselves to me to see how far you've come from the ape. It must be amusing at times."

She shook her head.

"You're hardly an amusement, Sparrow. The *Astron* is a very tiny village, the only one in a country that stretches to infinity in whatever direction you care to look. There are only a few of us, and we get to know each other very well. Hardly anything ever changes on board and if it does, it changes so slowly we don't realize it. Our lives are exactly like the lives of the generation before us. They're very structured, limited lives. They can't be anything else; they're the result of two thousand years of ship culture. But you lived your life back on Earth. You're very . . . unstructured. You're very human. Watching you reminds us of what it's like."

I recalled being stranded Outside and was suddenly angry.

"If I'm so valuable why did you let me go on the walkabout? I could have died."

She sighed.

"That's right, you could have. I told you that. As it was, we did our best to protect you. But keeping you locked up in a compartment would have defeated your purpose." With a touch of guilt, she added: "Telling you who you are would have done the same thing."

Squatting next to her, I was very much aware of her warmth, a very familiar warmth. At one point, she put a hand tentatively to her hair, then abruptly placed it in her lap. It was a touching moment; she had accepted that I was more than Sparrow even though she knew I was much less than . . . Hamlet.

That was one question I suddenly wanted to ask her, but I asked another instead.

"What was I to Noah?"

I could sense her sudden discomfort.

"His best friend. Aaron and Noah 'grew up' together."

"And Crow?"

"Hamlet took an interest. When Crow was very young."

Crow had probably been K2's age. As Hamlet, I had been a father to him. His reactions to me were a lot easier to understand now. He had initially deferred to me; it had taken him a while to accept himself as my equal and a friend. With luck, everybody's father eventually becomes their friend, but it hadn't been that simple for Crow or probably for Noah. Had I taken an interest in Noah when he was very young? Had he watched me go from father to friend to son?

"Laertes never existed," I said. "What about Nerissa, my mother?"

Ophelia shrugged. "She did. But she wasn't your mother."

It would have been nice to have had one—one that I remembered.

"Who makes the decision to flatline?"

"The Captain. But the necessity is apparent to all of us."

"When you take away a person's memories, that person dies," I said slowly. "The Captain murdered Hamlet. And you helped."

Her voice cracked.

"You think it was easy? It wasn't—but it was necessary!"

"If the Captain finds out I know who I am, he'll have me flatlined again, won't he?"

She nodded.

"And you'll tell him, won't you?"

She hadn't looked away from the projection since the moment she had slipped through the hatch and I wondered what attraction it held for her.

"Do you remember anything about Hamlet?"

I shrugged. "I know my life as Sparrow. That's all."

"Then continue being Sparrow," she said coldly.

I recalled Noah and Abel in sick bay and how anxious they were that I remember who I had been. I finally knew . . . but I did not remember. I was sure that the difference was crucial.

"For the first time in generations, something's changed, hasn't it?"

Once again, I could sense her shiver.

"In a few weeks, we'll be entering the Dark. We'll never survive. Once in it, most of us will choose to die like Judah."

The Dark was the connection; it had always been the connection.

"Hamlet was part of your mutiny." I grunted. "I'm not."

I started for the hatch. It was close to shift time and we wouldn't be alone much longer.

Behind me, she warned, "You can never admit that you know, Sparrow."

"Neither can you," I said. "Not to Noah, not to anybody."

Just before pushing through the shadow screen, I glanced back. Ophelia had run the projection to where I lay naked on the acceleration couch, her own image bent over mine, her fingers probing for broken bones. The real Ophelia was crying.

I hadn't asked what Hamlet had meant to her, but now I knew.

Part Two

For he who lives more lives than one
More deaths than one must die.
—from "The Ballad of Reading Gaol,"
Oscar Wilde

16

It wasn't long before I was excused from Coventry, though it might have been safer had I stayed in. For the first few time periods after learning about my history, I caught myself playing a game: Who had known me as "Hamlet" and who had known me as "Aaron" and how good were they at pretending ignorance?

After a week I noticed that some crew members frowned when they glanced at me and talked in low voices among themselves when I passed by. I was giving myself away with comments that had more than a trace of sarcasm and with knowing looks whenever they talked to me. They had accepted "Sparrow" while I was in the process of rejecting him.

I forced myself to forget that I had ever been anybody other than "Sparrow" and tried to project a mix of innocence and ignorance that I thought was appropriate. I spent more time with Tybalt and others outside the immediate ring of mutineers, glowered once or twice at Thrush to keep in character, and studiously ignored Heron. I was "myself" with Snipe more than with anybody else, probably because we spent most of our time wrapped around each other in her hammock rather than talking or working together.

The frowns gradually disappeared and I found it increasingly easy to become the "Sparrow" I had been before. Getting ready to explore a new planet helped, but even working with Ophelia I maintained the role. Once or twice she looked as if she were about to say something. I never gave her an opening.

I was always alert, watching for the sudden shift in attitude that would indicate that somebody knew *I* knew and my days as "Sparrow" were numbered.

It was easy to determine who had joined the mutiny and who hadn't been approached. Those who had joined frowned too much and were too conscious of themselves and their new status. They congregated in small clumps during mealtimes or in the corridors to talk among themselves, not yet aware that the best way to keep a secret is to forget you know it. Most of them were in Exploration, a few in Communications. With the exception of myself, I doubted that anybody had refused. They wouldn't have been approached in the first place unless the mutineers were absolutely sure of the response.

It was difficult to tell who had joined among the crew members in Maintenance since, without exception, all of them wore worried looks anyway. They knew better than anybody else the *Astron*'s chances of survival in the Dark. Tern, a thin, gawky engineering assistant, once tried to discuss the mutiny with me in the gymnasium. I discouraged him from talking about it, saying it was too public and too risky. I wasn't thinking of Tern so much as I was thinking of myself.

Then there were those on the sidelines. Myself, of course, though I wasn't the only one. There was Thrush, who observed his fellow crew members with quiet amusement. He had become his old smirking self, but with a certain detachment and a harder edge. And there were Banquo and Abel, both of whom worked too hard at maintaining poker faces and pretending they were unaware that anything at all was happening.

The crew was tense, excited and anxious about the upcoming exploration of Aquinas II. If any form of life were discovered, the mutiny would evaporate for lack of need—the *Astron* would finally be free to return home. But if the planet were as sterile as all the others, then the mutiny might spread like wildfire.

What should I do? I wondered. Join it? I was already inclined to. Or side with the Captain, realizing that if he ever found out I had joined the mutiny, "Sparrow" would be flatlined like Hamlet and Aaron had been? It was a decision I didn't have the courage to make.

The Captain had his eyes and ears among the crew, and I was convinced he knew every muscle twitch and stray thought of every crew member on board. He would have his arguments, his counterplots, and in the last analysis, he would have his powers as captain.

When it came to using them, I suspected he would be ferocious.

The one group on board not concerned with either Aquinas II or the mutiny was the very young. I found myself spending more and more time in the nursery, playing with the children and talking to Pipit. Ever since her decision to share Crow's compartment after the rape, she had become increasingly more mellow and content. As always, she seemed wise beyond her years, and I guessed that when Huldah went to Reduction Pipit would take her place.

One time period when I was in the nursery, another mystery presented itself, though I was unaware of it for a while, as I was of most mysteries on board the *Astron*.

Pipit had just finished leading the *begats* and drifted over to where I floated by the hatchway.

"Loon has moved in with Ibis," she said.

Loon, so good at spreading stories about the love affairs of others, had kept his own a secret. Ibis was his opposite: a quiet, thoughtful young woman, not particularly attractive. I didn't know her very well; she was a radio tech in Communications and most of my friends and acquaintances were in Exploration.

"That seems sudden," I said, surprised.

Pipit shook her head. "Not really. Ibis and I have always been good friends. She's spent a lot of time with us and Loon got to know her."

Pipit had probably engineered the romance, and I made a mental note to ask Snipe about it later. Snipe's flair for gossip had diminished, but I was sure she had some insight into Ibis and Loon that I didn't.

"He said he would give his life for her." Pipit laughed. "I think he was serious."

Loon was always willing to give his life for somebody, but if he ever had to, I suspected he would give it a little sooner for Crow than for anyone else. I suddenly wasn't sure of the right thing to say.

"I imagine you and Crow are glad to be alone," I fumbled.

Her smile faded and she gave me a troubled look. "I love Loon," she said slowly. "But he and I compete. And sometimes I lose. Too often." And then, hastily: "I'm very happy for him."

But she was obviously happier for herself.

"Spar-row?"

Somebody was tugging at my leg and I glanced down to see K2 wrapped around my calf.

"Come pray with me?"

K2 had grown a lot in the past few months but his diction hadn't caught up with the rest of him. He constantly surprised and delighted me, not the least with his ability to read me as easily as did the Captain. Right then, I decided I needed to play more than anything else.

I grabbed him around the waist and we went rolling through the compartment, the other children scattering to give us room. We bumped softly against the opposite bulkhead and I held him against the deck, tickling him under the arms. He squealed with delight and burst into a fit of giggling, joined by most of the others in the compartment.

Another roll around the compartment, only this time when we caught up against a bulkhead we hit it a shade too hard;

K2 took the brunt. His mouth turned down and he started to cry. I held him in my arms and said the usual words of comfort, then turned to stare in amazement at a compartment full of sobbing children.

"Are they always like this?" I asked Pipit.

She looked surprised.

"Of course. You hurt one, you hurt them all. And if you make one laugh, the others always feel it." She hesitated. "Most of them."

I settled in a corner and studied the children the rest of that time period. A number of mothers came to visit but there were many "fathers" as well. I found it fascinating to watch who had "taken an interest" in whom. Wren and Grebe were vastly proud of thin little Cuzco while Duncan, an engineer in Communications, played quietly with pudgy Denali. In general, the gentler members of the crew and the quieter children seemed to have an affinity for each other. In some cases, I was struck by the resemblance and guessed that natural father had taken an interest in natural son or daughter. But those cases were few.

I had frequently thought about the differences between the rest of the crew and myself; now it seemed as if they might be more subtle than I had imagined. There had always been a lot of hostility toward Thrush, and that had masked the lack of hostility between most members of the crew, the lack of any real malice. Even Loon's gossip and satires were meant to cause laughter, not hurt. Nor was there much competition among members of the crew, especially on station—they cooperated naturally when they worked together. They were also at ease with affection at almost any time and any place, something that had scandalized me at first and now made me envious.

Well, what should I have expected? It was a well-trained crew that had been working and living together for generations. But the crew's rapport with each other went deeper than that. Even their nonrefusal the first time when it came to sex hinted at something more complicated.

Maybe it was philosophical, I thought. If you knew that you and your fellow crew members were the only life in the entire universe, with what concern and respect would you treat each other?

The thought gave me great pause and I watched the children more closely. Right now they were too young for their character to have been shaped by philosophy. More important, there were a few who didn't join in the giggling or the infrequent crying but watched and frowned, obviously feeling left out.

The crew in microcosm. There was the bulk of the crew members, and then there were the Captain's men. If we found nothing on Aquinas II, the mutiny would spread very quickly, with the majority of the crew pitted against the Captain and a few followers. But unlike most of the rest of the crew, the Captain and his men were capable of violence.

A few time periods after that, I was once again approached to join the mutiny—and told I was indispensable. I had gone to the hangar deck to meet Snipe and playact with her in one of the historicals. They were heavily romantic and later we would go to her compartment and make love by the stream just outside her tent. It was exciting for both of us. I guessed that Loon would soon find out and spread the story around the ship; I didn't mind—if anything it would make more real the character of Sparrow, somebody my fellow crew members knew better than I did.

I had turned off the shadow screen and was floating to one side of the vast deck, staring at the stars overhead. I wondered how I could be so depressed when I had everything I wanted in life or even thought I wanted—a love affair with Snipe, a purpose in life, and, most of all, a knowledge of my background and who I had been.

But still, I was a chip floating on a sea of dissatisfaction. I *knew* who I was, but I did not *remember* who I was. It struck me as unfair to have lived so long yet recall only a small fraction of my life. I had my friends and lovers but there was no lifetime of shared experiences, no years of love and affection and growing up together. . . .

I was drifting, hoping solitude would jog me out of my black mood, when I felt the slight movement of air currents at my back.

"Snipe said to tell you she'd be late—a last-minute assignment from Ophelia."

The shadowy figure of Noah had materialized behind me. I had been staring up at the stars, absorbed in the view of Outside, and the ten percent of me constantly on the alert had let down its guard.

I winked the overhead shadow screen back on, let the glow tubes come up, and floated toward the hatch. "I'll meet her in her compartment."

"Sparrow."

I turned around, noting the worried look on Noah's face and his hands nervously twisting together behind his back.

"I've nothing I want to talk about, Noah."

"I'm sorry," he said, his eyes blinking furiously behind his thick lenses, "but I do."

I shrugged. "You're here."

He lowered his voice, worried that the Captain or some of his spies might overhear.

"I can't pretend with you, Sparrow. And you shouldn't have to pretend with me."

"Ophelia told you," I said coldly.

"She didn't have to. You gave yourself away."

"To everybody?"

He shook his head. "Not to everybody. But I know you better than most—and I've known you longer."

"You knew Aaron and Hamlet, you don't know me."

"Aaron was my best friend," he said with dignity. "I took an interest in Hamlet. I took an interest in you."

"There's a difference between us, Noah. I don't think anybody ever tried to murder Aaron or Hamlet."

"If they did, I never knew about it."

"Well, somebody tried to murder me," I said bitterly. "But nobody believes it."

His face glistened with sweat.

"I do." He hesitated. "For the first time, your life—your real life—is in danger."

It was one thing to know it myself, it was another to have it confirmed, and it was still another to wonder what he hoped to gain by telling me.

"Why?"

"Your memories."

"My memories?" I laughed. "I have no memories. It was you and Ophelia and the Captain and the crew—all of you—who agreed to flatline me."

"Neither Ophelia nor I could stop it. And at one time it was necessary."

Ophelia had told me that and I believed her. But Noah had plans in which I was the linchpin, and he had yet to tell me why.

"You wanted me to recall my memories when you and Abel came to sick bay," I said, suspicious. "Or were you just trying to make sure I had forgotten?"

He shook his head, the sweat flying off his nose and chin.

"I wanted you to remember. There's a window of opportunity when it comes to regaining your memories after a trauma . . . or flatlining. It closes a little with each time period that passes. In another year or so, you'll have no chance of regaining your memories at all."

"And Abel wanted me to remember as well?" I asked in mock surprise. Abel was the Captain's man, Noah must know that.

Noah read the insinuation in my voice and stiffened. "I would trust Abel with my life."

"Then you're more a fool than I." I wanted to remember my life as Hamlet, perhaps even as Aaron. They were closer to me, more immediate. Before that, I wasn't sure I cared. But Noah already *knew* my life as Aaron and Hamlet and I had the feeling he was after something more.

"What do you really want of me?" I asked, frowning. "It's not the same thing for both of us, I know that."

"I want you to remember," he said quietly. "All the way back."

I was incredulous. A hundred different lifetimes . . . "Why is that so important to you?"

"Not just to me, to all of us."

I stared at him, a thin, aging little man who had taken on the impossible role of opposing the Captain. I couldn't believe he had gotten this far, then guessed the only way he could have was if the Captain had let him. I suspected a trap somewhere had opened wide and Noah had walked right in.

"We can't win a mutiny, Sparrow. Not now. We know that. But there have been other mutinies before this. We don't know if they go back to the beginning; the computer has no true records of the first five generations. But the crew who started the first one must have thought they could win. They must have known a way they could run the ship without the Captain."

I was astonished. No true computer records for the first five generations! I struggled to hide my emotions.

"How does that involve me?"

His face became tight with tension.

"If you could remember—"

"Then you lose," I interrupted. "My memories are gone. I've tried to recall them. I can't." Then, sullenly and very much aware that I was probably saving my own neck: "I'm not a part of your mutiny, Noah."

His mouth straightened into a grim line. "You're of immense value to the *Astron*, Sparrow. But to some of those on board, you're more valuable dead than alive. The only possible reason is because they're afraid of what's buried in your memories."

Every time I had been flatlined, there was the slight possibility my memories might return when I recovered. But if Noah was right, until now nobody had ever tried to kill me because of it.

"What's so different this time?" I cried. "Why not before, when I was Hamlet or Aaron or a dozen others?"

"Because this time we're going into the Dark," he said bluntly, "and we'll never survive."

Once again Noah was forcing me to choose between him and the Captain and I couldn't make the choice.

"The Captain has his views," I said stiffly. "I've yet to hear them."

"You think you owe him that?"

I nodded.

Softly: "Then you should pay your debt as soon as possible, Sparrow. For all our sakes."

He touched the terminal pad. The glow tubes dimmed and the shadow screen disappeared, to be replaced by the canopy of glittering stars.

"Going into the Dark is death, Sparrow—inevitable death for everybody on board as life declines and gutters out a dozen generations from now. And probable death for everybody this generation. The more crewmen who decide to die like Judah, the fewer who will choose to keep on living."

He turned to face me in the gloom and for the first time, I saw faint tears in his eyes. When he spoke, it was more to himself than to me.

"We never knew what we lost when we lost Hamlet," he murmured.

I watched him go with a sudden surge of shame. Compared to the Captain, he was a nervous, unimpressive little man in a dirty, rumpled halter. I couldn't imagine anybody following him or being inspired by him. His only qualification was courage and then it occurred to me that perhaps courage was all he needed.

I left shortly after Noah had gone, to lie nervous and impotent with Snipe, then return to my own compartment and try to sleep. Hours went by before I finally drifted off, willing myself to return to the time when I slept in sick bay surrounded by all the faces of crewmen whom I didn't quite know but all of whom knew me.

I woke sweating and wet from a dream, swaying gently in my hammock and trying to recall exactly what it was I had dreamt. I had been me but I had also been someone other than me. Someone older and more sure of himself, more willing to take risks, more willing to gamble.

There had been a kaleidoscope of images of a planetary surface where I had been in charge of a landing party. A very young Tybalt with two good legs was my chief lieutenant and a slender black-haired girl was my tech assistant. We had slid, laughing, down slopes of methane ice, then stood on a cliff overlooking a frozen lake to gaze in awe at a bloated, reddish sun sinking below the horizon at sunset.

Later, back on board, the girl and I had rolled together in my hammock and made slow but impassioned love. I was awake now but I could still taste her skin upon my lips. Our lovemaking had not been as exciting as mine was with Snipe but it had been . . . familiar . . . and its very familiarity had somehow made it more fulfilling.

The girl was, of course, a very young Ophelia and I had been Hamlet.

It was then I decided it hadn't been a dream at all but the first faint trickle of returning memory.

17

The invitation to another dinner with the Captain came sooner than I had expected and I wasn't prepared, though there was probably no way I could have been. If I had discovered nothing at all about Sparrow's previous lives, how would I act? How young, how immature, how innocent? Would I give myself away by trying too hard, would I trap myself with a word that was out of character or a passing thought that never would have occurred to a seventeen-year-old tech assistant?

Thrush had not been invited, it was only the Captain and myself, and I thought immediately that I was lost. I was sweaty, nervous, and tongue-tied by the time I drifted into his cabin. When he turned away from the huge viewing port, I could see his eyes narrow with speculation.

"There's no more punishment, Sparrow. You were excused from Coventry early because we're going to need you below and I didn't want you harboring any grudges."

He clapped me on the back and guided me over to the port, where for a long moment we both stared silently at Outside. His hand still rested on my shoulder but it was no obvious attempt to gauge my reactions. Once again, we were to be friends, he and I, and this was to be a pleasant hour spent in casual conversation over a light meal.

My heart had thumped once when I saw his eyes narrow

and I had consigned my fate to the gods, promptly forgetting every artifice I had practiced in preparation for the meeting. I doubt that there was a time when I was more "Sparrow" than in that particular hour with the Captain. I was lucky because he misread my anxiety as fear of punishment and immediately tried to put me at ease. And having misread me at the start, he misread everything that followed.

Nevertheless, the conversation was anything but casual. The one thing I knew that he knew was that I had yet to join any mutiny, real or imagined. I was sure his eyes among the crew had told him that.

The meal itself was casual but bland, without Pipit's usual added tang. Escalus served it in silence, then settled in a corner, ostensibly ignoring me though I knew he watched every movement I made. Along with the meal, he had served drink bulbs filled with a reddish liquid. It had a slightly sour taste and I made a face when I sipped.

The Captain noted my expression and said, "Wine—it's usually served with a meal on Earth. You don't have to drink it if you don't want to."

But after the first sip, I decided I liked it and drank it as if it were water. The Captain smiled slightly but said nothing. Afterward, I wondered if his serving of the wine had been intended to loosen my tongue. But it turned out to be more of a help for me than a hindrance: For the rest of the hour I was very much Sparrow, without a thought for Hamlet or Aaron or any of the hundred others hiding in the recesses of my mind.

When we were through eating, he drifted back to the port and I joined him to gaze at the field of colorful jewels just beyond. It was a view I never saw when I winked off the shadow screen on the hangar deck and stared at the scattering of hard and unyielding crystal overhead. But rank had its privileges, as the Captain said, and he was entitled to look at whatever view he wanted. I couldn't deny its beauty.

He made no comment at first and I was aware once again of the weight of his hand on my shoulder and the emotional impact of touch, the real glue in any human relationship. Right then, it was my choice whether the captain was father, friend, or older brother.

"You use the computer a great deal, Sparrow," he finally said. I was too light-headed from the wine to react with any alarm. If he knew of my personal research, then he knew, I thought fatalistically. But his next comment was: "Have you ever studied Earth?"

I hadn't, and it struck me that perhaps I should have.

"Your friends gaze at the galaxy and see it as dead," he mused. "I look at it and see it as teeming with life."

He glanced at me and smiled and once again I was flooded with warmth, ashamed of myself for those few times when I'd had dark thoughts about him.

"I'll admit my prejudice—I believe the galaxy is filled with life because we come from a planet that is. There's no part of Earth that's not a home for life, Sparrow. I think we forget that life itself is so adaptable. On board the *Astron* we live at a constant temperature and humidity and pressure and we tend to think that life can only exist under the same kind of stringent conditions. But in actuality, it can exist almost any-place—and does."

This was going to be a lecture, I thought, and I'd had enough of lectures. Then I realized this was the chance I had always wanted. Why did the Captain think the way he did, when every exploration attempt had come up empty-handed? I couldn't believe it was purely because of conditioning. There had to be logical thought and theory behind his beliefs.

"Life is everywhere on Earth, Sparrow. Some fish exist in complete darkness, without ever seeing a ray of light. Others swim more than seven miles deep, where the pressure is a thousand times that at the surface. Some microbes exist in the middle of dry, cold rocks and some bacteria live in liquid that's boiling hot and as corrosive as sulfuric acid."

He was looking down at me now but I didn't meet his gaze, concentrating on the stars just beyond the port. I knew he wanted no interruptions until he had made his point.

"The Earth teems with life," he continued, "from the cold deserts of the Antarctic to the ocean depths. Scientists have found tiny animals that can be dehydrated until their moisture content is as low as two percent. They can even survive temperatures from thirty-three to three hundred and seventy-six Kelvin. They're dormant then but once you add water, they come back to life with no difficulty at all."

He left the port and drifted back to the table for another bulb of wine. I didn't refuse when he offered one to me, though I knew my tongue was getting thick and my movements uncoordinated.

"It seems impossible," I mumbled.

He shrugged. "The fact is that life as we know it is infinitely adaptable. And life as we don't know it? I can't imagine there being a limit. Somebody once suggested that life could evolve in lakes of ammonia or oceans of methane, that on some distant planet silicon creatures may be swimming in seas of molten rock. . . ."

He fell silent and I assumed it was my turn to say something. Of all the questions that I had once wanted to ask, cleverly phrased to hide my lack of conviction and my growing doubts, I couldn't think of one now.

"Life," I muttered, "how it begins . . ."

I thought of Thrush and couldn't continue, suddenly aware that the difference between the start of human life and the development of life itself were separated in complexity by millennia.

"The building blocks of life are all around us," the Captain continued gently. "They cluster on the surfaces of meteorites, they hide in the nuclei of comets, they float in the clouds of gas that obscure distant stars. Biology begins with chemistry, Sparrow, and there's no lack of chemistry out there. That's one thing your friends can't deny."

He turned away from the port and floated over to a hammock to settle in the netting and rub the stubble of his beard with the back of his free hand while staring at me over his drink bulb.

"We've seen our share of planets. Some are bubbles of gas, others solid rock. Some are covered with deserts, others have oceans of water. Some lack an atmosphere, others are blanketed with clouds and flooded with heavy rains of organic compounds. There's heat, there's lightning, there's billions of years of time, and yet your friends would have us believe the galaxy is lifeless except for one chance occurrence on a small planet orbiting a minor sun."

He cocked his head and squinted at me and I wondered if he felt the wine as much as I.

"Do you really believe them, Sparrow?"

I wasn't sure whether he expected me to answer or not. I wondered what Noah would say in rebuttal when I told him. And then I wondered if I should tell Noah anything at all. I was undoubtedly being watched and I realized I had played a fool's game up to now. I was important to the mutineers but for some reason I was equally important to the Captain. My memories, Noah had said, were vital to both sides.

The Captain was staring at me, his eyes large and intense, and I dared not blink or look away.

"Organic molecules are scattered all through space, Sparrow. Ultraviolet light can even produce them from mixtures of ethane, ammonia, water, and hydrogen, and the worlds that have those are legion. All you need then is energy and a liquid. It can be water or hydrocarbon solutions or perhaps solvents we don't even know exist. It's only a step to nucleic acids and proteins and after that life is inevitable. It took billions of years on Earth; on another planet it may only have taken a few million. Who knows?"

His voice dwindled off and he squeezed out the last of the wine from the bulb he held in his hand.

"But that's too simple, isn't it?" he asked bitterly. Then, to himself: "My God, the Ptolemaics are still with us. The sun and the stars no longer revolve around Earth but they cling to the hope that at least *we* are still unique. . . ." He said nothing for long minutes and I glanced over at Escalus, wondering if the Captain's silence worried him as well. He gave no indication of alarm and I tried to smother my own uneasiness.

The Captain's next statement shocked me because it echoed one that Ophelia had made.

"The belief in the utter uniqueness of life is a religious one, Sparrow; it has nothing to do with science."

He crumpled the now empty drink bulb and swam over to the port, turning back to me just before he touched the glass.

"You know how to use the computer better than anybody else. Study the data and make up your own mind." Then the slight smile slid away and I caught a glimpse of a face that was both sad and terrifying at the same time.

"I can't go back, Sparrow," he said in a low voice. "Too many crewmen have died for the mission and I won't make a mockery of their sacrifice."

I left then, half drunk from the wine and frightened by the implications of the conversation. He had told me to study and make up my own mind. I knew that the next time I saw him he would ask questions and expect me to have answers. But there were answers he wanted to hear and answers he didn't want to hear.

He was still trying to convince me and I was puzzled why it was so important to him. After all, I had been "Sparrow" for less than a year, and if he wanted it, I would cease being Sparrow tomorrow. But Noah was wrong in one respect. My memories could hardly matter to the Captain; he already knew everything that lay buried in them.

I wondered if he had tried to convince Hamlet or Aaron or any of the other crewmen I had once been.

I was convinced that he had—and also that he had failed.

My next meeting with the Captain was unexpected and hardly by invitation. There was an enclosed weightless handball court in the center of the gymnasium where I sometimes played with Hawk or Loon and where tournaments with crewmembers from Maintenance were occasionally held. I was good, the best player in Exploration, though playing under conditions of no gravity was hard, sweaty work. It required a knowledge of where the ball would be at any given moment and the ability of a contortionist, so I struck the bulkheads with the softer parts of my anatomy when I misjudged my direction or speed, as I frequently did.

Half a dozen time periods after the meal with the Captain, I was alone in the court, batting the plastic ball against the front bulkhead and waiting for Hawk to show up, when the Captain slipped in through the hatch.

"I asked your friend if I could take his turn."

I knew it was a game stolen from a busy schedule and I guessed he considered our discussion over dinner unfinished—and important. Within the confines of the court we would be alone for the first time, without Escalus to mount guard or carry tales back to his crew mates.

We threw fingers to see who would serve first. I won the serve and scored a fast two points; then the game seesawed back and forth. He won, 21 to 16. I noticed his hands weren't red or puffed even though we played bare-handed. At one time leather gloves or paddles were used, but that had been generations ago, and part of the masochistic thrill of the game was bare palm against hard ball.

Apparently the Captain played often. He was fast and adept at picking off balls in flight just before they hit the bulkheads. I consistently scored with corner serves where the ball rebounded parallel to, and scant centimeters away from, the metal walls. The Captain was very good—but then, I reminded myself, he'd had two millennia in which to improve his game.

So, I suspected, had I, which diminished some of my pride in beating my fellow crew members. I wondered if the Captain and I had ever played before in one of my other lifetimes and guessed that we had.

After the game I doubled over, my hands clasping my knees, trying to catch my breath. The Captain pushed over to one of the bulkheads and tapped on a palm terminal. The glow tubes darkened and the bulkheads faded away, to be replaced by projections of Outside—the Outside I was familiar with, suffocatingly black except for the brilliant, lifeless sparkles of the stars. Only the outline of the Captain against the crystal-strewn sky reminded me of where I really was.

"How many stars in our galaxy, Sparrow?"

It took a moment for me to find my voice.

"Billions," I chattered. "A hundred billion, maybe two."

"Subtract the numbers of red giants and super-giants, they exist too short a time for life to develop on any possible planets. Then take away the binaries and any three-star systems. The likelihood of planets circling them would be small to begin with and even if there were, their orbits would create conditions too erratic to support life. Forget the dwarf stars; if a star is too small it has no continuously habitable zone at all—chances are its planets would be perpetually frozen."

He had drifted close enough to me in the darkness so I could feel his body warmth. His voice was an insidious whisper in my ear, nibbling away at Noah's arguments.

"How many stars remain that are possibilities for life, Sparrow? Stars that are neither too hot nor too cold, neither too large nor too small nor too short-lived—stable stars of medium size that could serve as an incubator and then a nursery for life. How many, Sparrow?"

The glow tubes abruptly came back on and the walls of the court swam into view. The Captain was staring at me, his expression both thoughtful and suspicious. He had been playing cat and mouse with me; dinner had been meant to throw me off my guard.

"Well, how many?" he suddenly roared. "Take a god-damned guess!"

"I d-don't know," I stuttered. "Maybe a billion. Maybe ten billion."

"Good round numbers," he said with satisfaction. He tossed me the ball. "Your serve, Sparrow."

He had spoiled my game and came within a point of a whitewash before I fought my way back. I tried to force myself to forget he was the Captain and think of him as just another opponent, but I found it impossible.

At the end of the game, he said: "I asked you to do some studying, Sparrow. Do you know what the Green Bank equation is?"

I mumbled, "Yes, sir."

"It's a speculative equation for determining the number of communicating civilizations in the galaxy. You have to factor in the rate of star formation each year, then the number of stars that can support planets. Estimate the percentage of planets that can support life, the possibilities of intelligent life, the possibilities of a technical civilization arising, and then the lifetime of that civilization."

He caromed the ball around the corners of the compartment and caught it on the fly on its return. He had known where it was going to be every second of its journey. Complete control, I thought. He had meant that as a demonstration.

"What's the minimum figure for N, the number of communicating civilizations?" he suddenly asked.

I wildly plugged figures into the equation, then saw the obvious answer.

"One," I blurted. "It can never be less than one."

He nodded approvingly.

"That's right, Sparrow. The Earth makes it one. And the high end?"

"I . . . don't know," I said. "I suppose there are different estimates."

"In the millions, Sparrow—not a very high ratio but not so small, either."

"We haven't found any life—" I started to object.

"Because we haven't really looked," he interrupted. "But we don't have to investigate every possibility; we can eliminate the vast majority of the unlikely candidates at a distance.

The remaining possibilities are usually . . . very possible indeed."

He noticed my expression and raised an eyebrow. "You don't agree?"

He was pushing me and for that I was grateful. When pressed I had no thoughts at all of who I once had been. I could only be—and was—Sparrow.

"But we haven't found—" I repeated, sweating.

"—any life at all, though, like Tybalt, I'm not so sure we haven't run across traces of its former presence. But there's nothing wrong with the basic assumptions. It's a matter of . . . time."

He laughed, but there was a bitter edge to his laughter.

"'To hold infinity in the palm of your hand' is a bit of poetry, Sparrow. To imagine that the ordinary lifetime is a substantial piece of eternity is pure egoism. To the person who lives it, perhaps. To the universe, it's less than the tick of the second hand of a ten-year clock."

He threw the ball against the bulkhead again and caught it on the rebound without taking his eyes off me. He was reading me now, judging every twitch and grimace.

"Time is why the *Astron* is a generational ship, time is why I'm the captain. Many variables can be factored into the Green Bank equation, but the one that nobody figured on was the time needed for a ship such as ours to find one of those planets harboring life. The more time spent, the more lifeless planets eliminated, the greater our odds in finding one with life. And considering the time already spent, by now the odds in our favor are very great indeed."

"I'm sure they are, sir," I said, which was an inane reply but exactly what seventeen-year-old Sparrow would say.

He smiled. "One more game?"

I surprised myself. There are times when you play above your head, when no matter how good your opponent is, you can't lose. My serves became almost impossible to return and my saves were little short of phenomenal. He wasn't going to

win this game by staying in the backcourt and simply placing
his shots. But suddenly he was above me, behind me, below
me, off to one side, hawking the ball like no one I had ever
played before. He was moving so fast I seldom saw him push
off from one of the walls.

I thought I was moving just as fast, but he won the game,
21 to 19.

At the end of it, both of us glistened with sweat; if he had
suggested another, I would have refused—it wasn't in me. I
went to shake his hand and was surprised when he drew it
back.

"Sorry, Sparrow," he said with a tight smile, "I can't."

He held up his right hand so I could see that his index finger was puffed and bent back at an impossible angle. He had
broken it when he had skimmed too close to the bulkhead to
pick off a rebound. It had probably happened at the very start
but he had ignored the agony for the rest of the game.

Despite the smile, there was no friendship in his olive-black
eyes.

"Some advice, Sparrow, and I have no objections if you tell
your friends." His voice hardened. "I don't play to lose."

The computer verified everything the Captain had told me,
but it supplied no conclusion. The Captain and Ophelia had
started from the same point: There was life on at least one
planet in the galaxy. Earth. For the Captain, that was the vital
fact supporting all the other evidence that we were not alone,
that life was not only ubiquitous in the galaxy but that there
were millions of civilizations as advanced as our own.

For Ophelia and Noah, life had happened once, but despite
the flood of organic molecules to be found almost everywhere
you cared to look, the odds were against the miracle of life
happening again. It had taken half a billion years for primitive
single-celled organisms to appear on the infant Earth, simple
cells that could move and ingest organic molecules and repli-
cate. It had taken an additional two billion for cells of dif-

ferent types to learn how to cooperate and live symbiotically with each other, to share the chores of a difficult existence. By then the simple cell had developed a nucleus and with it the ability to change and become something better . . . and more complicated.

It had taken enormous periods of time, blind nature trying again and again and again. How many things had to go exactly right for all of that to happen? How many things could have gone wrong?

It had taken two and a half billion years to develop that first nucleated cell, an additional half billion plus for multicelled animals to appear, and another three to four hundred million before plants and animals struggled out of the oceans to thrive on the steaming beaches. After that, following each other in comparatively rapid succession, had come the early reptiles, the dinosaurs, the mammals, and finally the timid, brainy primates. Eventually, the first adventuresome ape dropped from the trees to shamble about on two legs, discovering to its delight that it had been gifted with a year-round sex urge and was destined to populate the primitive Eden.

After a point, the growth of life had been very logical and almost predictable.

It was the first three steps that had proved to be so enormously difficult. The role of luck had loomed far too large and those three steps had taken much too long—a total of almost three and a half billion years for the first multicelled creatures and a future filled with possibilities. One-quarter the lifetime of the universe itself.

It had happened once, but I couldn't imagine it ever happening again.

Both Ophelia and the Captain were right. Whether you believed life to be a one-time occurrence, never to repeat itself, or an inevitable development in the existence of a planet, yours was a religious belief.

Along with Tybalt and what I suspected was a minority of the crew, I had shared the Captain's.

My problem now was that I had lost my faith.

*   *   *

A few time periods later, I had my second dream about
what life had been like aboard the *Astron* generations before.
Again, I was Sparrow but not Sparrow—but not Hamlet or
Aaron, either. My name was Oryx.

I lived on a vastly different *Astron,* with all the tubes occupied by a crew more than three times as numerous. All the
glow tubes worked and the metal bulkheads were dry and
clean, most of them painted a soothing beige. Those that
weren't painted were so shiny I could clearly see my face in
them. The exploration suits were white and new, racked in a
compartment where everything had its appointed place. There
was no dust packed in the corners or coating the crates of
spare parts preserved in still-soft cosmoline.

I worked in Maintenance and envied those in Exploration,
who lorded it over the rest of us. I was still an icon of sorts, a
reminder of all that had once been back on distant Earth, but
few hung on my every word or watched me covertly to see
how I might react to different situations. The Earth was a
much more recent memory and hadn't yet receded into the
mists of fantasy.

I shared a compartment with a young girl who resembled
Ophelia a little and Snipe a great deal, and a technician my
own age who reminded me of Loon with a dash of Hawk
thrown in. Seal laughed a lot and loved to tease me; Bear was
kind and gentle. I was happy and lived much as Sparrow did,
looking forward with enthusiasm to each new planet we explored and longing to feel its surface beneath my feet. Standing apart from myself in the dream, I was mildly surprised
that it didn't make much difference who I slept with—Seal or
Bear, I loved them both. But I had been Oryx for a number
of years and my attitudes had changed greatly since I had last
been flatlined. In my dream, as Sparrow, I knew it wouldn't
be long before Oryx's memories would be erased once again.

There were more personnel in all divisions and there were
far more specialties than I knew as Sparrow. There were ma-

chine shops, electrical shops, stores, computer and biological labs. The equipment in sick bay was complicated and efficient and I wondered what had happened to it, then guessed it had been cannibalized over the generations. Instead of two doctors there were half a dozen, all with their areas of expertise. One even specialized in diseases of the eyes and the mouth; in my dream, I noticed no crewman who suffered from cataracts.

We didn't have a division mess but ate in a large dining compartment with magnetic plates on steel tables and light straps to hold us in the chairs bolted to the deck. It was as much a ritual as a meal, and one that everybody anticipated with pleasure.

One particular meal was etched in my mind after I woke, sweating and with a hammering heart. There had been the usual swirl of conversation around the table and much of it remained in my memory. A fat team leader named Meerkat who looked remotely like Portia had been talking in glowing terms about Eridani III, around which we were orbiting.

"It's a beautiful surface. If we could breathe the air it would be a great day for a picnic down there."

Next to her, Loris, a short, ruggedly-built Rover mechanic, picked at the meal on her plate.

"This looks like what they used to call ham. Probably doesn't taste like it but at least Lincoln's getting better."

Somebody else said, "Don't be hard on Lincoln; ever since he was hurt in the fall on Bishop VI he hasn't been the same around the food machines."

Meerkat again: "I'm looking forward to going back next time period, there's real visual drama where the hills meet the sky."

And Loris once more, holding up a drink bulb and squinting curiously at the contents: "I think this was called punch, diluted ethyl alcohol with some flavoring and fruit in it. I'd give a lot to sample the real thing."

Then there was abrupt silence. The Captain had floated in. He looked a little different to me-as-Oryx than he did to me-as-Sparrow. It was his eyes, I thought. They looked younger, they hadn't seen as much.

He said nothing but sat at the head of the table and quietly ate his meal. The conversation in the compartment started up again, but it was muted. Watching the crewmen as they nibbled at their food, I noticed their occasional glance at the Captain.

I was shocked. They lived in deadly fear of him and along with the fear went the sour smell of hatred. Few of them bothered to hide it. As Oryx, I knew why—but before the reason could come to mind, I woke up, sweating and clutching my hammock, overwhelmed by a deep sense of loss.

The scene in the mess hall matched the dialogue I had heard a few months before when I had explored the empty compartment with Crow and Loon. I had faces to go with the voices now: Bear and Seal and Loris and Meerkat. But I remembered little beyond my relationship with Bear and Seal and the talk around the mess table with Loris and Meerkat.

I lay there in the darkness, thinking about the dream and wondering why the fear and especially the intense hatred of the Captain by that very early crew. It hadn't been hatred for somebody who was cruel or somebody whose orders were unreasonable.

They hated him because of something he had done, something unforgivable that had frightened them badly.

Another chunk of my memories had returned and with it an intense foreboding. What would it be like, I wondered, if I remembered my one hundred lifetimes all at once?

18

The closer we came to Aquinas II, the faster the tempo of the drills and lectures. The tempo of our personal lives ran faster as well. It was probably much the same in a war. We knew we might not live through it, so we did as much living as we could beforehand. By now we had seen the cautionary projections once too often, and sapping our enthusiasm for the landing was the thought that some of us might not return. We were also afraid that if we found no life, there would be the journey into the Dark—a metaphor for death if there ever was one—or the possibility of mutiny and everything it implied.

Tybalt didn't help. He was preparing for more than the exploration of a planet that might or might not have been blessed with life. In every way he could, Tybalt made plans for his own version of a war. The Captain did little to stop him. In retrospect, I think the Captain probably encouraged him. The possibility of life might be pure fantasy but Tybalt's activities in organizing assault squads and defensive teams— 'ust in case—lent an air of reality to it.

Nobody said, "Eat, drink, and be merry, for tomorrow you may die." Nobody had to. Casual friendships flared into great passions and those of us who had paired off began to regret it when there was so much more of life yet to sample.

I can't remember what Snipe and I argued about—it was trivial and I'm sure I started it—but it ended with Snipe moving out of my compartment back to her tent by the peaceful stream. She never lost her temper, though I made a show of losing mine to mask my feelings of guilt. Snipe was hurt and wanted to talk about it but I told her, loftily, that there was nothing more to say. She stared at me, then said somberly, "There's sex and there's partnering—I thought you knew the difference."

After that, she was nothing but understanding, and that was a mistake. An argument might have brought us together; "understanding" drove us apart.

Similar dissensions shredded Crow's relationship with Pipit and within a few time periods we teamed up to rut our way through the *Astron*. We knew it was against ship's custom for anybody on board to turn us down, at least the first time, and we took full advantage. Neither of us was interested in asking a second time. My ego expanded rapidly. So did Crow's. Neither he nor I paid much attention to the looks of disapproval from fellow crew members when we paused in the corridors to compare notes and match scores. But it was hard to ignore Thrush's all-knowing smirk.

The Captain had said that sex was the fool's gold of the emotions and it seemed all too true. But while I didn't learn much about individual crew members, I learned a lot about the social structure of the ship. The dominant form of partnering was couples but triads were not uncommon and neither was the occasional small group. I was curious about all of them, and they about me. Even when my promiscuous period was over, I was surprised how much of my curiosity remained.

Two events brought my rutting to an end. The first was that Swallow asked me to bed. She was a plain woman—perhaps pretty or charming to others, but not to me. I tried to dissuade her by pretending she wasn't serious. But she was, and I had to remind myself it was ship's custom not to refuse the first time. Crow seemed to have no problem in similar situations, but I was different from Crow and I found the sex not only unpleasant but difficult.

The second event was more complicated.

My dreams didn't stop, though they were far more fragmentary. In most of them I saw myself as Hamlet. I helped raise an infant Crow as if he were my son and watched a young girl gradually grow to an aggressive and beautiful maturity. Eventually we became lovers. After more than one sleep period I woke still feeling Ophelia's breath on my shoulder and the touch of her fingers on my back.

One period I slept more fitfully than usual, never quite sure whether I was Hamlet or Sparrow. When I finally gave up on slumber, I slipped quietly out of my compartment and down the passageway to Ophelia's. I stole in through the shadow screen without announcing myself, pausing only a moment to get my bearings. I was in a cave on a hillside with a forest of tall pine trees spread out below. Constellations twinkled in the night sky and moonlight glinted off the snow that furred the branches of the trees. I could hear the occasional snap of a twig in the forest and I thought I saw the shadowy forms of wolves prowling among the trees, a thought confirmed a moment later by their distant howls.

Falsies weren't required to be original; Ophelia had been content to copy hers from the one Crow and Loon had turned into a "safe house." She was curled up near the embers of a fire and I felt my way over to her. It was easy to slide into the character of Hamlet, though a part of me still clung nervously to Sparrow.

I murmured, "Ophelia," at the same time lying next to her on the "skins" before the fire. She woke instantly, her muscles tense. She recognized me and started to push me away, but I pleaded, "Please don't," using the voice of Hamlet.

She closed her eyes and relaxed. I leaned into her, my arms sliding easily around her waist.

It was very strange. It was pleasant but not pleasant. I gradually realized that Hamlet could never be more than a role, that I remembered only bits and pieces of his life. Playing at being him was like trying to recognize a face in the splinters of a shattered mirror.

Mechanically, I aped the Hamlet of my dreams. When I was through I leaned against the cave wall, very much aware of the steel bulkhead at my back. Through it all, Ophelia had never responded.

"My God, I'm sorry," I murmured.

"Hamlet's dead," she said quietly. "You're Sparrow. Be Sparrow."

"I've been playing at being somebody else," I whispered in shame.

"You've been playing at being a fool," she said. There was no condemnation in her voice but the words stung.

For a few time periods after that I became a hermit, withdrawing into work and my library, burying myself in my books and my duties. I made a point of apologizing to my former bed partners until I realized that no apology was needed, that what had been of passing interest to me had been of passing interest to them as well. Emotion returned is usually in direct proportion to emotion invested, and there had been precious little of that.

I missed Snipe badly. It wasn't long before we were standing by her stream while I tried to explain myself. She was calm and considerate and—so I thought—totally uninvolved.

After I stammered my apologies, she said simply, "Why, Sparrow?"

I explained the pressures on board, the feeling that the number of my tomorrows might be limited and I had wanted to live as much as I could today.

"That's a surface reason," she said. "I don't believe it's the real one."

She was right and I knew it. My voice dried up. When I finally found it again, I sounded lonely and desperate. I was going to have to trust her if I wanted her to love me, and for some young men trusting somebody is amazingly difficult to do. It was for me.

I recalled what the Captain had told me and shivered. "You're going to grow old," I said in a cracked voice. "Some day you'll die."

"So will Sparrow," she said simply. "Probably before me."

I should have known. She and Ophelia had been too close. I had deluded myself as I had with Noah; she had to have known.

No matter how careful I was, sooner or later the charade would end and "Sparrow" would be gone, to be replaced by another seventeen-year-old tech assistant named Nuptse or Batura, whose best friend would be K2 and who would probably fall deeply in love with Denali.

That time would undoubtedly come, but until then I was Sparrow and I had Sparrow's life to lead.

Snipe and I resumed where we had left off. Shortly afterward, Pipit moved back to Crow's compartment. To Pipit's dismay, Loon soon followed. Ibis paired off with a young woman named Kestrel in Maintenance, though Loon visited her more often than friendship required and I guessed they had remained casual lovers.

I would like to say we all lived happily ever after, but happiness is hardly a constant in one's life. The unexpected is.

And part of the unexpected was that while Snipe and I were close, I always sensed a thin barrier between us but could never determine its cause.

For Ophelia, I had been her link to Hamlet, a constant reminder of him—until that sleep period when I tried to take his place and she finally realized Hamlet was gone for good.

I had awakened in Ophelia the memories of a Hamlet she had been trying to forget. What I hadn't known, what my dreams had failed to tell me, was that Hamlet and Tybalt had competed for Ophelia and Tybalt had lost. After Hamlet had been flatlined, somebody who looked like him had taken his place. There was no way I could ever be Hamlet, though

Ophelia might have had hopes until that moment when she awoke to discover an impostor lying beside her.

Afterward, I caught her looking at Tybalt with eyes suddenly soft with speculation. He had once wanted to partner with her, and he had also been Hamlet's best friend. There was little time for romance now, but Tybalt and Ophelia made the most of it. Love softened Ophelia's personality, her figure thinned, and her features lost their sharpness. Tybalt in turn seemed younger and less dour, more concerned with his appearance and less likely to make a show of favoring his crippled leg. He trimmed his moustache, darkened his beard, and walked around the gravity-plus gymnasium with only a trace of a limp.

A dozen time periods after they had found each other, both seemed edgy and distracted. Their match had been made with more enthusiasm than thought, something apparent even to them though they hadn't wanted to admit it. Ophelia was one of the leaders of the would-be mutiny and Tybalt was one of the Captain's staunchest supporters. Even at the beginning, I knew that each would try to convert the other despite whatever promises they made to never discuss it.

One time period Tybalt asked me to meet him after shift. I reluctantly agreed, knowing what he wanted to discuss. His compartment was as Spartan as any other, with a tiny locker, a hammock, some string paintings on the bulkheads, and half a dozen technical manuals on a small shelf. I took off my eye mask, curious to see the fantasy in which Tybalt lived, and was surprised when the compartment remained unchanged.

I guessed what had happened and said, "Can you restore the falsie?"

He shrugged and thumbed the palm terminal. A moment later I felt like gasping for breath. Wisps of fog swirled about my head, and if the falsie had been reality I would have been choking on methane. I was standing in a shallow valley of jumbled rock, the reddish sun low in the sky.

Then the fog lifted and I could see the alien ship that had crashed into a mountainside a kilometer or so away. It was bowed in the middle, a gigantic boomerang. It was a corroded olive green and there were obvious hatchways in the side through which nothing human had ever passed.

It was huge—half a kilometer from one end to the other. There were no signs of life and no sound except the rasping of the wind. Tybalt had picked that one moment of quiet just before the cannons speak or a voice cries "Charge!" or the rockets start falling.

The whole scene lay just outside the window of what had been Tybalt's compartment and was now his fort. At any moment lobster men with red chitin for skin would crawl out of the alien ship and lope toward the bunker where a brave Tybalt would blast them to kingdom come.

It was a strange mix of fantasy and pathos. If he had his way, Tybalt would never meet death via Reduction; he would die facing an enemy.

Then the falsie shifted and I was inside a bunker, looking at a desperate Tybalt who stared at me from the haven of his hammock.

I was torn between cynicism and compassion—part of me wanted to laugh and another felt like crying. I had come a long way since Tybalt had entertained me with his stories of exploration and battles with unseen enemies.

"Do you think there's anything out there, Sparrow?"

I had done as much research as possible but I guessed that Tybalt had as well. All I could offer were opinions and mine weren't necessarily superior to his.

"What do you think, Tybalt?"

"I know the possibilities. And I know what I saw."

He had seen what he had desperately wanted to see, but I could never convince him of that.

"And Ophelia doesn't believe in what you saw."

"We argued. We both knew we would. Ophelia . . . doesn't believe in anything."

He was talking to me as if I were a Senior and I wondered if he was talking to Sparrow or to Hamlet. Ophelia was frank and outspoken and I was convinced she was right. But she was going to pay a price for being right and she was going to make Tybalt pay one, too.

"You told me that about Ophelia months ago," I reminded him.

He drifted over to the bunker window and stared out at the landscape and the ship beyond. "They wouldn't have sent us on a useless mission," he said slowly. "Back on Earth, they must have had some reason for believing."

They'd had a thousand reasons, I thought. And every one of them had proved false.

I let him talk himself out. At the end, he said sadly: "I don't think Snipe believes, either."

I found out later that she, too, had been trying to convince him the galaxy was barren. Snipe had yet to learn that some arguments have no winners, only losers.

I floated up beside him and put my hand on his shoulder.

"You saw what you saw," I said gently, and once again saved my life.

Whatever doubts Tybalt may have had, he resolved—but at a cost. Ophelia and he grew distant and barely spoke. Tybalt took it out on the rest of us by staging drills on the hangar deck. It was hand-to-hand combat no matter how green our faces or how reluctant most of us were to hurt each other. Outside of his training zone, we could believe whatever we wanted, but when we were taking orders from him, we would believe as he did. Somewhere in the universe there were enemy aliens and if we ever met them, we would be prepared.

In his enthusiasm and devotion to what he considered his duty, Tybalt made the one mistake a commanding officer should never make: He lost touch with his troops. From hand-to-hand we went to simple weapons—pellet guns. It was Tybalt's idea to have some of the programmers create projections of alien life forms to use as target practice. When struck by the laser-aiming aid on the gun, the aliens promptly died in various realistic ways, all of them excessively gory.

Hawk, Loon, and I, plus Tern and Falcon, both from Maintenance, were scheduled to try out the new forms of target practice that Tybalt had developed. Tern was first. He turned out to be an excellent marksman, hitting the spidery alien directly in its lumpy forehead.

The head and face instantly disappeared in an explosion of shattered bone and a spray of red mist. A second later Tern's stomach self-destructed and for minutes afterward the rest of us devoted ourselves to cleaning up the area with whatever wipes we could find.

Tybalt stared at Tern with an amazement that quickly turned to anger and disgust.

"You're on report!" he snapped. Then: "You're up next, Loon."

"I think Tern killed it," Loon said, straight-faced. He made no move toward the firing position and the rest of us tried to smother our laughter.

Tybalt fingered the palm terminal and another alien suddenly appeared on top of a dune a hundred feet away.

"He didn't kill this one."

"If he saw what happened to his friend, maybe he'll go away." Loon suddenly sounded timid and a little frightened. He had realized his jokes weren't going to make the projection disappear.

"Get into position, Loon."

"No." This time Loon's voice had more strength to it, though his face was white with strain.

"Now!" Tybalt bellowed.

Loon threw the pellet gun away and we watched, astonished, as it drifted toward the far bulkhead.

"I won't destroy anything living," Loon said flatly.

Tybalt looked uncertain of what to do.

"All right, stand down, Loon—you're on report to the Captain. Hawk, you're next."

Hawk had to clear his throat twice before he finally managed to squeak: "I won't do it." Another pellet gun sailed toward the bulkhead.

Tybalt placed his hands on his hips and glared. "Any of the rest of you have the courage?"

None of us moved.

"What if it shot at you first?" Tybalt asked slowly.

There was more puzzlement than anger in his voice and I felt sorry for him. He had failed to see what was coming even though he had been getting signals ever since the drill started.

Hawk blanched and cleared his throat a dozen times but the words wouldn't come. It was a new idea to him, one he had never considered before.

"It's only a projection," Tybalt urged. "It's not really alive—you know that."

"It's a symbol of something that's alive," Hawk finally said, trying to explain the unexplainable to himself as well as to Tybalt. "The difference . . . isn't that great."

Tybalt stared at us for a full minute and we stared back with all the fascination that a bird is supposed to feel for a snake. Finally he said, "You're dismissed," and went to retrieve the guns.

I was the last one to the hatch, pausing when I heard Tybalt behind me.

"Ophelia and I could have saved ourselves the arguments. There isn't going to be any mutiny, Sparrow—they'll never fight."

It was one of the few times when I thought Tybalt was absolutely right.

19

None of us slept the last two time periods before our first landing on Aquinas II. We were ten thousand kilometers out and the planet was a swollen yellow-brown globe. To the eye, it was featureless except for an occasional streak of dirty yellow or black in the smog that hid its surface. But our instruments had penetrated the veil; we knew that there were mountains of rock and water ice, as well as oceans of methane, and that methane snow fell on methane ice caps.

On the one hand, the chances of life seemed promising but on the other, the intense cold ruled against it. Gravity was a little more than Earth normal, the terrain was rough, the atmosphere heavy and thick. Judging by the turbulent cloud cover, there were strong surface winds. Visibility would be limited and working in the high winds dangerous.

Despite the cold and the too-recent memory of the cautionary projections, the primordial soup presented possibilities. It was remarkable how we concentrated on them and ignored the dangers. Once we had landed, who would be the first to find life? Even the would-be mutineers were caught up in the lottery.

During the sleep period before the landing, we clustered in the various working spaces or in the compartments of friends. Close to a hundred crew members would be going down. My team included Hawk, Eagle, Crow, and Snipe. Ophelia and

Portia were the Seniors in command. Loon, Thrush, and Heron had been assigned to the team commanded by Tybalt and Quince.

I was grateful for the separation.

The team leaders and other Seniors kept to themselves but none of the younger would-be explorers like myself could sleep. My teammates and I found refuge among the cannibalized Rovers in Exploration, where we passed around some smoke and speculated about what we would find on Aquinas II. Snipe managed to get hold of a crude relief map of the landing area and we crowded around while Crow focused the rays of a portable glow lamp on it. Snipe and Crow were mutineers, but this was their first planet and they were as enthusiastic as the rest.

"Base camp should be here, to the north of this small mountain called Trefil. It's relatively flat but it won't take long to travel by Rover to the scarps and the highlands."

"It looks flat," Snipe said thoughtfully, "but it wouldn't have to be very rough to make travel difficult."

Hawk nudged me in the ribs. "What do you think our chances are of finding life, Sparrow?"

He and the others waited anxiously for my opinion, forgetting for a moment that I was only Sparrow. For all practical purposes planetary exploration was as new to me as it was to them, regardless of how many planets Aaron, Hamlet, and my previous incarnations had investigated.

The only planet I had memories of didn't exist.

I shrugged. "It's cold, probably too cold for life."

"Life as we know it," Eagle said, disappointed at my response.

"It doesn't mean it was always too cold," Hawk added.

Tybalt was not without a few star pupils.

"We should try and get some sleep," Crow said, yawning.

"Yeah, we should," Eagle agreed, and tied the end of his waistcloth to the rusted rollbar of a Rover so he wouldn't drift away. He crossed his arms over his chest and Crow dimmed the glow tube and for all of thirty seconds nobody said a word.

"What was the gravity?" Hawk suddenly asked. "One point one? It's going to be difficult walking around in our suits with that much gravity and the strong winds."

I swore silently and untied my own waistcloth from a convenient steering wheel.

"Don't worry, you'll be so heavy it'll be hard to blow you away." I pushed toward the shadow screen. I had decided to go to the hangar deck and sleep under the stars. The *Astron* was so oriented in its parking orbit that you couldn't see Aquinas II from there and the deck would probably be deserted.

The corridors were empty, though I could hear the hum of muted conversations behind the shadow screens that cloaked most of the working spaces and living compartments. I floated through the well that tied the decks together, passing by the one that housed the Captain's quarters. It was the only deck completely lit and I supposed the Captain was holding a meeting with some of the team leaders. The hangar deck was two levels away and I had just started to twist around for a landing when I felt the light touch of air currents at my back.

"Sparrow."

I grabbed at a nearby bulkhead ring to slow myself. When I turned, I saw the Captain close behind me, his eyes gleaming in the soft light from the glow tubes. For the first time, he was wearing something that looked like an official uniform—a skintight black halter that extended from his neck to his wrists and ankles. It was a moment before I noticed the fine tubing and realized it was the inner-weave for an exploration suit.

"I'll be going in with you," he said, smiling, then turned apologetic. "Not with your team—I'll be setting up the base camp a few hours from now." He clapped me on the back. "Aquinas II is the best possibility we've seen in generations, and God willing, I'm sure we'll find something."

Two thousand years of disappointments and he was still a true believer. I didn't know whether to admire him or be de-

pressed. His reaction was probably invariable, a conviction
that this time was it, that this time the long voyage was not in
vain. If Ophelia was right, he wasn't capable of any other
reaction.

"I'm looking forward to it, Sparrow. What about yourself?"

The Captain's spirit was catching. Once again I could feel
my emotions flip-flop towards him.

"My team can't wait," I said, which was true. "Neither can
I." Which was not true—the back of my mind was crowded
with second thoughts.

"Nobody can," he said. Then: "Where's your team? They
can't be the only ones sleeping, everybody's holding camp
meetings all over the ship. I'd like to talk to them."

The king, cheering on his loyal troops before the battle.

"Exploration—the glow tubes are out but they're probably
still talking."

He pushed off for the well. "See you down below, Sparrow."

It was then I said something I should have had the brains to
keep to myself, knowing it would come back to haunt me.

"What happens if we don't find anything?"

He spun around, no longer smiling.

"Then we'll just have to keep looking, won't we?"

I continued to the hangar deck, slipping through the
shadow screen and hoping nobody else was there. One dim
glow tube marked a distant well, but except for that, it was
completely dark. I was feeling along the bulkhead for the
palm terminal—its location light was out—when I ran into a
loose bundle of tether line that some idiot had failed to secure. Loose coils of line were one of the major hazards on
board; the spring and the tension in the coils lent them a life
of their own. I kicked at it, annoyed, and some of the coils
floated up around my legs and waist; I could even feel one
slide across my throat. I pulled at a loop and the line around
my neck promptly tightened.

Angered, I tugged various strands at random and then
heard the faint rumble of a take-up reel. Somewhere in the

dark somebody had turned it on, or else my tugging had triggered the reel into action. The rope grew taut and I flailed helplessly in the air as I was pulled toward the reel.

Would somebody else have the same idea and come up to the hangar deck to look at the stars and sleep? Initially, I had wanted to be by myself. Now I would have been grateful if the entire ship's company had joined me.

It was getting harder to breathe and I panicked, only wrapping the coils tighter around my body. But I was also making a lot of noise, crashing into the bulkheads while I shouted for help.

A nearby glow tube suddenly came on and a voice said, "Don't move, you're only making it worse."

He was behind me but I could tell by the voice who it was and I froze. Hands plucked at the coils around my waist, trying to unknot the line, and a moment later I was free to rub my throat and curse that it had to be Thrush who had saved my life.

His pale eyes narrowed with suspicion. "It's not like you to hide from all that enthusiasm below, Sparrow." I started to say something and he held up a hand. "You don't have to thank me—I didn't do it for you, I did it for me. If you'd choked to death, I'd be the first one they'd blame."

He disappeared through the shadow screen, leaving me to massage my neck and stare at the spot where he had been. In retrospect, I thought I had heard movement when I first came on deck. And what was Thrush doing there anyway? I shrugged; probably the same as me. I couldn't believe my struggles could wrap the line around my neck so tightly but neither could I believe that Thrush had flicked the switch on the take-up reel. His own logic was too convincing—he would be the first the crew would accuse.

It didn't occur to me until later that I had more enemies than one and that Thrush had indeed saved my life. He had told the truth when he gave his reasons, but he hadn't told the whole truth.

*   *   *

Aquinas II was hell.

It was storming and winds buffeted the Lander for almost an hour before we found a safe place to set down. We were frightened and sick; even Tybalt and Ophelia looked green around the gills. When little Quince ducked into the lavatory for five minutes, I guessed he had chosen to empty his stomach in private.

We settled in a rocky area half a dozen kilometers from base camp and two from a methane river that had gouged a rocky channel and left cliffs towering fifty meters on either side. Despite what we might have thought before, once on the planet's surface we all had hopes of finding living creatures in the eddies of the river or simple fossils in the stratum of the confining cliffs. It was a relatively young planet and none of us thought that any life forms would be very large or threatening. But I also knew none of us had forgotten the monsters Tybalt had conjured up for target practice.

The Rover had been weatherized and we huddled in its belly as it lumbered over rocks and forded small streams on its way toward the river. The wind howled around the metal hull while we fingered our way through the snow and smog with searchlights. We could see ahead for perhaps thirty meters; then everything was veiled by the swirling, dirty snow.

We didn't stop until we were near the river and boulders blocked the way. Portia ordered the hatches opened and we crawled out into the slush that was building up around the treads. I had a sense of déjà vu even though Aquinas II was vastly different from Seti IV. Was it really happening? I wondered. Or had I been drugged and stuffed into a data suit to fumble my way through another artificial reality, one as real to me as a genuine planet?

But there were familiar faces behind the visors of those

around me and their voices were comfortingly loud in my headset.

"Tybalt's team will explore the riverbank and descend to the stream itself." Another Rover had clanked up and Ophelia waved at the suited figures as they climbed out and trudged toward the river, maybe a hundred meters away. Before they had gone a quarter that distance, their helmet lights were lost in the driving snow. "Eagle, Hawk, and Crow, go with Portia. Sparrow and Snipe, follow me."

She turned toward a low-lying scarp another hundred meters in the other direction. The river originally had been wider and over the eons had cut itself two beds.

I followed Ophelia, fighting my way against the screaming wind, suddenly afraid that I might lose both her and Snipe in the gloom. My life-support systems were working at maximum but I could still feel the cold seeping through tiny chinks in my boots and sense it chilling the tips of my gloves. A small leak in the suit and I would freeze to death before I could get back to the Lander.

Ophelia was in the lead and I worried whenever she disappeared in a sudden swirl of dirty snow. It worried me just as much that the wind seemed to be getting stronger and I was losing traction because the slush was freezing in the grooves of my boots. If we hit a slope and I started to slide, there would be little I could do to stop.

Hamlet, I thought bitterly, would laugh at all of this; but then, he'd had twenty years of practice at being Hamlet and I'd had only a few months being Sparrow. It's easy to be brave when you've had the experience.

Ophelia's voice suddenly rattled in my headset. "There's a gully just ahead that splits in two."

A moment later the three of us were shining our helmet lights at the entrance, trying to peer through the snow at what lay beyond. The wind roared around us and there were moments when we had to hold onto each other for support. The gully, at least, would offer some protection so we could concentrate on work. We had our sample baskets and image cameras and what we had to do wasn't that difficult—pick up a few rocks, take a few pix of strata, and then return to the Rover and the Lander. Back on the *Astron* we would fill in the maps and make preliminary notations for the geologists.

And maybe we would take back a surprise or two.

"Sparrow, take the left leg. Snipe and I will take the right. Meet back here in thirty minutes. Take samples of anything that looks interesting—and watch your footing."

A few feet into the gully the wind died away, though I could still hear it shrieking overhead. The banks were several meters above my helmet and my radio headset's whip antenna just cleared them; I would be in touch with Ophelia and Snipe most of the time. We had orders to check in with each other every five minutes, and timers in our helmets to remind us.

Snipe, as always, sounded in complete control.

"Don't get lost, Sparrow."

"I'm not about to."

"If anybody could—"

"Keep the frequencies clear for reports," Ophelia interrupted, annoyed.

Snipe shut up and I concentrated on the ravine walls, at the same time keeping to the middle of the small gorge to avoid anything falling on me from above. The gully walls were rough and dark, worn by the winds and the spring floods of methane. I dutifully hammered at a rock or two and took some image pix of formations I didn't recognize. But I found no section of the rock walls that exposed different strata and thousands of years of planetary history.

The gully suddenly widened, its banks drifting away from each other.

"I think I've hit a lakebed," I said into my head set. "Can't tell the size."

"Keep to . . . sides . . . don't . . ."

Ophelia's voice was intermittent and weak and I glanced up with alarm, noting that the banks were now above antenna height. If I continued on, I would be out of contact. I hesitated, but in the back of my mind was the picture of Hamlet laughing as he skidded down a methane mountain. I decided to risk it for a few minutes more. At least I would be protected from the howling wind.

Two hundred meters farther on, the gully wall dropped off sharply to the right; I faced a solid blanket of fog and driving sleet. I could see nothing at all, though a heavy roaring sound came from somewhere within the fog bank. Then the unpredictable wind brushed aside the snow and fog like a curtain and I stared in wonder at a shallow valley a dozen kilometers wide. At the bottom was a small lake and at the far end, I could just make out a methane fall thundering over the valley's rim. *Falling liquids!* I had never seen liquids cascading in a fall, and the sight was both strange and beautiful. I could visualize the valley filling in the spring and the overflow racing through the gorge to the river beyond.

The air was filled with dirty flakes of drifting snow and the fall at the far end was half obscured by haze. But the scene was striking—and unsettling. Except for some of the compartment falsies and the artificial reality of Seti IV, I had never been in the open. Even during the landing and the trip in the Rover, the snow had closed us in. Suddenly the horizon was no longer determined by the snow and the fog or by a bulkhead one or two hundred meters away at the end of a corridor. My only experience with a limitless horizon had been on Seti IV; but the scene now before me had far more depth and detail than Seti IV had had and I could feel my stomach knot with sudden anxiety.

At the same time, it was humbling to realize that not only was I the first human being to see the valley, I was probably the first living creature in the entire universe to see it.

For just a moment, I thought I understood both God and the Captain.

Then the winds shifted, the valley disappeared, and I had to fight my way back to the gorge. I struggled through the slush to where the gully wall became a cliff twenty meters high. I was standing close to the rock face snapping image pix of the different formations when pebbles rattled onto my helmet. I glanced up. The rim above was actually an overhang where the rushing floods of methane had undercut the banks. I was staring at it, puzzled, when the puff of a small explosion just under the rim caused more pebbles and rocks to rain down.

I didn't move. Small explosions don't happen by themselves. Then my surprise turned to alarm as another rockslide tumbled down the bank.

Something was shooting at the overhang. And if it gave way, I would be buried under tons of rubble.

Another small explosion and another shower of dirt and stones. I stood there in shock and panic, forgetting all the research I had done but remembering with remarkable clarity all of Tybalt's stories.

My first thought was that Tybalt had been right.

I struggled back up the gully, staying close to the wall and looking for cover. The overhang might come down and bury me but there was no protection at all in the open except for the thick gusts of swirling snow.

Whatever it was followed me, firing another shot every few seconds. There were boulders at the bottom of the ravine, but nothing large enough to hide behind. Besides, my enemy was on the opposite bank, shooting down at me. There were a few caves in the ravine wall, but none into which I could squeeze. And if I had, I would have been a stationary target, sooner or later to be buried alive.

I slipped more than once in the slush, terrified that the sudden falls would loosen some of my suit disconnects. Then it would be a toss-up whether I froze to death or died breathing a mixture of nitrogen and methane so cold my lungs would turn to ice within a breath or two.

The pattern of shooting suddenly changed, with shots aimed at the ground before my boots, trying to drive me back under the overhang. The top of the gorge still towered above me, but a pile of boulders in the middle looked just high enough that if I climbed it, the whip antenna might clear the banks and I could call Ophelia and Snipe for help. But climbing the boulders would expose me even more. . . .

Or would it? I had already been exposed. A dozen times. And never been hit. Why try to hit the overhang, why not *me*? What reason required that I be crushed by a landslide rather than have my suit punctured so I could die from the cold or the unbreathable atmosphere?

Perhaps I had discovered life on Aquinas II. Perhaps creatures had evolved who were smart enough to make explosive weapons and who had a psychology strange enough to want my death and burial at the same time.

But I really didn't think so. The planet was young and I found it hard to believe a local version of Tybalt's aliens existed.

My alternatives were my fellow crew members. On a planet where simple walking was a hazard, a landslide would never be questioned. A suit with pellet holes in it would be.

I forced myself to forget my panic and consider the problem. Once I did, the answer was obvious. Unlike Ophelia, whom he had accused of believing in nothing, Tybalt believed in everything. His team would have gone in armed.

I ran for the boulders and scrabbled to hoist myself up, slipping off the ice-covered rocks several times before finding handholds. Any minute I expected to feel metal pellets tear through my suit, but the small explosions and rockslides suddenly stopped.

I hit the helmet squawk button with my chin. To keep down the babble, each team had its own frequency—nobody on Tybalt's team could overhear us.

"Ophelia! Sparrow here!"

Ophelia's voice, angry but relieved, echoed in my headset immediately.

"You're ten minutes late reporting in—"

"Somebody with a pellet gun!" I shouted. "They're shooting at me!"

"Position, Sparrow." I gave it to her and she asked the direction of the shots. Then Snipe came on, her voice shaky with worry.

"Seek cover, Sparrow, the walls—"

"—are dangerous," Ophelia interrupted. "There's an overhang in this branch as well. Use your own judgment on cover and continue toward the rendezvous point."

It was growing darker, which helped, and the closer I got to the canyon mouth, the stronger the winds and the more driven the snow. I feverishly hoped the weather would provide all the cover I needed.

I was the first to reach the ravine entrance and hid behind the Rovers a few meters away, crouching down and letting the snow cover me. It didn't take long before I was sure I looked like just another snow-covered rock.

It was five minutes before the other team members struggled into view. I came out from behind the boulders and counted them as they pushed through the screaming winds. Three missing.

Crow trudged over and said tentatively, "You all right, Sparrow?"

I nodded within the helmet. Ophelia had told them nothing and I felt too drained to fill them in. They would soon learn all about it.

A few minutes later somebody shouted and pointed toward the ravine's mouth at the three figures coming out. One was ahead of the other two, stumbling occasionally when he was pushed from behind. Ophelia and Tybalt followed. Tybalt, limping slightly, held a pellet gun.

We gathered around them and Ophelia reached out and scraped the snow off the visor of the first figure so we could see his face.

"We found an alien life form after all," Tybalt said grimly.

The face behind the visor was pale and strained, the eyes frightened but not so frightened they didn't fill with hatred when they saw me.

To my great surprise, it wasn't Thrush.

It was Heron.

Man's best friend.

20

Heron's court-martial was convened on the hangar deck. More than half the crew was present, even though it was a sleep period for many. With Banquo and Cato as his guards, Heron stood in front and a little to the right of the Captain, secured to the deck with magnetic lines, his hands bound behind him. His eyes were black holes in a pale, ugly face and he constantly licked his lips. Those close to him swore later that they could smell the stink of fear.

The audience sat in the few Rovers parked on the deck, clung to the sides of Inbetween Station, or had tied themselves to the rings on a nearby bulkhead. For the most part, they were silent and perhaps a little awed. Heron had tried to kill another crew member and that was something almost impossible to imagine. The few who glanced at him and could imagine it shivered with revulsion and looked away.

The lead actor in the drama was the Captain, who sat behind a small desk inside the hatchway. His halter was plain black but he also wore a black armband with a single gold star. It was the first time any of us had seen him wear anything indicating rank, and we were properly impressed. We knew the Captain held the power of life and death over us, but until that moment it had been an abstraction. Now it was reality and I could sense the unease in the crew.

There was no jury. Judgement was the Captain's responsibility, one he apparently wasn't required to share, according to the computer.

Heron had been charged with attempted murder. I was called as the first witness. I told what had happened as objectively as I could. I mentioned the incident in sick bay and the Captain listened intently. He hadn't known about it, which meant that Pipit hadn't reported it, and that surprised me. But in the end, he struck it as irrelevant.

"Why did you climb to the top of the boulders, Sparrow?"

I thought I had explained why, then realized he wanted me to repeat it so he could make a point. The proceedings had made me nervous to begin with and I felt even more so now.

"I needed the height so my whip antenna could clear the rim of the gorge and I could contact Ophelia for help."

He frowned.

"Wasn't that dangerous? Didn't you consider that exposing yourself in the open would make you an easy target?"

I sensed a trap.

"I took a gamble, sir."

The frown deepened.

"It would seem like a bad gamble, Sparrow. Something was shooting at you and yet you abandoned the only cover you had for the open area in the gorge. In your place, I would have assumed that would guarantee my being shot."

I suddenly wondered whose trial it was.

"I could have been killed at any time, sir. The only logical answer was that a fellow crewman was shooting at me. If I were shot while in the open, there would be pellet holes in my body and my exploration suit. The list of suspects would have been very small. A landslide from the rim above would have covered the evidence as well as killed me."

"It's still a gigantic leap of faith, Sparrow." He made a few notes on a writing slate, then asked, too casually: "You never considered the possibility of indigenous life on the planet?"

And that was the point he was driving at. Did I believe in life out there? Did I believe in the mission of the ship? Was I still willing to follow him?

I was right, this was far more than Heron's trial for attempted murder. I glimpsed Ophelia in the audience and she looked stricken; she realized it as well.

I needed time to think and made a show of clearing my throat.

"There had been no signatures of a technical civilization in the weeks before the landing, sir. And if I had stayed under the rim, it was only a matter of time before I was a dead man."

The Captain hunched forward in his chair.

"So you chanced the open to try and signal for help. Since you really didn't believe there was any life on the planet, your assailant had to be a fellow crew member. Is that right, Sparrow?"

I opened and closed my mouth several times before replying, then finally said, "I thought there was a good possibility of life, but not of beings so technically advanced they had pellet guns. It's a young planet." I hesitated again, then blurted: "I took the gamble because I had to. I was afraid all the time that I might lose."

He relaxed but didn't let me go without a reprimand.

"There's no timetable for the development of life and different levels of civilization, Sparrow—you can't use Earth as a measuring stick."

He had reinforced my premonition. Heron's trial wasn't going to be just about Heron. It was going to be about loyalty and faith, and eventually it would involve many more crew members in addition to Heron. If we had been on Earth, a good fraction of the crew would have fled the next time period.

"Sparrow—why would Heron want to kill you?"

It was no trick question but it was one I could not answer. Not in open court. And not when the Captain asked it. I finally said, "I don't know."

He raised an eyebrow.

"A man is filled with so much hatred for you that he's moved to murder and you have no idea why?"

The question hung there and I could do nothing but shrug.
I had no answer. He waited until the silence became smothering, then dismissed me.

The Captain's interrogation of Ophelia and Tybalt began
relatively routinely. Ophelia was crisp and respectful and I
thought I even detected respect on the Captain's part. He
scribbled another note on the slate and without looking up
asked:

"Why did you detach Sparrow to explore on his own?"

Ophelia's prompt responses suddenly slowed.

"We had limited time and I wanted to use the team effi-
ciently and cover as much ground as possible."

The Captain leaned back, tapped his teeth with his stylus,
and looked thoughtful.

"You didn't think it was risky sending a crewman into unknown territory by himself?"

"I didn't consider it dangerous. He knew the geology, he
could see what the terrain was like. And we were in constant
communication—" She stopped, realizing she had made a
mistake.

"But you weren't, of course. To investigate the gorge
meant that Sparrow would be out of touch with you for minutes."

I never thought I would see Ophelia sweat but she was
sweating now.

"I didn't realize that at the time."

The Captain smiled slightly. "You didn't foresee that he
would be so eager to fulfill one command that he might vio-
late another."

"No, sir."

"And you didn't foresee any danger from native life forms,
whatever they might have been?"

She knew it was a trap but her pride led her in without
hesitation.

"If there were any, it wouldn't have made any difference," she said flatly. "None of us were armed."

The Captain already knew that; he was making another point. But the points he was making weren't for the witnesses or the accused, they were for himself. He was building a case for whatever action he was going to take later.

"In retrospect," he said slowly, "I think that was a mistake. I'm sure Sparrow thinks so, too." He studied his slate. "You didn't believe in the possibility of life on Aquinas even before we landed, did you, Ophelia?"

She was white-faced, her voice hoarse.

"No, sir, I didn't."

He studied her, obviously weighing her and finding her wanting.

"Everybody's entitled to their opinion, Ophelia. But nobody's entitled to act on it if it endangers this ship and its crew. You've violated standard exploration procedures and shown a lack of common sense. You're relieved of your command."

There was a gasp from the assembled crew members.

In the front, at the Captain's right, Heron smirked at all of us.

The Captain called a recess and we filed out to report to our working spaces if we were on shift or to try and get some sleep if we weren't. It was mealtime in Exploration and we ate in silence while Pipit just as silently served us.

It was Thrush who stated the obvious. "It's not going well, is it?"

And it was little Quince who growled, "Shut up, Thrush."

Thrush started to object, caught the looks on our faces, then shrugged and took up his usual position in the corner. Nobody said anything to Ophelia, though one or two patted her gently on the back. Then Tybalt drifted over and they talked in low voices, his arm around her shoulder. When the meal was finished, the normal hum of conversation started again, though I heard no talk about the trial. Noah pulled out

the chessboard, nodded at me, and I joined him for a game.
He played badly and I scored an easy win.

"Another one?" I asked.

He shook his head.

"Not this time, Sparrow."

I lowered my voice so only he could hear.

"Ophelia's too valuable as a team leader," I reassured him.
"The Captain will reinstate her next time."

"You still believe in Kusaka, don't you, Sparrow?" he
asked bleakly.

"I suppose so," I admitted. "I've had more contact with
him than you've had—at least lately." I had my reservations
about the mission, but I had yet to lose my faith in the Captain.

He laughed without humor.

"Poor Sparrow," he murmured. "To have lived so long and
still be so innocent."

Tybalt was next and the Captain seemed genuinely glad to
have him as a witness. But then, Tybalt was a true believer;
whatever points the Captain wanted to make, Tybalt would
be glad to help.

He gave a detailed version of everything his team did after
the landing while the Captain nodded patiently.

"But you detached Heron to explore the top of the rim by
himself. Didn't you think that dangerous?"

"He was armed," Tybalt said, full of self-righteousness. "I
saw to it that everybody on my team was armed."

"With pellet guns," the Captain agreed. "Not exactly heavy
artillery on a planet we knew nothing about."

Tybalt looked confused.

"It was an exploration party, not an invasion," he said
slowly.

"I wasn't questioning the armament, just the wisdom of
sending a man off by himself."

A tinge of surliness crept into Tybalt's voice.

"It was his idea. I thought it a good one. So did other members of the team. We were pressed for time; we wanted to cover as much territory as we could while we were there."

The Captain fell silent, absorbed in his slate.

"I think I see," he said at last. "Heron volunteered to explore the rim and you detached him for that purpose." He glanced up at Tybalt, curious. "You said other members of the team thought it was a good idea. Who were they?"

Tybalt looked unhappy.

"Thrush, for one."

I snapped alert. I didn't know how the pieces fit together, but now it was obvious that Thrush had known Heron's intentions. Of course. Thrush always knew what Heron intended.

"Perhaps Thrush should have been the team leader," the Captain said wryly. Then: "Did you think the possibilities of alien life forms on Aquinas were very good?"

Just as Ophelia had, Tybalt was sweating heavily.

"Yes, sir."

"But you still let Heron go off alone."

Tybalt's voice was now thick with frustration as he tried to explain something he thought the Captain couldn't or wouldn't understand.

"I considered him a scout. An exploration party can't explore if they stay together. Tactically, it would have been just as dangerous if we'd split up. Heron volunteered to be a scout and I detached him as a scout."

"You're absolutely right," the Captain said sarcastically. "Detaching him as a scout was a good idea. Detaching him so he would be free to murder a fellow crew member was a very bad one."

Even from where I sat, I could see Tybalt start to tremble.

"I didn't know what he was going to do."

"Did you know how he was equipped?"

"Standard equipment—plus a pellet gun. We all had one."

The Captain shook his head.

"Did you know he had an RF detector as well as a gun? He

could determine the location of crew members on the other team. He could tell who they were by the numbers on their suits. And he could see them more easily from above than they could see him from below."

From the moment we had set down on Aquinas II, Tybalt had conducted his part of the landing as if it were a military operation. Thrush and Heron had known he would and had played on that. Sending out a scout would have had a lot of appeal to Tybalt. So Heron had been granted permission to go hunting and the game he had tracked was me.

"Did you know Heron and Sparrow were enemies?"

Tybalt glanced at Heron with contempt.

"Yes. But then Heron has no friends."

"Why?"

An uncomfortable shrug. "I suppose because he doesn't like anybody and as a result, nobody likes him."

The Captain looked annoyed.

"That's an inadequate answer. Everybody has at least one friend. Who was Heron's?"

Without any hesitation: "Thrush was the only one in the division who could tolerate him."

"Do you have any idea why Heron would want to kill Sparrow?"

It was a crucial question but Tybalt fumbled the answer. "They didn't like each other. Beyond that, I don't know."

The Captain sighed.

"You've been team leader for both Heron and Sparrow but you have no real idea why Heron has so few friends or why he and Sparrow were enemies. You should know the people in your command better than that." He tapped the slate. "You're excused, Tybalt. For now."

It was unfair. Nobody on board, with the exception of the Captain, had made more than half a dozen landings. Landings were too infrequent to breed proficiency, to teach the details of command. Tybalt was the best we had, a man who worked hard and who believed in the mission and worshiped the Captain. At least until now. For reasons I didn't understand, the

Captain had humiliated him before the crew, questioning his decisions and his professionalism. Once again I felt uneasy.

The next witness would probably be Thrush, Heron's one and only friend and a man for whom Heron would do anything.

I was curious to see what Thrush would do for Heron.

The Captain called another recess and I returned to my shift in Exploration. It was strangely silent except for the whisper of machinery and the occasional murmur of a command. The crew spoke to each other in monosyllables, and when Tybalt entered they stopped talking altogether.

Tybalt looked smaller and older than he had a few hours before. Strain had etched deep furrows in his forehead. He said nothing to anybody and showed no interest in what we were doing. He nodded briefly and disappeared into the headquarters compartment. I waited a moment, then followed him in.

"There's nothing I want to talk about," he said in a low voice.

"I wasn't going to talk." I felt around in my waistcloth and pulled out a small pipe. "Smoke?"

He lit it and inhaled for a long moment, then let the smoke drift out so it made a haze around his face. I flicked on the exhaust fan, looped an arm through a bulkhead ring, and waited.

"I don't know what he wants," Tybalt finally said, "but I don't think Heron has much to do with it."

"He should have known the answers to most of the questions he asked."

The smoke was doing its work and Tybalt looked more relaxed, the lines in his face softer.

"You're assuming something, Sparrow."

It was my turn with the pipe and I said, "What?" in a strangled voice.

"That he cares enough to actually want to know us."

It was one thing to hear it from Ophelia or Noah, it was another to hear Tybalt say it.

"I think he does," I protested.

He shook his head.

"He's seen a hundred generations of us come and go. We live too short a life. I'm surprised he even knows our names."

It was Tybalt's depression talking, I thought, not Tybalt. But I never forgot what he said and eventually it provided an answer when I had none of my own.

Everybody who could break away from their shifts was present when Thrush's turn came to testify. I was watching Heron when Thrush was called and was startled by his change of expression. The dull look of hatred was replaced by a combination of hero-worship, hope, and obsession. Heron had faith—he truly believed that Thrush's testimony would somehow make everything all right.

This time the Captain seemed more abrupt and on edge. I wondered if it was because he had thought ahead to the trial's consequences. At the end of it, he would have to pass judgment and I imagined he would find that difficult.

"It was Heron's idea that he be detached as a scout?"

Thrush was respectful but casual.

"Yes, sir, it was."

The Captain looked doubtful.

"It didn't happen to be your idea, did it?"

Thrush hesitated. I knew he was debating whether it was safe to take the credit.

"It was Heron who asked, sir. I thought it was a good idea and said so."

"Then you didn't think it was dangerous for Heron to go on alone?"

"I thought it was very brave of him. I also thought he could handle himself."

There was a flash of gratitude on Heron's face. But it wasn't an answer to the question and the Captain was irritated.

"I asked if you thought it was dangerous." The impatience in his voice made Thrush flinch.

"I did think it was dangerous, yes, sir. We didn't know what the native life forms might be like."

"Obviously Heron didn't think they'd be so dangerous. He wasn't interested in them, he was interested in Sparrow."

"I didn't know he was going to look for Sparrow," Thrush murmured.

The Captain suddenly changed the subject.

"I understand Heron is very good with a pellet gun."

"He should be, sir, he practices all the time."

My eyebrows shot up. An ordinary crewman who practiced all the time was to be commended. A would-be murderer who practiced all the time was to be feared.

"Your opinion, Thrush: Firing from the rim of the gorge, if Heron had wanted to hit Sparrow, he could have. Am I right?"

Thrush didn't hesitate. "Yes, sir."

"Even in those conditions of driving snow and poor visibility?"

"If he could see Sparrow at all, sir, he could have hit him."

The Captain stared at Thrush, thoughtful.

"So he was either trying to frighten Sparrow or Sparrow is right in his contention that Heron was trying to hit the rim above, to bury him in a landslide. What do you think?"

Thrush might have helped Heron make the case that he had tried to frighten me rather than kill me, but he didn't even try.

"I don't know, sir."

Heron looked puzzled. Thrush was damning him with faint praise, and he realized it but didn't understand why.

"You're the defendant's best friend, am I correct?"

"I'm a good friend, sir. I don't know if I'm his best friend."

A chasm had opened in front of Heron and Thrush was about to push him in.

"How would you characterize the defendant? Well liked? Well adjusted? Use your own judgment on the definition."

"I wouldn't say he was well liked, sir."

"Why not?"

"He means well, sir." Thrush turned and flashed a smile of support at the stricken Heron. "I get along fine with him but others don't."

"Explain."

Thrush did, and what emerged from between the lines of his testimony was a picture of a psychopathic personality whom Thrush could barely tolerate. What amazed me was not Thrush's self-serving monologue but the accuracy of his observations. He had known all along who and what he had been dealing with.

"Can you explain Heron's hatred for Sparrow?"

Thrush was cautious.

"He probably took offense at some small slight and brooded on it. I can't think of any other reason."

Only one more nail remained to be driven into Heron's coffin.

"You were on the hangar deck just before the landing?"

Heron turned an ashy white.

"I had gone up there to sleep, sir."

"Who else was there?"

"Sparrow, sir."

"Explain what happened."

Thrush did, complete with a description of how I had become entangled in the coil of tether line and how he had helped me out.

"You saved Sparrow's life." The Captain nodded his approval.

Thrush sounded modest.

"I was glad to help him, sir."

I swore quietly under my breath.

"Was anybody else on the hangar deck?"

Thrush managed to look appropriately uncomfortable in the role of a friend reluctantly testifying against a friend.

"Heron, sir."

"What was he doing there?"

"I don't really know."

"Is it possible he knew that Sparrow might go there, so he laid coils of tether line near the hatchway and once Sparrow had entangled himself in them, turned on the take-up reel?"

"I doubt it, sir." Pause. "Though I suppose anything is possible." He said it in a voice just uncertain enough to imply that it was probable.

Heron looked devastated. The Captain excused Thrush, located me in the audience, and told me to come forward.

"About that portion of Thrush's testimony which directly concerns you: Is his version accurate?"

"I didn't know Heron was there—"

"Answer the question, Sparrow."

Sullenly: "Yes, sir, that part of his testimony is correct."

"Is it your opinion that Thrush saved your life?"

At the time I had thought so. But I didn't want to admit it, not here and not now.

"Yes, sir," I finally said in a low voice. Those in the audience who knew my hatred for Thrush stared at me in amazement.

Thrush had managed to destroy Heron and paint himself as my savior all at the same time. I couldn't think of a reason for either.

Heron would be next, to testify in his own behalf, but there was no way he could save himself.

Thrush had made sure of that.

It wasn't until I was in my own compartment that I saw the flaw in Thrush's testimony. The Captain had known too much. There had been no more than three people on the hangar deck: Thrush, me, and, if Thrush was telling the truth, Heron. I hadn't mentioned the incident to anybody. Heron certainly wouldn't have, which meant that after the murder attempt on Aquinas II had failed, Thrush had gone to the Captain and betrayed the one man who idolized him.

Why? I wondered.

Then I realized with a chill that I had been the target all along. Sometime in the past Thrush had befriended a lonely Heron, who had returned casual friendship with all of his loyalty and devotion. He had begged to be used and Thrush had granted his wish. He probably hadn't been aware of the contents of the poisoned drink bulb when he tried to give it to me in sick bay—he had merely been running an errand for Thrush. But if I had died, the evidence would have pointed at him.

Then Thrush had found a way to cock a reluctant Heron as he would a pellet gun. The incident in Reduction was meant not just to prove that he was the alpha primate but also to make Heron mad with jealousy. But it wasn't Heron who had followed me to the hangar deck, it was Thrush. My talk with the Captain had given Thrush enough time to find Heron and suggest the plot. They planted the coils of line and turned off most of the glow tubes to darken the deck. At the last minute Thrush had deliberately aborted the plan and "saved my life."

He had done it to set Heron up as his insurance policy.

The cocked gun had misfired in the landing on Aquinas. Not only had Heron failed, which was forgivable; he had been caught, which was not. And to make matters worse, there was always the danger he would implicate Thrush.

But who would believe him, once I testified that Thrush had saved my life?

Heron was cross-examined the next time period. The hangar deck was crowded with crewmen, all of them hostile. I could feel the waves of emotion beat against Heron and watched him wither when he felt them. His face paled and his angry expression became one of deep hurt. Once he found Thrush in the crowd, his desperate eyes never left him except to look at the Captain when he was answering a question. I wondered how Thrush could stand it.

"It was your idea to have Tybalt assign you as a scout?"

Heron licked cracked lips and mumbled, "Yes, sir."

"When you found Sparrow, you intended to murder him. Is that correct?"

Once again, I could feel the revulsion of the crowd. Heron's face twisted with anguish. He couldn't bring himself to answer.

"Isn't that right, Heron?" the Captain repeated.

"Sparrow's . . . a good man," Heron whispered. The reddened eyes sought me out and I read his lips as he mouthed a silent *Forgive me*. He was sobbing now, the tears rolling down his face.

The Captain was implacable.

"You went to the hangar deck, knowing that Sparrow would be there shortly afterward. Is that correct, Heron?"

Heron nodded without speaking.

"You planted the coils of tether line just inside the hatchway, hoping that Sparrow would entangle himself in them. Once he did, you started the take-up reel. Is that also correct?"

Again, the hopeless nod. By now the expression on his face and every movement of his body begged for a mercy he knew he wouldn't get.

And then, for just a moment, the entire trial hung in the balance.

"Did you have help, Heron? Did somebody whisper all of this in your ear or was it your own idea from the very start?"

The silence was deafening. Thrush had been clinging to one of the Rovers and now looked as if he had frozen to its side. I had seen him show fear once before. He was terrified now.

Heron stared directly at him and again moistened his cracked lips. I thought the look of dull hatred and anger would return, but his expression made me look away. Heron was capable of many things in life, including murder, but sacrificing the only man who had showed him even a small amount of friendship and love, however stained and self-seeking, was beyond him.

"It was . . . my idea. Nobody helped me."

"Your hatred for Sparrow must have been all-consuming, Heron. Why?"

"Sparrow's . . . a good man," Heron mumbled once again.

"Then why, Heron?"

Heron hung his head and let the tears flow. He did not reply.

The Captain was silent and I thought that he was moved, that Tybalt was wrong, that he might even spare Heron. After a long moment, he made a final notation on his slate and stood up.

"The prisoner is condemned."

The shock was overwhelming.

We had lined up to leave when the Captain held up his hand. He was crisp, perfunctory—military in a way we had never seen before. I remember thinking how at one time most of us had loved and admired him.

Now, as in Oryx's generation, most of us were desperately afraid of him.

"We'll resume next time period. All ranks are to be present except those vitally needed for the operation of the ship."

Heron was going to die and so, apparently, were others.

21

It was strange how I reacted to Heron's sentence. My mind was filled with morbid thoughts about how it would be carried out. Was Banquo not only one of the Captain's men but also the public strangler? Would Abel give Heron a lethal injection? Or would they lock him in his compartment until he starved to death?

At the next meal, we stole glances at Thrush but nobody talked to him. Most of us half expected to see Heron at his feet, waiting for some errand to perform. As for myself, there was nothing more to fear from Thrush, or so I thought. He dared do nothing against me, since he would always be the prime suspect. And now that Heron had been condemned, there was no one to carry out his plots by proxy. From now on, Thrush would do his best to see that I remained alive.

Once condemned, Heron achieved a status that would have astonished him. Attempted murder had put him beyond the pale; but his appearance before the Captain had been so pathetic it captured most of the crew's sympathy. Even I agonized about the Captain's sentence—but what should be the penalty for attempted murder? Thirty periods on bread and water? Half a hundred lashes?

Considered in the abstract, death may have been a fitting punishment, but still . . . how was he to die? And how would the crew react once they realized that something living, something that could think, something that walked, talked, flexed its fingers and stubbed its toes, had been deliberately deprived of its life?

I knew a good part of the crew hadn't believed the Captain would sentence somebody to death. What would happen when Heron's death became a reality? What would they think? What would they do?

Heron preoccupied me not only because of the harsh sentence but because I suspected there were more trials to come and I knew what and who they would concern. After we left Aquinas II, we would change course for the Dark. But the Captain wasn't going to risk the journey with a mutiny brewing. He had tolerated it in past generations, but he couldn't afford to now. Heron's trial was the prelude to the crushing of the mutiny.

I was frightened, not for myself—I thanked God I had stayed clear of plotting—but for Crow and Ophelia and Noah and Loon and the rest of the mutineers. I tried not to think about it but others didn't have that luxury. After my next chess game with Noah, he folded up the board and handed it to me.

"This is yours now, Sparrow."

It was his most prized possession. I refused to take it, pretending I didn't know why he offered it.

"You need it for practice," I said. "Keep it."

He shook his head.

"That was my last game, Sparrow."

Nobody was paying any attention to us but I still lowered my voice to a murmur.

"You think the Captain will put you on trial?"

"He'll lose his ship if he doesn't."

"You shouldn't be telling me this," I warned him.

He shrugged. "You shouldn't be talking to me, either."

I felt miserable.

"I don't know what to say."

"Sparrow." He took off his glasses and wiped them with his sash, but his eyes never left mine. "You're very important to this ship and its crew. You have to realize that—and protect yourself from the Captain and Thrush."

"Thrush won't bother me," I said confidently.

He reached over and gripped my hand so tight it hurt.

"Don't be a fool. Thrush is like nobody else on board, and yet of all of us, you know him the least. Your ignorance will kill you, Sparrow. He's your enemy. He has been from the beginning."

He was patronizing me, I thought, irritated. Nobody knew Thrush as well as I did.

"And the Captain?" I asked sarcastically, then immediately felt guilty about my tone of voice. Maybe this was the last time I would see Noah, the last time he would give me lessons in either chess or life. But a perverse part of me also figured that as long as he was reading tea leaves, I might as well hear what he had to say.

He took his hand away, leaving the white imprint of his fingers on mine.

"The Captain," he repeated. His eyes were no longer focused on me. He was seeing something else, maybe a page in a ledger, perhaps something he had run across in the computer's memory or in the ship's fading medical records. "In your own way, you're vital to the ship, Sparrow. I imagine at one time you were vital to the Captain as well. You still are to us." Dryly: "But I'm not so sure you still are to the Captain."

I was torn between curiosity and sudden fear.

"Why?" I asked.

He shrugged. "If I knew, I would tell you. I was depending on you to tell me. I hoped you would remember."

They still wanted to know what was buried in my head. But if my memories were important to them, I was certain they weren't to the Captain—he already knew them, he had been there at the time. I discounted Noah's warning about the Captain but I wasn't as quick to discount what he had said about Thrush. Noah was right about my knowledge of him. In one sense, I had known Thrush intimately; but I really didn't know him at all.

Noah pressed the board in my hands and turned away.

"I'll be facing the Captain in a few hours. I want to spend them with Huldah." We were alone in the compartment now, the others having gone on shift. At the hatchway he turned and whispered more to himself than to me, "Watch over her, Aaron. At one time, you loved her, too."

He wasn't seeing Sparrow at all when he said it, nor was it just Sparrow who assured him if he were condemned, the entire crew would grieve.

The hangar deck was packed but the Captain was late and so was the prisoner, whoever he might be. I hadn't seen Noah but I had persuaded myself that he was wrong, that the Captain would leave a harmless old man alone.

When they finally appeared, the Captain floated in front with Noah trailing behind, followed by Banquo and Cato. Both of them wore black armbands to indicate they were in the service of the Captain, and I noticed a number of the crewmen in the audience were wearing them as well. The Captain expected trouble, I thought uneasily, or he was trying to intimidate us.

A murmur arose, which the Captain silenced with a glance. He settled behind his desk and Noah took Heron's place in front of him. The contrast was striking. The Captain was sleek, muscled, tanned, well groomed in a plain black halter that rippled when he moved. The appearance of power and the awe it inspired probably hadn't changed in two thousand years. He embodied all the authority of distant Earth, the hopes and fears of an entire race.

Noah was slightly bent over and disheveled. His arms and legs stuck out like bony rods from his rumpled halter, his thinning gray hair stood up over his ears and floated in front of his face so from time to time he had to brush it aside. He was nervous and at the start his voice quavered, but he was never without his dignity.

The Captain asked a few preliminary questions, then got to the heart of the matter.

"I understand there are mutineers on board and you're their leader. Is that correct, Noah?"

There was a gasp in the audience from those to whom mention of a possible mutiny was unsettling news.

"I would like to face my accusers," Noah said.

The Captain brushed this aside.

"Your request would be granted if we were on Earth and this were a formal trial. But of necessity hearings aboard ship are informal, an attempt to get at the truth."

"Will the sentencing also be informal?"

Noah was goading him, but the Captain refused to take the bait.

"Trials and sentencing are the responsibility of the Captain."

He studied Noah a moment. I think he realized he couldn't get the old man to confess to anything if he didn't want to and decided to tempt him instead. He suddenly became more casual, more the Captain I had talked to on the bridge.

"You have your views, Noah. It's safe to say they're different from mine and you believe they're right and justified. But I'm not so sure that everybody here knows what they are, and I think they're entitled to hear them." He looked apologetic. "I think you'd agree it's better to talk about them in the open than try and convince crew members secretly."

It sounded eminently fair, and it put the Captain on the side of the angels, encouraging open discussion instead of mutiny. It was also a trap and I wasn't sure that Noah, blinded by righteousness, would see it.

Noah looked uncertain. "For the sake of argument, then."

The Captain nodded in agreement and leaned back in his chair. "You don't believe there's life in the universe, do you, Noah?"

"Only what's on this ship and back on Earth."

The Captain smiled.

"Aside from Earth, Noah."

"No," Noah said slowly, "I don't believe there's any other life in the universe. I think it's a miracle that it happened even once."

The Captain jotted a note on his slate. "You have scientific proof, Noah?"

"The only way of proving there's life is by finding it and so far we haven't."

"And how much of the galaxy have we actually explored? A hundredth of one percent?"

Noah finally sensed the trap.

"Much less than that, unless you count the sweeps of the radio telescope. Then it's more."

"But still less than a hundredth," the Captain repeated, his eyes lidded.

There was a stirring in the audience. The Captain had made his point.

"You were unhappy with our progress, convinced the purpose of the *Astron* was futile. Is that correct, Noah?"

"That's largely correct," Noah said in a strained voice.

The Captain looked like he was going to push him on the point, then changed his mind. He didn't want to create sympathy for Noah by bullying him as he had Heron.

"So you and a few like-minded friends formed a group with the intention of . . . what? Taking over the *Astron*? And then what?"

"Returning to Earth," Noah said calmly. "The one planet we know that can support life."

I caught my breath. It was an admission of the Captain's accusation. The Captain made another note, then casually sprung the rest of his trap.

"You had doubts about the purpose of the *Astron* and whether we would succeed in that purpose. Why didn't you come to me with those doubts, Noah?"

The argument was changing now, but for Noah it was too late.

"You would never have listened—"

The Captain looked hurt. "I would have argued with you, but I think I would have listened. Perhaps you might have persuaded me. Or I you. But at the very least, I would have discouraged you from fomenting a mutiny, thus endangering others."

There was a muttering in the audience and I was afraid that Noah would wither in the face of it as Heron had.

Noah suddenly changed the subject. He had a forum and I suspected he was going to use it to warn the crew rather than defend himself, a cause I was sure he already considered lost.

"The *Astron* is wearing out," he said in a shaky voice. "It'll never make it through another twenty generations."

The Captain brought his open palm down on the desktop. The sharp sound abruptly quieted the whispering in the audience.

"We're not discussing the condition of the ship. That's in the hands of Maintenance! We're discussing a mutiny and your leadership of it and at no time have you denied that role!"

"It was for the sake of argument," Noah objected.

"Argument?" The Captain feigned a look of surprise. "Not argument, Noah. You admitted you formed such a group and you've told us its purpose. But when the *Astron* left the Earth two thousand years ago, it had a purpose far different from yours. Your ancestors enlisted in that purpose of their own free will and their Earth-born descendants were paid enormous sums of money because of that enlistment. That was a contract, Noah, one that can't be broken purely because it no longer suits the interests of one of the parties."

"Parents can't make contracts binding their children—"

"It's been done throughout history," the Captain sneered. "And those children who broke their contracts did so at their peril."

He waited a moment, then became conciliatory again, this time speaking directly to the crewmen in the hangar area.

"Few of you know the state of the Earth at the time of Launch. It was a used-up planet, a world of frontiersmen with

no frontiers, a world whose people doubted the value of their
existence because their own planetary system had proved barren. They took almost all their treasure and built this ship and
gave it a very definite purpose. It was to open Outside as a
new frontier, to find living creatures elsewhere and in so
doing, find a purpose to their lives. They knew it would take
time. They didn't expect the *Astron* to return early with a
message that there was nothing out there and their very lives
were an accident of nature!"

He fell silent and I stared at him, amazed. He had spoken
from the heart and I had to fight to keep from being swept up
in the jumble of emotions he evoked.

The Captain made one last notation on his writing slate,
pushed it aside, folded his hands, and looked at Noah with a
faint expression of sadness.

"You are charged with fomenting a mutiny. A mutiny not
only against me as captain but against the wishes of those millions in whose name the *Astron* was launched so long ago. Do
you have any final words to say in your defense?"

For the first and only time since I had known him, Noah
looked angry.

"You're not condemning me alone," he said quietly.
"You're condemning everybody on board. The *Astron* will
never make it through the Dark."

Sudden silence gripped the hangar deck. Many of the crew
had been thinking it and now somebody had voiced their
doubts aloud.

"You leave me only one choice, Noah, one that I regret
because you've been a valuable member of this ship's company." The Captain nodded to Banquo. "The prisoner is condemned."

He didn't look at Noah—but then, for him, there no longer
was a Noah.

We had started to file out when the Captain once again held
up his hand.

"We'll resume once more next time period."

It was obvious who was going to be called next. I managed to catch up with her in the corridor that led to the hangar deck.

"I'm sorry, Ophelia."

She looked at me without her usual arrogance and hostility.

"I was hard on you, Sparrow. I regret that." She smiled faintly and tried to make a joke of it. "You reminded me of somebody I knew."

"I presumed," I said. "I shouldn't have."

Her smile faded.

"When you get to know him better, say hello to Hamlet for me."

She kicked down the corridor back to her compartment and I stared after her, feeling admiration and guilt in equal amounts. Then I felt somebody float up beside me and turned to look at Snipe.

"Ophelia's a remarkable woman," she said. "I admire her." A faint flicker of a smile. "She's entitled to whatever's left of Hamlet."

Snipe was offering to share me, and I was touched.

"Do you mean that?"

Her smile faded. "She's entitled," she repeated.

It was my turn to smile, if only slightly.

"You're jealous, Snipe."

"I always have been." She looked away. "But I owe you to her."

It was Ophelia who had first introduced us, I remembered. And even though I was no longer Hamlet, it had been an act of generosity.

"Hamlet's dead," I said softly. "I'm just . . . Sparrow."

We went back to my compartment and she turned off the falsie of the library, then curled up beside me in the hammock. We didn't make love but merely held each other in silence and drifted quietly off to sleep in each other's arms. I was emotionally exhausted and wanted only to hold and to be held. I had no dreams at all.

When I woke, I sat on the edge of the hammock and lightly stroked Snipe's hair until she drifted awake.

"It's Ophelia's turn, isn't it?"

I nodded. "She'll start it."

"I think she'll be the last."

I was surprised.

"What makes you say that?"

"Pipit told me. She . . . sensed it last time. The Captain's afraid to call any more."

"Bad for morale," I grunted.

She shook her head.

"It would go too far, there would be no end to it."

We had breakfast in silence, then filed onto the hangar deck. I sat up front where Ophelia could see me, to lend whatever moral support I could. And then Ophelia herself came in and sat beside me. I was stunned. If not her, then who?

The answer shocked everyone. The Captain floated in, followed once again by Banquo and Cato. Accompanying them, and looking completely surprised at being there, was Tybalt. There had been no rumors and he hadn't been in custody long enough to be missed.

The Captain waited until the murmuring in the audience had quieted, then stared at Tybalt in silence, the expression on his face a carefully composed one of anger and hurt. Once again the charge was mutiny. We gasped.

"You've been a team leader for twenty years, Tybalt, one of the most experienced men on board. And one I trusted above all—"

"I've never given you reason not to trust me," Tybalt interrupted.

You don't interrupt the Captain, I thought. But he showed no anger at Tybalt's outburst.

"I thought I knew you," the Captain continued. "I would have trusted you with my life."

Tybalt looked bewildered.

"You still can."

The Captain slowly shook his head.

"Perhaps at one time. Not now." A glance at the slate. "Once you believed in the purpose of the *Astron,* that there was life elsewhere in the universe and someday we would find it. When did you change that belief, Tybalt?"

"I never have," Tybalt said, outraged. He still couldn't believe that he was on trial.

"You partnered with someone who didn't believe, someone who was closely connected to the mutiny, who was known as one of the leaders. Is that correct, Tybalt?"

Beside me, I could feel Ophelia stiffen. Tybalt couldn't deny it but neither could he admit it without confirming that Ophelia was one of the ringleaders. So he looked at the deck and said nothing.

"We all know you did," the Captain said easily. "It would seem unlikely you'd partner with somebody you disapproved of or with whom you violently disagreed."

Tybalt didn't reply, nor did he look up. The Captain frowned.

"If somebody is a loyal crew member and close enough to another crew member to know they're engaged in actively fomenting mutiny, that they oppose the mission of this ship and want to abort it, what do you think they should do, Tybalt? Keep it to themselves and thus betray not only the ship's purpose and everybody on board but everybody on Earth as well? Or should they go to the Captain and lay out the facts of the mutiny as they know them?"

That wasn't a lecture for Tybalt, that was a lecture for the rest of us. I wondered how many would now scurry to the Captain and tell everything they knew, naming names.

Tybalt finally glanced up at the Captain.

"I wouldn't betray my shipmates," he said in a husky whisper.

"A noble sentiment but a little late. You already have." The Captain nodded at me. "Sparrow was a member of your command; I'm sure he trusted you. But it was you who gave Heron the freedom to act as his assassin. Do you deny that

Heron asked for, and you granted, permission to move around the surface as he saw fit?"

"I didn't—"

The Captain brought the flat of his hand down on the table-top.

"You didn't know. Or so you say. Yet you knew there was bad blood between Sparrow and Heron. And you saw to it that alone of all the groups that landed on Aquinas II, yours was armed. Heron had a pellet gun. Sparrow did not. You knew that."

The Captain was picking and choosing evidence as he saw fit. What had been commendable three time periods before was now traitorous. I could sense the slow growth of anger in the audience. They all knew Tybalt and they all liked him. No one had doubted his loyalty, though I knew a few had questioned his wisdom in partnering with Ophelia, however briefly. But all of them had understood why.

"I was loyal," Tybalt said in a dull voice. "I've always been loyal."

The Captain shook his head in denial.

"You would have the court believe that you were an innocent dupe, that you had no idea what Heron intended. Yet you knew that he was armed and that he hated Sparrow. It stretches no one's imagination to speculate that you knew what Heron intended."

Tybalt gaped. "Sparrow was a friend."

"A friend who competed with you, however briefly, for the woman you later partnered with. Motive need go no further than that."

For a moment, I thought the Captain was referring to Hamlet, then realized he meant the one night I had taken Ophelia against her desires. The Captain had eyes everywhere. I waited to be called to testify, so I could deny the allegation.

The Captain made a final notation, then clapped his writing slate shut.

"I said I would have trusted you with my life. It would have been trust misplaced." Then Tybalt vanished for him as completely as if he had slipped through a crack in the deck. "The prisoner is condemned."

We stood there in silence, all of us too stunned to move. If we'd had to vote on the crew member most loyal to the ship and the Captain, there was no doubt who would have won.

I wondered why the Captain had done it, and then he obligingly told us. We had just started to shift toward the hatchway when he motioned us back.

"The trials are over." There was a grim smile on his face and I thought of a picture I had once seen in the computer's memory matrix, of a tiger. "I hope they serve as a warning to those who would betray the *Astron* or its purpose and thus betray the Earth itself."

Heron had been condemned for attempted murder.

Noah had been condemned for attempted mutiny.

Tybalt had been condemned as an object lesson.

In two thousand years, the Captain should have learned better.

In two weeks, we finished our job on Aquinas II. We found no life of any kind. Aquinas II was a windswept, lonely planet of water-ice mountains, lakes and rivers of methane, sudden storms, crater-marked plains, and smog dense enough to drastically limit visibility. It was a dirty planet with air we couldn't breathe and water we couldn't drink. A primitive planet, stillborn and barren. If only it had been closer to its primary, if only it had been warmer, if only there had been plate tectonics or deposits of radioactives—anything to heat up its chilly interior.

But it was a cold planet and a dead one. There were no tracks to mark the slow passage of an Aquinas snail, no tiny pathway indicating where an overburdened proto-ant had wandered, no trail of bubbles in the methane lakes or streams where something very tiny had scooted by, its flagella whirling. . . .

The disappointment on board was so devastating that some of

the crew were glad when it was announced we were leaving, even though they knew we were heading into the Dark. Nobody had computed how many generations it would take to cross it, and so far as I knew no studies had been done on the *Astron*'s ability to survive the crossing. But I doubted that the ship could.

Heron and Noah and Tybalt hadn't been seen since their trials and the speculation was they were being held somewhere on the Captain's deck. Ophelia, Crow, and Loon were present for meals but absent much of the rest of the time. More than once I was afraid the long arm of the Captain had reached out to take them into custody, that Snipe had been wrong and their trials would be announced at any moment.

When they were present, they ignored me and I ignored them. Guilt came with association and I knew they didn't want to put me in peril. My own motives were more selfish. I had grown to love "Sparrow" and had no wish to be flatlined because of the company I kept.

Half a dozen time periods later, when we were about to leave orbit, a stricken Portia broke the suspense and confirmed a rumor. Quince had told her the three prisoners wouldn't be sent to Reduction after all. They had been stranded on Aquinas II and would die whenever their air ran out or the batteries for their life-support systems were exhausted.

Tybalt had been right after all. The Captain didn't know us. If they had been sent to Reduction, they would have become part of the food we ate, the water we drank, and the air we breathed. In a very real sense, they would have been with us forever.

But stranding them on Aquinas II was like refusing somebody a formal burial back on ancient Earth. It went against the religion of the *Astron,* vague and undefined as it was, and it was something I doubted the crew would accept.

As for myself, while I didn't really care what happened to Heron, I cared very much what happened to Noah and Tybalt.

They were my friends, but I had done nothing to save them. It didn't take me long to realize I couldn't live with that.

22

We wouldn't leave orbit for twenty-four hours but the life-support systems of those stranded on Aquinas II couldn't function for nearly that long. I had no plan at all except that somebody would have to plead with the Captain to save the lives of Noah and Tybalt. And maybe Heron as well. If they could flatline my memories, perhaps they could do the same for his, and a newborn Heron might turn out to be a happy Heron and a credit to the ship.

But who would speak for Noah?

Or intercede for Tybalt?

Or plead for Heron?

I was very young; I had lived less than a year as Sparrow, and in my heart I knew the Captain's mind could be changed. Noah was an old man who led a mutiny so inept it hardly qualified as more than conversation. And if Tybalt had been tried by a jury, the Captain could not have found twelve crew members who would have condemned him as disloyal.

There was no logic at all in the sentences the Captain had handed down, and that should have warned me.

The first person I approached was Ophelia. This time I announced myself and received permission to enter. She was floating by the far bulkhead of her compartment, replaced now by a view of Outside. She looked much as the Captain usually did, staring moodily into infinity. She didn't turn when I entered.

"You're a fool, Sparrow. People will know you came to see
me and they'll report it to Kusaka."

I ignored her sarcasm and told her why I was there.

"You really think somebody could convince Kusaka to change
his mind? Forget it, Sparrow, there's nothing to be done."

"They'll die," I said.

"So will we all. Eventually." Her voice turned even more
bitter. "I should have been tried instead of Noah, Kusaka
knows that. And he knows that I was the one Tybalt partnered with, however briefly."

"Then why didn't he put you on trial?"

She shrugged.

"Perhaps he picked names at random." Her face twisted.
"Perhaps he figured that I would live longer than Noah and
therefore would be more useful to him."

"How much do you think Noah told him?"

"No more than Kusaka already knew."

There must have been a great battle of wits between Noah
and the Captain. The Captain would have wanted to know the
names of everybody connected with the mutiny, but Noah
wouldn't have revealed anything.

"The Captain has access to drugs," I pointed out, adding
reluctantly: "He'll use them on other mutineers."

"So? You can't tell what you don't know, I'm sure Kusaka
has already found that out. His only alternative was to make
examples of some of us and he chose Noah. It could just as
easily have been me—I thought it would be me—but maybe
Noah was more . . . expendable."

"And Tybalt?"

Sadness softened her features.

"Tybalt knew nothing. I never burdened him with useless
knowledge, even when we argued."

She was convinced there was nothing to be done and I was
increasingly unwilling to accept that.

"You must know somebody who could plead their case with
the Captain," I said. "We don't have much time."

I had pushed her too far and she got angry. "Don't blame

me for your own sense of guilt, Sparrow! If I could have volunteered to be tried in their place, I would have. Noah didn't ask and wouldn't have let me even if I had offered and Kusaka had agreed. As for Tybalt, you know nothing of what passed between us. And how sure are you that your assumptions are correct? Would it shock you if I suggested Kusaka might have made a lucky guess? But if anybody ever asks me, I don't know that for sure. As far as I'm concerned, Tybalt and I stole what time we could and at the end of it, we parted friends and thanked each other."

I felt foolish and turned to leave but she was still angry and stopped me at the hatchway to threaten me.

"I've told you more than I intended, Sparrow. But don't forget that you can be denounced, too, and your death as 'Sparrow' would be just as final as Noah's or Tybalt's, even though your body remained."

Unable to help Noah, Ophelia had lashed out at me in frustration—but it still hurt.

"I trust you, Ophelia—apparently more than you trust me."

There had been levels to the plotting that I never suspected. Implied in Ophelia's sudden outburst was that Noah had never been the head of the mutiny and that it was even possible Tybalt had led a life of elaborate deception. I didn't believe it—I knew him better than that—but Ophelia had introduced the worm of uncertainty and perhaps that's what she intended.

But I couldn't resist toying with a new idea. Maybe there hadn't been a series of mutinies over the years but only one, one that had lasted for generations. Ophelia's suggestions of complexity hinted at it.

The next person I went to was Huldah. At one time, if Loon was correct, she had partnered with both Noah and Abel, and Noah had become the ostensible leader of a mutiny while Abel had become one of the Captain's men. Or had he? In a moment of anger, Noah had once said he would trust Abel with his life. Wheels within wheels . . . Perhaps Abel had played both sides. But if he had, he had been a fool for underestimating the Captain.

*   *   *

Huldah was alone in her compartment, a sunken-faced old lady wrapped in several layers of black cloth for warmth, sipping at a bulb of Pipit's special tea and knotting a string tapestry. Her voice was tired but her eyes were alert and intelligent. Once again she had put aside the role of matron.

"Don't bother offering condolences," she said without rancor. "We both knew it would happen sooner or later."

I offered them anyway. "You know how I feel," I said. "How the crew feels." I floated there in silence, waiting for her to ask me the reason for my visit, then realized I had no time to be polite.

"I wondered if you knew of someone who could plead with the Captain for their lives."

"I have no influence with the Captain, Sparrow."

"I wasn't thinking of you." I lied—she might have had more influence than anyone. "I thought you would know of somebody who does."

Her fingers were unsteady as she tied another knot.

"There's no special person to whom he would listen—all of us are mayflies compared to him." She gave me a sidelong look. "Arguments might persuade him. Perhaps you know of someone who has persuasive arguments?"

The only crew members I knew of who might argue with the Captain were all Seniors, and of the ones I knew best Noah and Tybalt were dying on Aquinas II while Ophelia couldn't intercede and Huldah wouldn't. From the expression on Huldah's face, I had the uncomfortable feeling I was overlooking somebody but couldn't think who.

She tied a few more knots, then said impatiently: "You once shared the Captain's table with him. At his invitation."

"Thrush?" I said, disbelieving. "He wouldn't help me if I asked. And I wouldn't ask. Nor would the Captain listen."

"Thrush may be spoiled sperm"—she shrugged—"but he thinks like a scientist. And a scientific argument might carry some weight with the Captain."

"Why would Thrush do anything for me?"

"Not just for you, for Noah and Tybalt and Heron—for all of us." She was watching me with those too-alert eyes, gauging my reactions. She was very anxious that I see Thrush and ask his help.

There was something I didn't understand.

"Thrush raped your daughter—yet you're asking for his help through me."

She became impatient once again.

"I hope Thrush will lead a long and unhappy life and I've no doubt that he will—it's in his genes. I'll admit I'm using you, Sparrow; I can't go to him myself. But you know things about Thrush that he wouldn't care for the Captain to know. You could use them against him. For Noah's sake—and Tybalt's." She added under her breath: "For your sake as well."

But I knew of nothing with which I could threaten Thrush nor anything I could offer him. Nor could I think of any possible arguments he might advance that would influence the Captain.

Huldah was an old woman, I thought with a trace of contempt, and one in whom I had already placed too much faith. I wanted to ask more but she shook her head and bent low to pluck at the string tapestry. I was almost to the shadow screen when she stopped me.

"You underestimate yourself, Sparrow."

"It's because you ask the impossible," I said, angry. I had the feeling both she and Ophelia wanted me to play the hero.

"It's impossible only if you don't try."

I was young and could still be shamed into actions I would regret later. I turned and fled through the hatchway and down the corridors to Thrush's compartment. I didn't think about what I would do once I got there because if I did, I knew I wouldn't do anything at all.

I stood just outside his shadow screen and asked for entry, expecting to be turned away with a sneer. There was a moment's pause and then the shadow screen vanished and I was staring into what I later learned was a rain forest. Huge tree trunks soared for hundreds of feet into the air and the leafy canopy at the top was so thick, the sky was a patchwork of green. Brightly colored birds swooped through the branches and, high up, monkeys swung from limb to limb. Little things with lizard eyes scampered through the underbrush at my feet and lianas and creepers hung in front of my face. It was warm and humid and it smelled as I imagined a jungle should smell.

It was a masterpiece.

I knew of nobody else who had the ability to program a compartment falsie of such complexity. Once again I was forced to rethink my opinion of Thrush. He was more than just a scientist, and considerably more than an artist. It took an effort of will to remind myself that, for reasons I would probably never know, he wanted me dead.

It didn't take him long to remind me of that.

"Come in, Sparrow, don't stand out there in the corridor."

I ventured in, still amazed by his artistry, and too late sensed not only the shadow screen closing behind me but the hatch as well. Somewhere in front of me—or perhaps to the side or above me—was Thrush. I couldn't see him. Unlike every other compartment falsie, this one had not been designed around its meager furnishings. It had been designed to hide them as well as its occupant.

I felt for my mask, then realized I didn't have it with me. And Thrush, who was undoubtedly wearing his, could see that I didn't have mine.

I took a few steps and promptly banged into the hammock. There was no indication it was there. I would have to feel my way through the compartment, ignoring all the visual clues to my surroundings.

"I'm surprised you had the courage"—Thrush laughed—"though I can't say much for your judgment."

"Where are you?" I asked, ignoring the skip my heart had taken when he questioned my judgment.

"Not yet, Sparrow. Soon enough."

I tried to blank out the vegetation and orient myself in the compartment. I edged over to what had to be a bulkhead on my left and flattened against it, momentarily feeling safer. I fumbled for the thin strip of metal I had hidden in my waist-cloth and palmed it.

"The crew doesn't like me, Sparrow." Thrush's voice had suddenly turned sour and flat. "They like you better—but not much. Heron tried to kill you once, but you keep forgetting that you tried to kill me and came closer to succeeding than Heron ever did to murdering you. Nobody's forgotten that and you're a fool if you think they've forgiven."

A streak of excitement filtered into his voice.

"Didn't you stop to think, Sparrow? *You've* come to see *me,* it's not the other way around. And my guess is that you're carrying some kind of weapon. Have you got a blade, Sparrow? You're holding it right now, right? With your back against the bulkhead so I can't take you by surprise. Except I think I could. And if I killed you, Sparrow, I could plead self-defense and almost everybody would believe it."

I was sweating, the drops stinging as they crept into the corners of my eyes. My breathing was shallow and my ears strained to distinguish the sound of Thrush's movements from the rustle of the small things in the jungle around me.

"Are you afraid, Sparrow? I know you can't see me and I assure you that you won't hear me. Not in time."

I cursed myself again for being a fool. I started to slip around to my right, feeling for the hatchway, and bumped into an unexpected shelf. The sound seemed loud even among the shrieks and noises of the jungle. I tensed and swung the blade through the vegetation in front of me.

Thrush's voice filled with menace.

"Are you frightened, Sparrow? If you admit it, it might save your life."

He fell silent and I swore I heard a slight movement. He was right: By the time I knew where he was, it would be much too late. And he was right again when he said the Captain's case would be against me, not against him.

"I have to know, Sparrow."

His voice was savage and I guessed he was close by. I sensed my own emotions in his, remembered when I had held a strip of metal to his throat and would have cut it, hesitating only when I felt his tremor of fear. Now he wanted the same admission from me.

I shook my head and the sweat flew off in droplets. I wasn't going to win this time.

"So I'm afraid," I finally admitted.

The rain forest abruptly vanished. I was spread-eagled against the bulkhead, wriggling my blade foolishly in front of me, while a smug-looking Thrush floated behind the familiar ledge we all used as a desk. He took his hand off the terminal pad and showed large white teeth in a pale smile. On the hangar deck, I had spared his life only after he had shown fear. I had been the alpha primate then. Now he had spared mine, without ever leaving his position behind the desk. The possible fight, and winning or losing it, had all been in my imagination.

"That makes us even," he smirked.

"More than even," I muttered.

He clasped his hands behind his head, not afraid of me even though I still held the blade in my hand. He knew that he could reach the terminal pad before I could reach him and that I would never find him in the jungle he had programmed. He also knew I had a reason for coming to see him.

"We're the only two people on board who can play like this," he said smugly. "No, I take that back—a few could probably come close, Banquo for one. But very few of the others. We're not like them, Sparrow."

He was lumping me in the same category with himself; I was repelled, while apprehensive at the same time. Did he know I was aware of my own history? For a brief moment, I was sweaty with anxiety, then realized that while he might play with Sparrow, he wouldn't dare if he thought he was dealing with Hamlet.

"I think we're very different, Thrush—I would never have done to Heron what you did."

He sneered.

"Easy enough to say when you've never been in a position where it was his life or yours. He won't be missed by the ship—and though you don't want to agree, I would be."

"He idolized you," I said.

He shrugged. "Why not? Did anybody else take the trouble to befriend him? In the end, I treated him badly, but circumstances left me no choice. And if you recall, there was a time when you thought highly of me as well."

I bit back the hot reply that came to mind. On the hangar deck, when we had been so close I could feel his sudden surge of fear, I had asked him why he had wanted to kill me and was told he thought he was the better man. I had puzzled about that ever since. In the months that I had been "Sparrow," I had imagined the *Astron* was split into two parts—the Captain and his men against the rest of the crew. The Captain had a mission and was willing to go to any lengths to carry it out. But a large fraction of the crew wanted to seize the *Astron* and return home.

It had been a simple theory, but Thrush didn't fit into it. I knew what the Captain wanted. I knew what most of the crew wanted. But I didn't know what Thrush wanted.

Then I had one of the few inspirations of my short life.

"Do you agree with the Captain, Thrush? That there's life out there?"

"None of us will know for sure until we find it, will we, Sparrow?" He grinned. "If the Captain asked me, I might give him a different answer. As you did at the trials."

Were we that much alike? I wondered. Then I was curious what Hamlet had thought of Thrush, how Hamlet had handled him. Or if he had bothered.

"Now I've got one for you, Sparrow." Thrush's smile faded. "Why did you come to see me? The truth, please."

He was very much in control, very self-confident. Apparently we were mortal enemies; but right then, I would never have known it. If he had ever played a role in one of Snipe's historicals, he must have been very good.

"I need your help."

"I didn't think you could surprise me," he murmured. "I was wrong."

"I want to convince the Captain to save their lives." He knew who I meant.

His face became a pale mask.

"I was never that fond of Noah, and Tybalt's easily replaced. And you overestimate my friendship with Heron."

"You were never friends with Heron," I said. "*He* was friends with *you*."

A shrug. "I stand corrected."

Time was running out. I had spent half an hour with Ophelia and Huldah but I could easily spend half a time period with Thrush trying to coax him to do something he saw no profit in doing, only risk.

"I can prove you plotted with Heron on the hangar deck," I said. "There were other witnesses." It was too simple a lie and I cursed Huldah for urging me to even try talking to Thrush.

Thrush raised his eyebrows in mock surprise.

"A threat, Sparrow? Against me?" He smiled bleakly. "What is it you want me to do? Go to the Captain and plead for their lives?" Once again there was something in the back of his eyes that I couldn't read. "It would be more effective if you did that, Sparrow. He might believe pleading if it came from you; you're too innocent to have ulterior motives."

He drifted out from behind the desk. I stared at him in the light from the glow tubes and tried to hide my stare at the same time. I had been an idiot, I should have known. Why hadn't Huldah told me?

I had eyes but I had to learn to use them—and Huldah taught by example. She was intensely interested in the fate of those stranded below, but she had also wanted me to look at

Thrush in circumstances under which I could see him for what he really was.

Thrush opened the hatch and waited for me to leave.

"Do whatever you want, Sparrow, say anything you want. I can't go to the Captain and plead for them. Nobody can. All three of them endangered the *Astron* and there's no reprieve from that—nobody can be allowed to endanger the *Astron,* not even the Captain."

I paused in the corridor outside, just before he flicked on the shadow screen.

"If you were Captain," I said thoughtfully, "would you take the *Astron* into the Dark?"

It wasn't my question. It had come from somewhere in the back of my mind, perhaps from Hamlet, perhaps from Aaron. It surprised me as much as it surprised Thrush.

"I might."

"You wouldn't make it," I said.

He shrugged and turned back to the desk ledge and his terminal pad.

"The ship would, the crew might not. Not all of them."

The jungle and all of its noises suddenly reappeared, to vanish a moment later as the shadow screen flowed back in place.

I had the information I needed, but I had a good deal more than that as well and all of it totally unexpected. Thrush had been as badly gashed as I during our fight on the hangar deck. But now he was completely healed. I remembered Abel's look of surprise when he had inspected us three weeks earlier.

Ophelia had been wrong about the Captain's sterility. The skin color was a different shade, undoubtedly due to a recessive gene. But the sense of command was the same and so was the ruthlessness and the innate ability to manipulate people. So also was the attitude of one of those who was alone in life, stranded among the mayflies.

Thrush had once bragged that the Captain had taken a special interest in him. It had surprised me then but it didn't now.

Thrush, Thrush . . .

The Captain's son.

23

The Captain was not alone. Banquo guarded the hatchway to his cabin and I could see Escalus at his accustomed post inside, barring entrance to the Captain's private quarters. I even caught a glimpse of the Captain himself, shouting and gesturing angrily at somebody out of sight.

There was nothing I wanted more than to return to my compartment and the comforting arms of Snipe, whom I would comfort in turn. Tybalt had "taken an interest" in her long ago and she would be mourning him for a long time to come.

I dodged past Banquo, bursting in on a startled Captain, who had been arguing with a sweating Abel. For a moment, before Banquo grabbed me from behind, everybody froze. The Captain, interrupted in mid-sentence, glared at me, not quite believing that anybody would enter without first asking permission. Abel, who looked anguished, didn't take his eyes from the Captain's face; I had caught him at the end of an argument he had just lost. Escalus, frowning, had buried his hand in his waistcloth. I guessed he was clutching at some weapon he had hidden there.

I had forgotten the one Senior I might have gone to who would have pleaded for the condemned three. But apparently Abel had gone of his own accord to beg for Noah's life—and failed.

Then Banquo wrapped an arm around my waist and another around my neck, his sweaty forearm slippery against my windpipe.

"I have to see the Captain!" I squeaked. "Let me go—"

Banquo tightened his arm and my words were choked back into my throat. The Captain motioned and I was free to breathe and find my voice.

"You're late," he said sarcastically. He gestured at Abel. "I expected you before *him*." His voice was thick with contempt.

Abel paled. I took a momentary delight in his humiliation, then felt ashamed, realizing how much courage it had taken and how much it must have cost him in influence with the Captain. Noah had been his friend and, Captain's man or not, Abel had been willing to risk all.

The Captain nodded to Abel. "You can go. But perhaps we should talk again." The threat was unmistakable.

Abel fled, all dignity abandoned, and the dislike I had felt for him for so long vanished in a wave of pity.

"There's something on your mind, Sparrow?"

The Captain's voice was without its usual cloak of friendship. Both Banquo and Escalus were staring at me with half smiles and I realized that all three were waiting for me to repeat whatever pleas Abel had made. I stalled for time, stammering with embarrassment at entering the Captain's cabin without permission. I wondered furiously what Abel might have said.

Would he have pleaded for the return of the three to the ship and then begged for their lives? If so, what would have been the basis of his pleas? That they were innocent? That Heron was now harmless? That Noah was an old man with little influence among the crew? That the facts in Tybalt's case had been misinterpreted?

Abel had failed. But without even thinking, Thrush had given me the only approach that might work. Nor would I have to deny my ties of friendship with both Noah and Tybalt.

The Captain held up his hand to interrupt my torrent of

apologies for intruding. "You're forgiven, Sparrow—in the future, follow procedure."

He relaxed in his hammock and waved Banquo outside to resume his guard in the passageway. He let some friendship seep back into his voice but the dark eyes were bleak and calculating. I suspected I had played this scene many times before and I was merely repeating Hamlet or Aaron or God only knew who.

"You came here for some reason, Sparrow. What is it?"

I had trouble keeping my voice from shaking.

"Inventories, sir."

He frowned. "Inventories? Ship's business can wait—"

I shook my head.

"I don't think so, sir."

He knew why I was really there and had probably been wondering what approach I might take. I was sure he had assumed my pleas would be based on friendship or humanity. But I had surprised him and now he was curious.

"Explain."

"We're going into the Dark," I said, and rattled off our inventories of water, basic food constituents, and, most important, the vital supplies of trace elements on board—elements we would have difficulty replacing if planetfalls were limited to one per generation or perhaps fewer. I slowed when his eyes began to glaze.

"You have a point, Sparrow?"

I took my courage in my hands and gambled.

"We can't afford to lose their mass, sir. Or their trace elements." Once they were back on board, I'd worry about saving their lives.

He had lost track of what I really had in mind.

"Whose mass?"

"Heron's. And Noah's and Tybalt's."

He folded his arms and leaned back in his hammock, trying to read the carefully blank expression on my face.

"Noah was a good friend of yours," he said, too casually. "Am I right, Sparrow?"

I shrugged. "We played chess. He usually won. He talked about the mutiny with me. I refused to join it. But you know all about that, sir."

He knew I had been approached. He also knew I had rejected the mutiny or, at worst, had temporized.

"And Tybalt?"

"He was a good team leader," I said cautiously. "But I . . . hardly respected his judgment down below."

"And Heron?" The Captain was disbelieving. "You want to save the man who tried to kill you?"

I shrugged again.

"Eighty-five kilos of mass, standard distribution of elements." I took a deep breath and played the last card I had. "To leave them behind might . . . endanger the *Astron*." As Thrush had said, not even the Captain could do that.

His look terrified me but I kept my face frozen in an imbecilic expression of devotion to duty.

After a long moment, he turned and floated to the port and its view of Outside.

"Take a team below and get them," he said harshly.

I was out the hatch before he finished the sentence.

My down-below team consisted of Ophelia, Crow, and Abel, along with Grebe and Mercutio from Maintenance to act as porters—either made Banquo look small.

Noah and the others had been stranded on Aquinas II in the same area where Ophelia's team was originally based. The weather was no better than before and our Lander had to fight to make it safely to the surface. Once again we settled down by the methane river and its surrounding cliffs. Mercutio assured us that Noah and the others had been abandoned there, but when we turned on the landing lights, there were no signs of them. Any tracks they might have left were covered by huge drifts of methane snow.

After landing, it took time to prepare the sled and load the life-support supplies. Extra water, extra oxygen, plus emergency medical supplies in case Abel needed them before we got the three stranded crewmen back to the Lander. Full air tanks would last for four hours, and by my computations it had been a little more than three since I first approached Ophelia. We were running out of time.

"We're on a fool's errand," Ophelia muttered.

It was my turn to say curtly, "Shut up."

We loaded the Rover with sleds and supplies, then squeezed in after. We sat for a moment in silence, a tiny oasis of humanity on an alien world, searching for three companions condemned to death and stranded there. Only none of us had any idea where they might be.

Then I knew.

Grebe was at the controls and I tapped him lightly on the shoulder and said into my helmet microphone, "Drive to the gorge."

I had told Noah of my little valley with its thundering methane fall and how excited I was to be the only human in the universe to see it. On Aquinas II, it was one of probably very few areas where you could see more than a meter or two in front of your face. And I was sure it was one of the few places that might qualify as scenic.

"That'll take half an hour," Crow said, worried.

"Then we'll have to hurry, won't we?"

Everybody shut up then and we drove the two kilometers in silence. We located the gully, but it was impossible to get closer with the Rover. We quickly piled the extra oxygen cylinders on the sled and hauled it over to the mouth of the small canyon; it was probably the most difficult hundred meters I've ever traveled. The methane snow whipped around my helmet and visibility was so bad we lashed ourselves together with tether lines so even if we lost visual contact, we would still be physically linked.

By the time we pulled the sled to the entrance, we were exhausted.

"We'll leave it just inside the mouth of the gully," I said. "We'll have to carry the oxygen cylinders with us."

I had taken charge, but to my surprise, nobody questioned that.

It was a tired Mercutio who asked, "How far?"

"A hundred meters more, maybe less. We'll find them on a ledge overlooking a valley."

"You're sure of that?" Ophelia asked.

"No," I said.

A few moments later we were struggling between the cliffs, the wind roaring overhead. There was less snow inside the gully and the going was easier. I hesitated where the gully split into left and right legs, unable to remember whether I had mentioned the split to Noah or not, then headed into the left leg, toward the valley. If they had chosen the other leg, we would have to backtrack. I prayed we would have time to investigate both.

The wind died and we pushed through the slush with only the occasional curse to break the radio silence. At one point I untied my tether line and ran over to a group of three snow-covered boulders, each the size and shape of a crouching man, in the center of the ravine. I frantically scraped away the layers of frozen methane only to discover brown, pitted rock.

Twenty minutes into the gully, the canyon walls faded away. Directly ahead was the valley. Once again, the wind obligingly brushed aside the fog and I saw the methane river plunging over the distant rim.

I also saw three crumpled figures clustered together on the ledge, looking nothing like three boulders but very much like three space-suited crewmen who had fallen and been covered by the drifts.

Abel was in the lead and reached them first, moving remarkably fast for an exhausted fat man. He brushed away the snow that covered their suits, then sank down beside them. I expected him to report over his helmet phone but he said nothing at all.

The rest of us slogged up as fast as we could. The first body I looked at was Heron's. His faceplate was partly fogged over, but I could make out his eyes tightly closed and his mouth half open.

He had smothered in his own vomit.

Noah and Tybalt had chosen a faster way to die. They had opened their faceplates to let in the cold and the poisonous atmosphere. Their cheeks were ice, their eyes chilled steel. I started shivering and couldn't stop. I had never seen a dead man before—the closest I had come was Judah, when Crow and I visited Reduction.

I couldn't focus my thoughts. I wondered if Noah had liked the view, or if the fog had even cleared so he could see it. Or if Tybalt had finally realized the monsters of his imagination couldn't compare to the real ones back on the *Astron*.

I glanced at the time indicator inside my helmet. They should've had enough air for at least another fifteen minutes—with shallow breathing and minimum exertion, maybe a good half hour.

It was Abel who checked their gauges. His voice in my headset was bitter.

"They were sent down with half tanks. No one could have reached them in time."

Which meant that all the while I had been talking to the Captain, he had known they were dead.

He was waiting for me when we came back, floating by the huge port with Outside just beyond. Banquo nodded at me but made no effort to stop me or even make sure I announced myself. Escalus managed to make himself more inconspicuous than usual, though I knew the little man heard and saw everything.

The Captain turned away from the port and stared at me. I stared back in silence, failing to find the words that would express how I felt without giving myself away. He spoke first.

"Congratulations on recovering the mass, Sparrow. You were right, we'll need it."

Mass.

"They were dead," I said. "They had air for only two hours."

I had almost forgotten that I was "Sparrow," the young technician who once had idolized him.

He raised his eyebrows in mock surprise.

"I didn't know that was a concern of yours. You said you were interested in saving mass and trace elements. It was a practical argument." He shrugged. "I'll check to see who issued the equipment; they'll be punished. I wouldn't have denied them two more hours of life."

He was lying, I knew it. He had known about the tanks all along.

"They could have served the ship." My voice cracked with anger.

"Oh? You attended the trials, you know the charges, you heard the verdicts." He was suddenly suspicious. "You didn't think that stranding them was humane."

"You didn't see them," I said.

His expression softened. It took a moment to realize I had saved myself once again. I was outraged, but he expected that "Sparrow" would be outraged. If I hadn't been, I would have been flatlined the next time period.

"I've seen dead people before, Sparrow. It isn't a question of pretty or ugly, it just is."

"Did you really think Noah posed a threat?" I asked.

He turned back to the port, lost for a moment in the view.

"We're going into the Dark, Sparrow. I would be a fool if I thought that everybody wanted to go. But not because they want to return home—that was Noah's mistake. Home is here, it's the *Astron*. They're afraid to go into the Dark because it's new, because it's different, because they don't think the ship will make it. But the ship *will* make it. And so will a crew. Nobody's going to die because we're going into the Dark."

A crew. At first, I didn't pay much attention to his choice of words.

"Tybalt was innocent," I said bitterly.

He nodded.

"It hurt to lose him. But Ophelia isn't innocent and neither are a number of others. Perhaps they should all have been tried. And condemned. I chose Tybalt. Not because he was guilty but because he was innocent. I couldn't have tried all the conspirators. To have tried one who was actually guilty would have deterred a few, made them more cautious. To try and condemn a man everybody knew was innocent would deter a lot more."

He wanted to keep everybody in line. Including me—if I ever thought of joining the mutiny.

"Sometimes a warning is more important than justice, Sparrow."

"The crew will hate you," I warned.

He floated back to his hammock, where he made himself comfortable.

"This crew, perhaps," he said easily. "Maybe even a few in the next crew. But to the crew after that and all those that follow, Tybalt's death will be history, no more important in the long run than his life. Or anybody's life. Every three generations, God clears the stage for a new cast of actors, Sparrow."

Huldah had said the crew were mayflies to him. I had to remember that. I turned to go and he said, "You also forget something else."

I paused at the hatch. "What?" I loaded it with all the insolence I could muster. "Sparrow" wasn't going to forget Tybalt and Noah.

"Death buys a privilege that everybody eagerly seeks, especially those who overvalue living. There's room for new life on board." He let it hang there for a moment to give me time to realize just what he was saying. "Every man wants to father children and every woman wants to be a mother—it's built into the genes." He smiled cynically. "You might qualify for a chance at creating new life, Sparrow."

"I'd appreciate the opportunity, sir," I said stiffly and left. I suspected I was as sterile as Ophelia thought he was—and that he knew it. The only thing the offer meant to me was that he had decided to tolerate "Sparrow" a while longer.

I went back to my compartment and flicked on the falsie to surround myself with books and soft music. Snipe was on shift and I was glad to be alone.

A crew, the Captain had said, not *the* crew. I thought of the two empty cylinders that were a part of the *Astron* and the "dream" I'd had when I was a member of the fifth generation and the crew was three times as large. With the passing of the generations, the Captain had been slowly cannibalizing the ship. Now I realized he had been cannibalizing the crew as well. The ship was not quite a self-contained environment; there was a slow but gradual leakage of everything important for the maintenance of life. Every generation there would be fewer and fewer of us until finally there would be nobody left to return to the ancient kingdom of Spain. But that didn't really matter to the Captain.

It was then I finally joined the mutiny.

24

In a week, the Aquinas system was far behind; we watched and worried as the constellations slowly swung around in the sky. There was nothing but blackness ahead of the *Astron* now, while the glittering diamond dust of the stars shifted to our sides and rear. We were heading into the Dark and none of us knew how many generations it would take to cross it—or if we ever would.

I knew I was being watched, and not in my role as an icon for the crew. Unfortunately, everybody I knew in the mutiny was being watched as well. The Captain had known about Ophelia, which hardly surprised me, but he had also known about Snipe, Crow, Loon, and . . . who else? I thought of the "safe" compartment and wondered if the peep screen had been repaired, then decided it hadn't. Spare parts were in short supply and so ancient that most of them malfunctioned at the first opportunity.

But the Captain didn't need peep screens so long as he had informers. I guessed that there were a lot of them and that the would-be mutineers had been too naive about who they recruited or even approached.

It was easier to get together with Crow and the others than I thought. When we were alone, we exchanged a look or a nod and murmured a time, and half a dozen shifts after changing course we were sitting around an imaginary fire listening to the howls of imaginary wolves.

We didn't dog down the hatch—it would have been too obvious and it wasn't necessary. The shadow screens cut most of the sound as well as the light. But once inside and safe, we sat warming ourselves by the simulated flames and staring at each other in silence. Why should I assume that none of *them* were informers? I wondered. After all, the Captain would have his rewards as well as his punishments. But Crow and Loon were my best friends and Ophelia could have had me flatlined long ago. . . .

We sat there for a long moment, each of us speculating, and finally I decided to trust my emotions.

Ophelia beat me to it.

"We operate in cells," she said at last. "Only one person in each cell knows the name of a member in another cell. The Captain knows about me but I don't think he knows of many more."

They were better organized than I thought but I was sure Ophelia was naive, that the Captain at least suspected others.

Then I remembered when they had tried to recruit me.

"You put me at risk," I accused.

Ophelia shrugged. "You were a member before; Kusaka expected us to approach you. And we wanted you to know the arguments so you could check them yourself. You idolized Kusaka and we knew you'd refuse at first—and that your refusal would save you later on."

"And if he finds out now?"

"We'll lose our lives and you'll lose your memories."

That pretense was finally gone. Snipe reassured me without my asking.

"Only a few of us know that you're aware of who you really are Sparrow. Those here, Huldah, and Abel."

"You read minds?" I asked sarcastically.

"It was obvious what you were thinking."

I could feel the sweat start in the small of my back. Too

many knew and chances were it wouldn't be long before the Captain knew as well.

"What do you do about informers?" The mutineers couldn't use any sort of force to protect themselves, which meant informers had nothing to fear from them.

Crow laughed. "There aren't any—not really. We know who the Captain's men are and we mislead them with false information, or feed them real information that's not important enough for the Captain to act on."

"He acted on Noah and Tybalt," I said bitterly.

"We had just heard we were going into the Dark and there was resentment among the crew. We knew the Captain would do something."

But they hadn't anticipated that the Captain would condemn Tybalt as well as Noah. The attempted murder was a coincidence, a sideshow that had happened at the same time. Or was it? I suspected that Thrush, Heron, and the mutineers were all connected, though none of them may have realized it.

"You know all the Captain's men?" I asked, dubious.

Ophelia nodded.

"All of them. We can sense who's one of us and who isn't."

Ophelia was very brave and very confident and Hamlet must have loved her for those qualities. But I was more cautious than he had been and overconfidence irritated me.

"You underestimate the Captain," I grumbled. "He'll find out who all of the mutineers are and he'll chop off their heads one by one. The cells will slow him down but sooner or later there'll be informers. And you'll make mistakes in who you recruit."

Snipe shook her head.

"Ophelia's right, Sparrow. We know who we can trust."

They were all looking at me when she said that, nodding in agreement, and I felt the hair at the back of my head prickle. Another mystery that Huldah hadn't seen fit to tell me about.

"You want to seize the ship and return," I said, still playing devil's advocate. "But you can't run the ship without the Captain. The computer takes orders only from him. You told me so yourself."

Crow looked smug. "That's true, we can't run the ship without him. But he can't run it without us, either."

I wasn't too sure of that. "How many on the Captain's side?"

Everybody looked at Loon, who apparently kept track of these things.

"It's a sixty-forty split, Sparrow. More favor returning than continuing with the Captain."

"You can't force the Captain to agree," I said, disgusted for once by somebody else's innocence. "All he has to do is breed a new crew. Time's on his side. Your mutiny may be nothing but a rumor two generations from now." I hadn't forgotten the Captain's comments about Tybalt.

They fell silent but none of them looked worried.

"This hasn't been the only mutiny," Ophelia finally said. "During the first few generations there was another. The crew must have known it was possible to win—otherwise they would never have tried it."

Without them saying so, I knew they were depending on me. I remembered Noah telling me that the key to the success of their mutiny was locked away in my memories. Two of us would have had firsthand knowledge of that original mutiny: the Captain, who remembered everything. And I, who remembered nothing.

"You haven't told us," Crow said. For a moment, I had been lost in my thoughts.

"Told you what?"

"Whether you're with us or not."

"You can't sense it?" I said sarcastically. "Why else would I be here?" My sudden flash of anger was a cover for a sudden, wrenching feeling of loss. Ophelia was right, I had idolized the Captain, and it's hard to let go of idols—if nothing else, they're a bulwark against reality. Unfortunately, reality was something I could no longer avoid.

I was running out of time and I knew beyond all doubt that

my life as Sparrow was drawing to a close and I was hastening
the end by throwing in my lot with them. Sooner or later, the
Captain would find out about the new recruit.

My only comfort was that Hamlet would have been proud
of me.

Small comfort.

Sometimes it's the smallest events in life that lead to the
largest consequences. A missed bulb of coffee in the morning
can cause a nagging irritation that will lead to a fatal error in
judgment on some exotic planetary surface. A casual collision
in a passageway can lead to a brief apology, a slight show of
interest, an enthusiastic coupling, and permanent partnering.
I had seen both happen, though nobody was watching when it
happened to me.

Two weeks after leaving Aquinas, and one after my meeting in the "safe" compartment, I was half asleep in my hammock when Snipe came off duty and crawled in beside me.
We lay entwined and she murmured some question, I no
longer remember what, which started me thinking that everybody wanted answers from me but very few had ever offered
to tell me anything.

Huldah had warned me to use my eyes, but beyond that
had volunteered precious little information about my own life
or who I had been in the past. Ophelia and Crow had been
just as closemouthed—and so, for that matter, had Noah.
Perhaps there was some reason for their reticence, but if there
was, I didn't know it. I lay there, half asleep, feeling sorry for
myself, when it occurred to me that the mystery went deeper
than that.

Tybalt had confided in me, but nobody else had. There had
also been a fundamental difference between Tybalt and the
others, though at the moment I couldn't quite put my finger
on it. The Captain had taken me into his confidence as well,
though that had been calculated. Then I remembered the chil-

dren in the nursery: those who had laughed and cried in unison and those who had looked puzzled by it all. . . .

I yawned in the dark, decided it was foolish to spend more thought on it, and gave myself over to tracing lazy circles on Snipe's bare back until I was sure she was awake. We made slow and casual love and then she slipped off to sleep once more, leaving me to stare at the overhead and wonder about her curious lack of response and if romance had finally fled. I mused about it, then convinced myself I was merely suffering from the self-doubts that plague everybody in the early hours just before normal waking.

A moment later the hair prickled at the back of my head and I rolled slightly away from Snipe so there was a thin wedge of air between us. I suddenly couldn't bear the thought of touching her. I loved Snipe and I knew she cared for me, but sometimes, at some very basic level, there was a barrier between us, a barrier that I could neither identify nor penetrate and that extended into other areas of her life as well. There were those moments when I felt very close to Snipe . . . and was frustrated because I could get no closer.

That time period, a reason occurred to me and I felt my skin crawl. Those moments with Snipe were at the head of a very long list of questions that had been accumulating and I knew there was only one person who could answer them. But she probably wouldn't. Not of her own free will.

I would have to force her.

I waited until the passageway was deserted, then asked for entry. When she gave it, I slipped in, pausing only long enough to make sure no peep screen had been installed since the last time. The Captain had hardly trusted Noah but he hadn't bothered to monitor his living compartment; he knew Noah would have gotten around any monitor.

Huldah was sipping tea, but secured the drink bulb to the work ledge and settled back in her hammock, her eyes alert and watchful. She was neither matron nor oracle now. I realized with surprise that she was frightened of me. She had . . . sensed? . . . what was on my mind, and she also knew that I was unpredictable.

"You know all the *begats*," I said. When she nodded, I added: "Back to when time began. At least as far back as the computer keeps them and probably before. Isn't that correct?" I stole a line from Thrush then. "The truth, please, Huldah."

She nodded again but still said nothing.

"And you're teaching them to Pipit, right?"

Another nod.

"Who taught them to you, Huldah?"

She paled then and so did I. I was right and what I would get from Huldah was confirmation that I was right. And when I got it, my personal world would be smashed forever.

"It might not be good for you to know," she said.

I straddled her hammock and leaned so close my face was only a few centimeters from hers. She could not back away.

"You loved Noah and you love Abel," I said in a low voice, hoping that Loon's outrageous gossip was right for once. "Noah was stranded and it would take very little to convince the Captain to rid himself of Abel. Abel played both sides and funneled important information to you and unimportant information to the Captain. Someone with malice could remind the Captain that Abel is no longer of value to him."

She stared at me with sudden hatred.

"You wouldn't be merely an accessory," she said in a brittle voice. "You'd be as much a murderer as the Captain himself."

I quailed inside, but didn't dare let it show in my face.

"I have to know, Huldah."

"The Captain could be persuaded to do a lot of things," she threatened, "including flatlining you."

"All of us lead dangerous lives," I said. "Who taught you the *begats*?"

She shrugged. "My mother."

"And her mother taught her and her mother's mother taught *her*."

She nodded again, apprehensive, well aware what I was driving at.

"But you do more than keep the *begats*. The Captain gives out the birth allowances but you take care of the fine points of ritual, right? As your mother did before you and her mother before that. There's a birth ceremony and there's also an impregnation ceremony and no doubt they drink to the mother and the would-be father. Am I still right?"

"The crew needs ritual," she said harshly.

"A few mothers and maybe a hundred fathers," I said. "I've never seen one but it must be something like that. You and Pipit provide the wine and the blessing and the mothers have children by fathers chosen not by chance but by you. There's something in the wine, or perhaps there's something the mother takes before her next suitor presents himself."

"If you know, why do you ask, Sparrow?"

"I'm guessing," I said. "I'm asking you to confirm it." I then quit searching for a polite way to phrase it and said bluntly: "The Captain sets the birth allotments and picks the candidates, but he doesn't breed a crew, Huldah. You do. I want to know what kind of crew you're breeding."

I didn't think she would answer but she read the same expression on my face that Thrush had read when I held a blade to his throat. Would I have helped Abel on his way to Reduction? Generations later I'm not so sure, but at the time I was quite certain I would have.

Her voice turned sour with bitterness.

"Not like the one he started with. One that treasures life, one that values cooperation, one that experiences firsthand the emotions that another feels, one that's loyal to itself." She paused. "One that can share its memories . . ."

I wasn't sure of the last but life on board the *Astron* already encouraged the other noble attributes. Huldah wanted to engrave them in stone, to make them part of the genetic map.

She read me and said grimly, "They're not idealistic, Sparrow, they're practical. For life on board the *Astron*, they're survival traits."

"What you're trying to do is deprive the Captain of his crew," I said with sudden insight. "A crew loyal to itself ensures that in a few more generations the Captain would have a crew that was solidly against him."

"It will take five more generations," Huldah said calmly.

What was it Ophelia had said? *We can sense who's one of us.* Then I wondered if she had said that deliberately.

"Selective breeding?"

Huldah shrugged. "Small pockets of any species, separated from the main group, can change very fast. And they'll breed true. We've also been in outer space for more than two thousand years, subjected to continuous low-level radiation. We're dealing with a very small gene pool; our little branch of the human race is . . . malleable."

It hadn't been a series of mutinies, I thought again. It had been one long mutiny that had been going on for centuries, probably since the first generation. Having lost their first attempt, they had decided to take the long view, to breed a crew that would think and act as one and pit it against a Captain who held all the power that one man on board could possibly hold.

"More than half the crew is of different genetic stock from the Captain, right, Huldah?"

"In a sense."

"And different from me," I added bitterly.

She guessed what I was thinking.

"She loves you, Sparrow."

"What am I to her?" I asked cynically. "A pet?"

"We're different stock, Sparrow, not better, not worse."

"We can never be close," I said. If there was ever a time when I felt my heart break, I felt it then. Snipe had been the end of my loneliness.

She shook her head.

"Closer than most couples. Perhaps not as close as you would like."

"She would be closer with one of her own kind, is that right?"

Huldah hesitated. "Depending on the person . . . perhaps. But there's more involved than you think."

I thought of the children in the nursery and I thought of Pipit and Crow and Loon and Noah and Huldah and I was suddenly afraid for myself—and envious. Human relationships are based on a lifetime of trying to understand someone else's agonies and misunderstandings while they try to understand yours. Like the children in the nursery, we learn to empathize through pain as well as through laughter. The new crew would experience very little of that. There would be few misunderstandings and little alienation and what agonies there were would be shared by all, diminishing them for the individual. There would be little spiritual suffering— and the thought occurred to me that there would be little art produced because of it. If the crew ever found a planet on which to thrive, there would be few Beethovens or Van Goghs. But on balance, I wasn't sure they would be the losers.

As for myself and Snipe, once initial lust had been spent, I usually felt a stranger to her. There was a barrier I could not sweep aside. Too often we were no more than two people who liked each other and found casual release together. Now I knew we would never experience that blend of trust and desire that I had always hoped for. She would reach those heights of passion with someone else, but she never would with me. The new crew was capable of singing songs that I could never hear.

"You have more than most people ever have," Huldah said quietly.

I promptly accused her as I had Snipe.

"You can read minds? Is that part of the difference?"

"We sense what you feel and consequently what you must be thinking."

"No," I denied angrily, "you don't just read emotions, you

read minds." I was both right and wrong, but at the moment it didn't matter. "What does Snipe think of me?" I asked.

"In what way?"

I shrugged. "A Neanderthal must have been pleasantly surprised when it mated with a creature that possessed a superior nervous system. But I imagine it was pretty dull for a Cro-Magnon."

She looked away. "Neanderthal had a lot to offer. He was less gracile but he was stronger and a natural hunter. Cro-Magnon and Neanderthal interbred. Quite successfully."

"Neanderthal disappeared," I said.

"Perhaps. I prefer to think he bred up—or down, depending on how you look at it."

"I'm not talking about breeding," I said. "I'll live forever and because of that I'll have no children." I was hoping she would deny this, but Huldah said nothing. Then I had another thought. "You haven't explained Thrush," I said slowly. "Ophelia said the Captain was sterile."

"Ophelia doesn't know. Nobody knows." The ends of her mouth turned down. "The bastard child . . . We thought it was impossible, but the Captain had time and he was persistent. You don't have to have many viable sperm if you have two thousand years in which to separate them and save them in a generation chamber. But I doubt that even he will live long enough to have another."

I looked at her, unconvinced.

"And nobody knew? What about Thrush's mother? *She* knew."

"Thrush is one of the Uncounted. Phebe never told, and she went to Reduction shortly after delivery."

I was ready to curse the Captain, but Huldah shook her head.

"Voluntarily. Births are tightly controlled on board; one dies and statistically slightly less than one is born. To have a child outside of Ritual is to cheat someone else. Phebe went to Reduction out of guilt—and to make room for her son. In a sense, she committed suicide." She passed judgment then, which surprised me. "Mating with the Captain wasn't worth it. In a lot of ways."

Huldah and I were edging back into a wary friendship. I didn't think things would ever be the same between Snipe and me, but all of us were allied against the Captain.

"Why does Thrush want me dead?" I asked.

She shrugged. "If I had to guess, I would say envy was part of it. But I doubt he has reason to envy your immortality."

"The Captain passed it on." I felt no surprise.

"Perhaps. If he has, it complicates the future."

"You can read the future?" I asked, bemused.

"That gift I don't have," she said wryly.

"I'll ask anyway. When will I be flatlined again?"

She turned somber.

"I don't think you will be. But I don't think you'll be 'Sparrow' for very much longer, either."

I thanked her and backed out through the hatchway, waiting until the corridor was as empty as before. I didn't know what would happen when I went back to Snipe. I was no trained bear; I could not perform on command and I was afraid I would always be inhibited with her.

But Huldah had been right, there was more involved. If Snipe ever found pleasure elsewhere, I never knew it. She seemed content with me, though it took her a while to soothe my worries over an inferiority I could not even describe. Then it occurred to me I had my own barrier, one she could never breach. I would live a thousand years or more while she was condemned to an ordinary lifetime. She would flutter briefly around the candle but would be gone generations before the flame guttered out.

But she never complained, and because she didn't, I loved her all the more.

A few sleep periods after I had talked to Huldah, Snipe woke me gently and murmured, "You were having a nightmare."

I lay there in the hammock, sweating and trying to put together the pieces of a dream, knowing they really hadn't been parts of a dream at all, they had been more shreds of returning memory.

It wasn't of the ship this time, nor of shipmates generations in the past. It was of ancient Earth, and just remembering what I had seen in my distorted slumber made my eyes tear.

There had been huge cities clogged with throngs of people and there were ribbons of stone with small vehicles traveling on them. There were parks and oceans, lakes and streams and mountains and I remembered wishing that somehow Crow was with me so he could see it all firsthand. I was both a participant in the "dream" and an observer of it though, strangely, this time I could not remember my name. In fact, I could remember nothing of myself beyond—

I was in a Rover traveling on one of the ribbons of stone through a countryside so beautiful it made me want to cry. It was a late summer day, the drought-stricken hills like loaves of light-brown toast on either side. I could feel the wind against my face because the vehicle had no top, and there was a girl beside me whom I glanced at from time to time but who resembled nobody I was to meet later on the *Astron*. She was very pretty and very young.

The ribbon of stone curved over a hill and then straightened out as it approached a bay, alive with the white sails of distant boats and, closer by the shore, floating houses tied to piers that jutted out into the water. Crow would love this, I thought, once again in my role as observer. It far outdid the ancient city of Venice that he had programmed for his compartment.

There was a thin veil of sound in the dream—the wail of the wind itself, the noise of other vehicles as they warned one another of passing, a murmur from the distant, floating houses. I remembered wondering who I was and what I was doing there but my mind was blank.

It happened very suddenly. The girl beside me said something; I turned to look at her and almost missed seeing the small animal that scampered in front of the vehicle. I pressed my foot on the brake, we skidded, the Rover canted and rose above us and both I and the girl were catapulted through the air and onto the ground a few meters away.

I lay there, feeling the broken bones in my rib cage when I tried to breathe, embarrassed because I had soiled my clothing. My face hurt; I reached up to touch it and felt my broken nose. My hands were bloody when I took them away. I twisted slightly so I could see the girl, then looked away, regretting that I hadn't died as quickly.

It was another artificial reality, I thought in my dream, then realized with horror that it wasn't, that it had all happened in real time and a very real place. It was half an hour before I heard the wail of sirens and another dozen before I came out of the anesthetic and a doctor asked me who I was.

I could not remember and then he told me that I was seventeen years old and a student at a college whose name meant nothing to me and that my own name was—

But then the "dream" was jumbled and gone and I was in my hammock on board the *Astron,* holding onto Snipe while she stroked my head and my heartbeat gradually slowed.

I remembered nothing more but I knew without checking that that was the first time I had been flatlined, that it had happened naturally, that nobody had caused it.

And that some months later, in my lifetime in the "dream," I would regain all my memories and live my life as before.

25

The mutineers met again a few time periods later in the cave overlooking the forest. This time I felt like one of them, a plotter against the Captain, a man with a price on his head. I had begun to dream of ancient Earth and wondered how many shared the same dream and what I could say to persuade them if they didn't. Crow, Loon, Ophelia, Snipe, and I were in the mutiny together and I felt a warmth and bonding with them I had never felt before. I loved them all and would have given my life for any of them.

I had yet to learn that, at their highest levels, revolutions and mutinies inspire noble sentiments while at their lowest, they merely act as aphrodisiacs.

But that, I would find out in the weeks to come. What I realized at the second meeting was that instead of losing my purpose in life, I had found one that was both immediate and tangible: to seize the ship from the Captain and return to the planet from which we had come.

The only thing I didn't know was how it was all supposed to happen. To my amazement, the others didn't seem to know, either.

"I've been talking to Grebe," I said. "And Ibis."

"I've already talked to Ibis," Loon interrupted importantly. "She's one of us."

Ophelia and Crow stared at us and I shut up, feeling my

enthusiasm suddenly drain away. Loon and I had sounded very young, very amateurish, and I remembered before they told me that this wasn't a game, that it was deadly serious and lives could be lost, *had* been lost.

Ophelia nodded at Loon. "I can probably trust you about Ibis." Then to me: "What did you tell Grebe?" She was deceptively casual.

"Not much . . . really," I said, chastened.

"What did you—sense—about him that made you approach him in the first place?"

But, of course, I had "sensed" nothing about him. He had simply struck me as one who might be interested, so I had checked on him for the group.

"It won't be just your life, Sparrow," Crow said quietly. "It would be ours as well."

"You need as many of the crew on your side as you can get," I said, angry. "That means you're going to have to take chances." And then: "You wanted me to join you—what do you want me to do? Sit in a corner and try and remember something that happened two thousand years ago?"

"What we want you to do is to be friends with the Captain," Ophelia said carefully.

I stared. I had been friendly with the Captain in the past—as much as anybody in the crew aside from Abel and other informers—and the mutineers had done everything they possibly could to destroy that friendship.

Snipe touched my hand. "But you didn't know what was at stake then."

"You're reading me," I accused once again.

"It was your expression, Sparrow."

"We need somebody who's close to the Captain," Crow cut in.

Getting close to the Captain would be walking into the lion's den. I had avoided him as much as possible during the past few weeks, afraid he could tell by what I said or how I looked that I had joined the revolt against him.

I must have gone pale, because all of them tried to reassure me. Ophelia waited until they were quiet, then presented her own arguments.

"The Captain knows you've been approached before by us—and that you turned us down. And he likes you, he's interested in you."

"Of course he's interested in me. He makes the decision when it's time to flatline me."

"You can forestall that," Snipe said. "You know the signs that he'll be looking for."

I shivered. "He knows me, he's known me for thousands of years longer than he's known any of you. He can read me easier than you can."

Ophelia frowned, disappointed that I wasn't more enthusiastic. But she had been used to Hamlet and whatever I was in this lifetime, I wasn't Hamlet.

"You know him as well."

"I don't remember anything from one personality to another," I objected. "When I first met him, as 'Sparrow,' it really was for the first time."

"Are you so sure you remember nothing of him from before?"

I started to answer, then the words dried in my throat. To be truthful, the Captain had never seemed a complete stranger to me.

"It will be risky," I said lamely.

Ophelia shrugged. "It's even riskier to continue avoiding him."

I sat there in a sweaty silence, weighing all the alternatives, until Snipe said, "You're the logical choice, Sparrow. If you stay away, he'll suspect that something is wrong. Then it will be even more dangerous for you."

"What do you want me to do?" I murmured.

Ophelia looked thoughtful. "Just listen to whatever he says."

"I wouldn't dare ask him any leading questions."

"Nobody asked you to. But he'll say more than he thinks he's saying."

True enough, I thought. And so would I.

*   *   *

For a while, life went on as usual, though I could feel an increased tension in the crew. It wasn't so much what crew members talked about as what they didn't. Nobody complained openly about the *Astron*'s course change into the Dark or offered any bitter comments about the Captain. We were all acting as if we were in one of Snipe's plays, though our only audience was each other. Thrush, who had apparently guessed what was happening, enjoyed it immensely.

There were unanswered questions about Thrush and I promised myself that sometime I would answer them. Did he know he might live forever? Did he know he was the Captain's son? And what had been the Captain's purpose in fathering him? It couldn't have been the desire for immortality that most people seek when they have children: He already had that. For a while I spent as much time watching Thrush as he did watching me, but his occasional dinner with the Captain seemed a formality and I saw few other signs of familial friendliness. The Captain knew but apparently Thrush did not.

He and I took pains to avoid each other, with one exception: Thrush was now a frequent fixture in Exploration, practicing at the terminal pad. There were even times when I admitted he was as proficient a fingerman as I. But to what purpose, I had no idea.

I had been only casually friendly with other members of the crew, but now spent more time with Jay and Finch from Communications and Grebe from Maintenance. Jay and Finch were my age—"Sparrow's" age—and boasted a lot, telling me more about attitudes in Communications than I could ever have discovered by direct questioning. I was also becoming more adept at recognizing members of the "new" crew, not so much by how they related to me but by how they related to each other. Jay and Finch roughhoused quite a bit and got into more than one argument with each other, a dead giveaway that they were of older stock. I felt more comfortable with them than with many members of the new crew and we got along fine.

Grebe was a huge hulk of a man, as careful with his strength as Crow was with his. Along with Wren, he spent much of his time playing with Cuzco in the nursery; at least, they were there every time I dropped by to see K2. New crew, I thought, not only because of their gentleness but because they could sense Cuzco's moods and needs. In any squalling pile-up in a corner, they knew exactly where Cuzco was and whether or not she needed rescuing. And Cuzco knew when they were coming to visit while they were still floating through the outside corridor.

I liked Grebe and Wren a lot.

Corin had taken over Tybalt's role in Exploration, though I thought he catered too much to Thrush. Then it occurred to me that perhaps I was jealous. Apparently that occurred to Corin as well. I was soon invited into the small office for a little conversation and smoke. Corin had taken on many of Tybalt's personality quirks, though he never went so far as to adopt a belief in Tybalt's aliens.

"You miss Tybalt a lot, don't you?" he once asked.

I had just taken a puff and was holding in my breath, so I merely nodded.

"He was the best team leader we ever had," Corin said. There was a touch of sadness in his voice that I noted with approval.

He went on to praise Tybalt's good points and comment with humor on his failings.

"When you come down to it," I said, "he really only had one fault: He believed in monsters."

"He didn't believe in them enough," Corin said darkly.

I was becoming fond of Corin, though nobody would ever completely replace Tybalt in my affections. Then a sixth sense warned me and I put my emotions in check. There had been a time when I was fond of Thrush, too.

Within a month the lines were drawn and I guessed the

choosing of sides was almost complete. The tension was palpable. What would happen now, nobody seemed quite sure. Refuse to go on shift? Somehow that didn't seem to be what was needed.

Or what would work.

I finally reestablished contact with the Captain when I reported to him on inventories of life-support supplies on board. The report wasn't complete but I knew I didn't dare wait any longer or there would be questions as to why I had stayed away and whether I was still upset about Tybalt and Noah. I was—I always would be—but I couldn't afford to show it.

As always, he was standing in front of the enormous port, looking at a view of the galaxy that was overwhelming in its beauty. It was his standard view of Outside, a view the rest of us seldom saw: a computer-enhanced portrait alive with reds and greens and purples with vast streams of gas arcing through the middle, obscuring even greater wonders.

He turned and nodded when Banquo announced me. Noting the slates in my hand, he said, "Escalus, get Sparrow half a dozen blanks." I handed over the computations, then paused to admire the view. It was one I had never seen before and the Captain motioned for me to come closer.

"It's a computer simulation of the Great Wall, Sparrow."

Aside from the beauty of color and composition, I could make no sense of it at all.

"The great what, sir?"

"It's a wall of galaxies—half a billion light-years long, a quarter billion light-years wide, and fifteen million light-years thick." He floated closer to the port and pointed out three largely empty areas. "Did you know there were holes in the universe, Sparrow?"

How many times had he looked at Outside? I wondered. Yet he still took the same pleasure in it.

He drifted back to his desk and touched its terminal pad.

The scene faded, to be replaced by an angry splotch of color against a field of stars, with filaments of green and yellow gases splashing out from a small spot of white at the center.

"That's the remnants of the Bevis supernova, a star that exploded a thousand years ago."

It was beautiful; but for me, at least, it was an empty beauty. I didn't know what to say. His hand touched the pad again and probably the most spectacular view of all appeared.

"That's M2O," the Captain said with a touch of awe, "the Triffid nebula—as seen from Earth. If God's anyplace, I think He's there."

I stared at the swirl of colorful gases and tried to match it up with the view from the hangar deck. The most we ever saw were fields of crystal with very little color or dimension. They had their own beauty, but it was a quiet, cold, and distant beauty—the beauty of reality. I wondered if the Captain ever looked at the stars like that, but I knew he didn't. Nor did he see the Dark as we saw it, an area of emptiness as treacherous as any sea of quicksand on ancient Earth. He saw only the fire and the color and the possibilities in the star systems on the other side.

Something about the Captain's fascination struck me as odd and later, when I was alone with the computer, I researched it. The closest I could come to a name for it was "rapture of the deep," which deep-sea divers occasionally suffered from on Earth—the desire to go on and on, ever deeper into the sea. It was a hallucinogenic effect caused by the nitrogen in the bloodstream under conditions of high pressure.

I had no idea what caused its equivalent in the Captain, and more important, I knew of no way to cure it.

Another view suddenly appeared beyond the port and then another and still another.

"You don't see their beauty, do you Sparrow?" the Captain asked.

"Yes," I said simply, "I do."

There was a thin disappointment in his voice.

"But there are things more beautiful to you."

It was my turn to pause, wondering just how important my answer might be.

"There are views I value as much, sir."

He laughed. "The compartment falsies? I understand the one Thrush programmed is quite remarkable."

He lightly stroked the terminal pad again. This time I gasped.

The star-filled landscapes of Outside vanished completely. What was just beyond the port now was a carefully tended garden. There was a large pine tree in the foreground, with a limb heavy with needles coming into the scene from below, then a sweep of raked white gravel that curved from the base of the port around to the right, vanishing behind a nearby hill. The hill itself was covered with green shrubs and dark bushes with deep-red flowers. Several large rocks had been carefully placed in the middle of the wide stream of pebbles to deliberately break up the expanse of white.

"It exists in reality?" I asked, wonderstruck.

"It's a replica of the garden scene just outside a window of the Adachi museum in western Honshu. Look them up, Sparrow." He leaned forward to touch something I hadn't noticed at first—two flower petals lying on the field of gravel—then swept his hand upward. "The petals establish a line that pulls your eye to the rocks *here* and then up the hill."

"It's beautiful," I murmured. "And . . . different."

He smiled slightly. "From the stars? Not really. They both represent purity in nature."

He talked to me then, not as if I were a seventeen-year-old technician, but as if I were a true peer. And for the first time, I realized that I was. Of all the people he had ever talked to on the *Astron,* he must have talked to me the most often. Me, and all the crewmen I had once been.

It was the only glimpse I ever had of Michael Kusaka the man, rather than "The Captain." He talked of a culture I knew little about, of his home in ancient Japan, of the growing of bonsai and the elaborate nature of rock gardens and even the writing of haiku, something I grew to love myself.

> Constellations change
> But the shining stars still dance
> My heart is peaceful

I wondered why he was allowing me this glimpse of himself and decided he was still trying to persuade me of . . . what? And was it only "Sparrow" he was trying to persuade?

We ate and sipped some wine and then it was time to go. I picked up the blank slates from Escalus and thanked the Captain, wavering once again between seeing him as personal friend and seeing him as the man who had condemned Noah and Tybalt. But my heart had hardened, and no overtures of friendship could change the fact that the Captain had lied, murdered, and was leading the *Astron* to disaster.

He stopped me at the hatchway and smiled. "There'll be no mutiny, Sparrow." I immediately thought of Ophelia and Snipe and the others and felt my face go white. He read my expression, as I suspected he would, and added, "Don't worry about any of your friends."

Mass, he had called Noah and Tybalt.

I was halfway through the shadow screen when he suddenly said: "Do you believe in free will, Sparrow?"

I had no idea what he was talking about.

"I don't know, sir. Do you?"

He shook his head sadly and said, "No, I don't. I can't."

When I finally left, I caught a last glimpse of the view just outside the port. It was the one of the Triffid nebula.

Later, I searched the computer for the simulation of the garden but never found it. I think after the Captain had shown it to me, he erased it from the computer's memory matrix.

The next time period the new birth allotments were announced and the mutiny collapsed. Twelve births were to be allowed, far more than any of us had expected. I had thought the allotment would be three, to make up for Heron, Noah, and Tybalt. I hadn't anticipated a replacement for Judah, thinking his death would compensate for the natural attrition of ship's resources.

The tension vanished overnight, replaced by excitement and a wave of gossip about who the birth mothers and potential fathers might be. There would be a dozen mothers and almost a hundred would-be fathers, almost two-thirds of the male members of the crew. The odds were the best they had been for generations.

On a personal basis, the birth allotments meant nothing to me. It would be a charade if I were on the list of those eligible and the Captain knew it. For the others, it would be their chance to play God. Few things mattered more—the chance to create life, to watch via 'scope as it grew from a tiny cluster of cells to a fetus and then a living creature with the capacity to talk and think and wriggle its fingers and toes, a sponge for love that would return as much as it was given. . . .

The crew had searched for life for two thousand years, but the only place they had ever found it was on the *Astron*. To have a part in its creation was of vastly more importance—at least for the moment—than a mutiny or even the ship's venture into the Dark.

The creation of life would happen in the next year. The death of the *Astron* and everybody on it was generations away. Then I realized I was whistling in the dark. Judah's death could mean that extinction would happen this generation.

It was Ophelia who reminded me of the inevitable. She came to see me in the Exploration office. Corin had left to read the list of nominations posted outside the Captain's compartment, and for a few moments we were alone.

"You realize the rate of attrition won't support the allotments."

"I know," I said, "I took the figures to the Captain."

"Did he even look at them?"

I shrugged. "Who knows?"

She was driving at something but as usual wanted me to come to the same conclusions myself.

"What's the alternative, if the ship can't support them?" I ran the figures over in my mind.

"If the ship can't support them, then future allotments will have to be cut drastically."

She shook her head.

"It's too good a weapon, Sparrow. He may need it again."

I frowned, wondering what she had in mind, then went cold when I realized what it was.

"Involuntary shortening of the lifespan," I said slowly. "Or possibly more trials."

"Given a choice, Kusaka would prefer more trials," she said bitterly. "They'd serve a dual purpose—eliminate malcontents and bring the size of the crew down to attrition levels."

She was about to say more but Corin had come back with a broad grin painted on his face. He slapped me on the back.

"We're both on the lists," he said. I faked a smile and congratulated him. When I turned back to Ophelia, she had disappeared.

Four time periods later, it was my turn with one of the birth mothers. The corridor was decorated with colored scrim and models of a cross inside an ovoid—the Great Egg. Other crew members were waiting outside the compartments, their expressions a combination of solemnity and joy. I felt uneasy and nervous. It was a rite of passage for them. It was also barbaric and I wondered what I could compare it to. Maybe to the erotic duties of priestesses in some ancient temples, except that most of those priestesses were prostitutes and the worshipers knew it, paying for their favors with temple offerings.

This was as close as the *Astron* came to having a religion, and coupling with the birth mothers would probably be as close as any of the crew members came to religious ecstasy.

The smell of rut was heavy in the passageway, the crew members obviously ready for what awaited them within. I nodded to Tern, first in line outside Swift's compartment, and mumbled a few words of encouragement to Loon, who looked vaguely uncertain about it all.

Huldah pushed her way through the crowd, handing out small bulbs of wine and wafers, blessing both the crew members and the forthcoming happy events. I watched her intently, trying to decide if there was a difference among the bulbs of wine she passed out. But however she did it, she was more clever than that. The contraceptive drugs in the food had been eliminated during the ritual period and I guessed the bulbs of wine Huldah gave some would-be fathers were laced with fast-acting versions of the drugs. Huldah would control who was fertile and who wasn't. But she never told me and I never knew for sure until much later.

She made no sign she knew me. I swallowed the wine and chewed the wafer, then slipped through the shadow screen after Hawk slipped out. He looked as if he had just seen God.

Pipit was inside, lying naked on a hammock draped with various colored waistcloths. I had been used to seeing her with natural eyebrows and lips and with her hair in plaits. Now her eyebrows had been plucked and her lips smeared with red. Her hair lay loose about her shoulders; her olive skin gleamed with scented oil. She was too young, I thought. No amount of rouge and oil could make her look like a temple priestess, only a caricature of one.

I didn't know whether she had seen me or not. She had closed her eyes and lay back in the hammock, waiting.

"Pipit," I said softly.

Her eyes jerked open and I managed a smile, which quickly faded. Her pupils were small dots in her brown eyes. Before the ceremony had begun, she had been drugged. I wasn't sure she even knew me.

"I'm not here to 'create life,' Pipit," I said quietly.

"Sparrow . . ."

I caught the expression on her face and took her in my arms to calm her trembling.

"I'm all right," she whispered. "I knew it would be like

this. Huldah told me. It's . . . the way it has to be done." She hesitated. "I feel honored," she lied.

"Huldah will make sure the father is Crow," I said to reassure her. His name had been on the list and I knew that Huldah would match him with her.

She shook her head.

"Thrush was the first to see me."

The Captain's gift to his son, I thought, my mind flooding with anger. And Thrush would hardly have accepted Huldah's bulb of wine.

"I'm sure Huldah can take care of it," I muttered.

She stiffened in my arms and moved away, deliberately brushing the hair away from her face so I could see her expression. Her voice was cold and remote.

"It has its own life, Sparrow."

I had been foolish to suggest abortion and suddenly wished I had slit Thrush's throat when I had the chance.

"What about Crow?"

"He'll take an interest."

He would have no matter who the father was.

"Is there anything you want?" I asked.

"For you to stay a little longer," she said in a suddenly seductive voice, opening her arms to me. I lightly stroked her shoulder, then shoved out through the shadow screen.

That sleep period, I couldn't bring myself to touch Snipe, not because she was new crew and I was old but because I couldn't stand the thought of coupling.

26

The ceremony lasted for two weeks. During the final period I went back to see Pipit again, forcing myself to float down the corridor with its red and green banners and the ubiquitous cross-and-ovoid. Crow had visited her several times, once in the role of potential birth father, but I had the nagging feeling she might need to talk to somebody not caught up in ritual.

The corridor was crowded as usual, but few even noticed me, their eyes viewing glories to come that I had no desire to see. I was three shadow screens away when I suddenly flattened against the bulkhead. Abel had slipped out of Pipit's compartment. Fortunately, he turned down the far end of the corridor and never saw me.

Then my suspicions began to grow; I wondered if he had ingratiated himself with the Captain once again and had been spying on Pipit. She had helped Huldah out in previous ceremonies and now she was an actress in this one, heavily drugged and probably willing to say anything. . . .

I suddenly felt chilled. Snipe had said that Abel was aware I knew my past. If he were back in the service of the Captain, this time period might be my last as "Sparrow." . . .

I slipped down the corridor after him, catching a glimpse of his fat figure as he floated around a distant corner. Half a dozen turns later, I frowned, confused as to where he was going. He wasn't on his way to the bridge or to the Captain's quarters. He seemed to be drifting aimlessly through the corridors, stopping briefly in the engine compartment to talk to a few crew members there, then pausing equally briefly in the gymnasium, where he nodded at some of those exercising. Each time he stopped, he was another level lower in the *Astron*. But I never guessed his destination until he got there.

Reduction.

He slipped in through the shadow screen and I hesitated for only a moment before following. He hadn't been spying on Pipit, he hadn't dropped by her compartment to pry for information he could carry back to the Captain. He had gone to say good-bye.

"Abel."

He had taken off his cling-tites and was seated on the ledge, gently massaging his feet. It would have been a homey scene if it weren't for the equipment, the smells, and most of all, the open storage chamber against the rear bulkhead, its interior choked with a rust-colored mist.

"Close the hatch, Sparrow, it turns off the peep screen." When I had dogged it down, he said, "I didn't expect to see you here."

His voice was friendly, almost avuncular, with none of the harshness and arrogance of the Abel I had known. Even the planes of his chubby face had softened. For the first time in perhaps years, he probably felt safe. Once inside Reduction, you were beyond anybody's authority, even the Captain's. Your future then was between you and the Great Egg.

I waved my hand around the compartment.

"Why?" I asked.

He shrugged.

"Your life's been too short this time for you to know the customs—at least to know them from the inside, where it counts. When your life is over, you go to Reduction. It's that simple."

"When your life is over," I repeated stupidly.

"When that work of art you call your life is complete, when

one more brush stroke won't make a bit of difference." He looked somber. "When there's nothing to look forward to, when you can no longer help the ship or its crew, when your friends and your lovers are gone . . ."

He shook his head as I started to object.

"No false emotions, Sparrow. You've never liked me, you weren't supposed to. If you had, I wouldn't have been nearly as effective. As it is, there's only one last thing I can do." He suddenly smiled and winked and with that there was nothing left to remind me of the old Abel. "Cheat the Captain."

"I don't—"

He stripped off his halter and threw it in a waste chute. He was now naked, a fat old man who somehow hadn't shed his dignity with his clothing.

"I'm surprised you haven't guessed—or that Ophelia hasn't told you."

"Trials," I said.

He nodded. "There'll be much less resistance to them, at least for right now. And I was never . . . popular."

"On what charges?" I wanted to dissuade him from using the chamber, though I knew that if Abel went to trial, the Captain would be merciless.

"The right one, of course. Treason. I worked with Noah, the Captain must have guessed that—Noah and I were very close when we were younger. I never thought the arguments between us were convincing but I had to risk it. We needed somebody who could establish a rapport with Kusaka."

He cocked his head.

"I understand you're to succeed me. Dangerous job, Sparrow, especially for you. He's not an easy man to know. Or like."

He wrapped his flabby arms around his chest, trying to shield himself from the compartment chill. He glanced at the mist-filled chamber; I guessed it would be warm and comfortable once inside and he would merely slip away.

"There's nothing I can say?" I asked, feeling miserable.

This was an entirely new and likable Abel and I would know him for only a few minutes.

"Any way of dying is unpleasant, Sparrow, but the chamber is less unpleasant than most. And I'll still be with you." He deliberately made a joke of it. "Look for me at breakfast."

I thought of how much skill it must have taken to be humble and obsequious before the Captain and then protect what little influence he had acquired by being antagonistic to the crew. He had sacrificed any chance of making friends and in the end was willing to sacrifice his life as well.

"You were the greatest actor on board," I said. I meant it in a light vein but there was a note of sincerity to it that he found flattering.

"Why, thank you, Sparrow—that's nice of you to say."

He floated over to the chamber and tentatively dabbled a hand in the mist.

"What happens?" I asked, curious.

He was suddenly reticent.

"It's painless for me but I wouldn't watch if I were you."

I had to ask.

"You never told the Captain."

"Of your awareness? No, of course not."

The hand he had put in the mist now looked pale, almost translucent. I began to sweat, despite the chill of the compartment.

"Why hasn't anybody ever told me about myself?"

His expression became serious.

"We wanted you to remember, but at your own speed. Have you ever wondered what it would be like to recall all your lifetimes at once? A hundred different people live inside you, Sparrow. You'd have to pick one as the dominant personality and I imagine the others would object."

I had thought about that once before but didn't want to worry about it now.

"You ran the mutiny?" I asked.

He shook his head.

"Hardly. As much as anybody could be said to run it, I

suppose it's been run by you. You're the oldest living member, you've been one from the very beginning."

He noticed the stricken expression on my face and hastened to reassure me.

"That's only in a matter of speaking, Sparrow. Over the years, you've been the heart and soul of it but you've never had much of a role in the planning from generation to generation." His voice turned grim. "You've always been a member, but never for very long."

I felt uneasy.

"That's the trigger for flatlining, isn't it? When the Captain finds out."

He nodded. "One of them. Usually you're not urged to join unless it looks as if you've had a breakthrough, as if you might remember something important. And then you have to be prepared. We were in a hurry this time because of the Dark. . . ."

His voice trailed off. Neither of us had anything more to say to each other.

"Don't look so glum, Sparrow—there's no point to me starring in a trial for the Captain. To be honest, he's always frightened me. He's too inventive when it comes to ways of dying."

He thrust a foot into the swirling mist.

"I've said my good-byes to Huldah but give my love to Ophelia. Just the way it sounds. Old men have their fantasies, too."

He stepped into the chamber and let the thick mist wrap around him like a blanket. I had a glimpse of a peaceful face just before he made his final request.

"Privacy, Sparrow."

I turned my back, undogged the hatch and slipped out. On my return to Exploration I noticed Banquo hurrying through the corridors leading to the lower levels.

But Abel could rest easy. Banquo would arrive much too late.

*　　*　　*

There were no drills now, no demands for data, no expectations of a new planetary landing in another two years or five. There wouldn't be another one for generations. The sea of blackness ahead of us steadily expanded with the familiar constellations slipping to our rear.

The uneasiness on board began to grow again. The birth allotments had been only a brief respite from the growing fear of the Dark. Ophelia and the other members of our cell wondered when the Captain would realize that if the crew couldn't be bought, it might be intimidated. There would be another flurry of excitement nine months in the future when the birth mothers delivered, and after that . . .

After that, there would be no future, and we could expect more crew members to choose to die as Judah had.

But meanwhile Crow and I spent more time on the hangar deck running through the various training projections, this time more for entertainment than for knowledge we would never use. At other times Crow tinkered with the falsie for his compartment, reprogramming the images of the people in the square below and adding more rocket trails to the sky.

Eventually, even that palled. We still held drills but only Portia and Quince were serious about them. The rest of us were halfhearted, especially about the EVA maneuvers. Trainees were increasingly reluctant to go on them and Loon, predictably, was the first to refuse outright.

I could understand why. It was one thing to go into an Outside filled with stars. It was quite another when the only stars were behind the ship and ahead of you was a smothering blackness. Hawk and Eagle were the next to refuse and after that all EVA exercises were canceled.

The mutiny slumbered along, the clandestine meetings shorter and shorter. Originally, there had been the camaraderie of conspiracy, debates about how new members were to be recruited and power seized. It was easy to guess who the new recruits were—they seemed to think their new role required them to couple enthusiastically with as many other would-be mutineers as possible. Then the secret sessions deteriorated into bitching about the Captain and finally to round-robins of complaints about ship life in general.

It was my idea to turn the mutiny into a game, to make it fun as well as good training. I gave our cell a name—the Judah cell—and we drew assignments, the object being to find out as much as we could about the person whose name we drew. How they spent their shifts, what they ate at meals, who they saw in their free time and, if they happened to have a liaison with another crew member, exactly what they did.

Known members of your own cell weren't excluded, and the sport came when you got up at a meeting and told everything you had found out about a fellow cell member. Frienships were shattered, but only for the moment, and more than once a small bacchanal ensued when all was revealed.

I once drew Snipe's name but wisely refused to play with her as the quarry. Later I drew Loon's and reported at great length on his dalliances among the crew, not only with Ibis and her girlfriend but with Swallow and Grouse in Communications and with Crane in Maintenance. I almost—but not quite—felt ashamed when my report left him red-faced with embarrassment, while Crow clutched a nearby hammock and roared with laughter.

The next name I drew as part of the game was a member of another cell—Corin, my team leader in Exploration. Ophelia told me he had been a member of the mutiny long before she and Noah first tried to recruit me. My respect for him as a team leader had grown enormously and we had become friendly, frequently joking on shift or sharing smoke in his office.

I suddenly felt uneasy about my spying. The game had turned serious.

Now I found myself listening more than I talked. I quickly learned the difference between casual listening, when you concentrate more on what you're going to say next than on what the other person is telling you, and a professional awareness of content and nuance.

Corin led an unexciting life, vacillating between partnering with Gull in Communications and Raven in Maintenance. He worked out regularly in the gymnasium, though he never seemed able to lose the ridge of fat that circled his waist. He was old crew, not new, which meant he was even more of a mystery to the other members of my cell than he was to me.

His one character flaw wasn't immediately obvious—he simply took too much interest in crew members whom I knew were mutineers. He listened as carefully to me as I listened to him and was as difficult to follow about the ship as I knew I was. I had no desire for anyone to trace me to the weekly meetings in the cave compartment and it quickly became apparent that Corin also had appointments that he wished no one to know about.

I told what I knew about him at a cell meeting, careful not to draw conclusions. Loon looked bored and said, "Who cares if he has another life?"

But Snipe listened carefully to what I had to say. "Corin's an accomplished actor. I've watched him in a number of historicals. He could be acting now."

Ophelia frowned. "Those with contacts to other cells, ask for further information on him."

But on a ship where everybody normally knew everything about everybody else, few seemed to know much about Corin.

During the next dozen time periods, I finally tracked Corin to a remote corridor where he disappeared. The next time I followed him there, I allowed him just enough of a lead so he couldn't accuse me of stalking him, rounded the corner, and ran into Crow.

I guessed why he was there and asked, "Who did you draw?"

"Banquo."

We stared at each other, our suspicions confirmed. Both Banquo and Corin had come to this corridor and disappeared, no doubt together. We floated down it, glancing into empty compartments. It was Crow who mustered the courage to barge through the occasional shadow screen pretending he was giddy on smoke, then back out with apologies. Not many compartments were occupied; life was receding from this corridor, and soon it would be abandoned.

I hesitated at the large hatch closing off one of the two vacant tubes that had made up the original *Astron*.

"It's sealed," Crow said, dismissing it. "There's no life support in the deserted tubes anyway."

I took his words on faith but tugged halfheartedly at the wheel that secured the hatch, more out of curiosity than in any expectation it would open. It gave and when I pulled harder, the hatch silently turned on its hinges. There was no sudden hiss and while the air felt chilly, it certainly wasn't the cold of outer space.

"Small leaks," I guessed. "Given enough time, the pressure would have equalized and there would be enough heat transfer to warm it."

We peered in, saw nothing, then drifted through, closing the hatch quietly behind us and shivering in the chilly darkness. From one of the compartments there was the flicker of a glow tube and the soft murmur of voices. Only two, I decided after a moment. Corin and Banquo.

"Can you hear what they're saying?" Crow whispered. I shook my head and he said, "We should get closer." He started to drift toward the light.

I grabbed his arm. "Maybe they're almost through."

He hesitated, then followed me back out the hatch. We had barely made it into the next corridor when we heard Banquo and Corin leave.

"I wonder what they talked about," Crow mused.

"About us," I said. "About other cells." I was angry because in my mind I had built Corin up as something of a replacement for Tybalt. Now I felt like a fool. "He's a good listener. After this, his cell members will have to be careful what he hears."

*   *   *

Crow and I came back the next time period, eager for a chance to explore. We lingered a moment at the end of the deserted passageway, then slipped unseen through the hatchway into Section Two of the *Astron,* a primary residence tube that hadn't been in use for at least five hundred years.

The air was still—I could feel no stray currents against my face—and smelled strange. I suspected it was fresher than the air in the main tube, which was fouled by body odors and the stink of oil. Crow had brought a portable glow lamp and we made our way slowly down the corridor, stopping briefly in the compartment where Banquo had met with Corin. Some threads had adhered to the bulkhead where one of them had bumped into it, and their cling-tites had left faint marks on the oil-and-dust-caked deck.

There wasn't a great deal to see. When the crew finally deserted Section Two, they hadn't left much behind. Some lengths of worn tether line; a dirty food tray that somebody had thrown in a corner, the traces of food paste dried to a black scab; a soiled waistcloth; a string tapestry still sealed to one of the bulkheads . . .

In one compartment, I made a genuine find—a discarded volume of fiction, clinging by its magnetic headband to the underside of a ledge. Its pages crumbled when I opened it and we hurriedly left to avoid breathing the dust. In another, I noticed a terminal pad and drifted over to it.

Crow said, "If it works, you'll be talking to ghosts." I shrugged and positioned my palm on the still-resilient pad. "Let's see what happens."

I pressed, and much to my amazement the power light flickered on. The computer in Section Two was a slave to the one in the main tube and drew little power of its own. When the tube had been sealed off, apparently no one had thought to disconnect it. Curious, I retrieved the compartment inventory and turned on the falsie.

We were suddenly surrounded by phantoms, gray buildings

that towered into gray clouds overhead, gray storefronts with displays of gray dresses and suits and gray people walking by. There was no color and the forms were insubstantial and wavering; I could see the bulkheads through them and Crow watching me as I worked the pad.

"There's not enough power," I said. "Even if there were, it's not a very imaginative falsie."

"Street scene," Crow sniffed, playing the critic. "We've become more sophisticated since then."

But what city? And what street? And why did it seem so familiar?

I flicked it off and we continued down the corridor, pausing briefly in what was left of Section Two's Hydroponics compartment. The grow lights had been ripped out, probably as spares for those in the main tube, leaving only the metal troughs and the plastic mesh. Some dried roots stuck in the plastic crumbled to powder when I touched them. I shivered, and not from the chill.

Crow was right, there were ghosts all around us.

We drifted through a dozen more empty levels and found nothing. Finally Crow said, "Let's go back, I'm due on shift in an hour. There's nothing here."

I nodded and we retraced our steps. Three levels below the main one, I touched Crow on the shoulder and floated down a short corridor to Section Two Communications, or what was left of it—an example of the *Astron*'s redundancy. Like the other equipment rooms, this one had been cannibalized, though not completely. The receivers that automatically scanned the cosmic haystack for possible indications of life had been robbed of their chips and wiring. What remained was a terminal pad and a viewing globe. The equipment connected to the globe hadn't been stripped. I could still access the Section Two computer.

"I'm cold," Crow said, shivering.

"Give me a minute."

I powered up the pad, wondering what I should retrieve in the globe, then chose the last dispatch that had been received from Earth. I had seen only the scrawled messages posted every few months or so outside Communications in the main tube. The bubbles of RF information were still spreading out from that remote planet and every now and then we would skim the surface of a faint message.

Crow was clenching his thighs together, a sure sign we couldn't spend much more time there. He would have to find a waste chute soon but there weren't any operating ones in this section. And there was no possibility of pissing in a corner and hoping it would puddle there and stay.

"Look," I said.

"*Damn* it," Crow groaned, and drifted over to see what I was pointing at in the globe. At first it was vague and insubstantial, then the words firmed up and became readable. The message was a religious one and fragmentary at that, in a language that seemed only dimly related to what we spoke on the *Astron*. There were no scientific references in it at all.

"For Christ's sake," Crow said, his bladder temporarily forgotten. "It's a plea for better crops."

I retrieved the previous messages and we read about wars and famines, strange plagues and political movements. As I went further back toward Launch there were occasional passing references to the *Astron* and finally the familiar litany of best wishes and brief messages from the descendants of relatives left behind.

"How many years have gone by?" I asked Crow.

It was an effort for him to break his concentration.

"What?"

"How many years have gone by on Earth? The difference in elapsed time on board ship and back there?"

I hadn't thought much about time dilation before, but it was vastly important now. We had traveled far enough at high velocities so there would be a substantial difference. The years on Earth would have slipped by much faster than those on board ship.

"Maybe ten thousand—give or take a century or two."

The ship was a static society; nothing had changed much

despite the steady deterioration of the ship itself and the decrease in the size of the crew. But on Earth governments had come and gone, wars had been fought, minor ice ages had covered parts of the Northern Hemisphere, the very continents had drifted another few feet apart.

It struck me that the dispatches we were reading had little in common with those filed over the past few years by the Communications division in the main tube. According to those, nobody had forgotten us, the governments that had combined to send us were still in existence, and there had been a steady stream of exhortations to venture even further into the deeps. . . .

"I can't hold it any longer," Crow groaned.

"It'd be a sure sign somebody was here," I murmured.

I hastily powered down and we hurried back to the main level, cracked the hatch to see if anybody was coming, then slipped through and headed for the nearest waste chute.

Back in my compartment, we sat in thoughtful silence on the hammock until finally Crow said, "Who wrote them, Sparrow?"

"The dispatches in Section Two?"

"No, the ones our own Communications division posted."

"Probably the Captain. Who else?"

When they got that last dispatch, had that ancient crew tried to mutiny? I wondered. That would have been a crisis point for them, one as significant as the death of Judah and going into the Dark were for us.

"What did it mean?" Crow asked. "That last dispatch?"

"I don't know—but taken together they mean the Captain has no real authority. The governments that sent us have vanished, there's nobody depending on us, there's no one awaiting our return." It suddenly struck me as both tragic and funny. "There is no Kingdom of Spain, Crow."

He didn't understand the reference. Then he glanced at my hands and frowned. "What's the matter, Sparrow?"

I was flexing my fingers, balling them into a fist, straightening them out one by one, then curling them into a fist again.

Ophelia had done the same thing when she tried to convince me of the uniqueness of life. Then she had claimed the only life in the universe was on the *Astron* and in "that thin green layer of scum" covering our home planet.

Now I wondered what had happened to life on Earth. Putting the dispatches from Section Two in chronological order showed that disaster had followed disaster, the population had declined to some small farmers, the government to some sort of priesthood. Had wars and plagues reduced them to that? Had there been irreversible changes in the ecosphere? Had life itself survived?

"We have to return," I said.

But I wasn't sure there was anything to return to.

Perhaps that thin green layer of scum covering Earth had vanished completely and now the only life in the entire universe was that on board the *Astron*.

Part Three

*Mark keeps looking for
a truth that fits his reality
Given our reality,
the truth doesn't fit.*
—Werner Erhard

27

Anybody in the cell could call a meeting. Crow and I called the next one. Once again we met in the cave compartment. Ophelia was the first to arrive, followed by Loon and Snipe. They looked at me, curious, but I kept my face carefully blank.

I made no move to turn on the shadow screen after they entered and they guessed something was wrong. Loon looked apprehensive, glanced at Crow for explanations, received none, and turned back to me, frowning. Ophelia started to complain, took another look at my face, and shut up. Snipe made a show of studying her fingernails. She didn't like surprises and she wasn't prepared to like this one.

A moment later, Grebe floated in, followed by little Quince and then Malachi from Engineering, a frail, elderly man with a sharp mind who had many friends among the old crew. I didn't have the "sense" that Snipe and Ophelia had, but I could observe and investigate and I knew with certainty that all three were members of other cells. If any of the others knew, they pretended not to.

Once they had made themselves comfortable, I drifted over to the hatch and sealed it. This was the first time we had ever met in a sealed compartment.

Ophelia was quicker than the others.

"You've discovered an informer," she said with dawning awareness.

I nodded. "Corin. He's one of the Captain's men."

There was a shocked silence.

"The Captain knows about us?" Loon was terrified.

I shrugged. "He's probably always known about some of you." I devoutly hoped that I wasn't included. "But he's tolerated the mutiny because it's had no real leader since Noah." I turned to Ophelia. "You said you could sense a traitor."

She paled. "Corin's old crew, we couldn't . . . sense him. He'd been a friend of Noah's."

So much for their overconfidence. Corin had spent years ingratiating himself with Noah. For what? I wondered. A pat on the head from the Captain? Assurance that he would be among the next selection of would-be fathers? Maybe. If there had been fewer birth mothers, the competition would have been much tighter this time.

But I had more to talk about than a computerman turned informer.

"All Corin knows is what his cell members tell him. That can work to our advantage. But Corin's not that important."

Snipe took offense. "Sparrow, don't play games with us."

I nodded in apology, then told them about the Communications compartment in Section Two and the last dispatches received from Earth. When I was through, nobody said anything. I felt irritated. I had done my share; now it was up to somebody else. Or maybe they didn't realize the significance of what I had just said.

"What it means is that the Captain has no authority," I said with as much emphasis as I could. "He can't continue the voyage in the name of the governments existing at the time of Launch. We've heard nothing in five hundred ship years. For all we know, there's nobody left on Earth. At the very least, there's no technological civilization with the ability to send messages."

I knew what they were thinking. Michael Kusaka had always been . . . The Captain. He had been The Captain all their lives and all of their mothers' lives and their grand-mothers' lives going back for as long as they could remember their *begats*. He had been the highest authority on board and a father figure as well. It was difficult to accept him as any-thing else, and because of that—despite the trials, despite the course change into the Dark—there had been an air of unre-ality about the mutiny. It had always been serious but it had also involved a certain amount of playacting.

Now the Captain had lost the backing of any higher au-thority and the mutiny was going to be played out in earnest. The stakes were very real and so were the penalties. Noah and Tybalt hadn't been condemned in any sort of legal pro-cess—they had been murdered. The difference was enormous and for the first time, everybody in the compartment realized that if we lost, they would pay the same price.

Still, nobody volunteered to comment. They were waiting for me, as if somehow I knew all the answers. I realized I had challenged the one natural leader there, Ophelia. She wouldn't offer advice now unless I asked her.

"What should we do about it?" I looked at her when I spoke, forcing her out of her silence.

She glanced at Loon. "What are the numbers?"

He stumbled over his words, his voice still choked with fear. "The Captain has perhaps thirty who will . . . follow him. Maybe a few less."

"Cato's loyal," Malachi warned. "And all of Cato's friends."

"Why?"

Malachi was as frightened as the rest but he was older and did a better job of hiding his fears.

"Cato would follow the Captain to hell if he had to. I'd try to talk to him but I know he wouldn't listen. It would be dangerous."

The others were probably much like Cato—unquestioningly loyal and devoted, if only because that relieved them of mak-ing their own decisions. Huldah's breeding program had left behind some dross. Then I reminded myself that I, too, had once been loyal and devoted.

There was another silence and again I thought Ophelia would lead the discussion. But she said nothing and next time I didn't wait as long before offering my opinion.

"The Captain still runs the ship," Grebe objected.

I shook my head. "He runs the computer and the computer points the ship in the direction the Captain wants it to go. But he doesn't run Life Support, he doesn't run Maintenance, he doesn't run Engineering. He sets course but he doesn't run the ship."

"You want us to threaten him?" Grebe looked at me as if I had just suggested it. "Sabotage the water supply for a few time periods, convince him he can't do without us?"

"That's foolish," Ophelia said acidly. "You'd find yourself going to Reduction very early."

Loon came up with the most telling argument. "The pellet guns—the Captain controls the armory."

There was another long silence and again they waited for me to offer suggestions, to say what they were thinking before they thought it. I glanced at Ophelia once more, wondering why she wasn't doing that. She stared back, silent, a faint smile on her face.

"The Captain's men are all old crew?" I asked Malachi.

"So far as I know."

It was a simple equation. New crew wouldn't use violence. Old crew could be talked into it. Huldah's gamble had been the kind you won completely or you didn't win at all.

"We can't do things piecemeal," I said at last. "We can't threaten the Captain with shutting off the water supply; we can't turn off the odor scrubbers in the ventilation system and wait for him to come to terms. We'd suffer as much as he. Whatever we do has to affect him primarily and it has to be something dramatic."

Crow had almost as much trouble talking as Loon had. "The Captain would see through any bluffs."

"I'm not talking about a bluff," I said.

"How far will the Captain go?" Quince asked. There was a hint of aggression in his voice and I smiled to myself. A little man who wasn't afraid of the odds.

I remembered the handball game and the Captain continuing to play with a broken finger.

"The Captain will do whatever he thinks is necessary."

All the time I was talking, I was sitting in judgment on myself. I knew I sounded rational and pragmatic, confident. But I also felt uneasy about it. I was doing what I considered Ophelia's job.

Snipe summed it up and we were suddenly back to the beginning.

"You haven't told us how we can run the ship without the Captain."

This time I didn't wait for Ophelia to answer, nor did I look to her for tacit permission to speak.

"The real question is, Can the Captain run the ship without us? And the answer is, He can't."

"And you have some ideas as to how we can?"

It was Ophelia, challenging me this time, but I had no more answers. They had known each other longer than I had, they knew the ship better than I did. "That's what you're going to figure out—you and Snipe and Malachi. How can we force the Captain to do what we want? If it's a threat, it has to be decisive." I hesitated. "We have to be prepared to carry it out, we can't bluff him."

Playing the part of leader was a heady feeling—and deceptive. I was anything but confident; I could think of problems that none of them had even imagined.

"You mentioned the Captain's store of pellet guns, Loon—try to find any others. Crow will help you." Then, to Grebe and Malachi: "Both of you have friends among those still loyal to the Captain. Talk to those who can be swayed."

Grebe looked unhappy. "That'll be risky."

"Very risky." I felt more grim than confident and let some of it show. "At the end, surprise will be all we have, and the Captain will know almost as much about what we're going to do as we do. Once the mutiny starts, we'll have to improvise. We won't be able to stop it and, I hope, neither will the Captain. But he'll try—and he'll use force. We have to be prepared for that."

All of them looked a little frightened, even Ophelia. I understood their feelings because I felt the same way. I was as dubious as they were, as frightened as they were, but I couldn't afford to show it. Right then they needed encouragement, and encouragement was all I really had to offer.

"When you look at it from space," I said gently, "the Earth is very blue, covered with shreds of clouds that are blinding white. It has deserts and mountains, plains and lakes, rivers and vast prairies. There's life under every rock and in every drop of water. It's home—and it's time to go back."

The Great Egg would forgive me my small lies and extravagant hopes. I opened the hatch and they slipped out, a little less frightened and more determined than they had been before my pep talk. Ophelia was the last to go and she left with a look of grim satisfaction on her face.

She had always wanted me to act like Hamlet and at last I had.

There had been a certain amount of euphoria in acting the leader. Deep within I still had doubts about our chances and the final outcome, but doubt weakens purpose and I didn't dare admit my doubts, even to myself. Nor did I dismiss Noah's conviction that buried someplace in my memories was the secret of returning to Earth without the Captain.

On the other hand, there was always the chance of jogging my memory. What was buried in it might also be buried in the computer's and I spent the next dozen time periods doing my best to find out what the computer might remember that I had forgotten.

Eagle had now taken my place at the terminal pads and I had taken Corin's, though Corin still put in more shift time than anybody. And Thrush was often huddled over a pad in the corner, researching nobody knew what, though sometimes I thought he was there as much to watch me as to dance with the computer. Work remained, including logging in the signatures of distant stars, estimating the chances of planetary systems and the limits of their CHZ's—continuously habitable zones. But urgency had fled.

I knew Corin's schedule as well as I knew my own, and committed to memory those periods when he bedded down with Gull or Raven and when he might elect to put in extra shift time in Exploration. Eagle was there as little as possible—as Crow and I once had, he had discovered the dubious pleasures of continuous rut. Thrush showed up frequently but never stayed when I was there alone.

Which left those periods when I was by myself. I spent them searching the computer's memory matrix. It was, as Huldah had warned, unreliable. The personal history of the crew and the generation-by-generation records of the ship itself were inconsistent, not so much in content but in method of recording and presentation. Operating techniques of individual fingermen varied as much as their handwriting and within each generation you could distinguish between the different crewmen who had logged data or modified files. But studying the memory matrix for the first five generations confirmed Noah's comment that no true records existed. It was like going from a solid-colored blanket to a patchwork quilt.

There were occasional gaps in the early records and, more important, frequent mention of a virus infecting the neural net toward the end of the first generation. Beginning with the sixth, the patchwork-quilt effect disappeared and data logged was once again consistent in presentation.

I followed the memory matrix into various side paths and retrieved information about specific crew members, diets on board, the steady shrinking of the crew itself, information about planets explored, and all the minutiae of shipboard life.

And then I stopped, startled, and took my hands off the pad, watching the viewing globe go blank without even being aware of it. I had expected some raggedness, some "scar tissue" in the ship's memory, but there were no real indications that the neural net had ever been attacked by a virus.

What I was actually looking at was a selective erasure and rewriting of the ship's history for the first five generations. Not only could I tell where the excisions had taken place, I could see that the same individual had logged much of the data throughout that first hundred-year period.

It was well done, the work of a master fingerman. And the only one who could have done it was the Captain. He had effectively wiped the slate clean for the first five generations and written his own history of the ship. What had really happened, I would probably never know. But I could guess.

He must have originally intended to plant the stories about the virus, then simply leave the record blank for the next five generations. Apparently he had changed his mind, erased all references to the first mutiny, and altered the information logged by following generations.

The Captain and I were still the only ones who knew what had happened. There were no records of a mutiny—any mutiny—in the matrix.

The next time I was alone, I did some more personal research and reviewed all mentions in the computer of the various crewmen I had once been. I also checked the access codes to see if anybody else had become fascinated by my life history. The codes were like a library card, listing the names of all the interested parties who had accessed certain files. There was only one such person, but he had been very thorough.

What Thrush had been researching was me.

He had retraced my own steps through the computer's maze of memories and now knew all the connecting links, all the names of the crewmen whose lives I once had led, all the roles I once had played. What chilled me was not that he had done it but the reasons why. He had known I was a phoenix all of his life. What more had he hoped to find out?

"You're working late, Sparrow."

The display in the viewing globe had vanished before Corin floated in. I jiggled my thumb slightly and a sheaf of figures appeared. I yawned and wiped my eyes with the back of my hand.

"Inventory, Captain's request."

The Captain hadn't requested any, but I doubted that Corin would bring the matter up with him; even if he did, I had flooded the Captain with so many lists and figures lately that he probably wouldn't recall whether he had requested more or not.

"I can't imagine he'd be in a hurry," Corin said easily. His face was more affable than usual, a ready cover for any suspicion beneath.

"Supplies on board versus attrition rates for at least the next two hundred years," I said. "It will have a big effect on the number of birth mothers for the next few generations. I thought he ought to know."

Corin's face became appropriately somber.

"Venturing into the Dark is the worst thing the Captain could have thought of," he said in a low voice. Since he was a member of a cell, and probably suspected I was as well, I knew he wanted me to dig my own grave a little deeper. His eyes were a little too innocent, and I knew if I left now he would check my personal code to see what I had been doing.

I mumbled something noncommittal, then changed the subject. "I understand Gower and Raven have decided to partner."

He should have known Raven better, but out of the corner of my eye I caught his sudden look of consternation.

"She never said—" And then he vanished back through the shadow screen, intent on finding Raven. Sex was very open on board and few gave it much thought. But partnering was respected and interfering with it was a reportable offense. Raven would laugh it off, and Corin would be relieved and no doubt linger to cement their relationship. If he ever came back to me about it, I could truthfully say it was only a rumor, that it wasn't my fault he had overreacted.

Once Corin was gone, I retrieved the access codes again and studied Thrush's fingerprints scattered through the matrix. He had been tracking me with the aid of the computer and I wondered why. Then the answer was so obvious I couldn't believe it hadn't occurred to me before.

Thrush wanted to know what was buried in my memories as badly as the others did.

Two time periods later I was once again invited to the Captain's quarters for dinner. I had seen quite a bit of him lately, but primarily as a harassed crew member working hard on lists of information he had wanted or information I thought he ought to see. I had made sure our meetings weren't social; I hadn't wanted to give him time to notice my increasing nervousness when I was around him or my efforts to keep him from seeing that the "Sparrow" of six months before and the "Sparrow" of right now had become two different people.

I was a good actor but I was no miracle worker. This time our meeting would be social and this time he *would* see.

It didn't occur to me that he might not bother to look.

I showed up a few minutes early and was waved inside by a bored Banquo, who took only a moment to check my waistcloth for hidden weapons—a procedure now standard.

A few meters into the huge compartment I stopped. My heart felt as if somebody was holding it in his hands and had started to squeeze. The Captain was by the port, as I expected he would be. But he wasn't alone. Thrush was by his side and the Captain had rested his hand lightly on Thrush's shoulder while pointing out to him the wonders of a nebula that lay just beyond the glass.

He felt the air currents when I came in and turned slightly, saying: "Come over here, Sparrow, I want you to see this, too."

The sight was beautiful, as always. This time it was a well-defined explosion of orange-colored clouds around a few central stars, then more stars and bright streamers of gas half hidden by the hazy puffs of orange.

"NGC 2237," the Captain said quietly. "The Rosette nebula, as seen from Earth thousands of years ago."

I could understand the name. It looked like a huge interstellar flower, the petals of gas clearly defined around the stamens of stars in the center.

"Beautiful," Thrush breathed.

I felt my skin crawl. I was supposed to be above it all, a dispassionate observer who saw and noted everything the Captain did or said while never forgetting that I was a young tech assistant who idolized him.

But at the moment I was anything but dispassionate. To my dismay, I was intensely jealous of Thrush. Every other time I had been with the Captain, I was the one he took to the top of the mountain to be shown the wonders of the world below. I was the one whose shoulder he touched, the one he tried to impress with the beauty that lay just beyond the port.

"What do you think, Sparrow?"

I could sense him watching me, gauging my reactions and comparing them to those of Thrush. Or so I thought.

"I think it's gorgeous," I said. That much, I didn't have to pretend. The view was always gorgeous. It just wasn't real.

Escalus had outdone himself on the meal and the conversation swirled about me for five minutes before I gave up concentrating on the texture and spices and started to pay attention to what was being said.

"The other side," Thrush was saying with great conviction. "The population of older stars is denser there—naturally there has to be a greater chance of finding life."

The Captain's eyes glowed.

"I estimate we'll find it within a dozen generations at most." He glanced over at me. "Don't you agree, Sparrow?" Then he shook his head in mock regret. "But I forgot. You don't think we'll find anything at all."

"I never said that," I defended myself.

"But you think that," the Captain insisted. Both he and Thrush were staring at me with amusement and I remembered an image pic of two wolves stalking their prey just before the kill. I suddenly realized they had made common cause.

"No," I lied, "I don't necessarily think that at all."

"Sparrow's an optimist by nature," Thrush said, smirking. When he wasn't catering to the Captain, Thrush was studying me, and I knew he was thinking of ways to use me. I tried hard to hide my hatred of Thrush and at the same time flatter the Captain by paying as much attention to him as I could. But I suspected it was a losing game, though I couldn't quite determine when I had lost it.

"You'll be a hero when we return," the Captain said.

He and Thrush had wandered back to the port and I hastened to join them, still feeling twinges of jealousy over Thrush's taking of my place. Thrush, I noted, seemed to have blossomed under the Captain's touch. Then I felt the chills start. *When we return.* As if the Captain knew Thrush might still be alive then.

Before I had arrived, the Captain must have confirmed Thrush's paternity. Now Thrush knew he was the Captain's son and would live forever—it was the only thing that could account for his smugness.

In return, the Captain got an ally. One without scruples, one who was capable of murder, one who would do whatever the Captain wanted.

We talked some more and gazed in wonder at views of the Ring and Veil nebulas and finally a view of the Dark, that vast sea of nothingness that stretched before us with a faint suggestion of stars on the other side, like phosphorescent sands on a distant beach. I shivered inside, as always feeling small and insignificant in a tiny world that extended not more than five hundred meters in any direction. I was surrounded by the ship's company but I knew each and every one of the fewer than three hundred of them, and they were no protection at all against the sudden ache of loneliness I felt.

All the time I floated nervously around the compartment, sometimes leaving Thrush and the Captain alone by the port and returning to the table, ostensibly for another tidbit of food but in reality trying to see into the sleeping quarters just beyond. Loon had mentioned the Captain's armory; if it was anyplace, it had to be there. But Escalus was wary and I glimpsed nothing but a huge compartment filled with row after row of what looked like filing cabinets. I had heard it was forbidden for anybody to enter, even Escalus.

Then it was time to go. The Captain gave me a perfunctory handshake but gripped Thrush by the arm and patted him lightly on the back. It took an effort to fight my own hurt and resentment. I finally had to accept that my intellectual and emotional responses to the Captain were now vastly different. He had been responsible for the deaths of Noah and Tybalt and by extension, Abel, and he had acknowledged the paternity of my worst enemy on board.

And yet . . .

To me, he would always be The Captain. When I was fresh from sick bay he had imprinted me as thoroughly as any farmer had ever imprinted a duckling. I had become a mutineer, but I would always stand in awe of him, I would always wish for his touch on my arm, his light pat on my back, even the occasional scathing remark reminding me that I was very young and he was very concerned.

But when I left, I knew that things had changed forever. For a long time and for reasons I didn't understand, I had been important to the Captain. Now I was no longer important—and, I knew, I was much closer to being flatlined.

For whatever reason, the Captain could now do without me.

That sleep period Snipe asked no questions but took me in her arms and murmured in my ear and stroked my head and did what she could to reassure me.

But rejection was a small death at best. I was afraid a much larger one loomed just a few time periods away.

28

Things get worse before they get better. During the next few time periods they got much worse. The first indication I had of just how much worse was when a pale Loon told me that some of the Captain's men were holding target practice on the hangar deck.

I drifted up and watched half a dozen crewmen practice with pellet guns under the watchful eye of Cato. I thought of Tybalt when he had tried to instruct us before the landing on Aquinas II. I wondered if any of Cato's recruits would be reluctant to fire at the projection of an alien. Then I took another look and felt my stomach lurch. It wasn't an alien they were firing at, it was a crude projection of a fellow crewman.

I lingered for a few minutes and discovered there wasn't much difference between the old crew and the new after all. All but one of Cato's men missed the target and I was sure that the one who hit it, a young Communications tech named Robin, hit it by accident. But what interested me as much as the target practice itself was that all of them had tied a strip of red cloth around their upper arms. It was more of a uniform than anybody else wore; as a result the Captain's men stood out from the other crew members and there was an obvious camaraderie among them.

I kicked over to Cato, his mouth a thin line, his face shining with sweat.

"Captain's orders?" I asked.

He nodded but didn't want to talk and seemed more unfriendly than usual. It was obvious that I was now one of the enemy. He drilled his men for another half hour, with mixed results. If the mutineers were amateurish, I consoled myself, then so were the Captain's men.

"Do you think they'll actually fire on a fellow crewman?" I asked Cato when the drill was over.

He glared at me and growled, "They'll do what the Captain orders."

The next practice session, the Captain was on hand to watch and give a brief speech about protecting the integrity of the mission and the ship. The marksmanship improved dramatically. Would they willingly take the life of a fellow crewman? I had my doubts. Would they do their best to carry out the Captain's orders? Sometime soon there would be a conflict and they would have to choose between the two.

I still had no overall plan of my own, though somewhere in the back of my head I knew it would involve a confrontation with the Captain. Huldah's long-term scheme had been to deprive the Captain of his crew, to make it impossible for him to maintain the *Astron*. It still struck me as a good idea, though only now was I beginning to see what it might involve.

I was still thinking about it when I dropped by the nursery to see K2. As soon as I entered, he squealed and kicked off against the bulkhead, shooting straight for my midsection. I braced myself but he grabbed a floor ring just before he reached me and hit my stomach with only a slight bump.

"I'm practicin'," he said proudly.

"I'll bet you are." I glanced around for Pipit.

"She's visitin' Snipe," K2 offered.

He was reading me, and doing a better job than Snipe did. Then, a few minutes later when we were wrestling on the deck: "She's comin' back now."

I stared at him.

"How do you know that?"

He made an O with his mouth and his eyes widened. It was a secret and I wasn't supposed to know, though I had a feeling that nobody was supposed to know—certainly not members of the old crew. Was it just the children? Or was it all the members of the new crew? Huldah hadn't told me, but perhaps she had worried that somehow the Captain would wheedle it out of me.

Huldah and I would have to have another talk, but right then Corin was on shift and Ophelia had called a meeting of the cell. I ran my hand through K2's hair, kissed him lightly on top of the head, and then pushed out into the corridor.

We met in Malachi's compartment this time. Malachi turned off the falsie just as we were drifting in, but not before I raised an eyebrow and the others smiled. If Malachi wanted to live in a harem, who could fault him?

Ophelia waited until we had all arrived, then said without preamble, "Kusaka's announced the receipt of signals from the far side of the Dark."

I wasn't the only one who could drop a bombshell. There was a moment of consternation, and I asked, "Any confirmation?"

She shook her head. "Wren in Communications says it's not true."

Loon looked puzzled. "Why would the Captain lie?"

"He's not lying to our people," I said, "he's lying to his. He knows they'll believe him even though we won't."

Events were coming to a head faster than anybody, even the Captain, had thought. Each side would try their absurd, half-baked schemes first. Eventually things would spin out of control and somebody would stumble past the point of no return.

"So what do we do?" Ophelia was looking at me.

I was "Sparrow," but only to myself. To the others, I was the one who had been with the ship from the very beginning; like it or not, I was their de facto leader.

I shrugged. "Look skeptical and ask for proof."

"The Captain will invent some," Crow said.

"It's too late now if nobody in Communications will confirm it."

Crow looked unhappy. "Cato will."

"Then we'll have to remind crew members that Cato is one of the Captain's men. What about armories, Loon?"

He started ticking the points off on his fingers, afraid he might forget something important.

"There's only one that we know of and that's the one the Captain controls. We haven't found any others."

"You searched Section Two?"

He nodded. "Malachi and Eagle got together a team and we went through it thoroughly." He hesitated. "I think it's haunted."

By gray buildings populated with gray people, I thought, and wondered who had played fingerman with the terminal pad.

"What about Section Three?"

"It's sealed," Crow answered. "No air leaks at all. It was the first section to be abandoned, and afterward they pumped out the air and welded the hatch shut."

"No possible way of getting in?"

"Not unless you went in from the outside."

Snipe looked doubtful. "How many of the pellet guns still work?"

"A number have been used in target practice," I reminded her. "And Heron's worked well enough."

Loon ticked off the last of his fingers. "That leaves the Captain's armory. It has to be somewhere in his quarters."

Once again everyone stared at me. I was the only one who had access to the Captain's cabin, the only one who might have a reasonable excuse for going there. And the one for whom it was probably the most dangerous.

Crow said tentatively, "It's important to know how many guns they have."

I reviewed in my own mind the last few times I had seen the

Captain and the cursory examination I had given his quarters. Unfortunately, with both the Captain and Escalus watching, I had seen very little.

"What kind of a man is Escalus?" Snipe asked.

"A guard rat. Loyal."

"He sleeps there as well?"

I shrugged; I didn't know his schedule.

"He's fond of Plover in Maintenance," Loon said. "He spends his off-shift time with her."

Snipe frowned. "Are you sure?"

Loon looked surprised. "I thought everybody knew."

Snipe turned back to me.

"Where does the Captain sleep?"

"In the after compartment—the forward is used strictly for meetings, dinners, entertainment, that sort of thing. The compartment's organized around the viewing port."

Plots and intrigues were second nature to Snipe, probably because she had spent so much time studying the historicals. It took her only a few minutes to draw up a plan. When the Captain retired to sleep, Escalus was on his own time and usually spent it with Plover. Banquo would be on duty in the passageway but he might be decoyed away by a small disturbance on the same level. Snipe would talk to Plover and make sure she kept Escalus occupied. Which would guarantee me time alone in the compartment.

Provided Escalus left.

Provided Banquo could be decoyed.

Provided Plover would co-operate.

Provided the Captain had actually retired to sleep.

Snipe would let me know when Escalus went off duty and Quince and Loon would make arrangements for a disturbance in the corridor—two crewmen noisy on smoke, enough to lure Banquo away from his post but not enough to wake the Captain. We all agreed and they left.

All but Ophelia, who stayed behind, her face gray with strain.

"We have a plan to force the Captain to go back." I waited

for her to continue but instead she shook her head and said, "I'm not sure I should tell you, Sparrow. It's not dependent . . . on you." She hesitated. "It's your decision."

For a moment I was both hurt and insulted, then understood why she was withholding the information. Of all the mutineers, I was now the most important—and the most exposed. Ophelia knew as well as I did that I was hanging by a thread and the Captain could cut it at any time.

"Will it work?" I asked.

She nodded. "It has to."

That wasn't quite the same thing but I didn't pursue it. I would have to trust her.

"Then don't tell me. Not yet."

"I wish you luck, Sparrow."

It was Hamlet she was talking to and it was Hamlet who nodded his thanks.

It wasn't difficult to lure Banquo away from the hatchway and it took only a moment for me to slip into the Captain's quarters, two or three writing slates tucked under my arm in case the Captain was still awake. He would be annoyed but my seeing him early in his sleep period would hardly be enough reason to flatline me. . . .

Only one glow tube was on, which left most of the compartment in shadow. I froze, waiting until my eyes had adjusted to the gloom. The Captain's sling was empty and the only real light came from the after sleeping compartment and office. I could hear the low murmur of conversation and felt the hair on the back of my neck stiffen. The Captain was still up, talking to somebody—probably Cato. My armpits and palms were slimy with sweat and I debated leaving, though I was also tempted to edge closer so I could overhear the conversation or quickly search the cabin for any stock of weapons.

I hesitated, convinced I was being foolish. If he kept pellet guns anyplace, it would be in the after compartment.

The few slates I carried with me suddenly seemed like a

feeble excuse for being there. I made up my mind to go, hoping that Banquo was still occupied at the other end of the corridor. My courage had slipped away and my heart had started to race. Then I froze again. The huge port that took up one whole side of the compartment lacked its usual display and for once showed Outside as it looked from the hangar deck. It was as if the whole side of the ship were open to outer space. I had to fight a moment of vertigo, panicked that I might float out to be lost between the light dusting of stars on the left and the ocean of blackness on the right. . . .

Darkness and the Deep, I thought bleakly. Here we were, a group of frightened, chattering primates light-years away from the safety of the jungle, breeding and fighting within the steel confines of a tiny artificial world that had been launched millennia ago. Once it was gone, there might be no life left in the universe and no point at all to the vast explosions of matter and the whirling lumps of rock and bubbles of gas that filled the void and . . .

I swallowed my fears and started going through the compartment. If the Captain came in, I would try and bluff my way out. If Banquo interrupted me, I would do the same, though I doubted I could convince either one.

I drifted over to the Captain's desk. The viewing globe was empty and there was nothing else on the desktop with the sole exception of the ancient paperweight that I had first seen on the bridge. I held it for a moment, then carefully put it back.

I silently slid open the drawers in the desk, making sure that none of the contents escaped into the compartment. They held nothing but a few small writing slates. I pushed them shut, then floated over to the bookcases against the opposite bulkhead. I ran my fingers across the bindings, managed to read a few of the titles and fought down an urge to steal one or two.

It was an odd morality—I could lead a mutiny against the Captain but I couldn't steal one of his books.

From somewhere there came the tiny tick of a clock and once again I was paralyzed with fear. Time was running out;

they couldn't keep Banquo away forever and the Captain could wind up his conference at any moment. I shivered and groped my way past the bookcases, then turned to stare at the compartment. I had searched everywhere. Any armory had to be in the after compartment, as I had thought all along.

I took a final look at the huge port on my left, the Captain's desk and chair, his hammock for the occasional nap, and the row of bookcases—along with the dining table and the private food machine, the only real touch of luxury in a compartment almost as Spartan as those of the crew.

I started for the hatch, then grabbed a floor ring to stop myself. The dining table. With a cloth stretched taut over the top and reaching to the deck, anchored with magnetic lines. I drifted over, broke the magnetic seals and folded back the cloth. Beneath the table was a cabinet with metal doors. I felt for the latch and quietly forced it open.

Some of the pellet guns were still in cosmoline that had hardened to a rocky feel and appearance. I did a quick count. Perhaps twenty guns, plus tins of ammunition. Ten of them had been fired and I guessed that these were the ones issued for target practice. I wondered which one Heron had used when he had tracked me on Aquinas II. It was a morbid thought, but practical—if I knew which one it was, at least I could be certain that it worked.

The ones in hardened cosmoline I knew were useless—you would have to crack them out and the barrels were probably sealed with the stuff. But the other ten presumably worked; I guessed that they were all the firing power the Captain had.

I started to gather them all up, then realized I didn't dare. If the mutiny was to start the next time period, it would be different. But one gun might not be missed. I took what looked like the best one and a small tin of ammunition and stuffed them in my waistcloth. My possession of them wouldn't be immediately obvious to either the Captain or Banquo, though a quick search would not only mean flatlining, it would probably send me to Reduction.

I floated back toward the hatch, then hesitated once again.

There was still a low murmur of conversation coming from the after compartment, and curiosity quickly overcame prudence. I pushed toward it, keeping to one side to avoid being outlined in the light. I flattened myself against the bulkhead and peeped in. There was little to see: an outer compartment that was largely in shadow and a smaller one beyond, which held a sleeping sling and apparently little else. The Captain wasn't in sight but his voice was clear and I could make out specific words, though not the sense of what he was saying. He sounded as if he were in the outer compartment but I couldn't see him in the gloom.

Then once again the hair on the back of my neck stiffened. I had been there a good five minutes but I had never heard anybody else speak. It occurred to me that there were moments when even the Captain was alone and afraid, moments when he retreated to the after compartment and held long conversations with himself.

I was partly right and also, dreadfully, wrong.

By the next time period, the Captain knew that he had lost a weapon. When I went to see him on ship's business, he was in a thin-lipped fury, though he never indicated he suspected me. Banquo was the chief object of his anger and I was a silent witness to his brief interrogation. I had drifted in with some writing slates of supply statistics at the moment the Captain was facing a white-faced Banquo across his desk.

"You were on duty and a commotion started and you left your post. That's simple enough. It never occurred to you that it was a diversion?"

To my surprise, Banquo defended himself.

"It was my duty to investigate—you would have ordered me to if you had been awake. And the crewmen checked out."

"They wanted you to investigate because they knew I wasn't awake—wasn't that obvious?"

"I said I checked them out. I did my duty—"

It happened so fast I couldn't believe it. The Captain back-handed Banquo across the face, leaving a white welt that quickly turned red. Banquo fingered his cheek; he was livid with anger. He stood there a moment, trembling, a huge hulk of a man who had been loyal to the Captain all of his life and now, in an instant, had seen his loyalty shattered. Even though he was old crew, he had a built-in aversion to violence, and that had been stripped away as well. I had no idea what he would do; I don't think he himself knew.

There was an ominous silence, then the Captain said in a low voice, "I give you permission, Banquo—go ahead, strike."

The Captain was out of control, I thought with amazement. The veins in his forehead and neck pulsed with anger, his eyes were narrow with rage. Banquo stared for a moment; then his flush faded and he turned away without a word and pushed outside to the corridor to take up his post. I thought at first the Captain had faced him down, then realized the same thing Banquo had—if he had struck, the Captain would have killed him.

The Captain glared at me and snarled, "He probably took the gun himself," then nodded at the slates in my hand. "Leave them. And I don't want to see any more statistics for the next dozen time periods—or you, either."

I had been hovering there, quaking with guilt, and left as quickly as I could. It was a side of the Captain I had never seen before and hoped I never saw again. Sweating with rage, out of control, capable of murder . . . He was more than a match for all of us and I began to think we would never be prepared to deal with him.

Our final plan was simple, too simple. We would pick a specific time, then cripple the ship. We had a lot of work to do beforehand, from a final effort to subvert as many of the Captain's men as we could to a systems analysis of the ship's functioning so we could disable it with precise strikes. The end result would be to force the Captain to return to Earth. It had become an article of faith that he could not run the ship himself and that once we had convinced him of that, he would have to turn back.

In retrospect, it was all wishful thinking. I would wake in the middle of a sleep period realizing how flimsy our plan was and yet fail to find any fault with the logic. The Captain *had* to go back. . . .

But we had no textbooks on mutinies and ours was flawed from the very beginning. It lurched to a start long before we were ready, and whatever it was, it was no body blow to the operation of the ship. Everybody had their pet idea on how to cripple the *Astron*, tried that idea out first, and *then* told me about it. The mutiny never spun out of control because it was never in control.

The first blow was at Hydroponics, a blockage in a nutrient valve that wasn't discovered until three rows of soybeans had turned brown and useless.

Nobody raised an alarm; the withering could have happened in the natural course of events. And then a proud Ibis told me what she had done. I was harsh and probably frightened her but I desperately didn't want to warn the Captain of what we were planning.

The next assault came the following breakfast period and was a good deal more serious than turning off a spigot in Hydroponics. Halfway through the meal Snipe wrinkled her nose. At first I thought the food machine had malfunctioned or that one of the children in the compartment hadn't made it to a waste chute in time. Somebody, I never discovered who, had linked the waste-processing units with air support. We had long been used to foul air but we weren't used to the new odors and I doubted that anyone ever could be.

The last attempt was against the water system. Without warning, the drinking water began to taste like bile.

The three events in less than a dozen time periods convinced everybody it was no coincidence. More important, they alerted the Captain. His move was immediate and drastic. All the birth mothers were sequestered in an off-limits corridor with armed guards at both ends and no chance for anybody to see them without a permit.

The pressure was no longer on the Captain, it was on us. He had taken hostages and none of us knew what plans he had for them. But I couldn't forget the conversation with Ophelia about limiting the size of the crew once we ventured into the Dark.

The next sleep period I spent staring at the overhead and thinking of Pipit and the other birth mothers, wondering what the Captain might do next. Lack of sleep combined with an overactive imagination; what happened then was spontaneous and part of nobody's plan.

One of the Captain's men lost his nerve, I lost my temper, and the bloody revolt began.

29

The next time period we ate breakfast in silence. Loon worked the food machine, with mediocre results, though none of us had much of an appetite. Crow hunched by himself in a corner while Ophelia talked to him in low tones; then she gave up and pushed away, glancing at me and shaking her head. Corin was nervous and ate with a false heartiness. Thrush floated in, glanced around and sensed the mood, then slipped out. Crow's dark eyes followed him and I could feel the battle going on within—Huldah's breeding program would soon be put to the acid test. Then Crow handed his plate to Loon and kicked out into the corridor.

I pushed my own plate aside and started after him.

Snipe grabbed my arm. "You can't help him, Sparrow."

"I can't help any of them," I said bitterly. "But I can keep Crow from doing something foolish."

The detention corridor was four levels down, one above Reduction. There was a crowd of about thirty at one end, almost all of them new crew, arguing with the frightened Captain's man who had been assigned guard duty. A pellet gun was stuck loosely in his waistcloth but he made no move to touch it, trying to hold back the crowd with outstretched arms. I remembered him from Maintenance—a gangly twenty-year-old named Goose. He had probably become a Captain's man for the sake of the red strip of cloth around his upper arm and an occasional smile and pat on the back from the Captain himself.

I mingled with the crowd and listened to the rumors, some of which made my hair stand on end. An entire generation was to be skipped in birth allotments, the children were to be aborted, the birth mothers sterilized. . . . I caught up with Crow, who managed a twisted smile and said, "I'm just here to observe, Sparrow. For right now."

"Don't lie," I said. "What were you going to do?"

He looked away in uneasy agony. "I don't know."

"The Captain forbids any unauthorized personnel in this corridor!"

Goose's voice was high-pitched and nervous. The crowd was gradually pushing him back but none of them struck or threatened him. I glanced at the corridor behind me. The Captain must know of the commotion; reinforcements would arrive any moment.

"You've got no right!" somebody shouted, which struck me as odd since they must know by now that nobody had any rights, not in the Captain's eyes.

"Get the Captain!" I spotted Eagle and next to him, Hawk. Neither one could pass up this sort of excitement. But I worried that the crowd was playing into the Captain's hands. It was growing and I feared what might happen next.

Crow read me and said bitterly, "They won't do anything. They can't."

Huldah had emasculated an entire generation. . . . Then I wondered what they could do in any event. The Captain had the arms; he controlled the ship. And whatever else it was, this wasn't the type of demonstration that would convince him of anything.

I looked around the crowd and tried to locate the leaders. There were a few up front and several in the middle who were doing most of the shouting but it didn't look as if it were planned. It was a spontaneous demonstration of fear and anger, one of the many things we hadn't counted on.

Another of the Captain's men appeared at the far end of

the corridor—Cato himself—and I guessed others were slipping through the passageways behind us. I pulled at Crow and said, "Let's get out of here—we'll be trapped." He started to fall back and I turned to follow, then saw Tern at the front of the crowd, a little to one side of Goose. Tern was in love with Swift—I remembered him waiting outside her compartment during the ritual—and Loon had said they intended to partner after the birth of her child.

There were more Captain's men at the far end of the corridor now. I changed my mind and tried to force my way through the crowd to reach Tern, all the time shouting for the crowd to disperse. The demonstration would be a golden opportunity for the Captain to drum up trials of those who had disobeyed his edict.

"Tern!"

He heard me and twisted around for a brief glance, then continued arguing with Goose. I was almost up to him when he pushed Goose aside and shot down the corridor, yelling for Swift.

I think nobody but me heard the small report of the pellet gun above the shouting of the crowd. The air in the corridor suddenly turned pink with a fine red mist and there was an abrupt silence as all the actors froze in tableau. I'm sure at first they thought the air system had been sabotaged again. Then they realized what had happened and a low moan filled the passageway. I remembered playing with the children in the nursery. If one hurt, they all hurt.

And if Tern was dying, the new crew would feel each failing moment.

At the far end of the corridor, a Captain's man threw away his pellet gun and vomited into his waistcloth. He was probably the one who had fired, something he wouldn't forgive himself for as long as he lived.

I pushed past Goose and hurried up to Tern, who was floating motionless in the air. I caught him gently and turned him over to see the wound. He had been shot in the neck and blood was spurting in small red balloons from his torn throat to float away in the air currents or flatten in bright red splotches against the nearby bulkhead.

His lips moved as he murmured, "Swift?" Then his eyes glazed over and for the first time in my life as Sparrow, I saw something that was living—something that could think and talk and eat and make love—die. One moment he was alive, trembling in my arms, and the next he was gone. Whatever was Tern had vanished and I was holding something good only for Reduction.

The corridor had emptied except for several crewmen being held halfheartedly by the Captain's men. Everybody looked sick and those who had been close friends of Tern were crying. I remembered again Tybalt's abortive effort at target practice and Tern's refusal to shoot at a target symbolic of something living.

Huldah was right; she had needed five more generations. But she hadn't had them and the members of the new crew were going to pay a hideous price.

"You're responsible," a nervous Cato chattered at me, his teeth bared as if he were going to bite. "You and Ophelia, talking against the Captain. . . ."

"Get out of my way," I growled, and shoved him aside. I shot up the corridor toward the Captain's quarters, never realizing until later that if Cato had shot me in the back he would have been commended for his action.

I didn't know what to expect and I didn't particularly care, but this couldn't go on.

It didn't surprise me that the Captain was waiting.

By the time I got there, I remembered that I was supposed to be a young tech assistant who had once been close to the Captain and was outraged and frightened by Tern's murder. I could have avoided the Captain altogether but that wouldn't have been in character and would be just as dangerous as my bitter protests.

Banquo showed me in and went back to his post in the

corridor. The Captain was alone at his desk, checking some writing slates.

"Cato killed Tern," I said, the words tumbling out. "Tern was in the detention corridor but he wasn't doing anything, he—"

The Captain held up a hand. He looked puzzled and mildly concerned and I made the mistake of taking him at face value, of assuming that he didn't know, despite the peep screens at his back.

"Tell me what happened—from the beginning, Sparrow."

I took a deep breath and said that I had heard about a disturbance in the detention corridor, went to see what was happening and tried to get the crowd to disperse. I had shouted at Tern to leave but he had been worried about Swift—

"The guards were posted to keep crewmen away," the Captain interrupted, frowning. "If anybody wanted to see one of the birth mothers, they should have applied for a pass. It would have been granted."

"There were rumors," I said. "That detention—"

The Captain interrupted again. "It's customary to give birth mothers private quarters until their delivery date." I didn't know whether he was lying or not. Then, too casually: "What sort of rumors, Sparrow?"

He was friendly and sympathetic; there was no indication he would penalize me for telling the truth. When I was through, he shook his head in dismay. "Do you think any of those would have been good for the ship, Sparrow?"

"No, of course not," I said slowly.

"Then why would I have ordered them?"

"They were just rumors," I defended sullenly. "I didn't say I believed them."

"You tried to get the crewmen to disperse?"

I nodded. "I did my best."

He looked past my shoulder. "What happened down there, Cato?"

I twisted around. Cato had come in behind me, his expression one of fear of the Captain and anger toward me.

"A riot in the detention corridor. Some crewmen showed up and threatened the guard; apparently they wanted to take the birth mothers away. One of the crewmen broke past the guard and he was shot—not intentionally, the guard tried to shoot over his head."

"Your men need more practice," the Captain said dryly. He nodded at me. "Sparrow tells me he tried to get them to disperse."

Cato's mouth turned down at the corners.

"Hardly. He urged them on."

I started to protest but the Captain held up his hand to quiet me and said, "Return to your post, Cato, I'll talk to you later."

After Cato was gone, the Captain turned back to me, still friendly. "You shouldn't antagonize Cato, Sparrow. But I can't believe you'd urge a crowd to riot." He pushed out of his chair and drifted over to the port. It was the last time I would see him outlined against the vast expanse of the galaxy.

"What should I do, Sparrow? The crew doesn't want to continue with the mission, it's only myself and a few dozen crewmen who want to keep going." He clasped his hands behind his back, silent for a moment. Then: "What would you do if you were me?"

I was amazed that he had faced the truth so easily. Would he think of going back? I wondered. The Captain seemed open to my advice and the temptation was too great. I abandoned all caution and hastened to give it.

"Go back," I said. "We can't make it across the Dark."

I couldn't tell whether he was disappointed or not.

"You have the figures?"

I reeled them off from memory—the lack of supplies, the necessary cutbacks in crew size, the diminishing ability to actually maintain the ship—

The Captain held up his hand with a half smile.

"Did you know we've received signals in the waterhole frequency from the other side?"

He was giving me a last chance to recant, but I couldn't bring myself to accept the lie. I tried to argue around it.

"It doesn't change the figures." I stumbled over them once again. He stared at me and I finally saw beyond the look of friendship to the real face beneath. I had forgotten that he was a better actor than I had ever thought of being.

"But success is there, just waiting for our arrival," he mused. I wondered if he really believed what he was saying. He turned to gaze out the port. "You know, Sparrow, I've done the best I could, for a hundred generations. Until this one. And now people I thought I could trust are holding secret meetings, sabotaging the *Astron* . . ."

I couldn't beleve he was indulging in self-pity, and I was right—he wasn't. When he looked back at me, the thin veil of friendship had vanished altogether and his voice was savage and cold.

"Of all the crewmen on board, you owed me your trust, Sparrow. I befriended you when you needed a friend, I punished your enemies." By that, I knew he meant Heron, not Thrush. He smiled faintly. "You remind me of another crewman. Hamlet. You know him well, don't you?"

I was lost.

"You're the icon, Sparrow. But you know it. And because you know it, you're no longer useful to the ship. You wanted to know who you were and you found out. Poor Sparrow—a little knowledge was a dangerous thing. It turned you against me, against the mission, and against the welfare of the crew."

He suddenly hit his desk with his fist, showing me the same kind of out-of-control anger he'd shown Banquo.

"God, you take me for a fool! You're the leader of the mutiny; how could you assume I wouldn't know that?" He pushed over to face me and I could see the veins pulsing in his neck and forehead. "You're right about the crew numbers for the future. I regret them, but one thing I won't regret is that we'll no longer need an icon. But don't worry about being flatlined—not this time, Sparrow!"

I was going to be sent to Reduction.

He drifted back to his desk, dismissing me as completely as he had Noah and Tybalt when he had condemned them.

When I finally found my voice, I sounded very young and very angry.

"Your mission was to find life," I shouted, "but you failed because there isn't any! Instead, you're going to kill what little there is because you think you're God!"

His face had become friendly and placid once again. The words dried in my throat; I don't think he even heard what I had said.

"Of all the crewmen you've been, I think I liked Sparrow the best." He smiled, without malice, and there was honest regret in his voice. "That was because Sparrow liked me as well."

He was right, but that seemed like a lifetime ago. The bond between me and Captain Kusaka had finally snapped for good.

I suddenly felt air currents at my back and realized Banquo had come up behind me. What I did then was automatic, without any thought or warning. I doubled up, kicked off my cling-tites with one easy motion and braced my feet against the desk for leverage. A moment later I had shot past a startled Banquo and through the hatch into the corridor beyond.

Banquo followed, but it didn't take much to lose him in the crowded corridors and I suspected he didn't try too hard to catch me. But now Cato and the others would be looking for me and there was no place on board where I could hide.

Crow and Loon were alone in their compartment when I burst through the shadow screen without warning. I had fled through corridors filled with milling crewmen, their faces mirroring the shock of Tern's death. Whether they had seen it or not, I knew they had sensed it and were still reacting to it. Two of the Captain's men saw me and shouted but I evaded them in the jammed passageways.

Loon and Crow had been bending over something on the hammock and looked up at me, startled.

"I've been condemned," I said. "Cato and his men are after me."

Loon paled and it was my turn to read him. The mutiny was falling apart; nothing had gone according to plan.

I tried to sound confident; like everything else I had tried that period, it failed miserably. "I know where to hide—but I'll need help."

Crow moved away from the hammock and I caught a glimpse of what they had been working on. Laid out on the canvas were a dozen strips of metal, one end beaten into a rough handgrip and the other ground to a shiny point. I picked up one of them, tested the grip, and felt a wave of despair.

"Why, Crow? You'll never use them."

Loon scooped them up and wrapped them in the end of his waistcloth.

"We'll try." He sounded brave and pathetic at the same time.

I grabbed his arm. "Leave them. If the Captain's men find you with them, they'll kill you and claim it was self-defense." I knew intuitively that wars and riots had a life of their own; if the Captain's men became nervous enough, our little mutiny would end in massacre. "Find Ophelia, tell her I'll be in Section Three."

He left and I told Crow I had to get an exploration suit; if I were going to hide in Section Three, I'd have to enter from the outside. He didn't move.

"It's over, isn't it, Sparrow?"

His courage was gone, at least for the moment. I guessed that half the new crew felt the same way, devastated by Tern's murder and their first sight of blood. It's easy to lead when everybody wants to follow; it's far more difficult when nobody wants to. But Kusaka had left me with no choice. I would have to be everybody else's courage and lead as well as I could to whatever fate awaited us, even if I was followed only by my shadow.

I hugged him and said quietly, "It isn't over until I say it's over." I slipped out through the shadow screen. I didn't look behind to see if he followed, but I knew that he had.

The corridors were still filled with milling crewmen, but Exploration itself was deserted. I grabbed the suit that looked in best repair, then told Crow to take a spare helmet radio and stay in touch on the team frequency.

"What are you going to do?"

"Patch into the computer—wreck the ship." I said it with more confidence than I felt.

A ghostly smile surfaced then. "Wreck the ship? With us in it?"

I slapped him on the back. "Not wreck it completely, just enough to scare Kusaka."

A ghostly smile surfaced now and we sailed down the corridor, towing the suit behind us, doing our best to avoid colliding with fellow crewmen. We didn't meet any of the Captain's men until we were almost to Communications, where we ran into one floating around a corner. He tugged frantically at the pellet gun in his waistcloth and for a moment I thought he might shoot himself in the leg.

"I'll fire, Sparrow—the Captain wants you!"

We didn't stop. His first shot went wild; then we had kicked through the deserted gymnasium, turning abruptly into a passageway on the other side. One level down and we were at the airlock. Crow helped me into the suit, then grinned.

"Section Three, right?"

I nodded. "Tell Ophelia I'll try and disable the ship from there." With the Captain's men looking for me, there was no way I could remain in the main tube.

I took a portable glow lamp from the row against the bulkhead and stepped into the lock. The last I saw of Crow, he was still smiling, but the smile was painted on and I knew he had little confidence in his ability to stay alive. I was the one Kusaka wanted most, but he and Ophelia couldn't be far below me on the list.

A moment later the outer hatch rolled away and I stepped out onto the side of the *Astron* with no tether line as insurance, only my magnetic boots sticking to the pitted hull. Any sudden move and I could tear myself free and wind up another speck of matter lost in the immensity of the Dark.

The main tube was outlined by the warm glow of light coming from its ports. I gradually worked my way over the huge curve of the ship toward the third cylinder. The glow lamp's batteries were half exhausted by the time I finally located the outside hatch to Section Three. For a moment I thought it was corroded shut, then finally tugged it open. I slipped in, sealed it behind me, and manually cycled the inner lock.

There was no air, no heat, no light—only the silence of empty corridors and deserted compartments. I was fighting frantically against loneliness and fear when the helmet radio cut in.

"Sparrow?"

"Right here, Crow. Give me a few minutes."

Three lonely levels down I found the small satellite bridge. Like Communications in Section Two, it had been partially stripped, but the viewing globe and the terminal pad were still intact.

For a moment, I thought we had lost. Encased in my suit, I had no way of working the pad. And even if I hadn't been in my suit, at the temperature inside Section Three the pad would be anything but warm and resilient to the touch. I sat in the operator's chair, cursing silently to myself, then pushed over to the hatch and sealed it.

I opened the valve on one of my air tanks. The compartment was small; I might be able to pressurize it enough to survive. I watched the air as it escaped in a steady stream, freezing against the deck and the bulkheads. I tripped the levers on my suit heating units and over the next few minutes let the temperature rise until I felt I was roasting. But the frost disappeared from the bulkheads and a few minutes later my suit sensors measured a cold but thin and breathable atmosphere. I stripped off the suit and huddled over the heating units, praying I wouldn't freeze to death before the compartment warmed enough to be livable.

I put my hands on the terminal pad, felt my skin adhere to its surface because of the cold, then patiently waited for the pad to soften and spring to life. As in Section Two, there was residual power in the computer. I pressed my palms and fingers lightly into the pad, feeling my way through the programs and making the necessary connections so the terminal could feed off the power sources in the main tube.

"Sparrow? Answer." Crow sounded frightened.

My teeth were chattering and the air felt thinner than that on a mountain peak, but I was alive and well.

"I'm still here, Crow. For the moment."

The strain in his voice didn't go away.

"You're going to have company. Cato and two of the Captain's men are coming over."

I didn't need the interruption and at the moment I wasn't mobile, I was pinned in the compartment. They would probably guess where I was and head right for me. I moved my hand on the pad and powered the compartment's peep screen and the monitor in the airlock area. I thought I had lost my pursuers, then picked them up two corridors in. Three crewmen in exploration suits, armed with pellet guns and carrying portable glow lamps so they were visible on the screen as three bobbing smudges of light, populating the empty passageways with shadows that ebbed and flowed around corners and into deserted compartments.

Eventually, I would have to suit up and get out. But before I did, perhaps I could leave them with some lasting memories.

I caressed the terminal pad again and retrieved the compartment inventories. On the peep screen, the glow tubes in the corridors started to flicker on.

Then I activated every falsie in the section.

Section Three was suddenly a brand-new ship, with gleaming bulkheads and crowds of crewmen thronging its various levels. On the screen, the Captain's men froze with shock, unable to tell the real from the unreal. Exploration suits didn't come equipped with eye masks and I guessed the ghostly crewmen around them would slow their progress considerably. And maybe give me enough time to prepare some surprises for Kusaka.

I worked the terminal pad feverishly, trying desperately for control of the *Astron*'s life-support systems. I retrieved the code for the air-circulating and maintenance machinery, had momentary control, then felt it slip away as passwords were abruptly changed and electronic gates slammed shut. Heating and lighting were next, but I was milliseconds too late for each.

I thought it was Thrush fighting me for control, then realized that while he was good, he wasn't this good. I was fighting Kusaka and I was losing.

I finally leaned back, the sweat greasing my nose and gathering in globules in my armpits despite the chill of the compartment. I had been blocked from the main computer completely and it would be a very few minutes before Kusaka had control of the slave computer in Section Three as well.

"Sparrow?"

I didn't know how to tell Crow that we had lost, but I didn't get the chance.

"They're leaving, Sparrow."

"Who's leaving?"

"The crew." His voice caught. "They're deserting the ship."

I sat there, my hands still on the pad, not knowing what to say or think or do. Ophelia's final plan, I thought. It had taken great courage.

But I didn't think it was going to work. Not against Kusaka.

* * *

"I'm coming back, Crow. Meet me at the lock."

I didn't wait for him to reply but took a last look at the peep screen, noted that Cato and his men were only three corridors away, then hastily suited up, unsealed the hatch, and slipped out.

The trip back to the airlock took far more time than I thought. The crowds of crewmen in the compartment falsies, talking silently to each other in the cold near-vacuum of Section Three, made it difficult for me to keep my bearings. The corridors seemed far longer than they actually were and some of them led no place at all. But the ghosts gliding around me seemed strangely familiar.

The section had probably looked like this shortly after Launch, all chrome, stainless steel, and polish. I had probably known the crewmen—

My name was Byron and I was jammed in with half a hundred others at a lecture in Exploration. We were coming up on Lexus, a system with half a dozen planets, two of them in the CHZ. The lecture was boring and my attention had started to drift, focusing on a young man named Masefield two rows ahead, who was staring at me. I guessed why and, as Sparrow, was mildly embarrassed. As Byron, I was intrigued and looked boldly back. . . .

The memories were crowding up in my mind at a time when I couldn't afford them. I turned and plunged down a corridor, which ended abruptly in a small compartment, then closed my eyes to recall the various levels and passageways from the images on the peep screen. I reassured myself that the Captain's men were having even more difficulty than I was.

I got my bearings and a few minutes later opened the airlock, ignoring the ghostly operator who made a dumb show of asking for my authorization. I had just pushed into the lock when there was a shower of metal sparks from the frame. Cato and his men were two corridors away and one of them was firing a pellet gun. There was another shower of sparks and I slammed the inner hatch shut and secured it. The outer hatch cycled open automatically. I had just floated through when all the glow tubes in the airlock died.

Kusaka had gained control of the Section Three computer, but for the moment he had handicapped his own men more than me.

I waited for the outer hatch to cycle shut, then smashed the controls set in the frame. Cato and his men were now trapped in the section—three of the Captain's men I would no longer have to worry about.

But other things were now more important. My portable glow lamp flickered and died. The darkness was smothering, palpable. I took tiny little steps over the hull, unwilling to break the magnetic seal for more than a fraction of a second. I inched over the pitted steel, careful not to look at where the stars should have been and where there was now nothing.

Then it became difficult to breathe and I anxiously inspected the heads-up display in my helmet. The air was fine—it was my imagination, I had started to hyperventilate . . .

Where was the lock?

I felt a thin vibration through my boots. Once. Again. I got down on my hands and knees and crawled toward the vibrations, feeling for the thin crevice that marked the edges of the hatch. I beat against it with the dead glow lamp, wondering all the time who was sobbing, then realized it was myself. . . .

Beneath me, the hatch moved and a glow of golden light pulsed out. I tumbled inside, the hatch cycled shut, and there was the hiss of air filling the lock. Crow had suited up and was waiting, still holding the spanner wrench he had used to pound against the hull.

The inner lock opened and Crow quickly shed his suit and helped me out of mine. I stood there naked except for the inner-weave and he held me a moment while I shook with reaction. I would never go Outside again.

When I ceased trembling, he reminded me why I had come back.

"They're leaving, Sparrow. Everybody."

30

Ophelia and Snipe had taken the ultimate gamble and their audacity was breathtaking. But in the final analysis it was nothing but a bluff. We had underestimated Kusaka and I, at least, should have known better.

Crow stared at me the way I imagined he had once looked at Hamlet. He was expecting me to come up with answers.

"Where are they?"

"The hangar deck."

"What about the Captain's men?"

"They're there, too."

I kicked off against the nearest bulkhead and shot down the deserted passageway to the hangar deck, Crow following close behind. When we got there the hatch was closed and nothing I could do would open it. I put my ear against the seal and heard the faint shriek of the emergency evacuation siren within. The air pressure was dropping on the deck. Nobody could open the hatch now, not even Kusaka.

I leaped for the operator's terminal pad and the peep screen just above it, powered them up, and watched as the view inside wavered onto the screen and solidified. The Captain's men were firing pellet guns at the open hatches of In-between Station and the Lander; they didn't realize they could have rushed them without worry. In the long run,

Ophelia's bluff might not work with Kusaka—but so far it was working with his men.

I increased magnification and searched among the anxious faces looking out of the ports of the Station and the Lander, hoping for Crow's sake that Pipit was among them. I didn't see her, though she might have been among the crewmen in exploration suits who had taken shelter behind both vessels.

"What about the birth mothers?"

"They were freed. Two more crewmen died—Crane and Bunting."

Both had been friends of Crow.

"And Loon?" I asked.

Crow's voice came close to cracking. "He was one of those who stole an exploration suit."

On the hangar deck, a Captain's man frantically tried to work the compartment's control panel.

"What happened?"

"Ophelia called a rally. Everybody knew what was going to happen afterward." There had been no need to talk about it—Ophelia would have made sure of that so no informers would overhear and report it. "The Captain's men followed them and Ophelia started the evacuation procedure. They were trapped when the hatch closed."

"All of them?"

"I can't sense normal crew. I think so."

I worked with the pad, trying to bring up the sound so I could hear what was going on inside. I was still making the connections when one of the crewmen who had suited up crumpled.

I swore to myself but Crow reassured me. "He's all right, he was hit in a shoulder disconnect."

On the screen, several of the other figures grabbed their wounded comrade and rushed to the station's hatchway. I was praying they would make it when there was an explosion of sound from the peep screen.

"Exit hatches have been sealed. You have fifteen seconds to throw down your pellet guns and come aboard the station . . ."

It was Ophelia's voice on the station intercom. The firing suddenly died. Several of the Captain's men ran to try and open the compartment hatch manually, but with no success.

". . . *deck air's being pumped out, pressure is now ten p.s.i. You have only a few seconds left . . .*"

The sound now became tinny and faint in the thinning air. One of the Captain's men threw down his pellet gun and raced for the still-open hatch on Inbetween Station. Another second and the others followed. I saw Banquo among those who disappeared into the safety of the station just as the hatch closed behind them.

All action on the deck suddenly seemed frozen. I could no longer hear any sound and for a moment thought the speaker had died, then realized the air had become too thin for transmission. Then the shadow screen vanished overhead and the huge hangar doors rolled open.

On the screen, played out in miniature, Inbetween Station lifted on its jets and silently slipped into space, followed by the overcrowded Lander and several dozen tiny specks of crewmen in patched-up exploration suits. The crew of the *Astron,* drifting away into the Dark. There was nobody left on board now but Kusaka, Crow, and myself.

And Thrush.

"How long can they last?" I asked.

Crow was lost in the picture on the screen. I didn't think he heard me and I repeated it. "How long, Crow?"

"As long as their air lasts."

A dozen tiny patches of light could be seen in the portion of the sky where there was normally nothing but darkness.

"Will they come back?" Even to myself, I sounded wistful.

His voice was low and seemed far away.

"What for, Sparrow? Why not end it here? There's no future; Kusaka's killed it."

I searched his face, looking for the bluff behind the words, and didn't see it. I had forgotten that they were mayflies and the last of their kind, living on hope for generation after generation until this one.

"You're giving up," I said slowly. "You're committing suicide just like Judah."

He frowned, trying to put into words what all of the new crew instinctively accepted.

"We've done as much as we can."

A bluff's no good unless the other side is convinced you might carry it out. And in a way I was part of the other side; I was more like Kusaka than I was like them. Would they do it? Would they prefer to die now, or slowly dwindle over the next hundred years? For generations they had voluntarily gone to Reduction when their lives were complete, so that their next generation could live. But now they had seen the end of their generations. Their lives no longer served a purpose.

What would happen now depended on me. It had always depended on me, no matter what plans were made or what plots were hatched. I was the icon, the phoenix, trying to save the last of the human race, even though it was no longer quite human.

"Let's go, Crow."

He turned, his eyes still seeing the dwindling dots of light on the screen. Pipit, Loon, a dozen others—all the people he had loved and who had loved him were drifting away into the darkness.

"Go where?"

His eyes hadn't focused on me at all.

"To see Kusaka."

We kicked back through the levels until we came to the one that held my own compartment. I retrieved the pellet gun and the ammunition from the folds of the hammock where I had hidden them.

We sped back through the deserted passageways and memories of my life as Sparrow kept recurring as we passed the various compartments: Exploration, where Tybalt and I had shared a dozen smokes and I had listened raptly to his tales of aliens on the planets he had explored; the nursery and sick bay, filled with the silent squeals of Cuzco and K2 and the other children; the compartment where Pipit had fixed our meals and I had played chess with Noah . . .

Pleasant memories, memories I wanted to hang onto because they were what made me "Sparrow." I couldn't imagine myself without them.

The Captain's compartment was as deserted as the others, without even a shadow screen to close off the hatch. I hesitated, then floated through with Crow close behind me. I held the pellet gun nervously in my hand, wondering if Kusaka was alone or whether Crow had been wrong and some of the Captain's men had escaped the trap on the hangar deck and were with him now.

"You took your time," Thrush said.

He was sitting behind the Captain's desk, watching the various astronomical scenes roll across the port one by one, each spectacular view replaced after a few moments by one even more spectacular. The Triffid nebula, the Horsehead, the Lagoon, the bright pink of the region of Eta Carinae, the filaments of the Vela supernova and the bright red burst of the Rood, the purple fires of the Large Magellanic Cloud . . .

There was no other light in the compartment, so it was either bright or dim depending on the view just beyond the port. Shadows and colors flowed over Thrush's pale face, his own lack of color a perfect background for those flickering through the port. But Thrush was thumbing through the images out of idle curiosity; without Kusaka's sense of awe, they were shabby deceptions.

"Cato won't be coming," I said.

He looked faintly interested. "You lost him in Section Three? Good for you, Sparrow—I never cared much for him."

"Kusaka," I said coldly, "where is he?"

Thrush waved toward the after compartment.

"The Captain's in there. I imagine he's waiting for you."

"You stayed behind," I said.

"I'm not without"—he grinned—"filial feelings. Besides,

those who left only have air for an hour or so. They'll have to come back. It wasn't even a decent bluff, Sparrow."

He was very smug, very confident, but his eyes jumped nervously back and forth between me and Crow, who was staring at him with a terrifying intensity. I doubted that Thrush had ever given much thought to the differences between new crew and old—or maybe he hadn't even known there were any.

"It's not a bluff," I said. "You and Kusaka are going to have the entire ship to yourselves. Forever. Something to look forward to, Thrush, though you'll be sick of each other's company after the first thousand years."

His eyes narrowed; he was wondering what I knew that he didn't.

"I don't believe in suicide," he said firmly. "They'll be back." But in his voice was the tiniest shadow of doubt.

He had no weapon, at least none that I could see. No pellet guns protruded from his waistcloth and no knives or sharp-edged strips of metal clung to the bottom of the desk. Which only meant that he had hidden them well.

"You came to see the Captain, Sparrow. Nobody's keeping you from him."

"Not even you? When I turn my back?"

He pushed out from behind the desk and floated over to the hatchway leading to the after cabin. He bowed slightly and made an exaggerated sweep with his arm.

"I wouldn't dream of it, Sparrow. Go right in." His smile was unpleasant.

I ignored him and pushed through the hatchway into the compartment beyond. I could feel the sweat start to bead on my back. Something was waiting for me in there, something that Thrush was anxious for me to see.

In the dim compartment what had looked like rows of filing cabinets seemed to stretch on forever. I made a quick estimate—maybe nine hundred all told. Just beyond, I could see another compartment that was the Captain's sleeping quarters, brightly lit with glow tubes, though I couldn't see Kusaka himself through the hatchway.

I kicked toward it, pellet gun in hand, then caught a floor ring to slow down. I looked again at the cabinets. What a tremendous amount of storage space—and how unnecessary. The computer's memory matrix held far more information and most of the paper and plastic on board had crumbled long ago anyway.

Still, they had to hold something.

I drifted closer and for the first time noticed the thick tubes and cables that wound around the cabinets and plugged into each of them. They weren't cabinets after all, they were more like . . . the chamber in Reduction, like coffins standing on end. I pushed over to one and stared at it, the hair at the back of my head sticky with sudden fear. Grease and dust had caked on the front of it and I could see nothing. I reached out a hand and cleared a small circle with the heel of my palm. It came away black with grime but through the circle I could see a sheet of thick, clear plastic and behind that, something pink and fleshlike.

I wiped away more of the dirt and within seconds was looking at a naked woman, maybe thirty years old, her eyes closed, her lashes lying limp on her cheekbones. She lay there quiet and serene, not seeming to mind the silver tubes that filled the space around her and thrust into her body orifices like so many obscene fingers. She was an odd amalgamation of grease and metal and flesh; for a moment I imagined that oil flowed through her veins and that if she opened her eyes to look at me I would see the cold, impersonal flicker of a camera lens instead of iris and pupil.

I floated slowly down the row, scraping away just enough dirt from each cabinet to glimpse the bodies within, all of them hooked up to the silver tubes. My nightmare from sick bay had become real.

At first I didn't notice the small plaques above each plastic lid. When I finally did, I reached out and brushed away the filth so I could read whatever inscription had been put there.

Robert Armijo, electronic technician, a young man who reminded me faintly of Loon . . . Selma Delgado, biotech, a
slightly older woman who might have been Ophelia's grandmother many generations removed . . . Lewis Downes, communications engineer, a dead ringer for Crow . . . Iris Wong,
dark-skinned and very pretty, agronomist . . . Thomas
Youngblood, muscular and hairy, planetary specialist . . .
Richard Uphaus, very young and slender, his mouth slightly
open as if he had been frozen in mid-sentence . . .

There were hundreds of others, pinioned by the silver
worms like so many butterflies on a tray but looking as if they
could open the lids of their coffins and step out at any moment. They were all so lifelike and so familiar. . . . I *knew*
them but I didn't remember them.

I paused at the end of the row and stared at the last coffin.
It was empty, the plastic lid ajar, the silver tubes moving to
and fro in the air currents as if they were searching for another body. I hesitated, then wiped the dirt off the plaque so I
could read the name.

Raymond Stone.

The memories came rushing back then, without warning,
trampling whoever I had been as "Sparrow," reminding me of
a hundred other lives.

*"That was a bad accident, Ray—that's your name, you'll re-
member it and a lot more in another day or two. Accidents like
this, the initial shock is severe. I'm sorry about Susan but there
was no possibility of saving her. She died immediately. You'll
be out of bed in another two weeks but there'll be months of
rehabilitation. School? Not for a while, I'm afraid. But the
Academy has said you'll be readmitted next year and with good
luck and your parents' permission, you'll be an apprentice on
the moon shuttle during the summer, something to look forward to. . . . I do know how you feel about Susan. . . ."*

I was standing on the highest peak of Hubble V, the most
Earth-like planet we had explored so far, or so Shark claimed.
I could feel the cold seeping through my suit but didn't want
to go down yet. There were white puffs of clouds in a faintly

yellow sky and the rest of the range lay below me, the golden snow glinting in the sunlight. Perch was a hundred meters down the ridge and waved at me when I glanced his way. We would celebrate once back on board—he had found a bottle of brandy that somebody in the second generation had hidden two hundred years before. Then the snow suddenly gave way beneath his feet and my last glimpse of him was of a torn and battered exploration suit tumbling down the mountain side and bouncing off the rocky ledges below. . . .

My name was Garnet and I was in the Captain's cabin, staring out the port with the Captain by my side, his hand on my shoulder, while I gazed in awe at M31, the great spiral in Andromeda. "I've explored planets where red suns filled a third of the sky at dawning," he was saying. "I've seen worlds where the tides were made of molten rock, I've stood on planets in rain that had been falling for a hundred million years. . . ." His words flowed over me like warm water. I felt the pressure of each of his fingers against my skin and swore to myself that if he wanted me to, I would die for him. . . .

We had huddled together around a hologramed fire so real I could feel the heat. Dorrit had secured the hatch and Marley was trying to persuade me to join the mutiny. "There's nothing out there, Boz, we've explored a hundred different systems and three hundred planets and never found a microbe! The only life in the universe is on board this ship and back on Earth." As soon as I was free I reported them all to the Captain, then realized too late that I was going to regret it forever when they were sent to Reduction. . . .

I was hiding in Hydroponics, spying on Napoli, when she heard the rustle in the leaves and turned and saw me. "You're not supposed to be here," she said. I grinned and said I didn't care where I was supposed to be. I took her then, despite her wishes, smothering her screams with her own waistcloth. Roma found us and called Security and a week later I was court-martialed. The Captain told me afterward that I was too old, that I had been a member of the crew too long. I had never known who I was until then but the knowledge did me no good; the

next time period I was flatlined and the only thing I remem-
bered afterward was falling from a cliff. . . .

The memories crowded in, a hundred lifetimes, all demand-
ing to be remembered, to be made complete. I had been a
hero and I had been a villain, I had been everything it was
possible for a man to be, beloved by most, hated by some.
But whatever role I might have played, I was always the
phoenix, the reminder of Earth and everything that had once
been, the biological yardstick the crew compared themselves
to in an effort to determine the depth of their own humanity
and how much they might have changed.

But now I was flying apart, I couldn't hold them all, I
couldn't live a hundred different lives all at the same
time. . . .

The part of me that had been a crewman named Sparrow
suddenly realized why a crewman named Thrush had urged
me to enter the compartment. I would see and I would remember and then I would go mad with the accumulated memories of a multitude of lifetimes. It was what a crewman
named Abel had warned me would happen. . . .

I thrashed about, blundering into the preservation crypts
and cutting my arm when I smashed the lid of the open case.
The sudden pain cut through the psychological storm and all
the memories started sorting themselves out in sequence, like
amino acids in a kind of mental genetic code. I was mostly
Raymond Stone plus a little of Hamlet and a great deal of
Sparrow and mere touches of the rest. The others within me
fought for a moment and then reluctantly gave up. Raymond
Stone had been the first, Raymond Stone had precedence.

I turned back to the crypts and went slowly down the line
wiping away the grease and dirt from the plastic lids and the
plaques above. The faces behind the plastic were rosy or olive
or black or yellow but all were fresh and lifelike. I now remembered every one of them; I had been friends with them,

had gone to parties with them and sometimes to bed, had known their children and their parents. . . .

Bobby Armijo, the comedian in shuttle school; Selma, who played mother to us all; Lewis, who couldn't hold his liquor and was dangerous to drink with and apologetic for a full month after a binge; Iris, who loved all of us much too well but not often enough when it came to me; Tom, too witty for his own good and excessively proud of his Choctaw ancestry; Rich, who was like a brother to Iris and rumored to be more than a brother to Bobby . . .

I drifted past the row with tears streaming down my face, at first fighting the memories because they hurt too much and then finally acknowledging them. They had been my friends and my lovers and my enemies—and they had been my crew. Now they were dead, their shining faces and their lifelike skin a lie.

The readout screens above each case told the story. They were preserved in their nitrogen-filled crypts like so many sides of beef in a freezer. But the chemistry of life had stopped, their EM patterns had dissipated, their memories were dust, their appearance a fake . . .

I pushed toward the hatchway that led to Kusaka's private quarters. If Thrush was right, Sparrow's crew only had air for an hour and maybe a little more. I kicked forward.

My name was Raymond Stone.

I was thirty years old.

I was the return captain of the *Astronomy* and it was long past time to take her home.

31

Michael Kusaka was sitting in his hammock, watching me cautiously, trying to guess who I was this time and just how much I remembered. There was a pellet gun on the ledge that served as a bedside table but he made no move toward it. Sparrow knew him well but it was the first time I had seen him since the mutiny so long ago. I was amazed that physically he hadn't changed much. About my size; dark, smooth skin; damp black hair; a pencil moustache; and olive eyes that were good at smiling but masked whatever he was actually thinking.

Sparrow saw him differently—but then to Sparrow he was The Captain, while to me he was peer and friend.

"Hello, Ray."

I nodded. "Hello, Mike."

"We're a long way from home," he said.

"We couldn't get much farther," I agreed.

We were both nervous and fumbled for words. I stalled by looking around the compartment. It hadn't changed much since I had first seen it on a tour during pre-Launch, which meant that everything in it was *old*. The paintings coated with plastic that had been sealed to the bulkheads—views of the Grand Canyon and the Taj Mahal and the Brazilian rain forest, what was left of it—were yellowed and brittle. The library of maybe five hundred or so volumes, which I had coveted then and still did, were rimmed with dust and dirt. A music cube and a tiny stack of chips beside it looked welded to the bedside ledge. I wondered if the chips still played, then guessed that if the bulkhead paintings had survived, the chips had, too.

Holograms of Mike's family were also sealed to the bulkheads, while a few sat on the ledge, curling and colorless, behind the pellet gun. There was one of Sachiko, his fragile and beautiful wife, to whom he had never been close, who'd enjoyed a brief career in Hong Kong films and viewed science and space with distaste. And one of Matthew, his estranged son, who had died during an exploration of Venus. It had been easy for Mike to sign off on Earth and elect to spend forty years in space.

Except it had been a lot longer than forty years.

We had been the two indispensable members of our crews and the doctors had spared neither expense nor technique to make sure we were immune to disease and illness. None of them had anticipated long life as a side effect.

I made myself comfortable in the visitor's sling to one side of his hammock. As Sparrow, I was painfully aware of time ticking inexorably away. As Raymond Stone, I couldn't resist stealing a few moments to talk to a man who had once been my best friend.

"It's been a long time," he said awkwardly.

"A lot longer than it should have been." Inside, Sparrow raged with anger and fear—he was hard to suppress.

Mike passed it off. It was old home week and he played it to the hilt.

"When was the last time? Not counting shakedown."

"Relay Station." I couldn't keep from smiling. Relay had been the huge space station that grew like Topsy while serving as a jumping-off point for the Moon and the O'Neill colonies. We had thrown a monumental drunk, and the last I had seen of Mike, he was disappearing down a corridor with a too-fleshy woman named Rusty. She had been raucous but comfortable, and was the one woman almost the entire crew had

in common. Her rank had been Service Tech, First Class, a
euphemism for government prostitute.

"I know what you're thinking, Ray. She was overrated."

He managed a shadowed smile but his eyes were still too
busy judging me to join in.

"Maybe by you, not by me."

We fell silent and I thought of how close we had once been,
of whoring together in the Arizona training camps, of fishing
expeditions to Wisconsin for walleye and muskie, of racing on
San Francisco Bay in our daysailers. . . .

I glanced again at the holograms of Sachiko and Matthew.
If I were back on Earth, they would have been dead longer
than the pharaohs.

"What happened to the O'Neill colonies, Mike?"

The question took him by surprise. I could see him mentally review what he knew and what he thought he could
safely say. I wondered if he would lie and pretend that nothing much had changed aside from the passage of time itself,
that the dispatches he had written for Communications had
actually happened. He surprised me.

"All gone," he said matter-of-factly, "a hundred years after
we left. They never proved self-supporting and the participating governments cut back. Mitsubishi kept one going to the
very end but by then it was only a research station."

He had decided that most of me was Raymond Stone and
he could afford the truth. It still hurt to hear about the colonies, but I had guessed as much.

"And Luna City?"

We were both talking around what was really on our minds,
but there was a lot of catching up to do. Luna City hadn't
been much of a city—never more than a thousand people
lived there—but I had grown fond of the towering crater walls
and the silence.

"Same thing. It deteriorated into a research outpost and
then they decided it wasn't cost-effective, that nothing more
could be learned that couldn't be discovered with remote sensors and robotic installations. Within ten years they had mal-

functioned and the bean counters decided they weren't worth repairing."

"And after that, Relay Station no longer served a purpose, right?"

He took a sip from the drink bulb in front of him, then looked embarrassed that he hadn't offered me any. He waved it at me. "You want some? Ship brandy but better than nothing." I shook my head. He took another sip and continued. "Relay Station was disassembled by 2200. Don't ask me what happened to Rusty, she probably retired to a ranch in Mexico, fat and filthy rich."

If she was, it had been from tips; the government hadn't approved of sin and definitely didn't believe in paying much for it.

"What about the *Grand Tour*—they ever finish her?"

She had been the *Astronomy*'s bigger, better sister ship designed to be launched shortly after we returned.

"She was scuttled before they ever finished the hull."

While we talked, I watched Mike and compared myself to him. He had become The Captain and I had become . . . something else. I was a little fuzzy about the training but I knew I was never intended for the role of phoenix. I had been put in the Freeze before they ever left Earth orbit and I wasn't supposed to be revived until the first forty years were up and it was time for me and my crew to change places with Mike and his crew. One crew to take the *Astronomy* out and one to bring her back, that had been the plan. All of us were supposed to live out our lives as heroes back on Earth, and when we died, our ashes would be scattered over living dirt. . . .

"What happened, Mike? I mean, what happened between you and me."

The centuries between us had vanished. Mike and I and Relay Station had happened a week ago and Launch was yesterday.

He shrugged. "They screwed up. We all expected they would. The ship cost too much, they'd put too much into it." He tapped his head. "They wanted to hedge their bets so they rearranged my wiring. Programming, call it what you will. Don't come back until you find life or forty years is up."

"But you didn't go back at all," I said.

He frowned, searching for words to explain the unexplainable.

"They didn't realize they'd programmed two conflicting sets of instructions. Go back at the end of forty years—or go back once we'd found life? By the time the forty years had gone by, I knew that I was a long-lifer and didn't have to go back. That reinforced the programming for not returning until after we'd found . . . something." He laughed. "You always think you're going to find it over the next hill—in the next system, during the next decade. It's a gambler's disease, you want to throw the dice just one more time. And I always was a gambler."

He hesitated.

"I had no reason to go back, Ray—and I didn't have to, I was going to live forever." He grinned and suddenly became the Mike Kusaka I had hung out in bars with, the Mike Kusaka I had partied with, the Mike Kusaka who had been my best friend. "Everything they did to me, they did to you. You were going to live forever, too, except you were in the Deep Freeze and didn't know it."

It was hard to keep him in focus. One moment I was seeing him with the eyes of Raymond Stone and the next I was looking at him as Sparrow. The two views didn't coincide at all. To me, he was a friend. To Sparrow, he was The Captain— remote, authoritarian, the man who had sentenced three fellow crew members to suffocate on a cold and lifeless planet.

"The crew," I said slowly. "They didn't want to continue."

He looked away, his face now shadowed by the light from the glow tube.

"You know they didn't." He shrugged. "Most of the crew mutinied, maybe ten men remained loyal."

He was remarkably open, but inside me, Sparrow screamed it was a trick.

"You knew you could keep on going," I said. "You could run the ship—you were linked with the computer. But you couldn't run the ship all by yourself, you needed a crew."

He turned cynical. "Come on, Ray. We weren't out five years before Ilena had a kid. By the end of forty, there were sixty uncounted on board. It was obvious we could turn the *Astron* into a generational ship, breed replacement crews as we went."

"The mutiny failed," I reminded him.

"It almost didn't," he said dryly. "You were the return captain so they took you out of the Freeze and killed the rest of the return crew doing it. There was some shooting, some fighting, they were in too much of a hurry. . . ." His voice trailed off.

His telling was incomplete; he still hadn't told me why the mutineers had failed. They had needed each other, it should have been a standoff. Except . . .

I had been in the Freeze during most of the mutiny—the first I knew of it was waking up on a lab table with half a dozen needles stuck in my body and two frightened mutineers bending over me. After that, there had been a lot of shouting and the sharp reports of pellet guns. I had run through the corridors, trying to dodge the peep screens and the Captain's men, not really knowing why I was running but terrified just the same. They had finally caught me and stretched me out on the table once again with Mike looking down at me, holding a hypodermic and mumbling how I-honest-to-God-wouldn't-feel-a-thing. And then, darkness.

Noah and Abel would have been disappointed; I hadn't remembered anything important after all.

"You didn't put me back in the crypt," I asked, puzzled. "Why not?"

He made a bad joke of it.

"You can't refreeze meat, Ray. It loses its texture."

Some of Sparrow's anger crept into my voice.

"You flatlined my memories," I accused.

He looked at me in frustration.

"What the hell was I to do? You would have been the focus of a mutiny every generation that came along. I finally hid you in plain sight, like the purloined letter. It wasn't that difficult; you'd had amnesia before, from your car accident when you were seventeen. In a sense, it was your Achilles heel."

Not that difficult . . . I wondered how long it had taken him to program the artificial reality that was Seti IV and felt another surge of anger.

"I didn't have many options, Ray," Mike apologized. "And after all, you actually played an important role, you were needed."

He had been clever and resourceful and in the long run it really hadn't been his fault: The programming had proved too effective. It was what he wanted me to think. But he had left something out.

I thought I heard a clock ticking and guessed it was Sparrow within.

"They won't come back," I said.

He knew I was talking about Sparrow's crew and looked mildly surprised.

"You really believe that?"

"They won't come back," I repeated. "Not unless you return." I made the mistake of thinking I could convince him. I wasn't Sparrow now, I was his best friend. "You can't run the ship by yourself, and without the others you can't breed a new crew. It's time to go home, Mike."

I don't think he even heard me. He leaned forward in the hammock, his eyes bright with enthusiasm. Too bright.

"We don't need an entire crew, Ray. Three of us can do it—you and I and Thrush. All three of us are linked to the computer; we can seal off most of the ship and run Maintenance by ourselves."

The link to the computer was the key—but you had to be long-lived for the link to exist. Then, inside me, Sparrow warned that the best chess player is the one who convinces you his next move won't be the obvious one.

"It's been thousands of years, Ray," Mike said. "What have you got to go back to? You wouldn't have signed on if you didn't want to be an explorer."

The image of him and me and Thrush, voyaging forever into the great unknown, sickened me. Pipit, Crow, Ophelia, and the hundreds of others didn't matter: They were mayflies.

He watched the parade of emotions cross my face and his own expression hardened.

"I can't go back, Ray. I told you—they rearranged my wiring."

Neither side had been bluffing and that surprised me. The members of the new crew had made up their minds not to continue unless Mike turned back, and Mike couldn't.

No friendship can survive a lie if it's serious enough. And right then I watched my own friendship with Mike dissolve like tissue paper in the rain. The lie was simple and brutal and I hadn't wanted to look at it. Nobody but Mike had wanted to go on—he was the only one who had been programmed. He had to force the others.

"The mutiny had failed before you ever caught me, hadn't it, Mike? You pulled the plug on the return crew, didn't you? Nobody in your crew was going to live long enough to return so they had no choice but to breed their own replacements and hope that someday their children could go back."

His voice turned acid. "Don't think they didn't jump at the chance."

We sat there and stared at each other. With time, friends change. And there had been more than enough time. He'd had his friends among the first crew, at least at the start. But they must have told their children what had happened, and then their descendants avoided him and fell silent when he approached. A man already alienated had grown more distant with every generation until the crews became merely part of the machinery, maintaining the ship and exploring the planets until they were replaced by still another generation.

The movement was so slow I almost didn't see it, his hand edging toward the pellet gun. I could feel my own in my waistband and wondered if he had seen its outline.

Selma and Bobby Armijo, Lewis and Iris, Dave and Rich, and the eight hundred and ninety others who had volunteered for the Freeze and never woken up were suddenly vivid in my memory.

"Why didn't you just kill me, Mike? Why the purloined-letter routine?"

He looked surprised. "You were the return captain—if we'd found life, you'd be the one to take the *Astronomy* back. And if anything happened to me, you were my replacement. I couldn't kill my own replacement, Ray, that would've endangered the voyage."

Nobody could endanger the voyage, not even the captain. . . . Two thousand years ago, some minor bureaucrat in charge of programming had saved my life. And then, in anger, a jealous Sparrow made the mistake of saying the obvious.

"You've got one replacement, you don't need two."

Mike's hand closed around the pellet gun and he aimed it at my chest. He now sounded as indifferent as he had when condemning Noah and Tybalt at their courts-martial, but at least he solved the last of the mysteries.

"You're right, Ray. Thrush can act as my replacement. That's why I had him."

He fired. At the same time I jerked to one side, fumbling in my waistcloth for my own pellet gun. I never got the chance to use it. His foot caught me in the stomach and the gun went flying into the other compartment. I felt blood puddling on my skin where the pellet had grazed me; then we were grappling in the center of the cabin.

It had taken valuable minutes for my friendship with Mike to finally fade, to realize that his own for me had vanished two thousand years before. What power hadn't corrupted, time had. I had been impressed and affected by what he told me, as he had intended I should be, but he hadn't impressed Sparrow or Hamlet or the others inside me.

They had anticipated deception and prepared me for it.

He was strong and quick. But I didn't suffer from the sense of inferiority Sparrow might have had—I had beaten Mike before. He still had the pellet gun and I grabbed his wrist and cracked it against the ledge. He grunted and kneed me in the groin. I let loose and shot across the compartment, scraping my scalp on the hatch. When I shook my head, a thin stream of tiny red globules jetted into the air.

I turned back to him and saw his face fixed in the same intense look of concentration that he had when he played handball. He didn't play to lose.

I dove for him and he fired the pellet gun again. I twisted aside in midair, crashing into the bookshelf. The air was suddenly filled with bits of paper and plastic and I held my breath when I sailed through them. I grabbed his wrist with my hands and once more tried to loosen his grip on the gun.

We both had purchase now. He had wrapped his legs around one of the uprights his hammock was tied to and I had gripped the ledge with my own. It was a test of pure strength and he was stronger. The hand that held the pellet gun slowly swiveled until it was pointed dead center at my chest. He could just as easily have aimed at my head; I thought grimly that only our former friendship prevented it. It would have been too much even for him to see my features explode in a mist of bone and blood.

"I'm sorry, Ray," he murmured. "This isn't easy."

But it seemed all too easy to me. Inside, I could hear Sparrow silently screaming, not only because I might die and he as well but because if I didn't, I would probably kill his Captain. Sparrow had never quite recovered from that first meeting on the bridge.

I had kept my hand on his wrist and jerked it aside just

before he pulled the trigger. The gun misfired. Like every-thing else on board, it was corroded and falling apart. I wrenched it away and threw it in a corner.

Mike drove an elbow into my rib cage and I flailed back-ward. He was faster than me in maneuvering in no gravity. My back hit the bulkhead as he wrapped his hands around my neck, his thumbs pressing against my windpipe. I waited until he had set himself, then clasped my hands together and thrust them up between his arms, breaking the hold.

We flew apart, ending up at opposite ends of the cabin. Breathing was painful and blood was still misting out of my scalp. Across from me, Mike tried desperately to retain an appearance of calm but his skin was shiny with sweat and he was gulping air as hard as I was.

"In two thousand years, you were the only one I could really talk to . . . you were my last link to the original crews." He flashed a smile. " 'The universe is not only . . . queerer than we suppose, but queerer . . . than we *can* suppose.' That used to be your favorite quote, Ray." He held out a hand. "Come . . . with us," he pleaded, and I swore because I could feel a part of myself respond.

"Sure, Mike," I said, and felt no guilt at all when I butted him in the stomach a split second later and wrapped my arms around his waist. I held him in a bear hug and squeezed while he thrashed in the air, trying desperately to catch his breath. When he went limp, I loosened my hold and dragged him through the hatchway into the compartment that contained the preservation crypts of the return crew.

"Look at them, Mike. They almost look alive, don't they? Remember Selma? And Iris? There was a time when you thought the world of Iris. And Bobby? He worshiped you, he would have done anything for you, and eventually he died for you. Nine hundred men and women, Mike, and you mur-dered them all!"

"I had . . . no choice," he muttered, and turned away. I grabbed him by the hair and twisted his head so he was star-ing directly at the crypts and the silent figures within.

"You murdered nine hundred people to keep on going and you never found a goddamned thing! You don't want to go back now because that would be admitting it was all for nothing and you can't face that!"

He looked up at me then, his head wobbling, his eyes wide and filled with horror. For two thousand years the *Astron* had been his stage and he had played The Captain. Now the play was over and once again he was Michael Kusaka, an ordinary man who had lived too long and lost himself among the years.

"Every sleep period I ask their forgiveness," he whispered. "And they forgive me, Ray! They forgive me!"

I couldn't look at him. I was going to have to choose between pity and justice and I wasn't sure I could. Mike had become the Wandering Jew, pacing his five hundred meters of steel deck, praying for absolution every night and searching for it every morning. The only crews that had been real for him were his own and mine, the replacement crew, frozen in its preservation crypts. The crews that came after were faded copies, faces he never remembered, names he quickly forgot.

If Thrush had refused him, Mike would have gone into the Dark by himself, an alienated man whose alienation had finally become terminal.

For Mike, relative immortality had meant two thousand years of damnation.

He suddenly squirmed in my hands and I lost my grip, my fingers slippery with blood and perspiration. He darted out from under my arms, his fingers stretched out for my pellet gun which he had kicked into the compartment, where it was now floating a meter away. If he got it, I knew I wouldn't be as lucky the second time.

I scooped it up before he could touch it, flipping in midair so I was facing him, the pellet gun in my hand. I watched the color drain from his face and the sanity slowly return to his eyes.

I fought to catch my breath, the words coming out in short bursts.

"We're going back—"

He smiled and held up his hands. "You win, Ray."

His back was to the preservation crypts and over his shoulder I could see the dead faces of Selma and Bobby Armijo and Lewis and Tom and Rich. I was the captain now, and I knew the penalty for what Mike had done, both to my crew and to Sparrow's. I remembered how Sparrow had felt when he held the blade to Thrush's throat. I now felt the same way and inside me, Sparrow agreed.

I knew Mike hadn't meant what he said. And I knew Sparrow and I couldn't afford to lose. Not again.

"—without you," I finished.

I pulled the trigger of the pellet gun; at the same time, Mike lunged for me. The pellet caught him in the shoulder and he flew backward, crashing into the one empty preservation crypt, the one that had once contained me. There was a flash of blue light as the dead machinery sprang to life. In the glare I could see Mike's look of startled surprise fade to one of acceptance.

I thought, *Christ, it's still working!* and yanked him out. It was much too late. The skin on his face and chest was gray and hard, the soft tissues of his lips and eyes ruptured by the fine ice crystals that had formed almost instantly.

Michael Kusaka had been raised with a code of honor, but two thousand years had bleached almost all of it out of him. The faint look of acceptance at the end was the only indication that a trace of it still remained. Another time, another place, and if Mike had had a knife his losing might have ended with ritual and ceremony. Both of us would have felt better about it.

I floated by his side, remembering Relay Station and how we had once been friends. I cradled him in my arms and whispered, "Jesus, I'm sorry. . . ," while inside me, Sparrow wept.

Mike clutched my shoulders and pulled me close so I could hear him as he tried to work his frozen lips and tongue.

"No such thing as . . . free will, Ray . . . You had no choice, either. . . . You were programmed to go back. . . ."

Everything they had done to him, they had done to me, Mike had said. Two thousand years before they had wound us up and we had gone through our paces ever since, convinced we were masters of our own destinies. Mike had been programmed to take the *Astronomy* out and I had been programmed to bring her back. He had known about himself, but I had never known about myself.

Or maybe he had lied to the bitter end, unable to face the truth.

I held him, feeling the terrible cold of his chest and head and watching as he struggled for breath and the frost covered him until I couldn't see his face at all.

After a minute the air rattled out of his lungs for the last time and what I held in my arms was meat.

I drifted back to the outer compartment, gripping my side where I still bled. Crow was waiting for me. He looked sick and I wondered what had happened, then glanced over at Thrush, nursing a bleeding lip. Crow was holding a pellet gun and I guessed he had taken it away from Thrush. Crow had committed violence, and I was grateful that he had, but it would be a while before he forgave himself.

Both of them stared at me. I had looked seventeen when I pushed into the Captain's living quarters, but then I had thought I was seventeen. Now I knew my true age was thirty and I looked the part.

"He wanted to go in," Crow said. "I didn't think you wanted him there."

"You were right," I muttered, "I didn't."

I looked at Thrush and saw both of them through Sparrow's eyes at the same time I saw them through mine. It was an unsettling superimposition. Sparrow saw Crow as larger than himself, thickly muscled with heavy features and an odd air of saintliness. Thrush was handsome, lightly but well built, with a sly look and a seductive arrogance about him.

To me they were both kids, maybe twenty years old, one

pale and skinny and the other husky, with long hair and an open face that would someday get him into trouble with more women than one. The skinny one may have been arrogant at one time, but right now he was badly frightened.

Had Thrush wanted to help the Michael Kusaka who was the Captain or had he wanted to help the Michael Kusaka who was his father? They were one and the same but they were also quite different. It didn't matter. In trying to help Kusaka, Thrush had probably earned the right to his own life. When everything was over, I would have to talk to him.

I turned to tell Crow to call back Inbetween Station, the Lander, and the various floaters, but he read me before I could even ask.

"They're on their way."

"Lose any?"

"Maybe Finch—he might be beyond reach."

"Tell the Lander to try and pick him up." I wondered just how far their ability to locate fellow crew members extended.

He was almost to the hatchway when I said, "Was it a bluff, Crow?"

"I don't know, sir." But he looked stricken and that told me what I wanted to know. They hadn't run the bluff against Mike; they had known that he was programmed, that he wouldn't buy it, couldn't buy it.

They had run the bluff against Sparrow. They knew if they pressed him hard enough he would confront the Captain to try and save them and then . . . something would happen. They weren't sure what, but since the phoenix dated from Year One of the voyage, they knew something would. And they had gambled that the phoenix would win.

Lucky fools.

A few hours later, we gathered on the bridge. I sat in the captain's chair and could feel myself tied into every part of the ship. The chair was a giant terminal pad. The captain ran the ship not just with his hands but with every portion of his body. The chair itself was warm and resilient and I could feel my nerve endings tingle.

The last time I sat there had been during the shakedown cruise and I remembered the sense of power it had given me. It gave me the same feeling now but this time, I didn't relish it. I had lived a hundred lifetimes and come out of it with a far different view of life and my place in it.

They were all there—Ophelia, Snipe, Crow, and Loon, all looking expectant, while Grebe seemed apprehensive and Cato was frowning. Even Escalus was there, his eyes red-rimmed with grief; I knew I would have to watch him for as long as he lived. Finally, there was Thrush, his expression, as always, mocking.

Nobody was going to dispute that I was captain, but all wondered what I was going to do now. Ophelia, naturally, nominated herself as spokesperson.

"What are your plans?" she asked, but the question was a formality. Everybody on the bridge knew what I was going to do.

"We're going home," I said.

But I wasn't sure there was still a home to go to.

32

They got to Finch minutes before his air ran out so the only casualties were Tern, Crane, Bunting, and a member of the old crew, Gower. I had known him only vaguely and that bothered me. I would have to make a point of getting to know the crew better; I couldn't rely on Sparrow's memories of friends and acquaintances.

But what bothered me most was Snipe. I had become somebody she had never known, somebody she was uncomfortable living with. She could read me as well as ever, but the person she read wasn't . . . Sparrow. During the next sleep period we went through the motions of making love just once and found that it repelled both of us. After that, we were awkward and cold with each other and seldom found reason to talk.

We worked it out another sleep period when I accidentally brushed her face and discovered her cheek was damp with tears.

"What's wrong, Snipe?"

"I miss Sparrow," she murmured.

I stroked her hair and brushed her neck with my lips and a little of Raymond Stone dropped away and then more and more. "Sparrow" had lived perhaps a year; Raymond Stone had lived thirty and could look forward to . . . what? A thousand years? Two thousand? "Sparrow" would die when his generation on board finally died. Until then, he deserved his own life.

That sleep period Raymond Stone mentally slapped Sparrow on the back, wished him well, and quietly withdrew. Not completely; there were parts of Stone that Sparrow needed. But it was Sparrow who made love to Snipe, died the little death, and slept the sleep of the just.

Stepping into Mike's role as captain was easier than I thought it would be. The computer posed no problems and I set the course for the return to Earth. It would be a straight-line voyage with no star-hopping unless we got undeniable signals in the waterhole frequencies. We had been out a hundred generations at the time of the mutiny and I estimated it would take twenty to return. None of the crew, except Thrush and me, would ever see the Earth, though they realized their not-so-remote descendants would.

The former Captain's men posed a problem. I was blunt in warning Cato. He was resentful, but that I expected. He and his men did their job well and until such time as they didn't, I wouldn't interfere.

Thrush was another matter.

We had been on the return course for a month before I felt I had the reins of authority firmly in my hands. Once they were, I sent for Thrush. Crow ushered him in, then made himself inconspicuous by the hatchway.

I was mostly Sparrow then, with just enough of Raymond Stone to lend Sparrow some distance from his own feelings.

Thrush had changed very little. Pale, arrogant, suspicious . . . searching my face to determine how much of me was Sparrow and how much was Raymond Stone. He saw enough of Sparrow to be reassured and just enough of Raymond Stone to keep him off balance.

We stared at each other in silence. I waited while he became increasingly uncomfortable; finally he blurted: "When am I to be sent?"

"Sent where?" I asked, mystified.

"Reduction." His smile was sardonic. "You've won your mutiny but I'm sure you're worried about the possibility of others."

"Mutinies are composed of followers," I said quietly. "Not just leaders. Who would follow you, Thrush?" He colored and I shook my head, dismissing the fantasy. "If you go to Reduction, it will be because you want to go, not because I sent you."

I had been responsible for Mike's death and that was going to be hard to live down.

"You knew all along I was the return captain," I said, curious. "How?"

He seemed bemused.

"Being an icon was too . . . romantic. And even considering the practice time you spent with the computer, you were too good." He shrugged and for the first time sounded bitter. "The Captain should have sent you to Reduction half a dozen times and he never did. Only one explanation made sense—"

I cut him off.

"You're thinking emotionally and you're not the type, Thrush. What were the real reasons?"

He looked impressed and a little uneasy. He was used to dealing with Sparrow. Raymond Stone was unpredictable—and potentially threatening.

"Both you and the Captain were long-lifers and the roles you played fit a generational ship. But the *Astron* didn't have the redundancy that a true generational ship would have had; it fed upon itself and the crew. There had to be another explanation for the Captain and you."

Noah and Abel had undoubtedly come to the same conclusion.

"You wanted to be captain," I said.

He shrugged. "Perhaps sometime. What else was there to be?"

"And you would have gone with Kusaka?"

"I was curious." A glimmer of his old arrogance returned. "It's a big universe."

Mike would have gone because he had been programmed. Thrush would have gone out of a cold curiosity.

"You would have been inviting loneliness for centuries."

His face darkened.

"I'm lonely now."

There was a certain amount of self-pity in the statement, but it was also true. I wondered if alienation could be transmitted through the genes.

"You knew you were Kusaka's son?"

"Long before he told me." A brief grimace: "I never identified with any of the crew, and like you, I healed too fast."

He had logged computer time for the same reason I had—trying to find out who he was. It explained a lot. What he had discovered made him the prince-in-waiting and I his unwitting competition.

It was an uneasy moment of identification; I couldn't forget that he had tried to kill me. I couldn't afford him, but the *Astron* couldn't afford to be without him. He was the only true scientist on board.

"On the Lander, Thrush—you said you hoped I would die."

He looked surprised.

"You were Hamlet," he said. "I had no reason to like him."

From somewhere inside came confirmation.

"The drink bulb in sick bay," I said. "Was that you or Heron?"

His pale face suddenly shone with sweat.

"I knew Abel and Noah were going to ask you questions. I wanted to know the answers, too. But you would never have told me."

I smiled to myself. It had been a simple truth serum, but how was Sparrow to know?

"And the tether line?"

He shrugged. "Somebody's sloppy work."

If he was telling the truth, Sparrow had been a fool. But

considering all that had happened, Sparrow had the right. And Thrush was hardly blameless.

"And on Aquinas II? That was your idea, not Heron's."

He looked cornered, his pale lips lifting slightly away from his too-white teeth.

"Yes," he blurted, "that was my idea. But you tried to kill me on the hangar deck. You would have cut my throat!"

I had come so very close. . . .

"You drew first blood, Thrush."

He shook his head vehemently.

"I wanted to mark you, not kill you. What kind of a fool do you think I am? Kill the Captain's replacement? The crew's icon? I would have been sent to Reduction within the hour."

I continued, remorseless.

"On Aquinas II, you had decided I was too dangerous to live and tried murder by proxy. Of all the crew members, Heron was the only one who loved you, Thrush. The only one who would do anything for you."

He hung his head and said nothing.

"And let's not forget Pipit," I murmured.

He wouldn't meet my eyes. "You want me to agree I deserve Reduction? Then I agree."

I made up my mind.

"The *Astron* needs a doctor and you were Abel's assistant. He didn't like you, Thrush, but when it came to science, he thought highly of you."

"Whatever you say," he whispered.

He was a shade too humble and it irritated me.

"Don't you want to see the Earth? Aside from myself, you're the only one who will."

He shrugged once again. "It means nothing to me."

I thought of his compartment falsie and knew he was lying.

"I know the Earth firsthand, Thrush. I've seen birds whose wings beat so fast they can hover above the ground without benefit of updrafts and I've heard other birds imitate a human voice. There are animals that raise their young in pouches, slugs that excrete glue to coat the ground they travel over, and worms that live in the oceans at depths that would crush a submarine. . . ." My voice trailed away. I sounded like Mike so often had.

The old Thrush shouldered his way to the surface.

"You've seen a lot," he said sarcastically.

The *Astron* needed him but it needed him on its terms, not his.

"An ice volcano is not the highest achievement of the universe," I said slowly. "Neither are planetary rings nor a rock sitting in the middle of a lunar plain. You and I are its highest achievements, Thrush—we can think and we can feel and we can run and play games and pick our noses. There's nothing else in the universe that can do any of those."

He gave in then, making a great show of how little it meant to him. "If you want me to be the doctor—"

I cut him short, letting some of Raymond Stone's authority seep into my voice. "You'll do it because I tell you to, Thrush. And because nobody else is qualified." And then I sweetened it, but only a little. "I also hope you'll do it because you want to."

When he was at the hatchway, I said: "I'm sorry about . . . your father. At one time he was my friend."

"My father let you win," Thrush said proudly. "He knew all about the mutiny, he could have stopped it at any time. But even after he knew I could serve as his replacement, he didn't do it." He looked away. "Captain Kusaka committed suicide."

That was one of the few times I ever saw the real Thrush. It didn't make me like him any more but I understood him a little better. Everybody on board needed someone to "take an interest." The Captain never had until he knew for sure that Thrush was going to live forever. By then it was too late . . .

My first real test as captain didn't jump out at me all at once. I became aware of it bit by bit. Fewer and fewer crew members seemed to be wearing eye masks, preferring the comforting illusion of the compartment falsies to the reality of the ship as it actually was. A sullenness also seemed to be spreading through the crew, and too many of them fell silent when I passed.

"It's because you've taken away purpose," Snipe said one sleep period when we had curled up in the hammock.

"I haven't taken away purpose," I said, puzzled. "I've given it." She was silent, stroking my legs and tangling her fingers in the hair on my chest. "That hurts."

"Sorry," she said, not sorry at all. Then, trying to explain: "You've seen the Earth, Sparrow. They never will. Before, we went from planet to planet and while we never found anything, there was always the hope that we would. And we kept ourselves busy preparing."

Mike had made them promises and he was credible because he believed in them himself. If not *here*, he would say, then *there*. If not this generation, then next . . .

I could promise them nothing for twenty generations and I wasn't sure I could promise them the Earth even then. And they sensed it.

"They would rather believe in fantasy?"

"There's not much difference, Sparrow. What you promise, they'll never see."

She was right. I also knew I couldn't live with a sullen crew. I called in Thrush and told him what I wanted, then guaranteed I would get it by suggesting he couldn't do it. After that, I chose a time when almost everybody was asleep, stole up to the bridge and slipped into the captain's chair.

It took the entire period to identify all the compartment falsies as well as those for the various workplaces and assembly areas. I put each of them in a guardian shell, and when the crew woke they saw the *Astron* as it really was—small, dingy, with broken glow tubes and tiny compartments, ancient machinery and mossy bulkheads. Moments later they became aware of the sweat and the odor of human bodies that filled the air.

Ophelia was the first to push past Crow and ask for an explanation, her face white with anger.

"Why?" she demanded.

"They've grown too fond of shadows," I said.

"You've seen the Earth," she objected. "They haven't."

"They know where they've been but they don't know where they're going, is that it?"

I was the Captain, but she had known me too long as Sparrow and didn't bother to hide her sarcasm.

"You put it well."

"Then go to the hangar deck and take a look," I said casually.

She turned suspicious. "It's been off limits for the past half dozen time periods."

I left the chair and drifted to the corridor outside.

"It isn't now, Ophelia."

She hesitated in mid-tirade, then followed me to the well that led to the hangar deck. The news had already spread and outside the hatchway, the corridor was jammed. Inside, the crew gaped in awe at the prairie spread out before them. The huge expanse was a sloping hill of grass and wildflowers, while at the bottom was a small brook whose surface was broken by the frequent splashes of fish. There were little eddies in the stream and along its banks weeds hung over the water, acting as cover for a dozen croaking frogs.

Overhead, the sky was a light blue mottled with wispy white clouds. The touch of genius was the occasional bird that Thrush had programmed winging its way toward a distant plot of plowed land. A farmhouse topped a nearby hill; off in the distance was the barely discernible smudge of a city.

It was the third time I had seen it but it still took my breath away.

"I'll turn all the falsies back on," I assured Ophelia, "but I wanted the crew to know where we're going."

The sullen looks disappeared after that and there was more talk of when we would arrive at Earth orbit and what we might find. I gave Thrush full credit; he accepted the compliments grudgingly, but secretly, I think he was proud.

I was gambling that such a meadow still existed, consoling myself with the thought that those who admired the fantasy would never live long enough to be disappointed by the reality.

In one sense, birth is something that's best appreciated by the parents and maybe the attending doctors. For an outsider, it's a bloody, unpleasant, unaesthetic, barbaric business reminding us of the animals we are and the basic bodily functions we share with them.

But that was Raymond Stone's view and certainly didn't reflect that of the *Astron*'s crew. For two weeks the corridors were crowded with crew members watching the deliveries on peep screens and cheering wildly at the first cry of each baby. They gambled on the sex of each and the most beautiful was always the one that had just been born.

The women identified vicariously with the various mothers; none of the men openly claimed paternity but each secretly felt the baby of the birth mother he had been with was his.

Thrush was efficient and stoic, sometimes tending the mothers around the clock. One period, I went with him to sick bay, filled with nursing mothers and their bawling, lusty flock and was deeply moved. Life, I thought, with all its unlimited possibilities . . .

I looked around. "Where's Pipit?"

"In her compartment. She didn't want me to attend her after delivery."

His face showed no emotions, but his voice betrayed him.

"Healthy baby?" I asked inanely.

"A boy. You might recognize him."

It was a strange remark. A few minutes later I asked and was granted permission to enter Pipit's compartment. She was nursing the baby; Crow was beside her on the hammock, oohing and aah-ing and going through the fatherly routine I had already seen a dozen times.

"Hold him a minute," Pipit said proudly.

I did, and promptly regretted it. But that's what waistcloths are for. His skin was as olive as Pipit's and his eyes were almost black. I chucked him under the chin and he tolerated it a moment, his dark eyes staring somberly into mine, before crying for his mother.

I handed him back and congratulated Pipit profusely. I managed to control my shivering until I was out in the corridor, then let the goose bumps form. When young babies stare at you, they sometimes seem far older than their years, and very wise, as if they know something important that you don't. Unfortunately, by the time they learn to speak, they've forgotten whatever it was they wanted to say shortly after they were born.

That's more fantasy than theory, but when I looked into the dark eyes of Pipit's baby, I imagined I saw Michael Kusaka staring back.

When the excitement of the births had died away and the *Astron* had settled once more into routine, I asked Crow and Thrush and Ophelia to meet me in the captain's private compartment. It had been left exactly as it was when Mike had died. The nine hundred crypts sat silent, the figures within looking deceptively natural and lifelike, waiting patiently for the technicians to revive them. Ophelia and Crow inspected them uneasily, noting the names and the various professions. Thrush's face was as blank of emotion as my own. I didn't know whether he mourned Mike, but I mourned them all.

I waited a moment, then cleared my throat and said, "The return crew was cheated—they never had the chance to see Outside as the first crew did and neither did they have the chance to return to Earth to live out their lives and die there as they thought they would. They were my crew and my friends. . . ."

My voice trailed off but I had more control than to let myself weep.

"They never received much for participating in the voyage, but they've left us a legacy: themselves. Thanks to them, we'll arrive back on Earth with the same crew complement that we have right now, perhaps a few more."

They knew what I meant. The bodies of the return crew would go to Reduction and more than make up for the *Astron*'s losses during the next twenty generations.

"You'll supervise, Thrush. Pick a team. But attend to the job during sleep periods and close off any corridors you'll be using."

He nodded, but Crow and Ophelia still looked mystified, wondering why I had asked them to attend.

I cleared my throat again.

"I need witnesses to hear me read the service for the dead."

I had found the small book in Mike's library; now I opened it to the appropriate page and started reading in a low voice. For Selma and Bobby and the hundreds of others, it was the most that I could do.

When I was through I waved Crow and Ophelia away but asked Thrush to stay behind.

"Mike's in the crypt with my name on it. If you want to be left alone . . ."

He shook his head and said firmly, "No, I don't think so," then glanced around at the crypts and murmured, "I'm surprised they're still here."

I didn't say anything. Nobody would have helped Mike carry the bodies to Reduction and he would never have asked. The few words I had once overheard came back to me. He had lived for two millennia with nine hundred albatrosses hung around his neck. In imagination I could see him talking to them every sleep period, begging their forgiveness for the ten thousandth time.

The next few time periods I spent in the captain's chair in the outer compartment, staring at the simulations just outside the port. I refused to see anyone, even Snipe. The fourth sleep period by myself, Crow and Loon pushed through the shadow screen without announcing themselves. With them were two young women, Starling and Gull, whom I had never gotten to know very well, even during the time when Crow and I had rutted our way through the ship.

I glanced at them and waved my hand at the port.

"That's the solar system—Jupiter and its moons."

The two women looked at the view beyond the port and then back at me. They giggled and it occurred to me they hadn't come to look at simulations of Outside.

Oh, no, I thought, but Crow read me, nodded firmly, and said, "Oh, yes, Sparrow."

My heart wasn't in it, but they had brought some smoke and Loon played an old tune on his harmonica. Half an hour later our waistcloths were floating limply about the compartment and I discovered that despite everything that had happened, I was still very human and could smile and laugh after all.

Sometime during that period Crow murmured in my ear, "It's life, Sparrow." Crow had made his point and it was one that I never forgot.

Life is for the living.

33

As the months rolled by, I found myself regretting more and more that I was no longer a seventeen-year-old tech assistant. The problems of the ship were relatively easy to handle. The personal problems were trying. When I talked to Huldah now, it was difficult to see her as the matriarch on board. In my mind's eye I kept seeing her as she was when I was Aaron: She was very young and very pretty, with unwrinkled skin and large dark eyes that always smiled when they saw me. As Aaron, I had been a friend of Noah's and Abel's and all three of us had competed for Huldah. I remembered my hurt when she had finally dropped me, and how sullen I had been around Noah and Abel after that.

Strangely, I kept seeing the younger Huldah when we met and kept apologizing for it afterward until she finally stopped me.

"Sparrow, I don't mind being mistaken for a younger and prettier self. It's flattering—until you apologize for doing it."

We laughed, and once again I saw in her everything that I had admired when she was younger.

She was curious about the history of the ship and I filled her in from my own memories, surprised that her oral history was so accurate. For many months we met regularly every other time period and I would tell her about events in which I had played a part and remembered so well, but about which she had only heard at second or third or twentieth hand.

Then one period her interest seemed to flag. I noticed for the first time that she was becoming frail and her skin was turning translucent. She was failing and we both knew it.

The last time I saw her, we didn't talk about history but simply about Noah and Abel and us and the hurts and traumas of young love. I kissed her fondly when I left, knowing that we would never see each other again.

Her successor, as we all knew it would be, was Pipit, who now took Huldah's compartment and assumed the role of matron.

Snipe aged well, though there came a time when she pushed me firmly away in the hammock and said she loved me very much but the role she was playing was making her increasingly uncomfortable.

The next shift she showed up on the bridge with a young woman and announced that I needed an assistant recordkeeper and she had found one for me.

"You remember Denali, Sparrow."

Denali smiled and I smiled tentatively back. I had met her first in Pipit's nursery and had watched her grow into a young and beautiful woman. I remembered that Ophelia had introduced me to Snipe, and guessed that Snipe was now passing on the favor.

"A moment, Denali." I took Snipe by the hand and led her back to our living quarters.

"Why, Snipe?"

She stroked my cheek and said, "Look at me, Sparrow. See me as I am now, not as I was yesterday. Who will take care of you when I'm gone? I trust Denali."

Snipe remained a part of my household for many time periods after that, though eventually she moved in with Loon and Crow. Once again she had become interested in the historicals and fantasy; she and Loon had much in common. When I visited them, I noted that the unicorn, which had vanished shortly after we first partnered, had returned to graze by the stream. In the distance, outside a camp of tents with flying pennons, knights were jousting.

Ophelia and Grebe partnered for the remainder of their lives; then, one time period, both vanished, apparently having agreed to go to Reduction together. I missed Ophelia more than she could have guessed.

We made one stop at a system where Communications reported a signal in the waterhole. There were seven planets, two of which had possibilities. We explored both. On the second, we lost K2 in a landslide. I grieved for months.

And then one sleep period, a bowed and hobbling Snipe slipped through the shadow screen and said simply, "Will you go with me, Sparrow?"

We went to Reduction together and sat on the ledge and I held her tight, my arms wrapped around her thin shoulders. She murmured something to herself and I leaned closer to listen.

> "Wilt thou be gone? It is not yet near day.
> It was the nightingale, and not the lark,
> That pierced the fearful hollow of thine ear. . . ."

"'I have more care to stay than will to go,'" I said gently. She laughed quietly and pushed me away.

"Is that the best you can do?" she said with mock scorn and I found myself looking at the Snipe of sixty years before. I started to weep and she put her fingers on my lips as Pipit once had and said, "Shush, Sparrow." Then her voice thinned and she murmured, "Help me in, please."

I led her over to the chamber, undid her halter and helped her slide into the swirling red mists until only her face was visible. She smiled at me and said, "Privacy, Sparrow," then closed her eyes. I waited until she faded from view, then went back to my quarters and exiled Denali for six months.

A year later, I had one last party with Crow and Loon and a youngster to whom Loon had taught his songs and his skill with the harmonica. There was smoke for all and Denali and I floated near the window that opened out on St. Mark's Square, our arms entwined, and laughed as Loon and Samson and a young girl named Dido traded off playing duets.

When it was over and the others had left, Crow turned to me, concerned.

"Your face gets longer by the year, Sparrow. What's wrong?"

I hesitated, then shrugged. Crow and I had never kept anything from each other.

"You're getting older and I'm not," I said, my voice thick with regret.

A slight smile played around the corners of his mouth.

"You want to go to Reduction ahead of time, that's your choice, Sparrow."

"That's not what I meant," I objected.

He looked a little impatient with me.

"You're feeling sorry for us, am I right, Sparrow?"

I hesitated, then admitted it. "I guess so."

He shook his head in mock despair.

"You're the captain, Sparrow, but . . . you still don't know us very well."

I thought of the conversation I'd once had with Huldah about the new crew.

"You're right, in one sense I don't know you very well."

"The truth is, our lives are pretty full, probably more than yours, at least in a personal sense." He said it in a low voice, as if he were confiding a secret, and perhaps he was. "We're never lonely, Sparrow, we . . . share our memories. We're privy to each other's lives in a way that you and members of the old crew never can be. You can talk to each other about your lives, you can observe each other's lives, but you can't . . . live each other's lives. In a sense, we can." He smiled. "We see ourselves as others see us—you know the poem. But you may not remember the next line: 'It wad frae monie a blunder free us, An' foolish notion.' You can't really see yourself, Sparrow, and you can't really see us."

His comment hurt. If I had ever studied myself as closely as the crew once had, I might have discovered who I really was far sooner, if only through my anachronisms of thought and speech, which must have fascinated them. I had never looked at myself with the objectivity that the crew had; I had never listened to myself as closely as they had.

I had spent endless hours searching for my past in the computer's memory matrix. I could have saved myself endless time and trauma by looking within rather than without. Noah had been right: Somewhere inside, I had known.

"We don't go to Reduction because we're old," Crow continued. "We go because we've exhausted life. Abel tried to tell you that once."

I stared at him for a long moment, then said: "*You* feel sorry for *me*."

He nodded, his face somber. "I always have." He broke into another smile. "We all go back to the Great Egg, Sparrow. Life is finite, even for you—you won't live forever, if that's any consolation."

I hugged him when I left and we made plans to share a meal the next time period.

But when the next time period came, I ate alone.

To live your life with no regrets was the most important thing I learned from Crow. I settled back and let the generations roll over me, watching with fascination the never-ending shuttling of the genes as they wove the tapestry of life. It was a shock when in the eighth generation of the return, I played chess with a youngster named Ant and suddenly found myself pitted against Noah's basic game plan. I didn't believe in reincarnation, but I became convinced there were collective memories that could be passed along genetically as well as eye color or the shape of one's nose.

And during the ninth generation, when I saw a young man dragging his foot, I thought that fate had once again thrown the same combination and I was staring at Tybalt. It wasn't until two time periods later, when he was no longer limping, that I realized he had merely stubbed his toe—and in any event, an amputated foot was hardly a gene-linked trait. But I had wanted desperately to believe, I missed Tybalt that much.

The faces changed and I grew forgetful and knew I was being humored but didn't really object. I had a box seat at the greatest show in the universe. I gradually learned to recognize personality traits as well as features until I could follow entire families through the dance of life and predict in advance the basic character of the children of the birth mothers.

Nature repeated itself frequently, though never in quite the same way. But there came a time when I saw again the face of Crow and looked into the eyes of Snipe and heard Loon playing his harmonica in a distant corridor. I was developing a great fondness for humanity; I often wondered why Mike never had, and regretted that he had missed so much.

But I also had my dark periods when I would lie in a hammock on the hangar deck, stare at the unwinking stars overhead and think of the crew sleeping below. I felt crushed by my responsibility for them. They were the only life for thousands of light-years around, perhaps the only life there was in an interstellar desert populated by occasional lumps of rock or flaring globes of burning gas or bits of black capable of swallowing everything, including light itself. . . .

At such times I prided myself on saving the last few members of the human race, even though they were no longer quite human. But that didn't matter, they were alive. Genetic divergence was well under way and I knew if I lived long enough, someday I would wind up as the only true human being in a zoo of my own making. . . .

Thrush had become my best friend. We had been formal and distant for years after the mutiny, though I never had cause to complain about his work. He partnered with nobody, which worried me, and watched from the sidelines as Pipit's son, Baffin, grew to manhood. I think it was by mutual consent with Crow and Pipit that he never "took an interest," though I knew he itched to teach the boy some of his own skills.

Suddenly, or so it seemed, the boy was middle-aged, and finally elderly, and Thrush still had not changed at all. By that time both Pipit and Crow had gone to Reduction. Eventually Baffin vanished as well. The long life that Michael Kusaka had bestowed on Thrush had stopped with him. In all that time, Baffin and Thrush had never spoken a word to each other.

Once Baffin was gone, Thrush disappeared into his compartment and didn't come out until I sent a message asking him to share a meal with me.

Pipit's successor many times removed didn't have Pipit's flair with spices but the meal was more than adequate and to my satisfaction Thrush had a good appetite.

We ate largely in silence; after we had finished, he leaned back in his sling, his hands loose in his lap, and waited. He still looked the same but the arrogance had been replaced by an air of reserve. We tolerated each other, though I was beginning to think that it was a little more than tolerance. Of all the crew, only Thrush was left of those I had known as Sparrow.

"You and Baffin never spoke," I said.

He looked uncomfortable.

"Neither Crow nor Pipit would have encouraged it."

"But you would have liked to."

He looked away. "Yes, I would have liked to."

I didn't pursue it any further; the hurt was too obvious.

"I've somebody I want you to meet," I said.

He looked more polite than interested.

"Oh? Who?"

I grinned. "I think he's here now."

Aral had been allowed in by the corridor guard and now floated over to the table, his olive-black eyes wide with curiosity. He was seven years old and had never been in the compartment before, nor seen the simulations beyond the port.

"You know Thrush, Aral—he's the *Astron*'s scientist."

Aral clasped his hands behind his back and bowed formally, too shy to actually touch fingers. Thrush studied him, curious.

"Would you like to see the solar system, Aral?" I asked. He nodded, interest bright in his eyes.

There had been no simulation beyond the port, only the "off" sheet of gray. I played my hand over the terminal pad and a moment later, Saturn and its satellites filled the port.

Aral drifted over until his hands and nose touched the glass.

"That's Titan," he said, pointing. "And that's Enceladus, it's ice. . . ."

"Which one has life?" I asked.

He looked at me with a young boy's eager contempt for ignorance.

"There's no life, it's too cold!"

I laughed. "Would you like to see the Triffid nebula?"

We went through a dozen of the views, then I shooed him out.

"He needs someone to take an interest," I said to Thrush.

"Nobody has?" He looked surprised.

"The boy has his problems—one of them being he's too bright. How about you, Thrush?"

He froze up, disappointing me.

"Is that an order?"

"I ceased giving you orders generations ago," I murmured.

Thrush ignored the boy for a month, then thawed, and soon they were inseparable. Aral grew to be his assistant and eventually "took an interest" in a young girl who showed Pipit's talent for biology. I finally told Thrush that Aral was his great-grandson.

The next generation, Thrush started a school and even began to partner, usually with one of the mothers of his flock of students. We gradually grew closer until we regularly took our meals together and spent more than one sleep period planning the procedures to follow once in Earth orbit.

Then one time period Thrush drifted in unannounced with

a large mirror under his arm. He placed it on my desk and motioned me over so we could look in it together.

For the first time in generations, I started to tremble; Thrush had to put his hand on my shoulder to calm me. In the mirror, my own face looked back, unlined, unmarred by the passage of time. But Thrush's pale hair had turned silver and a crescent of fine wrinkles had formed under his eyes.

"You'll have to take the *Astron* in yourself, Ray."

Thrush lived fourteen generations. When he went to Reduction, he left me the cube of plastic that "Sparrow" had first noticed on the Captain's desk. The small blue and white flowers with their roots embedded in fine sand and tiny pebbles hadn't faded at all.

I made a silent promise to Thrush that when we landed, one of the first orders of business would be to replace the plastic cube and its frozen flowers with a vase of real ones.

Two generations before planetfall, I indulged myself and changed what had been a tradition on board. I took out the roster of the return crew and started assigning proper names to the children of the birth mothers. Robert Armijo and Selma Delgado and Tom Youngblood and Lewis Downes and Iris Wong and the others had never been able to return to Earth in person, but now they would do so, if only in name. It was my own small tribute to their memory and one that pleased me enormously.

The solar system had gradually been growing on the view screen; in the fifth year of the twentieth generation of the return we were once again in Earth orbit, high above a blue planet swathed in bands of white clouds. I had worried that the Earth would appear as a waterless rock covered with sand dunes like Mars, or hidden beneath the thick yellow smog of an atmosphere like that of Venus.

"Instrument readings, Crow?" I murmured.

"What?"

I looked over in annoyance at the husky engineer who had

taken the readings of the atmosphere. At first I couldn't figure out why he was staring at me, puzzled; then I recalled what I had said.

"Sorry, Lewis—instrument readings, please."

He had looked too much like Crow; the mistake had been a natural one. But it was one that I was making more and more and I wondered if I was coming to one of those watersheds in life, when you age suddenly and dramatically.

He recited the figures and I nodded as he went down the list. The proportions of oxygen and nitrogen were the same, though those of the rare gases had changed moderately and carbon dioxide was a little down. Much to my surprise, the ozone layer was intact—in the intervening millennia, it had reconstituted itself.

I raised my voice slightly.

"Bring up the magnification, Iris."

The view of the planet below grew alarmingly until we weren't more than a few hundred miles above the surface. It took two hours to make a complete orbit and I watched intently as we swung over the land and the oceans below. The Richat structures in West Africa, ancient reminders of meteor impacts, were the same. The outlines of the continents were also the same, though Baja California had finally separated from the mainland.

The mountains and bays and lakes for the most part hadn't changed, but Asia's Lake Balkhash had disappeared and it looked as if San Francisco Bay was completely filled in, whether by natural causes or by intent there was no way of knowing.

But what I was really looking for, I didn't see at all.

"Any signs of cities, Bob?"

I had almost called him Loon—but though he looked the same, I doubted that Bob Armijo had ever played the harmonica or danced through the corridors.

"None, Captain."

After a second orbit, Lewis drifted over and said, puzzled: "There's no detectable electromagnetic radiation of any kind."

No indications of technology or of human life, I thought, at least none as I had known it. I remembered the string of dispatches that Crow and I had found so long ago in the Communications department of Section Two.

"That's not good, is it?" I murmured.

Lewis shook his head, his brown hair floating in a halo around his face, and once again I thought of Crow.

"A team of us could take the Lander and go down," he offered.

It was tempting but dangerous.

"We'll try a probe first and bring back a sample," I said. He looked disappointed. "We've lived a hundred and twenty-two generations at a constant temperature and in a sterile atmosphere, Lewis. Send somebody down to the only planet we know of that has life and we could be dead within a week."

"Sorry, Captain, I didn't think."

"You're as anxious as I am," I said easily. "Send a probe and when we get it back, we'll see what's down there."

It was another half dozen orbits before I watched the probe dropping down through the atmosphere. We guided it under radio control toward one of the flat areas in North America, the part I remembered as farmland. We would bring back atmospheric samples and a core sample of topsoil for lab analysis.

Better the devil we knew, I thought. Nobody on board had any experience with a planet where there was life in every drop of water and under every rock and if you didn't eat it first, it would eat you.

For the next time period, all of us were nervous and ill at ease. Lewis and Iris and I practically lived on the bridge, and all of us were getting ripe, but nobody wanted to take the time to shower for fear he would miss something.

I was alone with my thoughts while we waited. With the members of the crew, conversation seemed to be falling into disuse and I knew it was because they sensed each other's feelings so completely and precisely that speech was used primarily for transmitting information.

I kept wondering if there was any life at all on the Earth. And, if there were, whether the crew could live with it. And what would the descendants of the crew be like in another hundred generations? Would they be content to remain on the Earth? I doubted it. Tybalt's fever dreams had become the stuff of legend. They had all been fiction and delusion, but there was no denying their impact as inspiration.

There would be a relaxation time and then they would go out again, maybe even crossing the Dark this time. Perhaps not so much to explore as to colonize, though that was a vastly long time in the future.

"Captain?"

I shook myself out of the half doze I had fallen into.

"The probe's back, Captain. We've built a P-3 containment on the hangar deck where we can open it."

I pushed out of my chair and kicked through the hatchway, and a few moments later half a hundred of us were gathered around the plastic containment watching while Iris manipulated the jury-rigged remotes to open the small drone and take out the core sample.

We held our collective breath as she slowly picked through the collection of dirt and stones.

For an agonizing moment I thought there was nothing at all, then—"Go back, Iris—gently."

The tiny scalpels felt their way back through the muck, stopping at the smudge of *something* that I had seen. They brushed away the grains of dirt, then carefully unfolded a splotch of green.

I stared at it, and for the first time in generations wiped away tears without embarrassment. I glanced up at the faces of Iris and Lewis and Bob and Selma but their features kept shifting and I found myself looking at Crow and Snipe and Ophelia and Loon and all the others with whom I had lived the most important life of my hundred and twenty or so.

"Do you see it?" I cried, and I was talking to all of them, Crow and Snipe as well as Lewis and Iris. "Do you see it?"

For centuries I had been a broken-field runner carrying a case of eggs across a plain filled with rocks and potholes—perhaps all the humanity in the universe, maybe all the life in the universe—and finally I was safely home.

In the containment, separated now from the dirt and sand that had crushed them, were several perfectly formed sprigs of clover. The first bit of life I had seen in almost three thousand years that hadn't been grown on the *Astron* itself.

I had gambled—and I had won.

The crew around me shouted and clapped each other on the back and for once used actual words to say what they felt.

I backed away and drifted over to the port and looked out at the Earth so close below.

I had no idea whether human beings were still living there or not.

But if they weren't, they soon would be.

EPILOGUE

We shall not cease from exploration
And the end of all our exploring
Will be to arrive where we started
And know the place for the first time.
—from "Little Gidding,"
T. S. Eliot

I was relaxed and alone on the bridge, having tired of the party on the hangar deck. I felt old. It was the end of the story. We had all come back—Aaron and Huldah and Noah and Abel and Michael Kusaka and Ophelia and Snipe and Crow and Loon and Thrush, all of us. In one form or another, we were all up on the hangar deck, drinking too much and storing up enough regrets for the next year and perhaps more.

We would take the Lander down and explore the Earth as we had any other planet, in exploration suits and with bottled air, and we would go through the ultraviolet sprays when we returned to make sure we weren't carrying some hardy bug that could kill us all. At the moment, as a life form, we were amazingly fragile, susceptible to every bacterium or virus we might run across.

Sooner or later we would have to abandon our suits and establish a colony, and then the mortality rate would be frightening. We would adapt, of course; we always had.

But my job was done. I could either hang around out of idle curiosity or let myself grow old—I was convinced it was a matter of will as much as anything else, though I had noticed the first faint lines around my eyes and a blemish on the back of my hand that I suspected was a liver spot. I had lived a very long life but I wasn't going to live forever. And if I ever got bored, there was always Reduction and my own belated return to the Great Egg.

I turned the viewing port up to maximum magnification, so I could see the coastlines and make out the bright spots of cities—if there had been any. And that bothered me. No cities, no EM radiation, no plumes of smoke from any factories below, no sparkles in the Sahara after nightfall marking the camp fires of the nomads . . .

I was searching the globe below for any indication of man when suddenly I caught my breath. I thought then of Mike and Noah—Mike, who had been mostly wrong but a little bit right, and Noah, who had been mostly right but a little bit wrong.

In their search for life in the vastness of the universe, neither of them had ever considered a third alternative.

That life might find them.

I readjusted the viewing globe while my thumping heart settled back into normal rhythm and I reassured myself that no race could have traveled this far through the empty void without developing as vast a respect for life as we had. . . .

In the viewing globe, the image leaped into sharp focus.

Sweeping into view, thrusting out from the terminator that gradually crept over the world below, was the outline of a huge, alien ship.

Something from Outside had beat us home.

THE END